Irresistible Darkness

ALSO BY RAVEN WOOD

To see the most recently updated list of books by Raven Wood, please visit: www.authorravenwood.com

CONTENT WARNINGS

Irresistible Darkness is a dark romance intended for mature readers. It contains violence and graphic sexual content. If you have specific triggers, you can find the full list of content warnings at: www.authorravenwood.com/content-warnings

IRRESISTIBLE DARKNESS

RAVEN WOOD

ISBN 978-91-989042-3-9 (paperback)
ISBN 978-91-989042-2-2 (ebook)

Cover design by Krafigs Design

www.authorravenwood.com

For all of you who need a ball of sunshine in your life.

A ball of sunshine who will also bash people's heads in with a bat if someone touches you without permission.

A murderous ball of sunshine.

Yes.

1

KAYLA

Guarding a rich heiress who is studying business at a fancy university should be a really comfortable job. One of those gigs that most bodyguards dream of landing. Because what's the worst that could happen? That they need to scare off some drunk frat boy who got a little too handsy at a party? That's probably the case for most assignments like this. But unfortunately for *my* bodyguards, they didn't get a normal client. They got me. And I have no intention of being guarded.

Music pulses out into the dark night from the open window above me. Holding on to the windowsill, I pull myself up until I can manage to swing one leg up onto the small ledge. I glance down at the bushes below. It's not exactly the first time I've climbed into an upstairs window, but I would still like to avoid falling into those bushes if I can. They're the scratchy kind. Not the soft kind.

Clenching my jaw, I heave myself up onto the windowsill.

"Uhm…" a guy says from inside the room. "Do you need some help with that?"

"I'm fine," I reply as I straighten on the small ledge before shifting my attention to the inside of the room. "I just need to..." Trailing off, I glare down at the mass of potted plants that takes up the entire windowsill inside the room. I groan. "Oh, come on."

A soft laugh sounds.

Looking up from the inconveniently placed plants, I find a guy standing just a step away. He has brown hair that has been slicked back in a stylish way, and gray eyes that glitter with both confusion and amusement as he watches me. He's a bit on the slim side, but objectively still very attractive. I wink at him as I start trying to climb over the potted plants.

"You do know that there's a front door downstairs, right?" the guys says, still watching me with a bemused smile on his lips.

I push aside a snake plant with my foot. "I'm aware."

"You're not a burglar, are you?"

"No." I nod towards the rest of the room behind him. "Would be kind of stupid to try to rob a place in the middle of a party when there's like a hundred witnesses, wouldn't it?"

He glances over his shoulder.

This is some kind of entertainment room or something like that. There's a large TV on the wall to my right, though it's not turned on. The people occupying the massive gray couch in the corner are too busy making out to watch anything. On the other side of the large room, four people are playing beer pong on a table that looks to be meant for table tennis. Another group is standing by the wall closer to the door, red plastic cups in their hands as they drink and talk.

The guy in front of me returns his attention to me right as I step over a plant with yellow flowers. "True. But it could also be the greatest tactic in the world. Reverse psychology. No one would think to rob the place during a party, which is why it's the best plan."

I roll my eyes at him before I turn around and grip the window frame for support. "Nah. I'm just trying to escape someone who doesn't understand the meaning of privacy." After swinging my other leg over the army of plants, I release my grip on the window frame. "It's—"

My words are cut off by a hiss as my foot slips off the edge of the windowsill. Flailing my arms, I try to get my balance back. But it's too late. My stomach lurches as I fall backwards into the room.

A huff sounds.

I brace myself for the impact. But I don't hit the floorboards. Instead, I land on top of something soft. And hard.

Blinking, I sit up and scramble around so that I'm no longer facing the window and the disgruntled house plants that are still glaring at me from the windowsill.

Another huff sounds.

I finish spinning around. And come face to face with the brown-haired guy I was talking to. The guy that I collided with when I fell. The guy that I'm now straddling on the floor.

"Wow," he says, and then chuckles as he raises an eyebrow at me. "At least buy me dinner first."

Clearing my throat, I lift my hands from where I was bracing them on his chest and instead push my long red hair back behind my ears before flashing him a sheepish smile. "Sorry."

He laughs again. "You sure know how to make a memorable first impression at least."

"That's what they say." I wink at him again before holding out my hand. "I'm Kayla."

Since he's still lying on the floor underneath me, it takes some maneuvering for him to reach up and take my hand. "Lionel." He smiles and shakes my hand. "Henderson."

"I'm—"

"Ms. Ashford," a stern voice snaps from the doorway. "What have I said about sneaking off like that? I can't do my job when you run off every chance you get."

"Aw, crap," I mutter.

"Ashford?" Lionel blinks at the burly man stalking towards us before meeting my gaze again. "As in *the* Ashford family?"

I grimace. "Yeah, I'm afraid so." Scrambling off him, I shoot to my feet and give him an apologetic smile. "I really have to go, but I'll see you around." I wiggle my eyebrows. "And thanks for the assistance."

Lionel sits up, looking very confused, and stares at me as I skirt around the room until my bodyguard, Max, is no longer blocking the door. Then I make a run for it.

"Ms. Ashford," Max snaps as I dart across the floor and skid into the hallway on the other side of the door. "We've talked about this. You have to stop doing..."

The rest of his sentence is drowned out by the thumping music. But it can't block out the sound of his feet stomping down the corridor after me. People leap out of the way as I hurry towards one of the rooms at the far end. Well, everyone except two blonde girls who are leaning against the wall opposite an open door, looking very suspicious.

"Is everything ready?" I ask as I reach them.

"Yeah," Jenn replies.

Her younger sister, Aurora, nods towards the open doorway. "But make sure you don't move the plastic sheet. If you ruin the floor, our housemates are going to kill us."

"I won't. I promise." I blow them a kiss. "Thank you."

But I don't have time to wait for their reply. Darting into the deserted room beyond, I push the door almost all the way shut. Then I grab the bucket waiting for me on the floor and leap up onto the chair by the wall. With steady hands, I balance the bucket on top of the door. Once it's in place, I jump back down and hurry over to the middle of the room.

I have just barely checked that the wide plastic sheet is still in place before the door is shoved open and Max storms across the threshold.

"Ms. Ashford," he growls. "My patience is at an end. If you don't—"

The bucket falls from the top of the door and tips down over him.

Red paint splashes down over his head, his black suit, and the plastic sheet that covers the floor.

He stops.

For a while, nothing moves. From the middle of the room, I watch as Max simply stands there. Red paint slides down his skin and clothes and drips down on the floor. That muted dripping is the only sound in the room.

Slowly, he looks down at his ruined suit. Then he wipes paint from his face before dragging his furious gaze up to me.

I grin. "It could've been blood. But it's not."

He forces out a long, angry breath. "That's it. I quit."

Victory pulses through me.

Raising a red-smeared hand, he stabs a finger at me. "Good luck finding another bodyguard. I know everyone in the business, and I will warn them all to steer clear of you. No professional bodyguard within a hundred-mile radius will touch you with a ten-foot pole."

Yanking his hand down, he flicks more paint onto the

plastic sheet before whipping around and stalking out the door.

A wide smile spreads across my lips as I watch him leave while I finally reply, "That's what I'm counting on."

My entire life has been monitored. For almost as long as I can remember, I have had a bodyguard lurking over my shoulder and watching my every move. But that stops now. I want freedom. Independence. And now I will get it.

Over the years, I have scared off dozens of bodyguards, but my father has always found someone else to take the job. But no more. After the absolute hell I put Max through, word will spread to everyone in the business.

I've finally won.

Because no one will be crazy enough to come anywhere near me now.

2

JACE

Noise. There is noise all around me. Loud thumping music from the massive speakers in the corner. Chatter from the mass of people around me. My own voice as I laugh too loudly at the joke that the guy opposite me cracked. And yet, it's still not enough to drown out the constant buzzing in my head.

Leaning forward on the couch, I snatch my glass of vodka from the table and down the rest of it in one go. It burns in my throat on the way down. But it might as well have been water, because it does nothing to numb the terrible restlessness that vibrates inside me.

I flex my fingers on the glass and then grab the half empty bottle on the table to refill it.

"What did I tell you?" the guy on the couch opposite me says to his friend as he slaps his arm with the back of his hand. "If there's anyone who can hold his liquor, it's Jace Hunter."

I laugh, again too loudly, and then hold out my glass in a cheers. "I'll drink to that."

They chuckle and clink their glasses against mine. They drink a mouthful. I empty my glass again.

Blowing out a long breath, I rake my fingers through my messy hair.

It feels as if there is a swarm of angry bees buzzing inside my ribcage. I just want to crack my chest open and release them. Or crawl out of my own skin before I start crawling up the fucking walls instead.

I flex my fingers on the glass again and then once more drag my other hand through my hair.

Distraction. I need a distraction. Something to block out everything that goes on inside my head.

"Hey, Jace."

I look up from my now empty glass to find an attractive brunette dropping down on the couch next to me. All around us, the party is in full swing. People are dancing on the floor to our left and others are playing a drinking game to my right. Blackwater University might be a school for hitmen, but we still know how to party.

Raising my empty glass, I give the brunette next to me a salute before I set my glass back down on the table. "What's up."

"What's up?" she echoes, and purses her lips in a show of exaggerated disappointment. "That's all I get?"

I glance at her from the corner of my eye while I lean back on the couch again. I'm pretty sure I fucked her at some point. Was it this year? Or last year? I can't remember. In fact, I can't even remember her name. And I don't care.

Just like everyone else at Blackwater, she's just one of the many meaningless distractions I've used in order to get some stress release and to get out of my own head for a little while. She doesn't matter. None of them do. *Nothing* matters.

"You don't remember me?" she continues, still with that fake pout. Then she flashes me a seductive smile. "I'll help jog your memory."

Before I can reply, she swings her leg over mine and twists so that she is straddling my lap. The guys on the couch opposite us whistle and cheer before laughing approvingly. The girl, whose name I still can't remember, places her hands on my shoulders and rolls her hips.

"Remember me yet?" she teases, looking very pleased with herself.

"Nope," I reply.

This time, the disappointment that flashes across her face is real. But it's gone quickly and instead replaced by a sultry expression. Climbing off my lap, she grabs my wrist and starts pulling me up.

"I suppose I'll just have to give you a more thorough demonstration," she says as she pulls on my wrist.

But I weigh probably twice as much as her, so unless I get up on my own, she won't succeed in pulling me up with her. I study her face. She's pretty. My gaze drops to her body. Toned and athletic, like most girls on this campus since she's here to become an assassin. But she also has some nice curves.

Ah, fuck it. I wanted a distraction, and I guess this will have to do.

Pushing myself up, I let her pull me away from the couches and towards the hallway that leads to the staircase.

"I still can't believe you don't remember me," she says, still holding on to my wrist as she weaves through the crowd.

Since I'm walking behind her, I can't see her face. But I can hear the disappointment and embarrassment in her voice.

To be fair, I get it. I was probably the best fuck she ever

had. A true night to remember. So the fact that *I* don't remember *her* must sting a little.

Yeah, well, I fuck a lot of people.

You were just a distraction.

Nothing we did matters so why would I remember you?

All of those responses flit through my head, but I still have enough presence of mind to not actually say any of that out loud. That would be a pretty dick move.

So instead, I simply say, "Sorry."

"I suppose we will just have to make tonight even more memorable then." She winks at me from over her shoulder as she starts leading me up the stairs.

I wait until she is facing forwards again to roll my eyes.

Fuck, I haven't even made it up the stairs yet and I'm already bored again. This isn't working.

Pulling my wrist out of her grip, I stop halfway up the steps. She jerks to a halt as well and turns around, blinking in surprise.

"What's wrong?" she asks.

I draw a hand through my hair. "I just... I've gotta..." Waving my hand around, I motion vaguely towards the front door. "I'll see you around."

Embarrassment floods her features, but her stammered reply gets drowned out by the noise of the music and the people crowding the hallway as I quickly stride back down the steps. I shake my head and roll my shoulders back as I set course for the door. The sea of people parts before me.

I swipe a half full bottle of rum from a side table as I make my way out the door and into the warm night outside. Raising it to my lips, I drink straight from the bottle as I walk through Blackwater's residential area where all the students live. I barely even know where I'm heading until I find myself in front of another house.

This one is silent and dark. Or at least, the ground floor and the upstairs level are. The real action is happening somewhere else.

My boots sink into the soft grass as I walk around the house and approach the door to the basement on the other side. The moment I yank the door open, noise drifts up towards me. I heave a sigh of relief. While drinking deeply from the bottle, I descend the stone steps.

A concrete basement lit by fluorescents in the ceiling meets me as I reach the bottom. It's nothing more than a semi large room. But it's enough for its intended purpose.

Cheers echo between the gray walls, along with the sounds of flesh striking flesh. I push my way through the crowd until I can see the middle of the room.

Two guys who are second-years, if I'm not mistaken, are fighting there in the square space that has been marked by tape. The taller one throws a punch that the other guy ducks before he delivers a blow to the tall guy's solar plexus. He goes down like a log.

More cheers rise from the crowd.

I take another drink from my bottle before shoving it into the hands of the guy next to me.

"I'm next," I call as I pull off my shirt.

All first-years and second-years in the room shrink back. But a blond guy from my senior class with a hungry glint in his eyes steps up and accepts the challenge. I roll my shoulders back and step into the makeshift fighting ring while he takes off his shirt as well.

That terrible restlessness still thrums inside me like a lightning storm trapped in a glass bottle. I rake my fingers through my hair. It feels as if light constantly flickers in my brain. I just need a fucking outlet.

The room quiets as I square up against the other third-year in front of me.

Hopefully, this will at least drown out the buzzing in my head.

Hopefully, it will make me forget for a few minutes just how fucking pointless my entire life is.

Lurching forward, I slam my fist into the guy's ribs.

My body aches and my throat is dry when I wake up. Fuck, I feel like I've been run over by a freight train. And I'm pretty sure my liver hurts.

Groaning, I blindly throw out a hand to grab my phone from my nightstand. But I just slam it right into what feels like the backrest of the couch in my living room. I must have passed out on the couch when I got home last night.

With another annoyed groan, I pull my hand back and instead rub it over my face. Then I heave a deep breath and open my eyes.

Three guns are pointed straight at me.

I blink, adrenaline pulsing through my body for a second before I recognize the three guys holding the weapons.

Drawing my eyebrows down in a scowl, I shoot them all a glare while sitting up and swinging my legs off the couch. "Get those fucking guns out of my face."

Eli, Kaden, and Rico just watch me in silence, still pointing their guns at me. I shoot my three brothers another glare.

Then I arch an expectant eyebrow at them, and Rico at last slides his gun into the back of his pants. Kaden holsters his as well, but instead slips out a knife that he starts spinning in his hand. Eli keeps the gun in his hand but uses it to motion at the combined kitchen and living room around us.

"The fuck did you do to our house?" he says. It's more of a demand than a question.

"It's not your house anymore," I remind him. "You all have already graduated."

"Technically, Rico didn't graduate," Kaden comments with a smirk directed at Rico.

"Shut up," Rico retorts.

Blowing out a forceful breath, I rake my fingers through my hair and then run my tongue around my parched mouth. How much did I drink last night? Clearly not enough, since that thrumming restlessness inside me is already back.

"How did you even get in here?" I mutter as I reach for the bottle of whiskey on the coffee table before me.

Kaden shoots me a look as if I've just said the dumbest thing ever while Rico quickly snatches the bottle from the table before I can grab it.

I glare at Rico, who just stares me down, before shifting my attention to Kaden, who looks like he's waiting for me to answer my own question.

"Yeah, yeah, you're elite assassins and mafia bosses," I mutter. "Whatever."

"We also used to live here, remember?" Rico says as he walks over to the liquor cabinet and puts the bottle there.

I let out something between a snarl and a sigh, and then push myself up from the cream-colored couch. Neither Eli nor Kaden makes any move to step back and allow me to pass, so I simply grab the back of the couch and jump over it instead.

"Pretty spry for someone who was passed out dead a

minute ago," Eli says, shooting me a grin and a look full of challenge.

However, before I can retort, Kaden speaks up. Or rather, issues a command.

"Drink some water," he orders. Then he nods towards my left shoulder. "And put some ice on your shoulder."

I raise my eyebrows in silent question while the three of them round the couch and approach the kitchen island as well.

"I saw you wince when you twisted around," Kaden responds to my wordless question.

"Of course you did," I mutter under my breath.

The bastard never misses a thing. I walk right past the freezer, but I do head for the sink since I actually am thirsty. After downing two entire glasses of water, I turn back to my meddling brothers and cross my arms over my chest.

They all look the way they usually do when I see them. It's not as often anymore since I'm still studying at Blackwater while all of them have left university and joined the real world.

Rico with his brown hair that curls softly looks the most like me. Which is interesting considering that he is technically our cousin and not our brother. Our hair is the same shade of brown, but my brown eyes are a little lighter than his. Ever since he left Blackwater, he has started wearing suits more often, though. Which is not something that I would ever willingly put on.

At least Kaden and Eli still wear their customary dark pants and tight-fitting black shirts complete with combat boots. As usual, Kaden has his knife holsters secured around his thighs and hips. That, combined with his sharply styled straight black hair and his dark eyes that always see too much, makes him look as dangerous and lethal as he really is.

And Eli is no better. His hair is also straight and black, but his eyes are a strange golden color. It would've made him look almost beautiful, if it weren't for the fact that those eyes of his are often tinted with a bit of insanity. Not to mention the scar that cuts through his eyebrow and ends at the top of his cheek. Or the other hundreds of scars across his skin.

"What are you even doing here?" I demand as I raise my eyebrows at the three of them.

"Dad has called a family meeting," Eli says.

I let out something between a groan and a sigh. "About what?"

"He didn't say. But he told us to go and get you." He jerks his chin towards the open doorway to the corridor. "So, get to it."

I narrow my eyes at him. But I know that there is no point in arguing, because our dear father does not take kindly to disobedience. So in the end, I just heave another sigh and reply, "Fine."

After taking a shower and changing clothes, I stalk down the stairs again. My brothers hear me coming and walk out of the kitchen at the same time as I reach the bottom of the stairs.

Something cold and hard smacks into my chest, and I catch it by reflex. Glancing down, I find an ice pack in my hands. I look up and meet Kaden's dark eyes. He shoots me a commanding stare and stabs a hand towards my shoulder.

I roll my eyes but then raise the ice pack and hold it against my shoulder. The coldness immediately seeps through my muscles and soothes the ache.

After locking the door behind us, we all climb into Eli's

Range Rover. I watch the gray concrete buildings that make up Blackwater University fade outside the windows to be replaced by fields as Eli drives us back towards the city.

When we reach our family home, Dad is already waiting for us in the study. Mom is nowhere to be seen, which isn't a good sign. It means that Dad probably timed this so that she wouldn't be here to calm things down. He has been threatening to kick my ass unless I pull myself together and stop drinking and fighting and neglecting my studies. And as I walk into his office, I can't help but wonder if he has finally decided to make good on that promise.

I left the ice pack in Eli's car, so I cross my arms over my chest and lock eyes with our father as I come to a halt on the other side of the desk where he's sitting. Eli and Kaden take up position on my left and right, with Rico on Eli's other side.

"Well, you wanted a family meeting," Eli says and lifts his shoulders in a lazy shrug. "Here we are."

Dad shoots him a disapproving look at the arrogance in his tone. But he raised us with the same arrogance and dominance that he himself possesses, so I don't know why he's surprised.

After holding Eli's nonchalant stare for another second, Dad shifts his sharp blue eyes to me. "The time for gentle guiding is long past now, Jace."

I force out an annoyed breath. "What is this? My intervention?"

He slams his hand down on the desk, making the pens jump and clatter. "Enough! Enough with the flippant attitude. I get reports from your instructors at Blackwater. And do you know what they say?"

"That I'm the best marksman in the senior year and at the top of the charts in every sparring competition?"

"That you barely show up to class! That you get into fights with anyone and everyone over the smallest things. That you smell like alcohol half of the fucking time."

My brothers cast me a glance from the corner of their eyes, but they say nothing.

I just hold our father's stare. "So?"

His eyes flash. "I will give you one chance to come up with another answer to that."

"If you're so unhappy with my performance, then pull me out of Blackwater."

"Pull you out of Blackwater?" Placing his palms on the table, he slowly stands up and leans forward over the desk while locking furious eyes on me. "You are *my* son. And you will finish your education at Blackwater just like your brothers have. Just like I have. Just like my father did. And his father before him. You are a Hunter and—"

"And maybe that's the problem!"

The words tear out of my chest with the force of a gunshot, and they're out before I can stop them. Anger and panic and desperation rip through me, shredding my insides as I stare at my father in the now dead silent room. My chest is heaving.

Dad looks shocked.

For a few seconds, all he does is to blink at me in stunned silence. Then the wheels start turning behind his eyes.

It sends another spike of panic up my spine. But it's too late to take it back now.

The fury drains from Dad's features and is instead replaced by confusion. Holding my gaze, he shakes his head slowly while realization finishes trickling through his mind.

Then he at last says the words that I have been trying to hide for years now.

"You don't want to be a hitman." It's half question, half statement.

Eli and Rico whip around to stare at me.

"What?" Eli blurts out. Confusion swirls in his eyes too as he looks at me. "You don't want to become a hitman?"

I glance towards him but don't reply since I haven't decided what to say yet. Thankfully, Eli's gaze shifts to Kaden on my other side and his frown deepens.

"Wait," Eli begins, now looking at Kaden. "Why the fuck are you not surprised?"

Both Rico and our father now turn to Kaden as well, blinking in surprise. Kaden just looks back at them with that customary blank expression on his face.

"Did you *know*?" Dad demands.

Of course he did. He always does, somehow. He even tried to confront me about it last year.

"Yes," Kaden simply replies.

"What the fuck," Eli says at the same time as Dad grinds out, "Then why didn't you say anything?"

Because I told him that I would shoot him in the head if he finished the sentence.

But Kaden doesn't tell them that. Instead, he just meets my eyes briefly before shifting his gaze back to the rest of our family. He lifts his shoulders in a casual shrug. "Because it wasn't my place to say."

Rico, who looked like he had been about to say something, just closes his mouth again and nods. Eli does too. Because they understand. We don't force each other to talk about stuff until we're ready. And we don't share secrets with outsiders. Including our parents.

But Dad does not look satisfied by that answer.

Displeasure flickers in his blue eyes as he fixes Kaden with a sharp stare. "For how long?"

"I've suspected it for about five years," Kaden admits. "And I've known for certain for a little over a year."

Five years? He has known how I feel about this for five years? That's news to me. I flick a glance at my brother again. He meets my gaze briefly, but neither of us say anything. Most people assume that Kaden is a pure psychopath who doesn't understand emotions. But I know that he can actually read them better than anyone.

"Fucking hell," Dad curses under his breath. He rubs a hand over his face before dragging it through his brown hair. Then he fixes me with a look full of disappointment. "You don't want to be a hitman. Why?"

"It's not—"

"Is it because you don't want to kill people?"

"It's not that."

"It's too dangerous?"

"Too dangerous?" I scowl at him. "Have you met me?"

"Too complicated then?"

"No. I can plan assassinations just fine."

"Then what the hell is the problem?"

"I just want a fucking choice!" I scream, the words tearing out from the very depths of my soul.

Dad draws back and blinks in surprise.

"I want a fucking choice," I repeat. My chest heaves, and fear and anger and panic rip through my chest again.

He shakes his head slowly, confusion once more marring his brows. "I don't understand."

"It's not that I hate the concept of being a hitman,' I explain. "I like the violence. The chaos. The power. But I *hate* that I don't have a choice."

Next to me, I can feel my brothers watching me. But none of them interrupt. Dad just continues staring at me, his mouth slightly open in surprise and befuddlement.

"I want to choose what I do with my life," I say. "I want to decide my own future. But I can't. Because I'm a Hunter, and that means that I must become a hitman. Whether I want to or not." Holding his stare, I shake my head. "So what's the fucking point? I can't choose my own life, so why even bother with it? It doesn't matter. Nothing fucking matters. So why the hell should I care if I never show up to class or pick unnecessary fights or that my professors think I smell like alcohol?"

The silence that descends over the neatly furnished study is so loud that I can practically hear it ringing between the dark wooden walls.

For quite a while, no one says anything. Once again, I can feel my brothers watching me. But I keep my eyes on our father. Indecision swirls in his eyes.

Then, at last, he breaks the crackling silence.

"I received an unusual request yesterday," he says carefully. "From the Ashford family."

"The real estate moguls?" Eli asks.

"Yes," Dad replies, but he keeps his eyes on me. "I've done some jobs for them in the past, but the one they offered yesterday was so odd that I was planning to refuse. But maybe I shouldn't."

"What kind of job?" I demand.

"Bodyguard."

I frown.

"I know," Dad says. "That was my first reaction too. Trent Ashford wants to hire a bodyguard for his twenty-year-old daughter who studies business at Ivy River University on the other side of the city. For at least the rest of the semester."

"What does that have to do with me?"

"I want you to continue our family's tradition and become a hitman. I'm not going to deny that. And I am disappointed in how you have handled your three years at Blackwater up until now. But..." He pauses for a few seconds, holding my gaze with commanding eyes. "I am open to making a deal with you."

I cross my arms. "What kind of deal?"

"If you can successfully handle this bodyguard job for the Ashfords, thereby showing me that you can get your shit together and act responsibly and professionally, then I will let you choose whether or not you finish your education at Blackwater and become a hitman."

My eyebrows shoot up. Our Dad isn't exactly known for his ability to compromise. He is used to giving orders and having them obeyed.

I stare at him. "You're serious?"

"Yes." He raises his eyebrows. "So, what do you say?"

"Deal."

He nods.

Relief and astonishment pulse through my chest. This is better than anything I could have hoped for.

Bodyguard to a twenty-year-old girl at a fancy business school?

How hard could it possibly be?

3

KAYLA

The disappointment and frustration pulsing through the air is so palpable that I can almost feel it physically vibrating against my skin. However, I keep the casual expression on my face as I sit there in the chair on the other side of Dad's desk. Leaning back nonchalantly, I cross one leg over the other while Dad finishes his lecture.

Though, *lecture* is probably not the right word. Perhaps tirade. Admonishment. Scolding. Yeah, those fit better.

"Do you have any idea how much your childish antics cost me?" Dad leans forward in his chair and angrily stabs his finger down on the glass tabletop between us. "Not only financially, but professionally too?"

I know that he is not actually waiting for an answer, so I just sit there in his pristine office in silence and hold his gaze. Sunlight streams in through the floor-to-ceiling windows that make up two of the walls in his penthouse office. The light plays over the white walls opposite them, and it glints in the sleek metal and glass furniture throughout the room.

"You've gone through eight bodyguards this year alone!" Dad continues, his blue eyes flashing. "*Eight*. And word has spread through their ranks. I'm lucky that my own bodyguards haven't quit out of solidarity too."

I roll my eyes. As if they would ever quit. His bodyguards have been with him for years. They're loyal to a fault.

"Don't roll your eyes at me," he snaps. "Do you have any idea how difficult it is to keep finding new bodyguards for you all the time?"

"You could just stop doing it," I say, raising my eyebrows expectantly. "And just let me live without being shadowed by a bodyguard all the time."

"After what happened to your brother? No."

Guilt twists my insides. Glancing down, I fiddle with the watch I always wear around my wrist. My brother's watch. Or it was supposed to be, anyway.

"It's not the same," I say quietly, still looking down at the watch.

"Are you seriously telling me that things wouldn't have been different if you'd had a bodyguard with you that day?"

"Well… no." I look up, meeting his gaze again, and then throw out my arms in frustration. "But this is nothing like that! I'm twenty years old. I'm a university student. I don't need a babysitter."

He draws his pale brows down in a look of disapproval. "A bodyguard is not a babysitter. It's someone who will keep you safe."

"From what?" The words tear out of my lungs, full of anger and exasperation. "We deal in real estate, for God's sake! It's not as if I'm a mafia princess."

"No, but I've still made enemies. Not to mention the risk that someone might kidnap you for ransom."

"Kidnap me?" Staring at him, I shake my head. "You can't be serious!"

"I am. Which is why—"

His words are cut off by a short beep from the office phone on his desk. After blowing out a breath, he presses a button.

"Yes?" he says.

"Sir," one of his assistants says on the other end of the line. "They're here."

"Great. Send them up."

He presses the button again, ending the call. Pushing his chair back, he stands up and then brushes a hand over his blond hair as if to smooth it down. Suspicion pulses through me as he buttons his suit jacket and straightens his cuffs.

"Send *who* up?" I ask, slowly rising to my feet as well.

Dad walks around his desk and moves towards the center of the room. "I've hired a new bodyguard for you."

"What?" Scrambling around my chair, I hurry after him. "But I thought you said that no bodyguard in this entire state would take the contract."

"I reached out to someone else."

"Who?"

"The Hunters."

Shock clangs inside my skull, and I jerk to a halt on the floor. Blinking, I just stare at my father for a few seconds while I try to process what he actually said. When time still doesn't make his words more logical, I quickly close the distance between us and grab his arm, turning him towards me.

"The Hunters," I echo. "The legendary hitman family that's connected to the Morelli mafia family."

Dad nods. "Yes. I've done business with Jonathan Hunter

before. Mostly retrieval jobs to recover some documents that were stolen during…" He gives his head a quick shake as if the details of that don't matter. "Anyway, I reached out to him about finding a bodyguard for you and he said that he has the perfect person for the job."

I just stare up at him with wide eyes. "You hired a *hitman* to protect me?"

"Yes. Now, be nice."

Before I can retort, the door is opened and two men stride across the threshold. I whirl around to face them.

The man on the right looks to be in his late forties, with straight brown hair and sharp blue eyes. Which means that he must be Jonathan Hunter. The guy walking beside him can't be anyone other than one of his sons. While their facial features are not overly similar, they're built the same. Tall and broad-shouldered. I swear, the younger guy is even more muscular than his father.

I study him.

Like his dad, he also has brown hair. But as opposed to Jonathan, whose hair is straight and neatly styled, this guy looks like he has just rolled out of bed. His loose brown curls are effortlessly messy in a way that makes him look annoyingly hot. And his light brown eyes glitter in the sunlight streaming in through the windows.

"Jonathan," Dad says as he holds out his hand to the legendary hitman. "Thank you for agreeing to this. I know that it was an unusual request."

"Anything for you, Trent," he replies as he shakes my dad's hand. "You know that."

Next to him, the younger guy flicks a quick assessing look over me. Then one side of his mouth tilts up in a small smile as he meets my gaze again. My heart jerks in my chest. Don't tell me that *this* is the guy that Dad has hired as my bodyguard?

As if the universe had heard my stunned thoughts, Jonathan draws back and instead motions at the younger guy. "This is my youngest son, Jace."

Dad reaches forward and shakes his hand as well. "Nice to meet you, Jace." Then he pulls his hand back and gestures at me. "This is my daughter, Kayla, who you will be guarding."

Jace shifts his glittering eyes to me and holds out his hand. "Kayla."

A ripple rolls down my spine at the utter confidence in his voice and at the way he says my name.

I'm still so stunned by the direction this has taken that I only manage to take his hand without actually saying anything. His hand is warm and strong around mine as he gives me a firm handshake.

This is the guy who will be my bodyguard? Up until now, it has only been middle-aged men. But this guy can't be more than a couple of years older than me. And why the fuck does he have to be this ridiculously hot?

"Dad, this really isn't necessary," I blurt out, and turn towards my father once Jace has released my hand.

Annoyance and embarrassment flicker in his blue eyes as he shoots me a sharp look. Then he turns back to Jonathan. "You'll have to forgive my daughter. I was just telling her about this arrangement when you arrived, so she's still a little surprised."

Jonathan waves his hand casually. "No worries." Then he nods towards the door. "Perhaps we should give them a moment to introduce themselves while we finish up the final details?"

"Yes, that sounds great." Dad turns to me. "Jace will start

tomorrow morning, so one of my guards will take you back to your apartment when you're done."

"No, wait," I protest, my mind still scrambling for a way out of this. "I don't need a bodyguard to—"

"Kayla." He shoots me a stern look. Then a smile slides home on his lips as he motions for Jonathan to follow him out the door. "This way, please."

"Jace," Jonathan says, glancing over his shoulder as he walks towards the door. "I'll meet you back at the car."

"Yeah," Jace simply replies, but he does turn slightly to watch our fathers leave.

I glare after my dad in both anger and frustration.

Then my gaze slides back to Jace.

My pulse flutters as I watch the way his muscles shift when he flexes his hand.

Fuck. This is the guy who is going to be living with me in my apartment now? It was bad enough when it was a random middle-aged man watching me every time I stumble home from a party drunk or every time I walk out of my bedroom with messy hair and morning breath. But now it's a guy my own age. And not just any guy. This guy.

I quickly rake my gaze up and down his body while he's still watching my father close the door on the other side of the room.

He's wearing a pair of jeans and a white t-shirt that only serves to accentuate his insanely sculpted body. And the way he's standing, the entire way that he carries himself, just screams effortless confidence. This is a guy who is both ridiculously hot and powerful, and he *knows it*.

"I know," Jace says.

A jolt shoots through me when I realize that he has just caught me staring at his body, and I snap my gaze back up to his face. His eyes glitter and there is a little smirk on his mouth as he looks back at me.

It immediately makes annoyance pulse through me.

If this guy thinks that I'm going to make this job easy for him just because he's hot, then he has another thing coming. In fact, I'm going to do the opposite. Just because he has the nerve to be both attractive and my age, I'm going to be even more of a demon to him.

He thinks that he can handle me?

He thinks that he can charm me with his glittering eyes and sexy smirk and smooth-talking voice?

Ha. Good fucking luck. I am going to drive him fucking insane.

"What?" I reply to his comment, and raise my eyebrows expectantly.

That cocky smirk stays on his lips. "I know what you were thinking."

"Oh?" I give him a flat look. "Do enlighten me."

"You were thinking that I look like I'm good in bed."

"No, I was actually thinking that you look like someone who preheats the microwave."

He opens his mouth to respond, but then pauses. His brows furrow as he frowns while staring at the wall behind me for a solid ten seconds. As if he is trying to figure out what that even means.

Then he blinks, apparently finally having realized that it was an insult, and snaps his gaze back to me.

"Hey, what the fuck?" he protests, shaking his head at me with a bewildered frown on his face.

"The fact that it also took you ten seconds to figure that one out isn't really helping your efforts to disprove my assessment."

"What are you—"

"But nice try, Sparky." I flick my hair back behind my shoulder and start towards the door. "I'll text you the address to my apartment. Don't be late."

"Hey, what the…?" he blurts out, but I just keep walking. "I…"

A wicked grin shines on my mouth as I saunter up to the door and push it open.

"It's *Jace*!" he calls after me.

I laugh under my breath while giving him a nonchalant wave with the back of my hand. Then I disappear out the door.

This is going to be so much fun.

4

JACE

Kayla Ashford is not at all what I was expecting. A twenty-year-old real estate heiress and university student… She should be ecstatic to have me as her bodyguard. I mean, come on. I'm hot. I'm funny. I'm a fucking delight.

But instead she hit me with that damn microwave insult. Which I have to admit was pretty clever. But still. So rude.

Oh well, if opportunity doesn't knock the first time, I'll just kick the door in and create a better first impression this time. Metaphorically, I mean.

Checking the number next to the apartment door, I make sure that it's the same address as the one Kayla texted me yesterday, and then I raise my hand to knock.

Almost half a minute passes. I'm just about to knock again when the door is pushed open.

"What?" a guy snaps as he glares out at me.

I frown at him. He's a few inches shorter than me, but he's built like a brick. Stocky, and with the neck the size of a bull. His head is shaved, tattoos cover his knuckles, and he's wearing a white tank top that has yellow stains underneath the arms. Over his shoulder, I can spot a guy who is similarly dressed, but who has greasy brown hair instead.

These are Trent Ashford's bodyguards? They look like thugs. And very *unimpressive* thugs at that.

Jeez, Kayla really should be thanking me for replacing them and lighting up her apartment with my dazzling presence instead.

"I'm here for Kayla," I say, giving Bull Neck an expectant look.

His eyes flash.

My stomach lurches as I'm suddenly hauled across the threshold. I blink in surprise as Bull Neck slams me up against the wall of the hallway inside, while Greasy Hair charges towards us.

"Calm the fuck down," I say. "She—"

Bull Neck swings his fist towards my face.

I ram my elbow down into his forearm, redirecting the blow while slamming my other fist into his stomach.

Air explodes from his lungs in a whoosh and he doubles over, losing his grip on me. But before I can deliver a kick to his face, Greasy Hair yells and swings a bat at me. Shoving Bull Neck away from me, I sidestep the bat and then grab it mid-air.

With a firm pull, I yank it from his grip while saying, "First of all, that's not how you hold a bat properly."

Greasy Hair jerks back in surprise and blinks at me.

"And secondly, you're not supposed to yell when you swing the bat." I spin the bat in my hand and then point it at him while raising my eyebrows. "Seriously? It's Bat Etiquette 101. Did no one ever teach you that?"

Bull Neck groans from my right and straightens to punch

me again. I quickly shift sideways and slam the bat into his stomach. He drops like a stone.

"I will fucking kill you!" Greasy Hair screams, and charges me again.

Rolling my eyes, I duck under his fist and then twist so that I can smack my bat into the back of his knee. He cries out and crashes down on one knee while I straighten. Before he can recover, I bring the bat down across his shoulder blades, making him collapse to the floor.

Behind me, Bull Neck stirs and tries to get off the ground.

I stride over to him and shove him down again with the top of my bat before I grab his arm and twist it up behind him.

A shrill cry of pain rips from his throat.

"Why are you screaming?" I say, frowning down at him. "I haven't even started breaking your arm yet."

His cry turns into a whimper. "Please."

"Now we're finally getting somewhere. Like I said, I'm here for Kayla."

"What do you want with me?" a girl's terrified voice suddenly cuts through the air.

I snap my gaze up from the whimpering man below me and stare at the source of the voice. A slim brown-haired girl, who can't be more than eighteen, stares at me with wide brown eyes.

I frown at her. "Who are you?"

"Kayla," she stammers, still staring at me with fear on her face. "Please don't hurt my brothers."

"What…"

Realization hits me like a shovel to the back of the head.

God fucking damn it. That little menace sent me to the wrong fucking address.

I draw in a deep breath through my nose to calm the irritation that flashes through me. Then I release my grip on Bull Neck's arm and straighten.

"Ah," I say, flashing the girl a smile. "It looks like I have the wrong address."

She just looks back at me with those wide brown eyes. Her brothers groan and start pushing themselves up to their knees.

After drawing a hand through my hair, I spin the bat around and rest it on my shoulder instead.

"Sorry for the intrusion." I raise my free hand to my forehead and give them a casual salute. "You all have a good day now."

And with that, I turn around and stroll back out into the corridor. While still resting my new bat on my shoulder, I pull out my phone and call Trent Ashford.

"Mr. Ashford," I say when he picks up. "It seems as though there must be a typo or something in the address that your daughter gave me. Could I trouble you for her proper address?"

Trent Ashford, who knows very well that it wasn't an accidental typo, apologizes several times and then gives me Kayla's real address. After we hang up, I type the address into Google Maps and find that it's nowhere near the apartment building that she sent me to.

While cursing that little menace under my breath, I head back down to my car and then drive to her real apartment.

I'm supposed to be relieving Trent's bodyguard at half past seven, and I manage to make it there with two minutes to spare.

Since I won't have time to head back to my car this time, I grab the duffel bag from my passenger seat straight away.

After slinging it over my shoulder, I snatch up the newest addition to my bat collection too and then start towards Kayla's door.

At exactly seven thirty, I knock on the door to her apartment.

A middle-aged man in a black suit opens it. He takes one look at me and then nods.

"Mr. Hunter," he says as he steps aside and motions for me to enter. "Come on in. Ms. Ashford is—"

"Who was..." Kayla begins as she walks out of a room a little ahead and to my right. But when she sees me, she trails off and jerks back in surprise. "You."

The other bodyguard turns towards her. "Since Mr. Hunter has arrived, I will be returning to my other duties now, ma'am."

I blink at him. Ma'am? Did he really just call her *ma'am*?

Kayla stares at me in stunned silence for another second before giving her head a quick shake and then returning her attention to her temporary bodyguard. "Yes, that's fine. You may leave."

"Thank you." He bows his head. "Have a good day, ma'am."

Incredulity pulses through me. He's acting as if she's the bloody Queen of England or something. If she is expecting me to bow my head and address her as *ma'am,* she's about to be incredibly disappointed.

I watch the guy leave while that incredulity still rings inside my skull.

Once the door is closed behind him, I at last turn to face Kayla.

It's only seven thirty in the morning, but she is already dressed and ready for school. She's wearing a pair of form-fitting jeans and a white dress shirt that shows off her curves. The pale shirt also makes her long, flaming red hair stand out in stark contrast as it spills down over her shoulders. In comparison to the fiery color of her hair, her blue eyes are calm and cool. Like a deep ocean.

Fuck, she's gorgeous.

And she's also scowling at me.

I flash her a smirk. "Surprised to see me? After you sent me to that dummy address?"

Drawing herself up to her full height, she tries to look down her nose at me even though she's an entire head shorter than me. "I have no idea what you're talking about."

"I'm not stupid, you know."

She scoffs and flicks a dismissive look up and down my body. "You sure look like it."

I draw my eyebrows down and open my mouth to retort, but before I can, she starts walking across the living room.

The apartment is large, but somehow still smaller than what I expected for someone who is as rich as she is. The door and the short hallway I'm currently standing in is connected to a combined kitchen and living room. The kitchen part to my right is full of stainless-steel appliances and gleaming countertops, and there is a massive oak table that forms a kind of barrier between the kitchen and the living room side. There is a corner sofa with pristine white fabric by the windows straight ahead, a fluffy white carpet underneath the glass coffee table, and some white bookshelves along the wall next to the TV.

To the right is the room that Kayla came out of, and to the left is another identical door.

I follow Kayla as she strides towards it.

She opens the door and then continues inside while speaking over her shoulder. "This is your room. It has a private bathroom through that door, as you can see. My room is on the other side of the living room."

Walking across the threshold, I study the bedroom that will be my temporary home.

It's decently sized and does indeed have a bathroom attached to it. There's a set of drawers and a closet by one wall, and a double bed with neutral gray sheets by another.

"But you will not, under any circumstances, be going into my bedroom," Kayla continues as she stops next to the bed and crosses her arms.

I unsling my duffel bag and drop it on the floor with a thud. Then I toss my bat onto the bed. Kayla frowns at it.

"What's with the bat?" she asks, giving me a look of genuine confusion.

Grinning, I lift my shoulders in a shrug. "You never know when you might need a good bat."

She lets out something between a sigh and an exasperated groan, and then rolls her eyes. "Anyway, you can unpack if you want. But I wouldn't bother getting too comfortable, if I were you."

"And why is that?"

"Because you won't be here long."

And with that, she spins on her heel and saunters back out into the living room.

I have to resist an overwhelming urge to shove her up against the wall.

She's such a little demon. Five minutes into the job, and she's already driving me crazy.

Shaking my head, I blow out a long sigh and instead just

follow her back into the living room. She grabs a bag that was leaning against the couch and swings it up onto the kitchen table.

"Alright, let's lay down some ground rules," she says as she begins sliding books into her bag.

She's not even looking at me, which just irks me even more.

"When I'm in class, you wait outside the lecture hall," she declares.

Crossing my arms over my chest, I scowl at her. "No."

Her hand stops halfway to her bag. Turning her head towards me, she stares at me with what looks like genuine surprise.

Huh. So apparently, she's not used to people refusing her orders.

"What do you mean, *no*?" she demands, that stunned incredulity bleeding into her voice too.

I just look back at her expectantly. "I won't be able to protect you from out there if something happens."

Anger flashes across her beautiful face, and she shoves the final book into her bag and then throws out her arms. "Protect me from *what*? Papercuts?"

"From any and all threats."

"There are no threats! I'm a business major at Ivy River, for God's sake! Where you come from, people might get kidnapped and killed all the time. But I live in the real world. And I don't need you to protect me."

"Apparently you do, since it's now my job."

"My dad is overreacting." She yanks up the bag and throws it over her shoulder while glaring at me. "I don't need a babysitter."

"Tough luck. Because you're stuck with me."

She lets out something between a curse and a snarl. After snatching up her keys from the counter, she stomps towards the front door and tries very hard to storm off dramatically.

I just chuckle under my breath and follow her out the door.

5

KAYLA

"Why are you following me?" I snap as I hear Jace walk out the door right behind me.

"It's my job." He raises his eyebrows in a show of exaggerated shock. "Man, I thought you were one of those people who don't preheat the microwave. But apparently, I was wrong."

I give him a flat look at his use of my own insult. But before I can spit out my retort, he turns around and closes the door while pulling a set of keys out of his pocket. I narrow my eyes. God damn it. I had planned on not giving him any keys, but it looks like Dad anticipated my actions and gave them to him behind my back.

Shaking my head, I just spin around and stalk towards the elevator. It's already on my floor, so I quickly push the button to open it and slip inside. Then I ram my finger into the button for the ground floor while begging the door to close before Jace can make it here.

A victorious grin spreads across my lips as the door starts sliding shut.

Right before it can close, an arm appears in the small gap.

The door immediately opens again.

I blow out an annoyed sigh.

"Going somewhere?" Jace asks with a smirk on his stupidly handsome face as he strolls into the elevator.

Crossing my arms over my chest, I shoot him a pointed look as the elevator starts descending. "You really are utterly clueless about what you're supposed to do when a woman storms off, aren't you?"

"Of course I am. Because no woman ever storms off when I'm in the room. Instead, they try to find excuses to stay."

"Wow, it really is massive, isn't it?"

"My cock?" He grins and gives me a quick rise and fall of his eyebrows. "Yes, it is."

Heat sears through my cheeks, but I manage to keep the dismissive expression on my face as I roll my eyes. "I was talking about your ego."

"Sure you were."

"Has it ever occurred to you that not every woman who looks at you wants to fuck you?"

"No."

"Jesus fucking Christ." Twisting towards him, I make a show of looking up and down his body and then towards the elevator door several times.

He gives me a befuddled look. "What?"

"I was just wondering how you fit through the door with an ego that large."

"I turn sideways."

A surprised laugh threatens to spill across my lips, and I have to bite the inside of my cheek hard to stop it.

The elevator door slides open with a *ding*.

Jace holds his arms bent out to his sides in the imitation of a gorilla and then turns around and walks sideways out of the elevator and into the lobby. I just stare at him, my mouth slightly open.

"Like that," he says, and flashes me a grin.

Once again, I have to swallow down a laugh.

It's immediately followed by a pulse of irritation. God damn it, he is not supposed to make me laugh. He is nothing more than an overbearing jailer who is keeping me from living a normal life. I refuse to be taken in by his dumb jokes and stupid charm.

With great effort, I wipe the mirth from my face and instead draw my eyebrows down in an unimpressed scowl. Stalking out of the elevator, I simply walk right past him and towards the glass doors that lead out onto the street.

To my great annoyance, Jace doesn't seem bothered by my rude dismissal in the slightest. He simply falls in beside me and slides his hands into his pockets as he starts down the street.

The morning air smells of mist and car exhaust, and the pale light of dawn glints in the windows of the building next to us. A few other people are hurrying up and down the street as well, passing us on the sidewalk on their way to work. Or to Ivy River, like me. I live within walking distance, so I don't need to worry about taking the car or finding a parking spot on campus.

"Why are you even leaving this early?" Jace suddenly asks from right next to me. With his hands still in his pockets, he glances down at me, looking genuinely curious. "Your classes don't start until nine."

I frown up at him. "How did you know that?"

"I memorized your schedule."

Heaving a sigh, I roll my eyes again. "Of course you did, Sparky."

"Don't call me that." He levels a commanding stare on me. "Just answer the bloody question for once."

For a moment, I consider saying something else to piss him off. But I can't come up with anything appropriately clever, so I just blow out a breath and shrug. "I'm meeting my friends for coffee before class."

"See? A simple answer to a simple question. Not that hard, is it?"

"And now you've just ruined it."

"Nah. I think we're going to make a great team, you and I."

Oh no, we most certainly won't. Because I am going to make sure that he quits before the week is over.

When we at last arrive at the coffeeshop, my friends are already there. With a cup of coffee in one hand and Jace trailing after me like a damn puppy, I approach Jenn and Aurora's table.

"Kayla!" Jenn calls when she sees me. "We thought you..." She trails off as her gaze slides over my shoulder and lands on Jace. Her blue eyes go wide. "Woah. Who's that?"

Aurora's mouth drops open as she also stares openly at Jace for a few seconds before snapping her gaze back to me. Her green eyes glitter as she grins at me. "Kayla! Did you get a boyfriend without telling us?"

"He's not my boyfriend," I reply as I pull out a chair and sit down at the table for four. "He's my new bodyguard."

Both of them stare at Jace as he comes to a halt next to the table. There's a very satisfied smile lurking on his lips.

"*That's* your new bodyguard," Aurora blurts out, still not taking her eyes off Jace.

He holds out his hand as if to shake hers. She takes his, but instead of shaking it, he raises it to his lips and gives the back of her hand a kiss.

A tiny squeak slips from Aurora's lips, and she looks like she's about to actually swoon.

An absolutely irrational sense of jealousy flashes through me.

"Jace Hunter," he says, smiling at her while still holding her hand.

"Hi," Aurora breathes.

"Jesus Christ, Aurora," I groan. "Don't feed his ego."

However, before either of them can respond, Jenn speaks up.

"Wait," she says, and blinks at Jace in surprise while he straightens and releases her sister's hand. "Jace Hunter. As in *the* Hunter family?"

He winks at her. "The one and only."

"Wow." She turns to me and gives me a knowing look. "This is just getting more and more interesting by the second."

"Not really," I try to deflect. Without even turning to meet his eyes, I flick my wrist at Jace. "You don't need to stand so close. You can guard me just fine from three steps away."

I can feel his eyes burning holes in my body, and the Carlisle sisters glance hesitantly between me and him. But in the end, Jace just takes two steps back. Not three. Two. But still, I consider it a win.

Once he has turned around to scan the coffeeshop, both Jenn and Aurora lean forward across the table and drop their voices to a whisper.

"Damn, Kayla," Jenn says. "He's hot."

"Yes," Aurora adds. "Smoking hot."

From the corner of my eye, I can see Jace's mouth quirk up in a satisfied smirk. So I make sure to keep my voice loud enough that he overhears me as well when I tell them, "You think? I have to admit, he's really not my type."

I can feel Jace shift his gaze back to me and see him drawing his eyebrows down, but I don't turn to face him. Instead, I just pick up my coffee and take a sip.

For the next twenty minutes, I try my best to ignore Jace's hulking presence right behind my shoulder while Jenn, Aurora, and I chat and drink our coffee. At least he blends in better than all the other bodyguards I've had. Marginally better, anyway.

All the others have been middle-aged men in dark suits who stand out like damn signaling beacons on campus. But Jace in his jeans and white t-shirt, and with his messy brown hair, looks like he's just a normal student here. If normal students also looked like they were carved statues of ancient Greek warriors, that is.

"Oh, by the way," Aurora says in an excited voice as she leans forward. "I think I'm going to ask Nichlas out for coffee tomorrow."

Jenn smirks and gives her a playful shove. "Then why were you flirting with Kayla's bodyguard just now?"

"Because I'm not a nun." She grins back and wiggles her eyebrows. "Like a certain someone."

"I'm not a nun! I just didn't want to date Henric Gutman."

"Oh come on, he has a nice smile."

"He has a pet lizard and a porn addiction."

"True. And that is never a good combo."

"Told you."

With matching grins, they raise their cups and clink them together.

My heart twists painfully.

I wish I had that.

I mean, we're friends and we have fun together. But I know that my relationship to them will never be what their relationship to each other is. Jenn and Aurora are sisters, with Jenn being only one year older. And since Jenn went to France for a year to work as an au pair, they are now in the same year at Ivy River.

And they're inseparable. They joke and laugh and tease each other and have each other's backs in a way that only siblings do. I only got to experience that for a short time.

Some people would say that I'm lucky that I got those years at least. But I'm not lucky. Having known what it's like is a fucking curse and it makes me feel even more lonely now that I'm all on my own.

A *bang* echoes through the room.

I leap up from my chair and whirl around as the sound of rattling silverware follows the bang.

Stunned shock pulses through my skull as I stare at the scene behind me.

"Ow," a miserable voice groans. "What was that for?"

Shaking my head, I blink to clear my vision. But the scene before me remains the same, which means that it is indeed happening.

Jace has slammed a guy down over a table. He has one hand on the back of the guy's neck and the other around his wrist as he bends the guy's arm up into the air behind his back.

All around us, the other people in the coffeeshop are staring at us with wide eyes. The barista is holding a cup towards a customer, but it's just hovering in the air because both of them are looking at us.

Embarrassment floods my cheeks.

I quickly shift my gaze back down to the guy who is bent

over the table with his cheek pressed against the pale wooden tabletop. Recognition flits through me.

"Uhm… Kayla," he croaks from his awkward position.

Oh God, it's that guy from the party. Lionel Henderson.

I snap my gaze to Jace and throw my arms out. "What the fuck are you doing?"

"He was sneaking up on you," Jace replies, scowling down at Lionel.

"He's a friend!"

Jace clenches his jaw in annoyance, but then finally releases Lionel. He doesn't step back, though. Instead, he remains standing there right behind Lionel, towering over him like the grim reaper himself.

Embarrassment and a hint of pain shine in Lionel's eyes as he straightens from the table and rolls his shoulder back into its proper position. And because Jace is standing so close, he has to carefully edge around him to get away from the table. I shoot Jace a glare. He just shrugs.

Lionel scratches the back of his neck and gives me a sheepish smile. "That was not how I had planned to say hi."

I chuckle. "Well, to be fair, all our meetings do seem to be a bit unconventional. Given that last time I saw you, I was straddling you on a living room floor."

Jace's gaze snaps to me.

It makes smug satisfaction ripple through me, and I don't bother suppressing the grin on my lips.

"A friend, huh?" Jace says.

"Yeah." I lift my shoulders in a nonchalant shrug. "We met at a party this weekend."

His gaze sharpens. "So you don't actually know him."

At the table, Aurora and Jenn watch the verbal sparring

match with rapt interest while Lionel edges a step away from Jace.

Anger sears through me at Jace's demanding tone. No one speaks to me like that. And certainly not my bodyguard.

"We need to have a talk," I declare, locking hard eyes on him. "Come with me."

Before he can even reply, I turn around and stalk towards the small, secluded corridor that leads towards the kitchen and the back rooms. The walls here are made of black tiles, and there is a fake plant in the corner to make it look a bit fancier. But the staff barely use this corridor at this time of day.

Once we're halfway down it, and away from the prying eyes of everyone in the coffeeshop, I spin around to face Jace.

"You listen to me and you listen well." I stab a finger into his annoyingly hard chest. "You do not treat my friends like that."

He stares right back at me. "If you met him at a party this weekend, he's not your friend. He's an acquaintance at best."

"It doesn't matter. You should not have done that to him."

He crosses his arms. "I don't like the look of him."

A frustrated sigh rips from my lungs, and I rake my fingers through my hair in annoyance. "Oh, so that's it, huh? It's because he's a guy."

"I never said that."

"Then why didn't you do the same thing to Jenn and Aurora?"

"I've already told you, I got a bad vibe from him."

I give his chest an angry shove, which unfortunately isn't enough to push him back. But he does uncross his arms and raise his eyebrows in silent question. Fury courses through me, and I shove at his chest again, trying to slam him up against the wall. It doesn't work.

So instead, I raise my hand and hold up a warning finger. "I will not tolerate this kind of macho bullshit. If you think that just because you're my bodyguard, you can stop other men from touching me, you're wrong."

"I never said that. You can fuck whoever you want." A devilish smile curls his lips. "As long as I'm there."

Heat sears through my veins. Embarrassment or anger or… something else.

I take a step forward, trying to back him up against the wall. But the bastard doesn't step back, so I'm forced to settle for glaring up at him instead.

"Let's get something straight," I say, infusing my voice with steel and unflinching authority. "*You* work for *me*. So when I give you an order, there is only one acceptable response. And do you know what that is? *Yes, ma'am.*"

His eyes glint, and he takes a step forward. And because of his sheer size, he actually succeeds in doing what I tried to do. Backing me up against the wall.

I try to stop before I reach it fully, but he plants a hand against my collarbones. With a firm shove, he pushes me up against the wall.

My heart leaps into my throat as my back connects with the black tiles.

Jace doesn't remove his hand.

While keeping one hand on my collarbones, pinning me to the wall, he presses closer until he can brace his other forearm against the tiles next to my head.

His intoxicating, masculine scent fills my lungs as he leans down, getting right into my face.

"I don't work for you," he says, his warm breath dancing over my lips with each word. "I work for your father."

My heart pounds in my chest as I look up into those gleaming brown eyes. I can't even feel the cold tiles behind my back anymore. All I can feel is his strong hand on my collarbones, his breath on my skin, and the warmth from his body.

I drag in an unsteady breath, trying to center myself again. Then I raise my chin and shoot him a threatening look. "I would choose my next words very carefully, if I were you."

A wicked smile plays over his lips as he cocks his head. "Threatening me now, are you, little demon?"

My pulse flutters at the nickname and the dark promises and threats in his voice. But I keep my chin jutted out defiantly and give him a stare full of challenge. "I can have you fired any time I want."

"No, you can't. Because if you could, you would've done it already."

I draw in shallow breaths and lick my lips, because he's right, of course. I can't have him fired. Which means that I don't actually have any power over him at all. None of my other bodyguards ever realized that. But somehow, Jace did. In less than a day.

"You—" I begin, but my retort is cut off abruptly as shock pulses through me instead.

My heart skips a beat as Jace slides his hand from my collarbones and up my throat. Drawing in a stunned breath, I just stare up at him.

A strange throbbing sensation pulses through my clit as Jace flexes his fingers around my throat before settling his hand there. He's not choking me, but there is still no mistaking who holds the power here now.

My pulse hammers and heat pools at my core.

"So, when *I* give *you* an order," Jace begins, echoing my words from earlier, as he holds my gaze with commanding eyes. "There is only one acceptable response. And do you know what that is? *Yes, sir.*"

My clit throbs and I have to press my thighs together.

Fucking hell. No one has ever spoken to me like this before. No one has ever treated me like this before. Because of who I am, everyone always jumps to obey my commands. No one ever gives *me* orders.

And my confused body doesn't seem to know how to react. I know that I should be angry. Or at least indignant. But with lightning flickering through my veins and my pussy throbbing, I can't deny that I'm also a bit turned on by this.

Fuck.

Maybe dealing with Jace is going to be a little more difficult than I had anticipated.

6

JACE

For the first time in years, I don't feel restless. I no longer feel the need to use buckets of alcohol or bloody fights or meaningless sex to suppress the overwhelming urge to crawl up the walls. It's such a strange feeling. That lack of restlessness. It makes me feel as if I'm bursting with energy. But in a good way, this time.

Kayla shoots me a glare as she strides into her lecture hall.

Amusement ripples through me. It's a good thing that I feel like I'm bursting with energy, because I'm going to need it to deal with this little demon that I have been tasked to protect.

Still, I don't really mind it. Because finally, I'm doing something that matters. This bodyguard assignment matters more than anything I have done at Blackwater for the past two years. It matters more than anything I have *ever* done. Because these coming months as Kayla's bodyguard is what's going to give me freedom for the rest of my life. So I will be dead before I let her ruin it for me.

She thinks that she can be an annoying menace?

She has no idea who she is playing against.

I grew up annoying the crap out of three older brothers whose mental state varies from arrogant and domineering to downright unhinged.

Menace is my fucking middle name.

"Let's sit in the middle," Kayla says to the Carlisle sisters.

Aurora flicks a quick glance at me while Jenn follows Kayla down the steps of the auditorium. I flash her a sly smile and wink. She flushes bright red and almost trips on the next step.

I suppress a smug laugh while she straightens and hurries after the others.

That is how women usually react to me. How they're supposed to react when I'm being charming and flirty.

But for some reason, Kayla seems entirely immune to my charm. Which is odd. And annoying. Usually, panties would've dropped by now. But instead, she just looks at me as if I'm something she scraped off the bottom of her shoe.

Except for our little argument in the coffeeshop. I could feel her pulse fluttering under my hand as I pinned her to the wall. Could see the heat that crept into her cheeks. She's not used to people speaking to her that way, or manhandling her like that, but it didn't look like she hated it either.

I file that information away for later and instead shift my attention to the annoying guy who showed up at the coffeeshop and decided to tag along.

Lionel Henderson. I drag my gaze over him. Brown hair that is slicked back from his face, gray eyes that seem to get very interested when he looks at Kayla, and fancy clothes that peg him as someone who comes from money. I don't like the look of him. I don't like the look of him at all.

Striding down the steps, I shoulder past Lionel so that I

can follow directly behind Kayla instead. He stumbles from the force of it and has to catch himself on the seats to his left. I don't bother stopping to see him straighten again. Instead, I stride down the row of seats and drop down in the one right next to Kayla.

She jerks back in surprise and turns to stare at me. Then she narrows her eyes.

Pointedly picking up her bag from the floor, she stands up and moves three seats to the right. I simply stand up and follow her.

Since I'm blocking the way, Lionel and the two blonde sisters are left awkwardly standing in the narrow space between the seats behind me.

After flipping the seat down from the backrest, I drop down on it and stretch my legs out.

"Stop," Kayla growls.

A few other people turn around to look at her. She gives them an embarrassed smile before fixing me with a furious stare. I just raise my eyebrows in a show of innocent confusion.

"You don't need to sit right next to me," she snaps.

"How else am I supposed to keep you safe?" I reply, grinning at her.

She draws in an annoyed breath between her teeth. Then she surprises me by climbing over my legs and walking back the way we came.

"Stay," she orders as she casts me a glance over her shoulder.

I narrow my eyes at her back. "I'm not a dog."

"Could've fooled me."

Before I can retort, she grabs the top of the seat in front of her and jumps over it and into the row ahead. Her friends blink at her in surprise, and even more students turn around to look.

After exchanging a glance, Jenn and Aurora jump the row of seats as well. Lionel follows suit. The blonde girls quickly settle themselves in the seats on Kayla's left while Lionel takes the seat on her right.

With a smug smirk on her lips, Kayla turns around and shoots me a look that I can only interpret as, *your move*.

Heaving a sigh, I push up from my seat and move towards them.

The soft murmur that was filling the lecture hall dies down as a man in a brown suit walks out onto the stage at the bottom. The room is shaped like an amphitheater, with curving rows of seats that slope down towards the stage.

I walk forward on silent feet until I reach Kayla.

Then I sit down in the seat right behind her.

Bracing my elbows on my knees, I lean forward until I'm so close that my breath caresses the back of her neck.

A shiver rolls down her spine as my breath dances over her skin.

Whipping her head around, she shoots me a lethal stare and opens her mouth.

But right then, the professor speaks up.

"Welcome back, everyone," he says.

Kayla grinds her teeth in annoyance but then turns back to face the professor. I let out a soft chuckle that also caresses the back of her neck. She swipes a hand under her hair, shifting it from her shoulder so that it falls down her back instead. It stops my breath from playing over her skin, but I still remain where I am. Hovering behind her like that just to piss her off.

"Today, I have a very exciting assignment for you," the

professor says. "These coming months, you will, in groups, be responsible for organizing an event. It can be any kind of event that you want, but it must be something that will show off your organizational skills. Which is what you will be graded on."

Kayla cocks her head and starts tapping her fingers on her thigh, as if she has already started planning in her head.

"There needs to be at least three people in each group," he continues. "But no more than five. And together, you will be responsible for organizing an event of your choice. You need to plan it and execute it, which includes finding funds, a location, a target audience, and so on."

I alternate between studying Kayla and sweeping my gaze around the auditorium while the professor finishes his instructions. All students listen attentively and take notes. I grimace. As much as I hate to admit it, Kayla is right about one thing. I doubt there will actually be any real threats to protect her from in here. These people aren't like the students that I'm used to at Blackwater. These people are polite and mild-mannered. Nonviolent. They would never instigate some kind of attack because they would be too worried about ruining their designer clothing.

"We should do a silent auction," Kayla says.

I shift my attention back to her, realizing that the professor has finished speaking. All around us, people are talking and moving around, probably splitting into groups.

"Is it okay if I join your group too?" Lionel asks from Kayla's right.

Kayla, who was looking at Jenn and Aurora, turns towards him. All three of them seem a little surprised for a second, but then they all smile. I suppress the urge to smack Lionel's head into the backrest.

"Oh, of course," Kayla says.

He smiles. "Thanks."

I flex my hands as that same violent impulse bubbles up again. Leaning back in my seat, I cross my arms and just watch in silence as they begin discussing the assignment.

Though, the more I listen, the more I realize that they are not actually *discussing*. Kayla has taken charge and is more or less stating how they should set up this silent auction. There is no hesitation in her tone. No handwringing. No apologizing for her opinions. She owns herself and dominates the situation with complete and utter confidence.

Uncrossing my arms, I discreetly shift a hand down and adjust myself.

Because God damn, Kayla is fucking hot when she bosses people around like that.

She's good at it too.

It really is too bad for her that she ended up with me as her bodyguard. Because no matter how bossy she tries to be, no matter how hard she pushes, in terms of confidence and sheer swaggering arrogance, she will never beat me.

She wants to be a little demon?

I will be the fucking king of hell.

7

KAYLA

It's still dark outside the windows when I climb out of bed and sneak over to my closet. I haven't done this particular thing since last year, because it annoys the neighbors. But Jace is turning out to be a real pain in the ass, so I can't go easy on him.

I hated the way he sat right behind me like that in class yesterday. It made me feel like a prisoner.

Sliding my closet door open, I crouch down and push aside a stack of sweaters so that I can reach the small box in the back. After lifting the lid, I move aside some other items from my stash and then pull out the canister I was searching for. I leave the box like that since I'll be returning my anti-bodyguard equipment to it soon. Straightening, I brush my free hand down my sleep shorts and top.

With the canister in hand, I walk over to my door and edge it open.

Since it's only five o'clock in the morning, the rest of the apartment is dark and quiet. But I still check to make sure that Jace isn't lurking out there before I slip through the door and into the living room.

Yellow light from the streetlamps outside falls in through the windows and illuminates the room enough for me to see where I'm going. I tiptoe across the hardwood floor until I reach the door to Jace's room on the other side.

His door has been left slightly open, probably so that he can clearly hear if I call for help. Which I have to admit is kind of thoughtful of him. But it unfortunately still doesn't change the fact that I don't want him here.

How can he not understand what it's like? How can he not understand that his presence here, and everywhere I am every day of the week, makes me feel like a prisoner? That it makes me feel like I'm being suffocated. He is living *in* my apartment, for God's sake! I have no privacy. No freedom. Doesn't he understand what it's like to feel trapped?

Shaking my head in frustration, I slink in through the gap in the door and sneak into his bedroom.

My heart skips a beat when my eyes land on him.

He hasn't even closed the blinds, so the light from the streetlamps outside falls in patches across the bed. And across his body.

Standing by the foot of the bed, I watch him for a while.

His perpetually messy hair is equally messy in sleep. But when those loose curls are tumbling over a pillow it's somehow even more sinfully hot. Suddenly, I just want to run my fingers through his hair and make it even more messy.

My gaze slips down to his body.

He has kicked off the cover at some point because it now only covers one leg and half of his hip, leaving the rest of his body on full display. And since he only sleeps in a pair of boxers, it leaves *a lot* on display.

Fire sears through my veins.

God, I thought he was hot just wearing that damn t-shirt. But shirtless... the man is a damn masterpiece.

I stare at his broad shoulders and firm pectorals and perfectly sculpted abs while slowly shaking my head in disbelief. Does he do anything other than work out? With a body this perfect, he has to be one of those health freaks who only eat chicken and eggs and who spend every waking moment in the gym.

Shaking my head once again, I shift my gaze back up to his face.

His features are smoothened by sleep, making him look almost... innocent.

Guilt slices through my insides, and I glance down at the canister in my hand.

It's technically not his fault that he's here. My father is the one who hired him and who is insisting that I need a bodyguard. Not Jace. He is literally just doing the job he was hired for.

A flash of anger pulses through me.

Gritting my teeth, I tighten my grip on the canister and shove all traces of guilt out of my mind.

It doesn't matter if he's only doing his job, it's making *me* miserable. And I want him gone. If he didn't want to deal with my shit, he shouldn't have accepted this contract. Nothing is stopping him from just getting another job. But him being here is stopping me from living my life. So I will give him hell until he quits.

I straighten my spine and give myself a determined nod before sneaking around the bed until I'm standing right next to Jace instead.

Then I lift the air horn canister and blare it right in his

face.

A loud blast cuts through the room, shattering the silence like a smashed mirror.

Jace shoots up from the bed.

I chuckle, but the sound is cut off halfway through by a yelp.

My stomach lurches as I topple backwards when Jace practically tackles me to the floor. I hit it hard enough to knock the breath from my lungs. A huff rips from my throat and I drop the air horn canister. It clatters against the floor before rolling away.

I try to gasp air back into my lungs, but before I can even begin to draw a breath, Jace's massive body lands on top of me.

His hands are like steel bands around my wrists, slamming them into the floor above my head. I try to use my legs to push him off me, but it's impossible because they're spread wide on either side of his hips rather than underneath him.

I snap my gaze up to his face.

Fear floods my chest like cold water.

His face is lethally calm, his mouth pressed into a thin line and his eyes sharp. And there is a terrible sense of danger radiating off him.

I try to suck in another breath underneath his powerful body.

Fuck.

Maybe surprising an assassin with an air horn in the middle of the night wasn't such a good idea after all.

Then Jace's eyes focus on my face, and recognition blows across his features. He blinks. And then frowns.

In a matter of seconds, that terrifying danger evaporates

from his features and is instead replaced by something like exasperation. Or maybe annoyance. Or both.

At last, he pulls back enough for his chest to stop crushing mine. I suck in a desperate breath, finally refilling my lungs.

But he doesn't climb off me.

His hands remain around my wrists, pinning them to the floor, and his hips are flush against mine. With his body between my legs like that, I can feel the massive bulge of his cock through the thin fabric of our clothes.

Heat sears my skin, and I suddenly become acutely aware that Jace is naked except for his underwear.

I try to yank my hands out of his grip and wiggle out from underneath him, but it only makes me grind my hips against his.

Another wave of heat pulses through me.

"What the hell are you doing?" Jace demands above me.

I scowl up at him, desperately praying that the heat I can feel radiating from my cheeks isn't visible in the gloomy light. "What does it look like? I'm trying to get you off me."

"Yeah, I can see that." He gives me a flat look. "I meant with the air horn."

My gaze drifts towards the canister now resting against the leg of the bed a short distance from us. Oh. Right. That. Well, uhm…

While taking an extra second to look at the air horn, I scramble to come up with a scathing remark. But it's annoyingly difficult when I'm hyperaware of how his cock is pressed between my legs.

At last settling on something, I turn my gaze back to him and arch a haughty eyebrow. "You were late. My usual bodyguard would be up by now."

He scoffs and flashes me a smile full of challenge. "No, he

wouldn't. Because you get up at six, and your bodyguards always get up at a quarter to six."

Surprise flits through me.

His smile turns into a smirk as he raises an eyebrow. "I've memorized your schedule, remember?"

Yanking against his hands, I squirm underneath him again while shooting him a vicious glare. "Just get off me."

"No."

I stare up at him incredulously. "What?"

"First, you're going to apologize."

"For *what?*"

"For sneaking into my bedroom uninvited and blaring an air horn in my face." He tuts and shakes his head. "That's a very rude thing to do, little demon."

Anger flickers through me, and I struggle against his hold yet again. "First of all, this is *my* apartment. I don't need permission to enter any of the rooms in it. So if I want to be in your bed—"

"You want to be in my bed?" he interrupts, and gives me one of those damn smirks that makes my heart flip.

"Bed*room*," I snap, once more trying to block out the embarrassment with fury. "I was going to say bedroom."

"Sure you were."

"God fucking damn it!" I yank and squirm against him furiously. "Just let me up."

"Apologize."

"Like hell!"

"Then I guess we're staying right here."

A snarl rips from my throat, and I struggle hard on the floor. But my wrists might as well be locked to the ground with metal shackles. No matter how much I try to pull my arms down from where he keeps them trapped above my head, his hands around my wrists don't move a single inch.

I buck my hips, trying to throw his body off me.

My pussy grinds against his cock.

I draw in a sharp breath between my teeth as a jolt shoots through me.

Above me, Jace watches me with glittering brown eyes while amusement plays over his lips.

Another snarl tears from my chest.

"Apologize," he orders, that wicked smirk still on his face.

I clench my jaw. "No."

"I can do this all day."

"I'll miss class."

"That's not my problem. My job is to guard you."

My heart jerks as he abruptly leans down and slants his lips over mine, just shy of touching. I suck in an unsteady breath while heat pools at my core.

"And I can do that just fine from right here," he finishes, every word like a caress over my mouth.

The feeling of his breath on my lips like that and his solid weight between my spread legs and his hands pinning my wrists to the floor make my heart pound in my chest. Absolutely insane images flash through my mind. But before I can dwell too much on them, Jace pulls back as abruptly as he leaned down.

Still keeping me trapped underneath him, he cocks his head and gives me a smug look full of challenge. "Now, apologize."

I grind my teeth as I glare up at him in silence. But if the past few minutes have taught me anything, it's that I won't be getting off this floor unless he lets me. Forcing out an annoyed sigh, I break eye contact and instead tilt my head to stare out at the rest of the room.

"Sorry," I press out.

"Eyes on me." The sheer command in his voice sends a pulse through me.

I drag my gaze back to his. Then I have to draw in a bracing breath before I manage to repeat, "I'm sorry."

"I'm sorry, *sir*."

Disbelief clangs through me. He can't be fucking serious? I stare up at him with wide eyes.

He just smirks at me. Challenge dances in his eyes like tiny flames as he holds my stare.

When he does nothing to indicate that he was joking, I blurt out, "You can't be serious!"

"You give me shit, and I'll give you shit." He tightens his grip on my wrists and levels a hard stare at me. "So we can either make each other's lives hell, or we can be civil. Your choice."

I grind my teeth and glare up at him. But Jace doesn't budge. I force out a long, calming breath that does absolutely nothing to calm the wildfire in my veins. Then I at last press out the words he wants to hear.

"I'm sorry, sir."

His eyes gleam, and he lets out a soft chuckle. "Good choice."

I'm pretty sure a growl slips past my lips.

With that smirk still in place, he slides a very deliberate look down my body. Another wave of heat ripples through me. Then he at long last releases my wrists and climbs off me.

The moment his weight is off my body, I push up into a sitting position. Jace, who is already on his feet, reaches down and offers me his hand to help me up. I slap it away.

Shooting to my feet on my own, I cast him a sharp look before stalking back to my own room.

We can make each other's lives hell, or we can be civil.

Arrogant fucking bastard. He forced me to apologize and made me address him as *sir*.

I will be fucking dead before he ever sees any civility from me.

8

JACE

Well, I did give her a choice. But I suppose *making each other's lives hell* it is, then.

It has been almost an entire week since I started this job, and I'm already exhausted. Every day, Kayla Ashford finds some new way to drive me crazy. It helps that I grew up with Eli, Kaden, and Rico, who have all done nothing but mess with me for twenty-two years, but the little demon that I'm supposed to be guarding still somehow manages to infuriate me.

How can one person be so fucking difficult?

I don't even understand why she's so against me. I'm literally just doing my job. Which is to *protect* her. Plus, I'm funny and hot as fuck. How can she not enjoy my delightful company?

At least I will be getting a little break from her tomorrow. I have every Sunday off since Trent Ashford apparently wants them all to spend family time together every Sunday, which means that his bodyguards handle security for Kayla as well as Trent and his wife.

And right now, I'm very glad that it's Sunday tomorrow, because I have a feeling that tonight is going to be a particularly exhausting ordeal.

Sneaking out of the bookshop, I quickly skirt around the building until I reach the back. There is a trellis secured to the wall there, and it runs up to the upstairs window. A massive ivy plant snakes up the wooden support.

I move so that I'm standing in the shadows behind the hedges that cover the area below the windows. And then I wait.

Less than a minute later, the upstairs window is cracked open and flaming red hair becomes visible.

Remaining in the shadows, I watch as Kayla scans the small garden behind the bookshop. But there is only one decorative lamp on the wooden wall a little farther down, so there is no way that she can see me in the gloom.

Once she's satisfied, she quickly climbs up onto the windowsill.

Her sleek legs are steady as she swings herself around and then starts nimbly climbing down the trellis.

My cock hardens as I watch her perfect ass move in the skintight little black dress she's wearing.

Did she actually think that she could fool me with this? No one goes to a bookshop on a Saturday night dressed like *that*. And her plan to lose me in the twisting aisles while she ran upstairs to climb out the window? Ridiculous. Who does she think I am? An amateur?

I grab the item that I secured to my belt for this specific reason before we left her apartment.

Raising my hand, I wait until Kayla is past the halfway point on the trellis.

Then I blare the air horn in my hand.

She cries out in surprise and loses her grip on the wooden trellis.

Red hair streams through the night like a fiery waterfall as she falls through the air and lands right in one of the thick bushes. I hook the air horn to my belt again and stroll up to her.

For a few seconds, she doesn't move. Just lies there in the middle of the thick, green bush with her red hair spilling out all around her and those stunned blue eyes of hers staring up into the darkened sky. As if she can't process what just happened. I stop right in front of her.

Arching an eyebrow, I smirk down at her. "Going somewhere, little demon?"

She snaps her gaze to me, and realization slams home on her features.

"Ugh," she growls, and slams her hand down into the already half flattened bush before shooting me an incredulous look. "Seriously?"

"You're the one who left the air horn in my room," I point out.

She starts trying to untangle herself from the branches so that she can climb out of the bush. "You could've given it back."

"Why would I do that? When I could watch you fall into a bush instead."

"You are unbelievable!"

"No, you are the one who's unbelievable. Did you really think that I bought your little I'm-going-to-the-bookstore act?"

Her hair gets caught in the leaves, and she practically rips the tiny branches away from her long red strands while she glowers at me. "It could've worked."

"No, it couldn't." I nod towards the poor bush that she's mangling. "Now, do you want me to help you out so that I can follow you to the party you're really going to?"

She scoffs and shoves the branches aside before finally stalking out of the bush on her own. I heave an exasperated sigh and shake my head. Stubborn woman.

"How did you know that I was going to a party?" she mutters while she brushes leaves off her dress.

I reach up and pick a few twigs from her hair. She starts in surprise and her mouth drops open a little, but she doesn't slap my hand away.

After gently disentangling the twigs from her hair, I toss them down on the grass and give Kayla a pointed look while replying, "Because no one makes an effort to look that hot just to go to a bookstore."

She jerks back a little again, once more looking genuinely surprised. Then she recovers and instead lets a smug expression settle on her features as she raises her eyebrows at me. "You think I'm hot?"

"Of course I do. Everyone does." I stab my finger at her pointedly. "And you know it. So don't try to pretend otherwise. False modesty doesn't suit you."

For a moment, it looks like she doesn't know whether to be flattered by the compliment or annoyed by the admonishment.

In the end, she just huffs and rolls her eyes.

"Fine," she says, though it sounds more like a sigh. "I'm going to a party. And since you're already here, I suppose I'll let you come too."

I snort. She doesn't *let me* do anything, and we both know it.

"Just make sure that you don't stand too close to me," she

finishes as she flicks her hair back behind her shoulders and starts towards the street.

Chuckling under my breath, I follow her.

I will promise no such thing.

Music pulses around me. I once more sweep my gaze over the large living room and scan the faces of everyone in here. Most of them are dancing and jumping with smiles on their faces. Some are laughing and talking in groups while drinking from their red plastic cups. All of them are in various stages of inebriation.

It's so strange to be at a party while not actually *being* at the party. Normally, I would be one of the people getting drunk and making out with some hot stranger. But now I'm standing here, completely sober, in the middle of a crowd of dancing university students, and being utterly fucking boring. It's not like me at all.

My gaze drifts back to Kayla, and a small smile blows across my lips.

At least I can have fun by annoying the crap out of her.

She's dancing with her friends Jenn and Aurora, swaying her hips and throwing her arms up over her head. Her back is to me, which I'm sure was a very deliberate choice, so I can't see the expression on her face. But she appears to be having fun. She has tried to sneak away from me three times since we got here, but it looks like she has given up on that. At least for now.

A blond guy approaches her from across the packed living room. His gaze roams over her body. It sends an irrational flare of rage through me, and I flex my hand. I should've brought one of my bats.

The blond guy smiles as he looks up at Kayla's face again while closing the distance to her.

I take a threatening step forward and level a death stare at him.

His gaze darts to me, and he screeches to a halt on the polished wooden floor. Glancing between me and Kayla, he licks his lips. Then he turns and quickly walks away.

Kayla stops dancing and turns to stare after him as if confused.

Then she whirls around.

Fury pulses across her gorgeous face as she locks eyes with me. "Stop doing that!"

I just hold her angry stare and lift my shoulders in a nonchalant shrug. "I'm not doing anything."

"You've scared off every single guy who has tried to approach me!"

"It's not my fault that they have such an inferiority complex that they can't stand to be in my presence."

"Asshole."

"Demon."

She blows out an annoyed breath and then turns around. Jenn and Aurora cast confused glances between the two of us, but Kayla just shakes her head and starts dancing again. I watch her perfect body move to the rhythm of the beat. The Carlisle sisters throw their arms up and dance as well.

After about two minutes, a guy in a pink shirt starts towards them.

I cross my arms and lock a menacing stare on him.

He blinks and then quickly scurries away.

Vicious curses cut through the thumping music as Kayla whips around to face me.

"You fucking…" Trailing off, she grits her teeth and shakes her head at me.

Then a scheming glint appears in her blue eyes. With a seductive smile on her face, she closes the distance between us. I narrow my eyes at her.

"Ah, so this is why," she says, that little sexy smirk still on her lips. "You're scaring off all the other guys because you want me to dance with you instead."

Uncrossing my arms, I just give her a flat look in response.

She chuckles and lifts her hand.

A ripple courses through my body as she slides her fingers over my collarbones before drawing her hand down my chest. My cock hardens.

"Like this?" she says, a taunting note to her voice.

However, before I can retort, she drops her hand and instead turns around so that her back is flush against my chest. Then she starts dancing. Her ass grinds against my cock with every sway of her hips.

"Or like this?" she says, casting me a knowing look over her shoulder.

Blood rushes to my cock at the feeling of her body writhing against mine. The impulse to grab her hips and press her harder against me almost overrides my self-control. Drawing in a silent breath to steady myself, I remain perfectly still.

"Is this supposed to affect me in some way?" I mock, making sure to keep my voice bored and disinterested.

She arches her back slightly, pushing her ass more firmly against my cock as she rolls her hips to the music.

A jolt shoots through me.

Clenching my jaw, I flex my fingers and once again blow out a long breath through my nose. My cock aches.

Kayla chuckles and then turns around to face me instead. Her eyes glitter with devilish delight as she tilts her head back and meets my gaze.

"Do you know one of the many reasons why women are superior to men?" she asks, raising her eyebrows while challenge dances across her features.

I just look back at her with what I hope is bored disinterest.

"We can hide it when we're turned on." With a wicked smirk on her lips, she flicks a pointed look down at my hard cock. "You cannot."

My hand shoots out.

Sliding it through her silken hair, I thread my fingers through the long strands at the back of her neck and grip her hair hard. My chest heaves and fire licks through my veins.

A smug smile curls her lips.

I use the firm grip on her hair to tilt her head back.

My pulse pounds in my ears.

Kayla just looks up at me with gleaming eyes, daring me to… To what? Punish her? Kiss her? Shove her up against a wall and act out all of the images that flashed through my mind when she was grinding her ass against my cock?

"Uhm, what's going on?" a terribly annoying voice says.

Kayla and I just continue staring each other down. A silent dare.

Blowing out an impressed breath, I shake my head at her and then release my grip on her hair. Those smooth red strands slide over my hand as I let my arm drop back down. Kayla flashes me a victorious smile and then turns towards the sound of the voice.

"Nothing," she replies. "What's up, Lionel?"

I drag my gaze to the annoying interruption. Lionel is standing next to Aurora and Jenn, his confused gray eyes shifting between me and Kayla.

"We're just about to start a drinking game," he says. "Never have I ever. Do you wanna play?"

"Yes!" Aurora cries, and claps her hands excitedly before grabbing her sister by the hand. "Come on, Jenn."

"Yeah, yeah, of course," Jenn says as she lets Aurora lead her in the direction that Lionel pointed. Twisting her head, she meets Kayla's eyes over her shoulder. "You're coming too, right?"

Kayla flicks her hair back while a wicked grin spreads across her face. "Naturally."

I heave a sigh. Oh, great. A drinking game. This will no doubt make Kayla even more difficult to handle.

While Lionel takes the lead, Kayla surprises me by walking next to me instead of trying to slip away.

"You're playing too," she announces.

Glancing down at her, I frown as we make our way towards the kitchen. "I'm working."

"So?"

I just give her a flat look.

A small groan escapes her throat. "Alright, fine. How about this? If you play with us, I promise that I won't try to sneak away. For the rest of the night."

Raising my eyebrows, I just look back down at her.

"I'll stay where you can see me and I'll even let you walk me home without trying to ditch you," she promises, giving me a perfect look of innocence.

Amusement ripples through me. I know exactly what she's doing. She is planning to drink me under the table so that, even if she doesn't try to actively sneak away, I will be too drunk to keep a close eye on her.

Clever.

But what she doesn't know is that I've spent the past five years drinking heavily to escape the feeling of being trapped and suffocated by a future that I can't choose. I'm not a lightweight by any sort of standards. I could drink her under the table ten times over before I even start to feel intoxicated.

A grin pulls at my mouth as I meet Kayla's scheming eyes.

"Deal."

9

KAYLA

This is the perfect plan. Given his sculpted body, Jace must be a health freak who no doubt treats his body like a temple. He probably never drinks alcohol because it would mess up his perfect body. So I will easily be able to drink him under the table. And I don't even need to make him pass out or anything. Just drunk enough to make it difficult for him to keep track of me. Then I can enjoy the rest of the party without him looming over me like a bloody god of death.

Four people look up from the massive dining room table when we reach it. Three girls and one guy. I've never met them before, but Ivy River University is huge, so it's not really that surprising.

"Alright, everyone, this is Mitch," Lionel says as he points to the guy.

Mitch tosses his black hair out of his eyes and raises a hand. "What's up."

We all give him a nod while we start pulling out chairs.

"And this is Trina," Lionel motions to one of the blonde girls next to Mitch before pointing to the one with stunning green eyes. "And Felicia." His hand moves to the brown-haired girl on the other side. "And Rebecca."

"Hi," they say in unison and smile at us.

Chairs scrape against the pale wooden floor as we all join them around the table. It's one of those massive tables with room for ten people, so we all fit comfortably around it. Just like most students at Ivy River, the guy who lives here is rich. Or his parents are, anyway. And they're out of town, which is why he decided to throw a party.

I glance around the beautiful kitchen and dining room. The marble countertops are now littered with red plastic cups and empty bottles and cans. One of the pale wooden cabinets has been left open after someone no doubt searched for more glasses. Or maybe more alcohol. And the grand painting of a sunlit beach on the white wall opposite me now hangs a little crooked. Cleaning all of this up is going to be a pain. For the guy at least. Or rather, for the people he has no doubt hired to clean for him.

"And this is Kayla," Lionel says from where he is now sitting next to me. Then he motions to the Carlisle sisters on my other side. "And Jenn and Aurora." A frown pulls at his brows as he turns to Jace, who is sitting right opposite me. "And, uhm… I'm sorry. What's your name again?"

Jace just keeps holding my gaze with those penetrating eyes of his for another second. Then he leans back in his seat and draws a hand through his messy brown hair while giving the rest of the table a confident grin.

"Jace," he says, his warm brown eyes glittering in the light from the ornate lamp above the table. "The name's Jace."

Aurora, Trina, and Rebecca all watch the way his muscles shift underneath his white t-shirt when he moves his arm like that. Lust burns in their eyes. I suddenly find myself scowling.

"Are we playing or what?" I demand, my words coming out with a little more bite than I had intended.

Lionel blinks and looks over at me in surprise. I catch myself and make a show of rubbing my hands together instead, as if I'm just excited. Lionel buys it completely and flashes me a smile before reaching for a bottle of vodka from the ones waiting in the middle of the table. Jace, on the other hand, slides his gaze back to me and smirks. I give him a dark look.

"Alright, the game is simple," Lionel begins while Mitch starts sliding shot glasses across the table. "You say *never have I ever* and then you finish the sentence with something that you have never done. And then everyone who has done that takes a shot."

Jace chuckles while he grabs another bottle of vodka and leans over the table to fill my glass first. Once it's so full that I'll barely be able to lift it without spilling the alcohol, he winks at me and then starts filling his own glass. To his credit, he pours as much alcohol into his own glass as he did mine.

On my left, Lionel scowls at the way Jace laughed at his instructions. "What?"

"I just love how you felt the need to explain the rules of a drinking game that everyone here has no doubt been playing since high school," Jace replies, without even looking at Lionel, while filling Felicia's glass.

Everyone else at the table chuckles softly and nods in confirmation. A hint of red creeps into Lionel's cheeks. I shoot Jace a glare, which he pretends not to notice.

"Alright, who's first?" Mitch asks once everyone has a shot ready and waiting on the table.

"Me," I say quickly. With a wicked smile on my lips, I look straight at Jace as I say, "Never have I ever beaten someone up."

Jace raises his eyebrows and gives me a flat look that I can only interpret as, *seriously?*

I just look back at him expectantly.

He lets out a huff of amusement and then picks up his glass. Mitch does too.

"Mitch," Rebecca blurts out, blinking at him in surprise. "What the hell?"

"What?" he replies, pausing with his shot glass halfway to his mouth. "Some guy was trying to hit on my sister even after she said no, so I beat him the fuck up."

Jace shoots him an approving look and leans across the table to clink his glass against Mitch's. "Oh, I'll drink to that."

Mitch grins at the approval, and both of them down their shots.

Pain twists inside my chest. Victor would no doubt have been that kind of brother too. The protective older brother type who would beat someone up for disrespecting me. The kind of brother who would've stroked my hair while I bawled my eyes out about some guy who broke my heart in high school. Someone who would've always been there for me.

But instead, I've been alone most of my life.

My fingers tighten around my shot glass, and I have to resist the urge to fiddle with my watch.

"Alright, Jenn, you're up," Aurora says, and nudges her sister in the ribs.

"Oh, uhm..." Jenn clears her throat, looking like she's scrambling for something to say.

Shrugging off my painful thoughts, I force my mind back to the plan at hand. To drink Jace under the table.

Discreetly leaning over, I whisper in Jenn's ear. She gives me a small nod and a quick smile.

"Never have I ever fired a gun," she declares, echoing what I told her to say.

Jace lets out a soft laugh and shakes his head at me while picking up his glass again. His eyes gleam. "If I didn't know better, I would think that you're trying to get me drunk."

I flash him a devilish smile. "I have no idea what you're talking about."

"My turn!" Aurora announces. Mischief sparkles in her green eyes as she says, "Never have I ever gotten my dick sucked."

All three guys groan and roll their eyes at her.

"Oh, come on," Mitch protests. "That's cheating. You don't even have a dick."

"It's called playing smart." Aurora winks at him. "Now, drink."

All three of them take a shot.

"Watch your back," Mitch says, and grins at Aurora as he sets his empty glass down and refills it. "Revenge is heading your way."

She just laughs and wiggles her eyebrows.

"Never have I ever had a threesome," Trina says.

A jolt shoots through me when Jace picks up his glass and drinks again. Felicia does too.

"Felicia!" Trina squeals and gapes at her friend. "You've never told me that!"

"There's not much to tell," she replies with a shrug. "It was a pretty disappointing night, to be honest."

Jace slides his gaze to her, and a sly smile plays over his lips. "Sounds like you just didn't have the right partners."

Heat creeps into Felicia's cheeks, and she almost drops her now empty shot glass. A small noise comes from the back of Aurora's throat while Trina stares at Jace with open longing.

Annoyance ripples through me.

"Mitch, your turn," I say, cutting off any further discussion of this particular topic.

A smile full of challenge spreads across Mitch's face as he looks straight at Aurora. "Never have I ever had my pussy licked."

With that victorious smile still on his lips, he waits for all six of us girls to drink.

Only Rebecca does.

Shock pulses across his face as he stares between the other five of us.

Aurora shrugs. "You'd be surprised by how few guys are actually willing to reciprocate."

The rest of us nod in confirmation.

Jace clicks his tongue and shakes his head in disapproval. "Once again, you've clearly not been fucking the right kind of guys."

This time, all of the other girls glance towards him with longing in their eyes. But Jace only looks at me, his intense gaze searing through my soul.

An absolutely insane image flashes through my mind. An image of Jace getting down on his knees, draping my leg over his shoulder, and eating me out while I writhe in pleasure against a wall.

My clit pulses.

Pressing my legs together under the table, I give my head a quick shake and force that stupid image out of my mind.

The game continues. Most of the statements are about sex now. I drink on some of them. Jace drinks on every single one. Well, except on his own turns, of course. He always uses those for a targeted attack on me.

My head is buzzing with alcohol, and I've started giggling at the stupidest things, which means that I'm starting to get seriously wasted. I reach for the bottle of vodka after downing another shot, but my fingers fumble and I almost knock the bottle over.

From across the table, Jace quickly reaches out and wraps his hand over mine, steadying my hand and the bottle.

Electricity shoots up my spine at the feeling of his hand over mine like that.

It makes me irrationally angry, and I try to yank my hand and the bottle out of his grip. He just raises his eyebrows expectantly. A frustrated sigh rips from my lungs. Releasing the bottle, I let him fill up my glass instead.

Through narrowed eyes, and a vision that is slightly blurry at the edges, I watch him pour vodka into my glass with a completely steady hand.

How the hell is he not drunk yet? Because of all the sex statements, he has been taking more shots than anyone at the table. Yet he appears entirely unaffected while the rest of us are giggling and fumbling and slurring our words. I swear, Aurora almost toppled over in her chair when she leaned over to jab her sister in the ribs. But Jace is just sitting there, smirking at us as if he has been drinking water instead of vodka.

Drawing my eyebrows down, I fume in silence while everyone finishes refilling their glasses.

On the other side of the table, Felicia leans over and places a hand on Jace's arm while Trina and Rebecca bat their long lashes at him as well. Even Aurora is eyeing him like she's starving for his attention.

During the course of the game, all of them have unconsciously shifted closer to him. Leaning a little forward in their seats. Twisting their bodies a little more in his direction.

I watch the way they all try to catch his eye or get his attention or make him laugh.

But Jace simply refills Mitch's glass and gives his arm a slap while chuckling at something he said.

I wonder if he even notices that people seem to gravitate towards him. As if he is a radiant sun that everyone is circling in the hopes of being bathed by his brilliant light for a few seconds.

That irrational anger inside me grows.

"Alright, how about this one?" Mitch says, his voice now significantly louder after all the shots he has been downing. "Never have I ever fucked more than four people in the same night."

Jace smirks and picks up his glass.

A booming laugh escapes Mitch's chest as he pounds his fist on the table while Jace downs the shot.

The image of five girls worshipping Jace's body all at the same time flashes through my mind.

"Man, you are a fucking legend," Mitch says, and slaps Jace on the back.

"Or a whore," I snipe, that crackling annoyance still pulsing inside me.

Jace snaps his gaze to me, anger flashing in his eyes.

I flinch at the intensity of that rage.

It's the first time I have seen true fury in his eyes. Even

after all the bullshit I have pulled this past week, I have never seen him get truly angry. Except now.

"Being experienced does not make me a whore," Jace says, holding my gaze with hard eyes.

Guilt twists inside me, because I didn't even mean it. I was just angry and frustrated. But before I can respond, Felicia speaks up.

"Of course not," she says, once again leaning over to place a flirty hand on his arm. "We hate it when guys say things like that to *us*, so why would we say that to them?"

Embarrassment burns through me at the truth in her words.

I clear my throat and push to my feet. "I think I need to get some water."

But the thing about drinking while sitting down is that you don't feel just how drunk you really are until you stand up.

My legs wobble as I awkwardly climb off the chair and take a step away from the table. I immediately have to throw out a hand to steady myself on the back of Jenn's chair.

Lionel jumps to his feet and wraps an arm around my waist for support. "Here. You should probably go and lie down for a bit." With his arm still around my waist, he starts walking me away from the table. "Come on, I'll take you to a quiet room."

I gasp and almost fall over when Lionel's body is suddenly ripped away from mine.

Jace's dark voice cuts through the room like thunder. "Back the fuck off."

Spinning around, I find Lionel bracing himself on the table that Jace no doubt threw him into. Jace is now standing between me and Lionel. His arms are crossed over his broad chest, and there is an unforgiving look on his face as he stares Lionel down.

Lionel's cheeks are red with indignation as he straightens from the table and throws his arms out in frustration. "I was helping her!"

"You do not put your hands on her body unless she gives you express permission to do so," Jace growls at him.

My heart skips a beat. At his commanding tone. At the power that pulses from his body. But most of all, at his word choice. He didn't say that Lionel is not allowed to touch me. He said that he's not allowed to touch me without *my* permission. Meaning that my will, my choice, is the deciding factor here. Not anyone else's.

The realization sends a pulse of warmth through me.

But before I can do anything, Jace uncrosses his arms and turns back to me instead. "Come on, let's get you home."

I'm still a bit dazed, and very drunk, so I just nod. Then I turn to the others at the table, who are watching Jace with expressions varying from surprise to adoration.

"Bye, guys," I manage to say while my head spins from the alcohol. "I'll see you later."

"Uhm, yeah," Mitch replies, casting a hesitant glance at Lionel, who is staring daggers at Jace.

The girls wave and call out goodbyes as well. Aurora even winks at me while casting a sly look between me and Jace. I just roll my eyes at her and then start towards the doorway.

Music and laughter and loud voices envelop us as Jace and I make our way through the elegant but now very messy house and towards the front door.

Warm night winds wash over us as we step out onto the lawn. I draw in a deep breath and close my eyes. But that only makes me stumble a step to the side, because my legs are still far too unsteady.

A firm hand appears on my elbow, steadying me.

I open my eyes to find Jace there. He raises his eyebrows in silent question. I just clear my throat and start down the small path that leads to the street. The world sways around me.

Once we reach the street, I turn in the direction of my apartment. But I have to throw out a hand and brace myself on a metal pole because the abrupt turn made my head spin.

Clearing my throat again, I start forwards.

I only make it five more steps before I trip over something.

Jace's hand shoots out, grabbing my arm and stopping me from falling on my face. My hair swings over my eyes as I look down. I drag a clumsy hand through the long strands, pushing them away from my vision as I raise my head again while straightening.

A deep sigh sounds from right next to me.

Then Jace scoops me up into his arms instead.

Lightning pulses through me.

While shock still rings inside my skull, I tilt my head back and stare up at Jace while he starts us down the street. But he doesn't look down to meet my gaze. Instead, he simply keeps carrying me in his arms as he walks back to my apartment.

Heat, both from embarrassment and something else, washes through me at the way my body is pressed against his chest and the way his strong arms are wrapped around me. I study his handsome face in silence for a few minutes. The streets are dark and deserted around us.

"I didn't mean it, you know," I say quietly after a while.

"Mean what?" Jace asks, still not looking down at me.

"I don't think you're a whore."

He says nothing for a few seconds. And he still isn't

looking at me. Guilt and regret twist inside my chest like snakes.

"Then why did you say it?" he asks at last.

"Because I was jealous," I admit in a soft voice. "Because I wish that *I* was more experienced."

Finally, he glances down at me. His steady gaze searches my face, as if checking to see if I'm just making this up. I'm not. I do wish that I was more experienced.

I want to do stupid shit and have kinky sex and try crazy things too. But it's very difficult to do that when there is always a man in a suit watching my every move. I've had a few boyfriends, of course. And I've had sex with them. But it's always hard to get in the mood for that when I know my bodyguard is standing right outside the apartment door.

Jace can apparently tell that I was being sincere, because he nods in acknowledgement. Then he returns his gaze to the street ahead.

The warmth from his body wraps around me, seeping into my bones and soothing my soul, as he holds me tightly to his chest while he carries me down the next street.

Countless questions swirl in my mind, but I know that I shouldn't ask any of them. I shouldn't make any effort to get to know Jace. Not when I'm trying my best to get rid of him. But there is one question that I can ask. One question that I can convince myself is strategically important for my plan to make him quit.

"Why did you take this job?" I ask.

Jace says nothing. Only turns the corner and starts us down the street that leads to my apartment.

"You're an assassin," I push. "You kill people. You don't protect them. So why did you agree to take this job?"

Only silence answers me. From a few streets over, a car

alarm starts beeping. Someone honks their horn from that direction as well. Mist and car exhaust mingle in the night air that fills the city.

Just when I think that Jace is not going to answer, he replies with a single vague sentence.

"I have my reasons."

10

JACE

"Who pissed in your cereal this morning?" Eli says. And even though I have my arm draped over my face so I can't see him, I can still hear the smirk in his voice.

I groan, still slumped on the couch with my arm over my face. "Kayla fucking Ashford."

"Wait, seriously? She actually pissed in your cereal?"

A huff that is half amusement and half exasperation rips from my chest. "No. But I'm sure the only reason she hasn't done that yet is because she doesn't actually eat breakfast. She does everything else she can, though, to be a fucking menace who—"

My words are cut off as something hard slams into my chest.

"Ow," I growl, yanking my arm off my face and sitting upright.

Glaring down, I find my own bat now lying in my lap after it smacked into my chest. I draw my eyebrows down and look up to find Kaden standing in the doorway to the living room with a nonchalant expression on his face.

Eli huffs out a laugh while dropping down on the couch opposite me. It creaks underneath his weight as he lands and swings his feet up on the coffee table. Rico strolls past and casually kicks Eli's feet down from the table before he shoves my legs off the couch as well and sits down next to me. Eli shoots him a threatening look that Rico responds to with a grin full of challenge.

I snatch up the bat in my lap and spin it in my hand before pointing it at Kaden, who is still watching me from the doorway with cool dark eyes. Narrowing my eyes, I level a hard stare on him.

"You don't just throw bats at people," I warn.

From next to me on the couch, Rico snorts and cuts me a sideways look. "*You* are the last person who gets to lecture someone about throwing bats at people, Golden."

"One, don't call me that. And two, let me rephrase." I level my bat threateningly at Kaden again. "You don't just throw a bat at the owner of said bat. It's—"

"Bat Etiquette 101," both Eli and Rico finish for me, and then chuckle in unison.

"Exactly," I say.

"Yeah, you do," Kaden argues as he at last pushes off from the doorframe and starts towards the couch. While dropping down next to Eli, he gives me a pointed look. "If the owner of that bat left it blocking *my* hallway."

"*Blocking* the hallway?" I roll my eyes and put the bat down on the coffee table in front of me. "Now you're just being dramatic."

Kaden slides out a knife and starts twirling it in his hand.

"If I wanted bats all over my house, I would be marrying you. Not Alina."

"Yes, where is Alina?" I ask, glancing around their neat living room.

Just like Kaden's room was back home, and back at Blackwater, his and Alina's house is freakishly neat and clean. He has always preferred things organized, and it shines through now as well.

There is not a speck of dust on the pale wooden furniture, and the two white couches that we're occupying don't have a single stain on them. Sunlight streams in through the windows and glints against the silver decorations around the living room.

I suppress a smile as my gaze drifts across the light colors. That is something Kaden had to give up. He prefers dark colors. Dark wood. Black fabric. But Alina doesn't. She likes it light and airy. And Kaden is whipped as fuck when it comes to Alina, so whatever she wants, she gets.

"She's out with Raina and Isabella," Kaden replies, still nonchalantly twirling the knife in his hand.

I snap my attention back to his face. "What?" Incredulity pulses through me as I stare between my three brothers. "You let the three of them go out alone. *Together*."

Rico clears his throat and lifts one shoulder in a shrug. "We've preemptively paid off the entire police department."

"Just in case they set the whole city on fire," Eli picks up, and waves a casual hand in the air. "Or, you know, kill a bunch of people or something."

An astonished laugh escapes my chest, and I shake my head. "And this is why I'm still single."

Eli, Kaden, and Rico exchange a glance. Knowing smiles spread across their lips. I scowl at them.

"What?" I demand.

Kaden snickers and cuts me a look. "For now."

"What does that mean?"

"It means that you've been talking an awful lot about Kayla Ashford in our group chat."

"So," Rico begins, drawing out the word, before I can retort. "What's she like?"

I shoot them all a threatening look, which they all just answer with a wicked grin. Groaning, I slump back against the backrest again and rake my fingers through my hair.

"I'm telling you, she's fucking crazy," I mutter.

Eli arches a dark eyebrow. "Crazy or insane?"

Letting my hands drop back down, I frown at him. "Is there a difference?"

"Yes."

"I don't know." I shake my head at him in befuddlement. "Both?"

Kaden shrugs, still not missing a single spin with his knife. "She can't be worse than Raina."

"No one is worse than Raina." I hold up my hands to illustrate two separate groups. "There are insane people. And then there's Raina. She's not in the same league. Hell, she's not even playing the same sport."

"Hey," Eli cuts off, shooting me and Kaden a threatening look. "Watch your mouths about my girl."

Kaden just shrugs again. "She would probably take it as a compliment."

Eli considers for a second, and then tips his head to the side as if conceding the point. "True."

"So no, she's not worse than Raina," I continue. "But she's still driving me crazy!"

All three of them exchange another knowing look and then smirk at me.

"Stop smirking," I mutter. "I'm serious. I have never met anyone who is as infuriating and tenacious and as utterly incapable of following orders and as immune to my charms as..." Trailing off, I shoot them all a dark look. "You're smirking again."

They chuckle.

Rico wiggles his eyebrows at me. "Yeah, I mean, Kaden is the one getting married in a couple of weeks, but I'm sure we could make the priest stay for a second wedding right after as well."

"Yeah," Kaden adds, his dark eyes glinting as he holds my gaze. "And I'm sure I can find that French maid costume you keep talking about, so that *you* can practice wearing it instead."

I scowl at both of them. "Shut up. I'm not..." Trailing off, I sit upright again as a realization crackles through me like a lightning bolt. "Oh, fuck. Your wedding. It's on a Saturday. I need to find someone to cover Kayla that day."

"Bring her," Kaden says with a casual shrug.

Shaking my head, I stare at him. "Haven't you been listening? She's crazy. And annoying as hell."

"So are you, and you're still invited."

"Fuck you."

He smirks. But there is a sparkle in his eyes. Kaden talks a lot of shit. In fact, we all talk a lot of shit and take every opportunity to mess with each other. But when push comes to shove, we have each other's backs without question. Every day of the week. Or at least, I hope so. But maybe that has changed now that they know that I'm not sure if I want to be a hitman.

As if his mind went down a similar path, Rico turns to me with a serious expression on his face. "I've been meaning to ask. Well, *we've* been wondering…"

Panic shoots up my spine. I'm pretty sure I know where this is going, but I manage to keep a casual expression on my face as I meet his gaze and raise my eyebrows in silent question.

"Why didn't you tell us?" he asks, his serious eyes searching my face. "That you didn't want to become a hitman."

That panic ripples through me again, mixed with dread this time. I can feel Eli and Kaden watching me as well.

"It's not that I don't want to be a hitman," I begin, trying to choose my words carefully. "Like I said, I do actually enjoy it. But I just… I want a choice."

He gives me a small smile. "Yeah, I get that."

And he does. I know that he truly does understand. Out of all of them, Rico is probably the one who most understands what it's like to feel trapped in a life that you haven't chosen.

"But still," Eli picks up from the white couch across from me. His golden eyes are also serious as he studies my face. "Why didn't you tell us about that?"

How could I? When they're all so perfect. Eli, the ruthless killer who will without a doubt surpass our father as the most legendary Hunter assassin. Kaden, the calculating schemer who makes people flinch just by looking at them. Sons that our parents can be proud of. Sons that will accomplish great things and carry on the notorious Hunter name. And Rico, the powerful leader who will rule this entire state one day. The pride and joy of Federico Morelli.

And then there's me.

How could I ever tell my brothers that I might not want to

join them down this path? That I might not want to become a hitman. That I couldn't stand the thought that this was going to be my life whether I wanted it or not.

I didn't want them to see me as weak. I didn't want them to see me as a failure. As someone unworthy of being their brother. Of being one of them.

So that's why I didn't tell them.

But how could I ever explain that to them now?

Clearing my throat, I push to my feet and do my best to give them all a casual smile. "I'm just going to grab something to drink."

They watch me in silence, but they say nothing. And they don't try to stop me as I walk back through the living room and towards Kaden and Alina's kitchen.

And I fucking love them for that. I love them for not pushing me. For not forcing me.

Maybe one day I will tell them, but not today.

Not right now.

Because right now, I need to keep myself together firmly enough to survive this semester of guarding Kayla. Nothing is going to stop me. No matter what, I am going to make it to the end of the semester. Because I need to have the choice to decide my own future. I need it more than anything.

11

KAYLA

Quickly climbing out of bed, I sneak over to my dresser and open the top drawer. Through my closed bedroom door, I can finally hear Jace walking out of his room and into the kitchen. He always gets up before me and is ready and waiting by the time I leave my room. But not today. Today, I plan to surprise him.

Since he is apparently completely unfazed by all the annoying things I do to make his life miserable, I'm going to switch tactics and try something else. Instead of subjecting him to what are essentially irritating pranks, I'm going to make him uncomfortable. I'm going to make him squirm in his seat and nervously glance over his shoulder as he worries about someone seeing him. Seeing me. Seeing us.

After stripping out of my sleep shorts and top, I search through my underwear drawer until I find the sexiest lingerie that I own. They're made of black lace, and they perfectly accentuate my curves.

On the other side of the door, I can hear faint clinks and thuds from where Jace is moving around in the kitchen.

Once I'm finished getting changed, I brush my hair and let it flow down my back. Then I put on some makeup too.

By the time I'm done, the noise from the kitchen has stopped. A chair scrapes lightly over the floor as Jace no doubt sits down at the table.

I check my appearance in the mirror. A wicked smirk spreads across my lips as I draw my hands over my hips and then turn to look at myself from all angles. In only a pair of black lace panties and a bra in the same material, I look like any man's dream. And Jace's nightmare.

A silent laugh rolls from my chest. Let's see him sweat now as he worries about how my father will react if he finds out that Jace has seen me dressed like this.

With a sultry sway of my hips, I at last walk out of my bedroom and into the combined kitchen and living room.

Jace is seated at the table, eating breakfast. He is fully dressed in a pair of jeans and a white t-shirt that contrasts against his slightly tan skin. His brown hair is, as always, effortlessly messy in a way that makes me want to run my hands through it. The muscles in his forearms flex as he cuts into his food.

Surprise flickers through me, and I lose that swaggering in my step for a second, when my gaze lands on the plate in front of him. Or rather *plates*. There is one plate full of scrambled eggs and bacon, another one that contains something that looks like a panini, and a third one is piled high with fruit.

I've known that he eats breakfast, of course, since I've sometimes heard him in the kitchen when I've woken up early. But I've always just assumed that he eats hardboiled eggs or something similarly boring like most health freaks. Not *this.*

My gaze darts between his face and the little feast he has made for himself. There's a sparkle in his eyes and a small smile on his mouth as he eats. As if he truly savors the food.

It surprises me so much that I forget what I'm doing for a moment.

Jace starts looking up from his plate.

I lurch into motion again. With that seductive sway in my hips, I saunter across the floor and towards the table where he is seated.

He turns towards me as he catches the movement in the corner of his eye, and opens his mouth as if to say something.

Then his gaze lands on me.

And he jerks back slightly in his seat as surprise pulses across his face.

His stunned gaze quickly flicks up and down my body.

I give him a sly smile, and wait for him to start glancing over his shoulder in worry.

He doesn't.

Instead, he quickly wipes the astonished expression from his features and simply returns his attention to his food while casually saying, "Morning."

"Morning," I reply as I walk up to the table.

"Shouldn't you get dressed?"

"I am dressed."

He looks up from his food again and casts a deliberate glance up and down my body while raising an eyebrow. "You're going to school like that?"

I wait for heat to flood his cheeks when he draws his gaze over my half-naked body. But it doesn't. The infuriating bastard doesn't look affected at all. After that first moment of surprise, he is acting as if he's looking at a mediocre landscape painting and not my hot fucking body in lace lingerie.

Annoyance ripples through me.

But I make sure to keep the irritation off my face as I arch an eyebrow at him. "Last I checked, this was my kitchen. Not uni. And I can dress however I like in my own home."

Jace watches me in silence for a few seconds. Then he shrugs. "Alright."

And then he goes back to eating.

Curling my fingers into a fist, I fume in silence as I glare at the frustrating man at my kitchen table.

After blowing out a discreet sigh of exasperation, I give my body a short shake to get rid of the annoyance. I'm far from done. Let's see him ignore me when I turn up the heat.

I walk over to where I put my bag last night and move it over to the edge of the couch, which is straight in Jace's line of sight. Then I stroll over to the bookshelves where I keep my course books and pull out a few. After sauntering back to my bag, I position myself with my back to Jace and drape my hair over my shoulder.

Then I slowly bend over and start putting the books into my bag.

The position puts my ass on full display in those tiny lace panties. And when I'm bent over in that suggestive pose, there's no way that Jace isn't blushing. Or glancing nervously around the room as if he's worried that my father will suddenly materialize and kill him for looking at me.

While sliding the final book into my bag, I angle my head and discreetly glance back towards the table.

Jace is holding his panini now, biting into it with a completely unaffected expression on his face.

I grind my teeth.

God damn it. What do I have to do to get a reaction out of this guy?

Shoving my bag shut again, I straighten and flick my hair back behind my shoulder before turning around. Jace chews his bite of panini, watching me with a casual look on his face.

Maybe he needs it a bit more up close and personal.

With a sly smile on my lips, I walk back to the kitchen table until I'm standing on the other side of it, right opposite Jace. Holding his gaze, I lean forward over the table and reach for his plate of fruit. If I was any closer, my tits would be in his fucking face. He has to react now.

But Jace just keeps his eyes on my face, not once letting his gaze slip down to my cleavage.

I curse him in my mind.

Then I pick up a strawberry from his plate.

He sets down his panini and takes a sip of orange juice. "If you want breakfast, make it yourself."

"I don't eat breakfast," I reply as I bring the strawberry to my lips and bite down.

Shaking his head, he lets out a huff while shooting me a pointed look. "Yeah, I can see that."

Still leaning forward over the table so that my breasts are on full display, I lick my lips as seductively as I can before I take another bite of the strawberry. Jace's eyes remain on mine. He doesn't even glance down at my lips. Not even once.

Fucking hell, what is it with this guy?

I pop the final piece of strawberry in my mouth, placing it deliberately on my tongue and then sucking my finger on the way out.

Jace curls his hand into a fist on the table and shakes his head again before pushing his chair back.

"And now I've lost my appetite," he says as he gets to his feet and quickly starts turning around as if to leave.

Humiliation washes through me.

But then I see it.

The massive bulge in his pants.

Shock pulses through me at the sight of it. God, he must be painfully hard if his cock is straining that much against his jeans.

Straightening in a flash, I quickly skirt around the table before he can walk away. He jerks back, coming to an abrupt halt as I stop right in front of him.

With a wicked smirk on my lips, I tilt my head back and lock eyes with him. "Liar."

He frowns down at me with what I have to admit is impressive nonchalance. "About what?"

"Losing your appetite. In fact, I'm pretty sure you're actually struggling to... *contain* your appetite."

"Keep telling yourself that if it makes you feel better."

"Uh-huh." I shoot a pointed look down at the bulge in his pants. "So that's not your cock standing at attention for me?"

A muscle ticks in his jaw, but he doesn't reply.

"Oh, I see," I taunt, flashing him a devilish smile. "It's not your cock. It's your gun. Man, I didn't realize that the groceries were giving you so much trouble that you had to keep a gun in your pants while making breakfast." I flick another knowing look down at his crotch before raising my eyebrows in a show of innocent curiosity. "Or perhaps it's a pet snake that I have yet to meet. I didn't realize that you were a reptile guy. I have to warn you, I'm not a fan of snakes—"

My mocking words are cut off by a yelp as Jace surges forward.

Grabbing my wrist, he twists me around and pushes my

arm up behind my back while his other hand locks around the back of my neck.

A huff escapes my lungs as Jace bends me over and shoves my chest down against the smooth wooden tabletop. He keeps one hand on the back of my neck, holding me down, while the other keeps my arm twisted up behind my back.

I blink, my mind scrambling to catch up with the sudden turn of events.

Before I can get my wits about me, Jace places his foot against the inside of mine and pushes outwards in one firm motion, widening my stance.

My heart skips a beat as he steps closer, his hard cock pressing against my ass.

"Is this what you want?" he demands, his commanding voice pulsing through the air and vibrating through my soul. "For me to bend you over the table and fuck you?"

Heat sears through me at his words.

"Answer," he snaps.

A jolt shoots through me, and my clit throbs. At the effortless command in his voice. At his dominating hands on my body as he keeps me bent over the table. At the feeling of his cock pressing against my ass.

And suddenly, all those ridiculous images that flashed through my mind during the party flicker across my vision again. Images of what Jace must have looked like when he participated in all those adventurous sexual activities that he admitted to when we played *never have I ever*. And I once again can't help but wonder what it would be like to fuck someone as experienced as him. What it would be like to fuck *him*.

Anger quickly follows the thought, burning away those ridiculous images.

I yank against his grip on my wrist while planting my

other palm on the table, trying to use it as leverage to push myself up. But I might as well have been pushing against a rock wall. His hand around the back of my neck keeps me mercilessly pinned to the table.

A snarl rips from my throat as I retort, "I wouldn't fuck you even if you were the last man on earth."

"Likewise."

"Good."

"Great." He gives me another shove down into the tabletop, as if to truly rub his power over me in my face. "Now that we've established that, I'm going to allow you to get up. And then you are going to go back into your room and put some fucking clothes on. Understood?"

I slam my free hand into the tabletop. "I will not be—"

"I said, am I making myself clear?" The sheer command in his voice sends a pulse straight through my soul.

Grinding my teeth, I struggle on the table again. But no matter how hard I try, I can't get free. So in the end, I force out, "Yes."

"Good."

He releases my wrist and neck and takes a step back. I shoot upright and whip around to face him so fast that my hair smacks into his cheek on the way past. With fire burning in my eyes, I glare up at him.

Power ripples from his muscular body as he stares me down.

Raising his arm, he stabs a commanding hand towards my bedroom door. His unflinching gaze remains locked on me.

"I said," he begins, his voice dripping with authority. "Get. Dressed."

Electricity shoots up my spine.

No one ever orders me around. Or manhandles me. No

one ever exerts power over me like this. I'm an Ashford. I give the orders.

But Jace doesn't seem to give a shit about that. He acts as if the world belongs to him. As if everyone should bow at his feet. Me included.

Narrowing my eyes, I glare up at him.

He just keeps staring me down in silence, pointing that commanding hand towards my room.

A faint snarl rips from my lungs as I spin on my heel and stalk away.

But no matter how angry this damn bastard makes me, I can't block out the memory of how much my clit throbbed when he bent be over the table like that.

12

JACE

She wants to play dirty? Fine, I can play dirty.

Lounging on the white couch in the living room, I pretend to scroll on my phone while I watch Kayla from the corner of my eye. She usually finishes up her evening read through of her study notes right about now and then heads back to her room to take a shower.

My phone vibrates in my hand as a text appears on the screen.

Marcus Jones: *I'm here.*

I discreetly glance at Kayla again. Seated at the kitchen table, she frowns down at the notebook before her and underlines something. She continues reading for another few seconds. Then she glances at the clock on the wall and sighs. Putting her pen down, she stretches her arms over her head before rolling her shoulders back.

Returning my attention to my phone, I send a quick reply.

Me: *Give me a minute.*

Marcus is a second-year from Blackwater who I've partied with on occasion. He is, all things considered, a pretty chill guy. And he, just like most people at Blackwater, will jump at the chance to help out a Hunter in the hopes that I will put in a good word for him with the Morelli family.

At the table, Kayla gets to her feet and starts packing up her books and notebooks. She is now standing in the exact same spot she was standing in this morning when I bent her over that table.

My cock hardens just at the memory.

Does that little demon have any idea just how fucking difficult it was to sit there and pretend to be completely unaffected while she sauntered across the room looking like the hottest fucking thing I have ever seen in that black lace lingerie?

And when she slid her hair over her shoulder and bent over to pack her books? Fucking hell, I thought the wood was going to crack from how hard I was gripping the table leg. And then she had the fucking nerve to stroll up to the table and lean over it. It took all of my self-control to keep my eyes on her face.

But then she just had to go and suck her finger like that.

Damn infuriating woman.

I was so fucking turned on that I thought I was going to lose my damn mind.

My cock throbs again at the mere memory.

Clenching my jaw, I stare down at my phone while Kayla finishes putting her books away.

Anticipation quickly pushes out the frustration. Kayla might be good, but I'm better. And there is nothing I love more than playing dirty.

Without so much as a glance in my direction, she strides across the room and disappears into her bedroom. The door shuts behind her with a click.

The moment it's closed, I leap up from the couch and hurry across the floor. Moving on silent feet, I sneak up to Kayla's closed door and press my ear against it.

After a few seconds, the sound of another door being closed reaches me. Then everything goes silent.

About half a minute passes.

And then the sound of splashing water echoes as Kayla turns on the shower in her private bathroom.

I sprint over to the front door and unlock it. After a quick look back, I open the door and slip out into the hallway outside the apartment.

A guy with brown hair and dark brown eyes is standing there a couple of steps away. He's holding a large box in his hands.

"Hunter," he says, and nods in greeting when he sees me.

"Marcus," I reply as I close the distance between us. "Thanks for coming through for me on such short notice."

"Yeah, of course. Anytime."

"I'll have her back to you safe and sound in about ten minutes."

He nods. "Alright. I'll just wait here."

I reach out and take the box from him when he holds it out to me. After another nod in thanks, I turn around and disappear back into the apartment. Hurrying over to Kayla's door, I press my ear against it again.

The sound of splashing water still echoes from inside.

Taking a step back, I set the box down on the floor outside the door before I straighten again and carefully push down the handle. I open the door to reveal Kayla's deserted bedroom. The sound of water is louder now when there is no second door to block it.

I spare a quick glance towards the closed door to her

bathroom while I crouch down and open the lid of the box Marcus handed me.

A wide grin spreads across my lips.

Freya looks up at me.

I reach into the box and gently pick her up.

Then I walk into the room and put the corn snake right in the middle of Kayla's bed.

Freya the corn snake is apparently as chill as her owner, because she just curls up there on the soft cover. I give the friendly snake a salute before backing out of the room and quietly closing the door behind me again. But I remain standing right outside.

The noise from the shower continues for another five minutes. After a short silence, the sound of the bathroom door being opened drifts towards me.

Anticipation crackles through me.

With my ear against the door, I listen to Kayla's footsteps move from the bathroom and across the room towards where her closet and dresser are located.

She makes it about halfway.

Then a scream shatters through the air.

I immediately open the door and move forward until I can see her entire bedroom.

And what a sight it is.

Kayla, with only a fluffy white towel wrapped around her body, is scrambling away from the bed and pressing herself against the wall next to her dresser while Freya the corn snake lifts her head to look at the source of the loud noise.

Another squeak rips from Kayla's throat.

Satisfaction ripples through me, and I let out a smug laugh.

Kayla snaps her gaze to me, panic and fear still flashing over her beautiful features.

Leaning one shoulder against the doorframe, I cross my arms over my chest and raise my eyebrows nonchalantly. "Problem?"

Disbelief pulses across her face. Yanking up a hand, she points frantically towards Freya. "There's a snake on my bed!"

"Yes."

"What do you mean, *yes*?" she practically shrieks that final word.

Challenge bleeds into my tone as I hold her stare. "I thought you said just this morning that you wanted to meet my pet snake. Well, here she is."

As if on cue, Freya slithers a couple of inches across the bed.

Kayla lets out another high-pitched cry and jerks back so fast that she loses the grip on her towel. It flutters down to the floor, leaving her completely naked. But she doesn't even seem to notice as she tries to climb up onto her dresser. However, her moves are so frantic that she can't get a solid grip on it, so she just ends up backing farther into the corner instead.

My gaze quickly drifts over her body. Blood rushes to my cock. Fuck, it should be illegal to be that hot.

"Get it out of here!" Kayla snaps, her eyes still locked firmly on the snake.

"She's a *her*," I respond, shaking my head in an exaggerated show of disapproval. "Not an *it*."

"I don't care! Just get it out of here."

"Say please."

At long last, Kayla tears her gaze from the snake and whips around to face me. Utter incredulity pulses in those beautiful blue eyes of hers. Once her attention is no longer on Freya, she seems to process the rest of her situation too. Her gaze snaps down to the towel now lying on the floor halfway between the bed and the corner she is huddled in.

She stares between the bed and that pile of white fabric as if she desperately wants to go back and grab the towel but can't bear to get closer to the snake. I just watch her while smug amusement tugs at my lips.

In the end, she decides to just cover herself up with her arms instead.

Standing there naked in the corner, with one arm over her tits and the other hand over her pussy, she stares at the snake on the bed for another few seconds before dragging desperate eyes to me.

I raise my eyebrows. "Need some help?"

"Yes," she presses out between gritted teeth.

"Say please."

"Please."

"Please, *sir*," I coax.

Her eyes flash with fury and the promise of revenge as she screams, "I will fucking kill you!"

Freya shifts a little at the loudness of her voice.

A whimper spills from Kayla's lips, and she presses herself farther into the corner.

"How are you going to do that when you're about to be bitten by a venomous snake?" I reply, and lift one shoulder in a casual shrug.

Fear pulses in her eyes as she snaps her attention back to the snake. I suppress a laugh. Freya is a corn snake. She's not venomous. But Kayla doesn't need to know that.

"If I die, you won't just lose your job," she says as she adorably tries to threaten me. "My dad will fucking kill you."

"Who says you're going to die?"

"If I get bitten by a venomous snake, I *will* die, you idiot!"

"Nah. I'll just suck the venom out of the wound." With a sly smile on my lips, I make a show of raking my gaze over her body. "Better hope she doesn't bite your inner thigh. Or your tit."

A truly murderous expression descends on Kayla's features like the shadow of death, and she glares at me with hellfire in her eyes. I grin back at her.

"Like I said, little demon," I begin, keeping that wicked smile on my lips as I level a hard stare on her. "You give me shit, and I'll give you shit."

"You fucking son of a—"

But the rest of her curse is cut off by another whimper as Freya moves on top of the bed again. Kayla edges impossibly farther into the corner.

"You want my help?" I taunt. "You know what to say."

The muscles in her jaw flex as she grinds her teeth while glaring at me as if she's imagining the sound I would make if she shoved a knife through my heart. But then Freya moves again, and the rage is replaced by fear as she glances towards the snake now occupying her bed. And then finally, resignation washes across her features.

Shifting her gaze back to me, she drags in a bracing breath.

"Please, sir," she begs.

Smug victory pulses through me, and my cock throbs at the sound of those submissive words on her tongue.

I smirk as I hold her gaze. "Good girl."

Her naked body trembles as a shudder rolls through her.

And I don't think it's out of fear or revulsion this time.

13

KAYLA

He's not supposed to fight back. When I do annoying shit to them, all my other bodyguards have just taken it. They have gritted their teeth and endured it in stoic silence until they can't take it anymore and finally quit. But Jace retaliates. He is not at all intimidated by my power and station as the Ashford heir. And I'm not sure how to feel about that.

Running a brush through my hair, I untangle the mess that it turned into when I slept. Morning sunlight filters in through the windows of my bedroom and illuminates the pale walls. From the other side of my closed door, I can hear Jace bustling around in the kitchen. Which is odd, since he normally always eats breakfast before I even get out of bed.

I glance towards the closed door with suspicious eyes. Is he planning something?

But after my little strip tease two days ago, and his revenge with the snake, I haven't pulled anymore pranks or done anything to mess with him, so there should be no reason for him to plan something in return. Maybe he just decided to eat a little later than normal today?

As I return my gaze to the mirror and the red strands I'm untangling, my mind drifts back to that evening two days ago when I walked out of the shower to find a damn snake on my bed. I didn't see that coming. At all.

A shudder rolls down my spine at the memory of that terrifying beast slithering around on my bed. Ugh. I fucking hate snakes.

And even though I wanted to kill Jace for putting me through that absolute horror, I can't help but be a little impressed. I've done a lot of shit to my bodyguards, so I have quite the repertoire to compare it to, and I have to say that the stunt with the snake was a nice move. Not only did he tie it back to my comment about the snake in his pants that morning, he also accurately deducted that I'm terribly afraid of those slithering animals. And not only that. He also managed to actually procure a snake.

I made that snake comment in the morning, and come nightfall, he had managed to put one on my bed without leaving my side for even one second. As a master of pulling shit on people, I have to say that that move was impressive as hell. Not that I would ever admit that to him, though.

Setting down my brush, I pull my hair up in a ponytail and then smooth down my shirt. After one last glance in the mirror, I walk across the room towards my door to find out what it is that Jace is cooking up in the kitchen. Literally or figuratively. Since I have been civil to him for the past two days, there should be no nasty surprise waiting for me when I open the door. But the keyword in that sentence is *should*. Because with Jace Hunter, you never know.

The scent of food meets me when I stroll into the kitchen.

I frown towards where Jace is standing, his back to me, in front of the stove. Something sizzles in the frying pan, and there is a distinct scent of herbs filling the air.

"What are you doing?" I ask as I walk over to where I put my bag yesterday.

It's already packed, but I still flip through the books to make sure I didn't forget any of them.

"Making an omelet," Jace replies without even turning to look at me.

I just shake my head at him and finish checking my bag. Glancing at the clock, I note that I need to leave in about ten minutes. So if Jace plans to eat an omelet, he's going to have to do it quickly.

While setting my bag down again, I glance towards Jace. He holds the frying pan by the handle and shakes it back and forth a little. Then he uses the pan to flip the omelet like an absolute professional. I blink at him in surprise.

He sets the pan down again and then finally turns towards me. I quickly clear the impressed expression from my features and instead just raise my eyebrows nonchalantly. For a second, I swear I can see amusement tugging at his lips. But then he just raises a hand and points it towards the kitchen table.

"Sit," he orders.

I start slightly at the effortless command in his voice. Then irritation ripples through me instead, and I narrow my eyes at him. "You don't give me orders. I give you orders."

A sly smile plays over his lips as he rakes a highly deliberate glance up and down my body before meeting my gaze again. "We both know that I could *make you* sit in that chair if I wanted to."

Heat pulses through my core.

"But I'm not," he continues. "I'm asking politely."

"No, you're not. You said, *sit*. That's a command. Not a request."

Amusement sparkles in his eyes. Then he sweeps a hand towards the table again. "Please have a seat."

Surprise clangs through me, and I'm pretty sure I jerk back a little as I blink at him. I hadn't expected him to actually… ask politely.

Still a bit stunned, I find myself walking over to the table and pulling out the chair. Jace turns back towards the stove again, but I swear that I can see the edge of a smirk before his back is to me again. It makes me hesitate halfway down to the chair. But in the end, I just blow out a sigh and sit down completely. I have eight minutes before I need to leave, and nothing else to do, so I might as well see where this is going.

Once I'm seated, Jace slides the omelet onto a plate and then grabs some utensils. I watch him through suspicious eyes. He starts walking to the table. But instead of skirting around it to sit down with his plate opposite me, he sets the plate down in front of *me*. Then he walks around the table and sits down opposite me without his plate. The wooden chair creaks a little underneath his muscular body as he shifts his weight until he's comfortable.

Completely befuddled, I look between the omelet and his face. He just looks back at me as if this should somehow make sense.

When no other explanation is forthcoming, I at last nod down at the plate and ask, "What's this?"

"It's called breakfast." Leaning back in his seat, he flashes me a brilliant grin that somehow makes my heart flutter. "It's a meal that people eat after they wake up. You see, the word breakfast comes from *break fast*. Since you've been fasting while you've been sleeping and now you're breaking that fast with a meal."

"Yes, I know what breakfast is. But what is it doing in front of me?"

"You only drink coffee before you go to class in the morning."

"So?"

"Caffeine is not a food."

"The coffee bean comes from a plant. Which means that coffee is basically a salad."

He gives me an incredulous look. "I'm going to pretend that you didn't say that."

Rolling my eyes, I throw out my arms. "What's wrong with drinking coffee?"

"Nothing. But you need to eat some actual food too. Breakfast is the most important meal of the day."

"Wow, thank you, Mr. Public Service Announcement."

"Just eat." He stabs a hand towards the omelet and gives me a look dripping with authority.

For a few seconds, we just stare at each other from across the table. A silent battle of wills. But I know that refusing to eat just makes me petty and childish, so in the end, I blow out a long breath in annoyance and shake my head at Jace while picking up my knife and fork.

A victorious smirk spreads across his lips.

I give him an irritated grimace and start cutting into the omelet with more force than necessary. He just watches me with that damn smirk on his stupidly handsome face.

Stabbing the piece of omelet I cut off, I shove it into my mouth.

I'm just about to shoot Jace an indifferent look when I stop short.

Different tastes blend and mix and enhance that single bite of omelet in a way that makes me feel all warm inside. I start in surprise. And then cut off another piece of omelet, because this has to be some kind of mistake.

But when I eat that second bite, the feeling is even stronger. There's cheese and some kind of thin salty ham and garlic-seared mushrooms and fresh herbs, and it's all warm and buttery from the pan. I quickly cut another bite and put it in my mouth.

A moan escapes my throat, and my eyes flutter as I savor that incredible taste.

Then I suddenly remember that I'm not alone at the table, and I snap my gaze back up to Jace.

He has his head cocked and he is watching me with an expression that I can't quite read. That smug smirk from earlier is gone, and instead, there's a soft smile on his mouth. It does strange things to my heart.

"You made this?" I ask while both confusion and amazement swirl inside me.

It's a really stupid question, I know that. I literally saw him making the omelet when I walked out of my bedroom. But I still need to ask because... well, because I can't quite wrap my head around the fact that someone like Jace can make food like this.

He lifts his broad shoulders in a casual shrug. "Yeah."

"Why?"

"I like food."

"Yeah, I mean..." I trail off for a few seconds, trying to figure out what it is that I'm even asking. "I mean, why did you make it for me?"

Another casual shrug. "Like I said, breakfast is the most important meal of the day."

For a few moments, we just watch each other from across the table. Jace is leaning back in his chair, his hands nonchalantly resting in his pockets, and a faint smile on his mouth. He's the picture of casualness. But there is a glittering sparkle in his eyes now. And it makes my heart skip a beat.

Tearing my gaze from his, I continue eating and savoring the taste with each bite.

Jace just watches me in silence, but that sparkle remains in his eyes. As does the faint smile on his lips.

Once I've finished every single crumb, short of actually licking the plate, I look up and meet his eyes head on again.

"This was…" I begin, searching for the right word. "Delicious."

His lips quirk up in a smirk. "I know."

I give him a flat look. "You're supposed to say, *thank you*."

"No, *you* are supposed to say thank you."

Heat floods my cheeks. Because he's right, of course. He made breakfast for me and I haven't even said thank you yet. But I'm not used to people doing thoughtful things for me like this. I'm rich and powerful enough that I'm usually the one who is asked to do kind things for others. And something as simple, and yet as extraordinary, as randomly making breakfast for me is not something anyone has ever done before.

Clearing my throat, I manage to press out a bit awkwardly, "Thank you."

As soon as it's out of my mouth, I realize just how rarely I say those particular words. At least in these kinds of circumstances. They sound almost strange on my tongue.

Across the table, Jace's smile turns into a full-blown smirk.

I immediately regret thanking him, even though the food was incredible.

I'm not supposed to thank him. Or enjoy the food he makes. Or feel any sort of gratitude towards him at all. I'm not supposed to like him. I'm supposed to get him the hell out of here so that I can finally live my life without a bodyguard looming over me every step of the way. I need to remember my mission. Make this job so unbearable that he quits.

"Aww, look at that," Jace says, with a grin on his face. "I'm growing on you."

I give him a flat look. "Yes, like fungus."

He chuckles and simply gets to his feet before reaching over to grab my now empty plate. I scowl at his back as he walks over to the dishwasher and puts the plate and utensils into it. Why didn't he take the bait?

In fact, why is it so bloody difficult to faze him? My rudeness and insults and annoying stunts never seem to hit the way they normally do. Jace just takes it all in stride. Always shrugging casually and smiling while that unshakable confidence pulses from his entire soul.

But I refuse to give up. I will make him quit. No matter what.

14

JACE

My two days of relative peace are apparently at an end. After I made her breakfast this morning, she spent the entire day trying to ditch me and sneak off alone. I have a feeling that it's because she has started to actually like me a little bit. And why wouldn't she? I'm awesome.

Soft evening winds swirl down the street, bringing with them the smell of warm asphalt and car exhaust. Since everyone is trying to get home from work at the same time, the cars covering the street are barely crawling forwards. The sidewalks are full of people too, bustling one way or the other. I scan our surroundings for threats while I follow Kayla towards some mysterious location that she refused to specify beforehand.

I also watch *her*. Watch the way her red ponytail swings across her back. The way her hips sway slightly. The way she walks with her spine straight and her chin held high.

There are lots of other people heading in the opposite

direction, but they all shift aside for her. As if that is the natural order.

Kayla Ashford moves through the world as if it belongs to her.

And it's hot as fuck.

We reach a tall building made of white stone. It's designed to look like one of those fancy buildings from England's Victorian era, and I recognize it immediately.

Surprise pulses through me when Kayla starts heading for the front door.

"This is where we were going?" I ask as I follow her.

"Yes," she replies without even looking at me.

Pulling open the door, she strides inside. She doesn't bother holding it open for me, but I was prepared for that, so I yank up an arm and catch the door before it can slam into me. Despite Kayla's nonexistent manners, I find myself getting incredibly excited.

Among other things, this building houses a restaurant called *La Fleur*, which is one of the best restaurants in town. It has a waitlist several months long. For normal people, anyway. Being a Hunter has its perks. But even despite my ability to skip the waitlist if I want to, I've still only been here twice, because I haven't really had that many occasions to visit.

I glance down at the jeans and t-shirt I'm wearing. Kayla is dressed in chic black pants and a stylish shirt that makes her look like she has just stepped off a fashion runway. Her clothes fit the dress code. Mine do not. I'll most likely need to pull the Hunter card to get inside.

But it doesn't matter. I'm still ridiculously excited. If she is here to eat alone, then I might as well claim the second seat at the table and eat too. This is turning into a fabulous day.

The moment that thought has finished passing through my mind, we turn the corner and find a group of people who instantly darken my mood.

Lionel Henderson is standing at the entrance to La Fleur along with Jenn and Aurora Carlisle. Which means that this is probably a meeting for her event planning group. Kayla must have organized this via group chat, because she sure as hell hasn't been talking about it so that I could hear.

"I'm telling you," Aurora says to the smartly dressed woman standing at the entrance. "We're supposed to be meeting our friend here."

The woman gives her a patient smile. "As I have explained, the waitlist is three months long. Unfortunately, you cannot simply go inside because your friend is here."

"That's not what—"

"Aurora," Kayla says as she closes the final distance to the four of them.

They all turn to look at her. Jenn and Aurora offer her a smile while Lionel shoots an annoyed look at me. The woman at the front desk startles slightly.

"Ms. Ashford," she blurts out.

"They're with me," Kayla says.

"Oh, of course." She glances to Lionel and the Carlisle sisters before meeting Kayla's eyes again. "I'm so sorry, ma'am. I didn't realize that—"

"It's fine." Kayla waves a hand in the air, dismissing the issue. "Is our table ready?"

"Yes, of course."

The woman flicks a quick glance between the four of them, who are all dressed in at least semi-formal clothes, before her gaze lands on my jeans. An apologetic expression descends on her features, and she looks very uncomfortable, as she raises her eyes to meet mine.

"I'm sorry, but the dress code states that jeans are not permitted in the dining room," she begins.

Next to me, I can feel Kayla smirking at me in smug victory. She thinks that she is so clever. Bringing me here without telling me beforehand so that I will have to wait outside because I'm not wearing proper attire. And it might have worked. If I had been anyone else.

Saying nothing, I just continue holding the woman's gaze. She opens her mouth as if to repeat the statement, but then she blinks as if finally recognizing me. Her gaze quickly flicks up and down my body before once again settling on my face. True realization at last floods her features. She remembers me from when I was here last time.

"Mr. Hunter," she says, sounding a little breathless and worried.

I incline my head in acknowledgement.

"I didn't realize…" she begins before trailing off. Abruptly taking a step to the side, she motions for all of us to enter. "Please, follow me."

Kayla frowns deeply at her before shooting a frustrated look at me. I just grin back at her. Her family might be powerful, but so is mine.

We all follow the woman through the elegant dining room. Glittering chandeliers hang in the ceiling and pristine white tablecloths cover the tables. There is a pleasant murmur throughout the already full dining room as the other patrons talk softly while eating. I glance at the food on their plates as we pass their tables. My stomach rumbles.

Then we reach the table, and our guide starts looking uncomfortable again.

"Ms. Ashford," she begins, and gives Kayla an apologetic look. "When you reached out this afternoon, you mentioned that there were four of you so... well..." She motions awkwardly at the table for four. "But I'm sure we can—"

"That won't be necessary," Kayla interrupts as she strides around the table and takes a seat. There's a smug smile full of challenge on her beautiful face as she nods at me. "He's not here to eat."

"Oh, well, then please have a seat while a waiter brings over menus for you."

I narrow my eyes at Kayla, who just continues smirking at me while her classmates pull out the other three chairs and sit down as well. Holding her gaze, I shake my head at her. I make her a delicious omelet this morning, and she responds by taking me to one of the best restaurants in town only to make me stand next to the table while she and her friends eat. Damn, she really is a vicious little demon, isn't she?

"I can't believe you managed to get a reservation at La Fleur in just a few hours," Aurora says, grinning broadly at Kayla. "We've been on the waitlist for weeks."

"Oh, it was nothing." Kayla shrugs casually. "My parents and I come here a lot."

Lionel frowns at the glittering dining room around him before shifting his gaze to Kayla. "Yes, very impressive. But why are we here? I thought we were going to have our event group meeting in the library. I almost didn't make it in time since you changed the location on such short notice."

"Ah, yeah, sorry about that. After class this afternoon, I was just hungry and found myself really craving some food from La Fleur. I hope you don't mind. It's my treat, of course."

Lionel visibly relaxes at that. I watch him. Huh. So maybe he's not quite as rich as he looks.

"Of course we don't mind," Aurora says with a bright smile. "We're always down with being treated to meals at exclusive restaurants."

Then she laughs and winks at Kayla as if it's a joke, but I'm pretty sure that she actually meant every word of that.

I study Kayla again while the waiter appears and places menus in front of the four of them.

Since my family is connected both by money and blood to the Morelli mafia family, which is the most powerful mafia family in the entire state, I've grown up surrounded by people who want nothing more than to use my connections for themselves. I learned early how to handle it, and truth be told, I don't actually mind it. In fact, I find the constant attempts to get into my good graces quite convenient. And fun. I love holding power over other people.

But I wonder how Kayla deals with it. Because she's the sole Ashford heir, she must be surrounded by people who want to take advantage of her too. I've always had my brothers to laugh off the ridiculousness with. But she's an only child. I wonder if that makes the experience different for her.

"Alright," Kayla begins once they have all ordered their food. "Let's get our group meeting underway then."

"Right," Jenn picks up and nods. "We need to decide how we are going to obtain the items for the silent auction."

"Wait, hold on," Lionel says. "We can't just start with the items. First, we need to figure out how to get funds."

"That's what I meant," Jenn protests, and gives him an exasperated look. "I said *obtain* the items. I didn't say buy them."

"What do you mean *obtain*? What are you going to do? Steal them?"

"That's so not what I said."

"Then what—"

Kayla clears her throat, interrupting their argument. Both of them turn to face her. Aurora, who was preoccupied with tasting her wine, does the same.

"Look," Kayla begins. There is a neutral expression on her face as she meets their gazes and waves a hand to indicate the restaurant around them. "I'm very rich. I can easily front the money for the items."

Jenn smiles and Aurora claps her hands excitedly.

"That would be amazing," Jenn says.

Her sister nods enthusiastically. "It would save us so much work."

Across the table from Kayla, Lionel grimaces and lets out a disapproving sound.

"What?" Jenn snaps.

I'm starting to like Jenn a bit more now, because she seems to be as annoyed by Lionel as I am.

"This is an assignment," he begins. "We're supposed to work to solve it. Not take shortcuts that are only available to Kayla."

My eyes narrow. Do I detect a hint of jealousy in his tone?

However, before I can get a proper read on him, the waiter returns with their food.

Heavenly scents drift through the air as he places the plates full of absolutely delicious-looking food in front of the four Ivy River students.

My stomach rumbles.

Kayla casts me a wicked little smirk that I pretend not to notice.

That God damn little demon. I will get back at her for this.

"Was there anything else I could get for you, ma'am?" the waiter asks Kayla once he is done.

"No, that will be all," she replies.

"Of course. Enjoy your food."

Something flickers in Lionel's eyes as he watches the exchange, and he shifts slightly in his seat while pursing his lips.

It takes me another few seconds to identify the emotion. But once I have, his reaction to Kayla's offer to front the money for the auction suddenly becomes clear as well.

He is uncomfortable with her money and power.

The realization stuns me so much that I just stare at him for a while.

Lionel was relieved that she was going to pay for his meal today because he probably can't afford it. But he is also deeply unsettled by the thought that Kayla is both wealthier and more influential than he is.

What a pathetic fucking idiot.

Only weak men get uncomfortable in the presence of a powerful woman.

"Oh, this looks so good," Jenn says with a grateful nod to Kayla before she picks up her utensils.

That breaks Lionel's grumpy spell, and he grabs his knife and fork too.

While they all dig into their food, they continue discussing how to get funds and obtain the items for their silent auction. Lionel continues to argue that they can't use any of Kayla's money for it. I alternate between scanning the dining room for threats, casting discreet glares at Kayla, and pretending that I'm the one eating the incredible food on the table instead.

"How about this?" Jenn suddenly says, sounding very

excited. "What if we do things for people, for businesses, like help them out with stuff, and in return we ask them to donate something to our auction?"

Considering looks blow across their faces.

"Oh, I like it," Aurora says.

Kayla nods. "That could work."

"Sure," Lionel adds. "How about we do it on Sunday?"

"I can't." Kayla shakes her head. "Sunday is family day." Rolling her eyes, she lets out something between a laugh and a sigh. "Dad is very big on that. But what about Saturday?"

"God, no," Aurora protests, and waves her hands. "We'll be too hungover. We're going to that huge costume party tomorrow, remember?"

My gaze snaps to Kayla, who winces.

She keeps her eyes firmly on her group members while I stare daggers at her. A party, huh? She very conveniently neglected to tell me about that.

The others don't seem to notice because they just continue trying to decide on a day. But Kayla and I will be having a private little chat about this later.

"So, Monday, then?" Aurora at last says.

Kayla and the others nod.

"Sounds good," she says.

For the first time since they sat down, Lionel's gaze shifts to me. Disapproval laces every line of his face as he gives me a frustrated look. "Must your guard dog always be lurking like this?"

I flash him a psycho smile that would've made even my brother Kaden proud. It makes Lionel flinch. But he recovers quickly and shoots me another contemptuous stare.

"Unfortunately, yes," Kayla says, and tosses her flaming red ponytail over her shoulder. "Just ignore him. That's what I do."

Moving closer, I make sure that I am truly looming over her where she sits at the table. She clenches her jaw in annoyance, but refuses to look at me. I almost chuckle. She can't throw out that kind of bait and not expect me to retaliate.

I remain there, lurking right behind her, the entire rest of the dinner. Once they're finished and Kayla has paid for their food, she practically shoots out of the chair and storms away as if to put as much distance between us as possible. I simply slide my hands into my pockets and follow her.

The street is dark and almost deserted when we at last step out of the restaurant. After saying goodbye to the others, Kayla and I start down the sidewalk. She tries to outpace me, but my legs are so much longer that she would need to jog to actually do it. So after a while, she stops trying and blows out an annoyed sigh as she is forced to walk next to me.

When we're halfway back to her apartment, I break the silence.

"What costume party?" I demand.

She lifts her shoulders in an impressively casual shrug. "I thought I told you about that."

"Right." I give her a flat look. "Sure you did."

We continue walking in silence down the street.

The streetlamps cast warm pools of light on the dark asphalt, and light from the buildings we pass shine out into the warm night.

I let a sly smile slide home on my lips as I glance down at Kayla. "So, what are we going as?"

Her brows furrow in confusion as she looks up at me. "We?"

"Yeah." I shrug as I continue strolling along next to her

"Since we're going together, we might as well do a couple's costume."

Incredulity pulses across her features. Then she shoots me a hard stare and stalks ahead. Her words cut through the warm night with the sharpness of a blade.

"We are not doing a couple's costume."

15

KAYLA

Apparently, we are doing a couple's costume. I'm dressed as a sexy policewoman, for reasons that Jace is about to find out very soon, and he is dressed as himself, which is a hitman. He even wore all black for the occasion. Black pants, black combat boots, and a tight-fitting black shirt that shows off every inch of his sculpted body and makes girls turn their heads to stare at him as we walk through the door and into the grand building where the party is in full swing.

Cop and criminal. Technically a couple's costume, which Jace has pointed out no less than five times already.

The smell of perfume and spilled alcohol hangs in the air like mist as we make our way through the packed hallway and towards the ballroom on the other side of the building. As opposed to the party last weekend, this one isn't hosted by just a single person in their own home. This massive costume party is hosted by none other than Ivy River's Society for Dramatic Arts. And say what you will about drama students, but they do know how to throw a party.

"I'm impressed," Jace comments from right next to me.

"Of course you are," I reply. "I'm sure you've never seen a party like this at your university."

Turning to face me, he levels a pointed look at me. "First of all, we throw *epic* parties at Blackwater. And secondly, I meant I'm impressed that we managed to make it all the way here without you trying to sneak off even once."

I roll my eyes. "As if hitmen know how to party."

"Uhm, excuse me…" He stares at me with a look of absolute affront on his face while gesturing up and down his own body. "Have you met me?"

"Unfortunately, yes."

"Oh my God," an excited voice interrupts before Jace can retort.

Both of us turn to find Aurora skipping towards us, her green eyes sparkling with joy. She's wearing a white gauzy dress with gold accessories that make her look like some kind of Greek goddess. Her long blonde hair is styled into loose waves, and it ripples behind her as she comes to a halt before us.

"Are you wearing a couple's costume?" she says.

"No," I mutter at the same time as Jace says, "Yes."

She lets out a little squeal and grins. "You guys are adorable." A sly smile plays over her lips as she looks us up and down before she gives me a conspiratorial wink. "And hot."

Well, she's right about that at least. I'm wearing a short navy-blue skirt and a low-cut top with a fake badge that imitates a police shirt, and a leather belt around my waist with handcuffs hanging from it. I *am* hot. And Jace is…

Actually, it doesn't matter what Jace is. He's not supposed to be here, and we're not wearing a couple's costume. So whether he's hot or not is irrelevant. He might as well be dressed as a house plant for all I care.

Next to me, the seriously overconfident bastard is smirking at the compliment, and probably at the poorly hidden lust that burns in Aurora's eyes too. I let out a silent scoff. I'm about to wipe that smirk off his mouth and turn him into a wallflower.

"Speaking of hot," I begin. "I'm going to grab something to drink."

"Good plan." Aurora flashes me a mischievous grin. "Jenn and I started drinking before we even left our house, so you have some catching up to do."

A sharp jab of pain spears through my heart at the casual reminder that that is what siblings do. Drink and get ready together before heading to a party. Together. I could've had that too. But instead, I'm stuck with a fucking bodyguard.

"I was just heading to the bathroom," she continues, and points down the packed hallway. "But Jenn is in the ballroom with Lionel and those guys we met at the party last weekend."

"Great," I reply with a smile as I shove aside that flicker of pain. "I'll meet you in there after I grab something to drink."

"Yes, we will," Jace adds, putting just a hint of emphasis on the word *we*.

We, huh? I suppress another scoff and a wicked smile. We'll see about that.

While Aurora continues towards the bathroom, I turn around and start in the direction of the basement. Jace falls into step beside me. There is a slight smile lurking on his lips as he strolls along there next to me while also watching the crowd. And the crowd is watching *him* too.

Several guys scowl at him as we pass, jealousy and annoyance clear on their features. Most girls cast discreet glances at him, but a fair number outright stare too. Their hungry eyes track Jace's every move as he raises his arm to drag a hand through his messy curls. After raking their gazes over his sinfully hot body, they shoot envious looks at me.

I just scowl back at them. If they only knew how annoying and frustrating Jace really is, they wouldn't be so jealous of me.

"I thought you were getting something to drink," Jace suddenly says.

"I am," I reply.

"We've passed the kitchen."

"So?"

Before he can retort, I round the corner and start down the white marble steps that lead to the storage room underneath the ground floor. Jace, who assumed that we were heading straight forward, has to skid to a halt and then backtrack to follow me.

"You know," he begins as he hurries to catch up with me again. "Everything would be so much easier if you actually communicated with me instead."

"Because you're such a master of communication yourself."

"I thought the snake in your bed was a pretty obvious message."

My gaze darts to him. But he only wears his customary casual smile, so it's impossible to interpret if he meant that as a threat or as a double entendre.

I shake my head at myself. I don't need to understand Jace Hunter. I just need to get rid of him.

We reach the bottom of the stairs. Only stacks of chairs and tables piled on top of each other meet us there. Most of them have been pushed up against the walls, but the space is still packed to the point that there is almost nothing left of the floor. Not to mention that there is a sliding gate made of iron separating the stairs from the storage area.

There is a confused frown on Jace's features as he scans the odd space before us. "What, exactly, are we doing here again?"

I twist around so that I'm in front of him instead. Then I let a sly smile curve my lips as I start backing him towards the sliding gate. Cocking my head slightly, I look up and meet his gaze.

"I just wanted to get you alone for a minute before we rejoin the party," I say, my voice coming out low and sultry.

Even more confusion pulses across his face. And I'm not sure if that confusion is the reason for his lack of resistance, but he lets me back him across the floor.

"Kayla," he says, a cautious note to his voice.

His brown eyes are full of suspicion as he studies my face. I just keep moving until his back connects with the sliding gate. The metal lets out a rattling sound at the impact. I close the distance between us until I'm standing only a breath away. I can almost feel his chest brush against mine when we breathe, and an involuntary tingle ripples down my spine. While holding his gaze, I slide my hands over my waist. Jace makes no move to touch me. But he doesn't try to leave either. He just watches me with those intense eyes of his.

"Aurora was right, you know," I say. "You are hot."

At last, a smirk replaces the suspicion on his face, and he grins down at me. "I know."

A laugh that is half surprise and half exasperation rips from my lungs as I shake my head at him. "You're very cocky, aren't you?"

"False modesty is pointless. Own who you are."

His words spear right into my soul with unexpected

accuracy. Because I actually agree with him. It's why I never apologize for being rich. Why I never feel bad about being powerful even though I have done nothing to earn it. I am who I am. And I own every inch of it. So the fact that I apparently share that sentiment with Jace surprises me so much that I almost forget what I'm doing for a second.

Recovering quickly, I force that revelation aside and instead focus on what I came here for.

My heart pounds as I reach up and draw my hand over Jace's shoulder.

A shudder rolls through him the moment my hand touches his body.

And once again, I almost lose track of my mission.

While trying to keep my mind from wandering down ridiculous paths, I slide my hand down his arm. Heat pools inside me at the feeling of those hard muscles underneath my palm. I reach the end of his shirt sleeve and trail my hand down his forearm. His skin is warm against mine.

"Kayla," he says, that cautious note now back in his voice again. "What are you doing?"

Holding his gaze, I flash him a smile full of mischief. "Something I have been thinking about doing all week."

Fire flickers in his eyes for a second. "Really? And what's—"

The moment he's distracted, I strike. In two quick moves, I snap one side of the handcuffs that came with the costume shut around his right wrist while locking the other side to the iron sliding gate behind him.

Jace blinks in genuine surprise.

That alone makes victory pulse through me like glittering fireworks.

I leap back out of his reach before he can get his wits about him again.

Standing halfway between the bottom of the stairs and the gate, I study Jace while a wide grin spreads across my mouth.

He stares at me for a few seconds before looking down at his now shackled wrist. I managed to lock the manacles to a spot where two rods intersect, which means that he can't slide the handcuffs up along the bar. Instead, his right hand is now trapped at waist level.

A metallic rattling noise comes from the gate as Jace gives his restraints a small tug.

That wicked grin remains on my mouth.

The veins in Jace's forearm shift as he flexes his hand. It makes a pulse of heat sear through me. In that tight-fitting black shirt and with his messy brown hair falling down over his forehead as he looks down at his handcuffed wrist, Jace is illegally attractive.

My gaze drifts down to the manacles again.

And God fucking damn it but he looks hot as hell when he's handcuffed too.

"Really?" Jace tears his eyes away from his shackled wrist and looks up to meet my gaze again. Raising his eyebrows, he gives me a look of both exasperation and incredulity while he gives the handcuffs another little tug. "*This* is what you brought me down here for?"

"Naturally." I toss my hair behind my shoulder. "Why do you think I dressed up as a policewoman?"

"So that you would be able to handcuff me."

"Exactly."

A sly smile blows across his handsome features as he rakes a suggestive gaze over my body. "I didn't realize you were into role play."

My cheeks heat, but I manage to shoot him a disinterested

stare. "Don't flatter yourself, pretty boy. The only reason I handcuffed you was so that I would be able to enjoy the party without having you glued to my side."

"Is that right?"

"Yes." I give him a mocking smile as I take a step back towards the stairs. "So, have fun down here while I go back to the party and get drunk and dance with my friends and fuck strangers in dark rooms. If you're a good boy and say please, I might even come back down here and release you before I leave."

A wicked glint appears in his eyes. "Been planning this all week, have you?"

"Yes."

"Impressive."

"I know."

"But you forgot one thing."

I arch a cocky eyebrow at him. "Oh?"

"Yeah." The smile on his face turns outright villainous. "You forgot the importance of high-quality equipment."

"What's that supposed to—"

He yanks his arm forward in one quick motion.

And the handcuffs *snap*.

I gasp and jerk back in shock.

Broken bits clink down on the marble floor, and for one second, I can only stare at them in stunned surprise.

Jace, however, doesn't hesitate.

Shooting forward, he closes the distance between us again in a matter of moments. I scramble backwards, trying to escape up the stairs. But it's too late. His arms wrap around my waist and yank me off the first step. I suck in a hiss as he spins me around and shoves me up against the wall.

Air escapes my lungs as my chest hits the marble wall.

Placing my palms on the cold stone, I try to push myself away from it. Jace just grabs my right wrist and yanks it down from the wall before twisting it up behind my back. His knees dig into the back of my thighs as he uses his body weight to keep me pinned to the wall.

Leaning forward, he places his lips right next to my ear. "So that's how you want to play it, huh?"

Lightning skitters across my skin as his warm breath dances over the shell of my ear.

"Then fine," he continues, his lips almost brushing my skin. "That's how we'll play it."

Faint metallic clinking sounds. Then something cold appears against my wrist. I try to yank my arm back but Jace keeps it mercilessly trapped behind my back. A very ominous click sounds. Followed by another.

Then Jace at last releases me and steps back.

I yank my arm down while whirling around towards Jace, and then snap my gaze down to my hand.

Disbelief pulses through me.

My right wrist is now handcuffed. Not with the ones I brought, since half of them are still stuck to the iron gate. No, this is another pair of handcuffs. Ones that look much more professional. And sturdy. But that's not the worst of it.

One side of those handcuffs is locked around my wrist. The other side encircles Jace's left wrist.

I drag my gaze up to his face, but no words make it out of my mouth.

"As opposed to the cheap toy *you* brought," Jace begins.

And then he demonstrates just how cheap and low-quality my handcuffs were by breaking what remains of them from his right wrist until the cuff falls to the floor in pieces. Shock crackles through me. Because even though they might have been a toy compared to real handcuffs, it would still take serious strength to just shatter them like that.

Jace raises his other hand, lifting my right hand with it as well since it's trapped to his.

"Mine are the real deal," he finishes. Mischief sparkles in his eyes as he casts a pointed look at our joined wrists. "So good luck trying to ditch me now, little demon."

For a few seconds, all I can do is to stare at him in complete disbelief.

Then reality snaps back into me like a hard slap to the face.

"Ugh," I growl, giving his muscular chest a hard shove. "You are unbelievable! Who even walks around with a pair of extra handcuffs like this?"

"You did."

"I was on a mission!"

"So was I."

"God fucking damn…" Another snarl rips from my chest as I shoot him a vicious glare. "Asshole."

Then I whirl around and storm up the steps.

Or I try to, at least.

My movements come to an abrupt halt as my arm doesn't follow me up the stairs. I jerk back, almost falling down the steps as I'm pulled off balance. Twisting back around, I stare between my wrist and Jace, who is still standing on the floor below.

"What are you doing?" I growl.

He just raises his eyebrows at me, completely unfazed by the venom in my voice. "What does it look like?"

I stab a hand towards the corridor at the top of the stairs. "The party is up there!"

"So? I'm not here to party. I'm here to guard you. And it

seems to me that'll be a hell of a lot easier down here than up there."

"I don't want to be standing here all night! I want to go up there and dance with my friends."

"Tough luck."

Wrapping both hands around the handcuffs locking us together, I try to forcibly pull him with me as I start backing up the stairs.

I might as well have been trying to pull a mountain up those steps.

Jace simply stands there on the floor, watching me with raised eyebrows while amusement dances across his face.

A vicious curse rips from my chest as I try to pull him up the first step again.

He doesn't move one inch.

Deciding to switch tactics, I stalk down the steps instead and move until I'm standing behind him. Then I try to push him forwards instead.

Once again, I would have had better luck trying to move a fucking bolder.

"Come on!" I snap, frustration welling up inside me.

I make another three attempts to get him to move before I'm forced to admit that it's impossible.

Stomping my foot down on the floor, I grind my teeth as I glare up at his stupid smirking face.

Music and laughter and the sound of people chatting drift through the corridor upstairs. I glance longingly towards it.

"You want to go up there and dance with your friends?" Jace asks.

"Yes," I all but growl since he damn well already knows the answer to that.

He wraps his free hand around my jaw in a highly

commanding move that sends a pulse through my spine. "Say please."

I glare up at him in silence for all of two seconds before I force out, "Please."

His lips tilt up in a satisfied smile. "Good girl."

A shudder rolls through my body. I draw in a sharp breath and yank my chin out of his grip while desperately trying to ignore the throbbing sensation in my clit.

Thankfully, Jace doesn't comment on it. Instead, he simply starts up the steps.

I scramble to catch up with him before he changes his mind.

The smell of perfume and spilled alcohol once more fills my lungs as we return to the packed hallway upstairs. Several couples are making out against the walls to our left and right. I glance at them while we make our way back to the carved double doors that lead to the ballroom.

The back of Jace's hand brushes against mine when we have to squeeze through a gap in the crowd. It sends a jolt through my body, and I try to snatch my hand away. But because of those damn handcuffs, it only makes his hand follow mine and bump into it again. I can practically feel Jace's smirk even though I'm not even looking at him.

With a scowl on my face, I stalk forward.

We have almost reached the open doors to the ballroom when I'm abruptly jerked to a halt. Throwing out my free hand, I spin it in the air to keep my balance as my other arm remains far behind me. Once I have my balance back, I twist around to see what caused it.

"Give me that," Jace orders as he snatches a bat out of the hand of some guy who is dressed up as a baseball player.

The guy, who was half turned away from Jace, whirls

around. Anger flashes in his pale eyes.

"Hey, what the fuck!" he snaps.

Then he jerks back as he comes face to face with Jace's menacing presence. Jace expertly spins the bat in his right hand and then places the top of it straight against the guy's chest. Power and utter dominance pulse from every inch of his muscular body.

"If you don't know how to properly hold a bat, you shouldn't bring a fucking bat," Jace says, sounding surprisingly offended.

I stare at him in bewilderment. It's just a bat. Is he some sort of baseball aficionado or what?

The Ivy River student shrinks back and holds up his hands in surrender, clearly not interested in picking a fight with the biggest guy at this whole damn party. "Sorry."

"You should be," Jace declares.

Then he promptly spins the bat again and rests it against his shoulder before turning around and starting towards the ballroom once more. I stumble after him.

"Bloody amateurs," Jace mutters under his breath. "Not one of them knows proper bat etiquette."

"Uhm…" I say, very eloquently.

However, before I can figure out what to even ask, we round the corner and walk into the ballroom.

I've been here before, so I know that this massive room is very elegant when the sun falls in through the gleaming windows and illuminates the pale walls and the frescos in the ceiling.

Right now, however, it's dimly lit, packed with people, and full of strobing lights in neon colors. It might as well have been a night club in a concrete factory for all the attention people spare the beautiful decorations around the room.

"Kayla!" Jenn calls, and waves a hand at me from a short distance away.

We start towards her and the rest of their group. Aurora is dancing with that guy Mitch from the party last weekend. Though dancing is probably not the right word. More like grinding herself against him while he has his hands on her hips. Both of them look like they're a few minutes away from sneaking into a private room.

I grin at Aurora and give her a nod of approval. *Go for it, girl.*

Trina and Felicia are dancing together, their blonde hair rippling as they jump to the beat of the music.

Lionel, who was facing Rebecca, immediately snaps his attention to me when Jace and I reach them.

"We were starting to think that you had gotten lost," Jenn says to me as she laughs, evidence that she is as drunk as the rest of them appear to be.

I wink at her. "We just had some stuff to sort out first."

"Well, I'm glad you're here now."

Before I can reply, she tilts her head up to the ceiling and starts dancing.

"Me too," Lionel says from my right before I can start dancing as well. His gray eyes are full of hope as he meets my gaze and smiles. "I was actually wondering if you want to get some air. Just you and me."

I grimace and raise my right hand, showing him the handcuffs that trap me to Jace. "Unfortunately, I'm dragging around like two hundred and fifty pounds of dead weight at the moment."

Lionel jerks back in surprise. Then anger flashes in his eyes as he snaps his gaze between the handcuffs and Jace's face. "You handcuffed her to you?"

A smile that is half threat and half challenge slides across Jace's mouth as he looks Lionel up and down. "So what if I did?"

"Handcuffing someone without their permission is illegal."

The threatening smile on Jace's mouth turns into a sly smirk as he shifts his gaze to me. "You hear that, little demon? Maybe I should file charges against you."

"Come try it." I match his wicked smile and wiggle my eyebrows at him. "I would bury you with elite lawyers who charge more a month than you make in a year."

He laughs. A full, genuine laugh that makes his eyes glitter.

It sends a ripple of warmth through my soul.

"Just uncuff her," Lionel demands, ruining the rare moment.

Jace drags his gaze to him and simply declares, "No."

"You can't just—"

"Can we please drop it?" I interrupt. "I just want to dance."

Before either of them can start arguing again, I turn away from them both and throw my free arm up into the air, tip my head back, and dance.

Music pulses through the air, beating in tune with my heart. I grin up at the ceiling. Then I try to raise my other arm too.

It doesn't move.

Turning back to Jace, I find him simply standing there on the floor, watching me. He still holds the bat he stole in his right hand, leaning the smooth wood against his shoulder, while he keeps his left hand down by his side. And my right hand with it.

I yank pointedly against the handcuffs and give him an expectant look.

"What?" he asks, looking back at me with mock confusion.

"I said that I wanted to dance."

"So dance."

"It's difficult when you refuse to move your arm."

"How is that my problem? I agreed to let you come here and dance. I never said anything about my own participation."

Narrowing my eyes, I glare at him. He keeps a nonchalant expression on his face, but I swear I can see him trying to suppress a smile too.

Fine, he wants to be difficult? I can be difficult. In fact, we've only scratched the surface of just how fucking difficult I can be.

A grin full of challenge slides home on my lips as I close the distance between us instead. This move worked wonders last time. And now, I'm going to make it even worse for him. I won't stop until he fucking blows his load in the middle of the dance floor. Let's see how cocky he is then.

With my eyes locked on his, I raise my free hand and wrap it around the back of his neck. Then I slide it down towards his chest while I start swaying. I'm so close to him now that my breasts brush against him with every writhing move I make.

From behind me, Aurora whistles suggestively before laughing. The sound is full of approval. Some others laugh too. And a little to my right, I swear I can feel Lionel scowling, or maybe glaring, at us. I ignore them all as I dance closer to Jace.

A muscle feathers in his jaw, and his body is suddenly rigid.

Twisting around, I dance exactly like I did at the last party we went to. Moving to the beat of the music, I grind my ass against Jace's crotch.

Satisfaction pulses through me when I can feel his cock harden instantly.

A wooden clattering sounds from right next to me, and I glance down to find the bat hitting the floor.

Then Jace's free hand lands on my hip. But he doesn't do what Mitch did earlier, who let his hand follow the sway of Aurora's body. Instead, Jace digs his fingers into my hip as if he is trying to stop my movements.

With my other arm twisted rather awkwardly behind me because of the handcuffs, I simply ignore his demanding hand and instead continue dancing. My ass brushes against his cock over and over again. I can practically hear Jace's teeth crack from how hard he is clenching his jaw.

And because I truly am a little demon, I use that moment to bend forward, giving him a clear image of what it would look like if he actually was fucking me from behind.

He sucks in a sharp breath between his teeth.

I chuckle as I straighten and then continue to grind against him.

His fingers tighten on my hip. "I would suggest you stop that. Unless you—"

"What?" I cut him off, my voice pulsing with challenge "Unless I *what?*"

He yanks his left arm, and since it's locked to mine, the movement makes me spin around to face him instead. His free hand shoots up and wraps around my jaw. Fire burns in his eyes as he stares me down.

"Stop," he commands, his voice coming out low and rough

Realization flashes through my mind. It's followed by a brilliant idea. I know just how to make him take these handcuffs off.

"Fine," I reply, making sure to sound defeated. "This is

giving me a headache anyway. I need to go somewhere quiet and sit down for a moment."

"Oh, are you okay?" Jenn asks from behind me.

I can't turn to meet her gaze since Jace still has his hand locked around my jaw, but I assure her, "Yeah, I'm fine. I just need a minute."

Jace keeps his eyes on mine for another few seconds. Then he nods and lets his hand drop back down. I immediately turn to my friends and give them a smile.

"I'll be right back," I promise.

Aurora and Mitch are already lost in each other again, but Jenn smiles back and gives me a little wave. Trina, Felicia, and Rebecca haven't even been paying attention to us, so they only continue dancing. Next to them, Lionel glowers as he nods in acknowledgement.

I start towards the door.

Jace bends down and picks up his bat before following.

Thankfully, he doesn't stop me as I weave through the sea of drunk people and make my way upstairs. I know that there are several lounge rooms up here. I walk until I reach one that's unoccupied.

After going inside, I close the door behind us and lock it. Then I stride over to the dark red couch by the wall and drop into it. Since he has no choice but to follow, Jace does the same. The carved wooden frame creaks, and the soft cushions let out a huff as his massive weight lands on them. Twisting to the side, he places the bat on the cushions next to him with more care than any bat deserves. If I didn't know better, I would think it's because he's feeling guilty about simply dropping it on the hard floor back in that ballroom earlier.

Ignoring Jace's odd behavior, I slide down so that I'm lying almost flat on the couch instead. It's so wide that I can rest the back of my head against the bottom of the backrest while the entire rest of my body, except for my legs, is still on the seat. Jace arches an eyebrow at me but doesn't comment.

However, my slouched position leaves his arm in a mildly uncomfortable position, so he slides down the backrest too until he's half lying down as well.

"You have a headache?" he asks.

To my surprise, he actually does sound concerned.

"Yeah," I reply, keeping my voice neutral. "I just need to release some tension. Then I'll be fine."

"Tension?"

Instead of answering, I slide my right hand between my legs. Because of the handcuffs, it makes his hand follow as well until it's resting on my thigh. I keep my eyes on the beautiful landscape painting on the beige wall opposite us as I push my skirt up and move my fingers towards my pussy.

"Kayla," Jace says, his voice dark and full of warning.

I ignore him and instead push my panties aside so that I can reach my clit. Jace's hand rests on my bare thigh only inches away from my pussy now.

Leaning the back of my head against the couch, I close my eyes and blow out a long sigh as I start stroking my clit.

Next to me, I can feel Jace's body tensing up. His fingers flex where his hand rests on my thigh.

That small movement sends bolts of electricity up my spine even more than the work my fingers are doing.

"Kayla," Jace says again. His voice is hoarse this time.

A wicked smile threatens to spread across my mouth, but I manage to keep my expression neutral as I continue rubbing my clit until pleasure starts building inside me. I squirm a little on the soft cushions.

Jace squeezes the hand he has on my thigh into a fist.

I let a moan slip past my lips.

Jace draws in a long breath between what sounds like tightly clenched teeth.

At last, I crack an eye open and glance over at him.

Just like I expected, he is clenching his jaw hard and his entire body is as taut as a bowstring where he sits next to me. I shift my gaze up to his eyes.

A jolt shoots through me.

Because what I wasn't expecting was the searing fire burning in his eyes as he stares down at my hand.

I barely remember to keep my fingers moving while I try to process the expression on his face. Since it proves more difficult than I anticipated, I abandon that effort and instead concentrate solely on my plan. To make him uncuff me.

While continuing to stroke my clit, I shoot him a look full of challenge. "If it makes you uncomfortable, you can always remove the handcuffs."

Jace snaps his gaze from my hand and up to my face. For a few seconds, it looks like he is trying to reorient himself or get his wits back. Then his expression clears, and a matching look full of challenge and forbidden promises settles on his handsome face.

My stomach flips at the sight of it.

Before I even know what's happening, Jace sits upright on the couch, twists so that he is facing me, and then grabs my hips with both hands. The movement forces my hand away from my clit. But before I can protest, he shifts my body up and to the side so that my legs are resting along the length of the couch instead and my head is on the seat cushion on the opposite side.

I suck in a surprised breath while lust burns through me at how effortlessly Jace moves my body into his desired position.

Blinking, I stare up at him with wide eyes as he straddles my right thigh.

"Uncomfortable?" Jace echoes as he places his free hand on my left thigh and pushes it sideways, spreading my legs wider. His eyes glitter in the golden light from the chandelier above us. "The only thing that's making me uncomfortable is watching you work to relieve your own tension. That should be done for you. By someone who knows what he's doing."

I try to sit up from the couch, but Jace places his hand against my chest and pushes me back down. My own free hand shoots up and wraps around his wrist. But he keeps his hand there on my chest, pinning me to the soft cushions.

A devilish smile graces his lips as he moves our handcuffed hands over my thigh and towards my pussy until he can push aside the fabric of my panties. "Allow me."

Lightning crackles through my veins as his fingers brush against my clit.

I suck in a gasp and try to arch up from the couch.

Jace just keeps his hand on my chest, holding me firmly in place as he starts stroking my clit with slow tantalizing movements. His eyes remain locked on mine, cataloging every expression on my face.

He rolls my clit between his fingers.

A tiny whimper spills from my lips, and I tighten my grip on his wrist.

It makes a sly smile blow across his features.

He shifts his hand so that he can continue to rub my clit with his thumb while his index and middle finger trail down to my entrance.

My heart slams against my ribs.

Drawing in unsteady breaths, I hold his intense gaze as my very soul flutters.

He pushes one finger inside me.

A moan escapes my lungs.

Closing my eyes, I throw my head back against the cushions again as Jace slowly pushes his finger farther in. His thumb continues working my clit, making pleasure spear through my belly with each firm stroke.

Jace moves his finger in and out a few times. Then he adds a second finger.

My eyes fly open again, and I stare up at him while my pulse thunders in my ears. A faint smirk plays over his lips as he pushes both fingers deeper. Then he pulls them out again.

I drag in shuddering breaths.

His thumb rubs over just the right spot on my clit.

Another moan rips from my throat, and I squirm against the couch.

The smile on Jace's mouth widens.

While rubbing his thumb over that exact spot again and again, he starts up a steady pace with his fingers.

Pleasure pulses through me with each thrust and each precise move of his thumb. I grip his wrist harder. My heart pounds in my chest.

I writhe and squirm on the soft red cushions as Jace pushes me closer and closer to an orgasm.

It feels as if my heart is going to break through my ribs.

More whimpers fall from my lips as the tension inside me soars towards unbearable levels.

"Please," I moan, throwing my head from side to side. "Oh God."

He curls his fingers on the way out.

Pleasure shoots through me like a lightning strike.

I gasp into the white-painted ceiling as my pussy tightens around his fingers and release crashes through my limbs with enough force to make my body tremble. I hold on to his wrist as if it's the only thing keeping me in this world.

Jace continues rubbing that perfect spot on my clit until it feels as if my brain is melting.

My inner walls flutter around his dominating fingers as he keeps pumping them inside me.

"Oh God," I gasp again.

Pleasure spikes through my spine with each thrust of his fingers. My clit throbs and black spots dance before my eyes as Jace wrings every drop of pleasure from my soul and prolongs the orgasm until I feel like my brain has left my body.

My chest heaves and my heart hammers so loudly in my chest that my ears are ringing.

Once the orgasm at last fades, I just lie there on the soft red cushions and stare up into the ceiling while I try to piece my mind back together.

Every bone in my body feels like it's made of jelly. I don't even know if I can stand up right now. I'm pretty sure I will just crumple to the floor if I try. So I simply lie there, my chest heaving, and drag my gaze to the man still straddling my thigh.

Jace's brown eyes glitter like golden sparkles, and there is a victorious smirk on his lethally handsome face. His messy curls fall down over his forehead in a way that makes my already exhausted heart clench.

This was not how I had planned for this to turn out. At all. And I'm pretty sure I just lost this round.

But God damn, what a sweet loss it was.

16

JACE

I probably shouldn't have done that. In fact, I know that I shouldn't have done that. I really, really, shouldn't have done that. Fucking hell, why did I do that?

The memory of Kayla squirming underneath me as I pinned her to that couch and fucked her with my fingers has been playing nonstop in my mind ever since we left that room last night. The way her beautiful blue eyes widened as pleasure flooded her features. The way her cunt pulsed around my fingers. The way her legs shook slightly. The way she was gripping my wrist. And those moans… God, those moans and whimpers that spilled from her luscious lips as she gasped for air between waves of pleasure.

I can't get it out of my head.

But I need to. Because I crossed a massive fucking line last night. No, I didn't even cross it. I bloody cartwheeled right over it.

Shaking my head at my own recklessness, I add some dried tomatoes, basil, and mozzarella to the omelet in the pan.

I'm supposed to be guarding Kayla, for God's sake. Not

fucking her with my fingers while wondering what it would be like to fuck her for real. I was supposed to be professional. I *need* to be professional. Because I need to make it to the end of the semester and complete this job assignment so that I can choose my own future. That's what matters. That's the goal. That's the prize that I need to keep my eyes and my entire focus on.

Despite myself, I smile as I flip the omelet in the pan while my mind yet again drifts back to Kayla. Because I have to give it to her, she sure knows how to keep things interesting.

For as long as I can remember, I've felt restless and bored almost every minute of every day. I get bored of things and people almost before I have even started playing with them. And I expected this to be the same.

Guarding a rich university student? I fully expected to be bored out of my mind before the end of the first day.

But God damn was I wrong.

Handcuffing me to a gate in the basement? Pleasuring herself with the same hand that is shackled to mine?

A chuckle, full of amusement and approval that I will never admit out loud, rumbles from my chest.

There is never a dull moment with Kayla. And I have to admit that I'm actually starting to enjoy this assignment a little.

The door to her bedroom opens on the other side of the apartment. I keep my back to her as I slide the omelet from the pan and onto a plate. Just like every morning, I've made her breakfast. Because breakfast is important, and I know that she won't eat it if I don't make it for her.

She might roll her eyes and groan and argue with me about anything and everything, but she always eats the breakfast I make for her.

Grabbing a set of utensils, I walk over to the table and set them down in front of the chair she usually sits in. She watches me in silence as she closes the distance to the table as well.

In the dim light of that fancy room at the party, what we did on that couch felt right. But now, in the light of day, there is a strange tension between us. As if neither of us knows how to act now.

Kayla clears her throat as she sits down. The utensils clink faintly in the crackling silence as she picks them up.

I consider sitting down opposite her, as I usually do, but decide against it. Instead, I walk back to the kitchen and start cleaning up.

She eats in silence. Only the soft dings of her fork connecting with the plate break the oppressive stillness in the room.

"I'm sorry," I blurt out when the tense silence reaches unbearable levels.

Rolling my shoulders back, I turn so that I'm facing Kayla at the table again. She hasn't finished eating yet, but she has still turned around in her chair to look at me. Surprise flickers in her eyes.

"What I did in that room last night," I continue, holding her gaze. "I shouldn't have done that. That was unprofessional."

Disbelief, and something that almost looks a little like hurt, flashes across her features. It's gone in a second, replaced by anger. Pushing up from the table, she gets to her feet so that she can turn around and face me fully.

"Unprofessional?" she echoes, raising her eyebrows and staring at me with incredulous eyes.

I stare right back at her. "Yes."

"You put a snake in my bed. But you somehow think *yesterday* was unprofessional?"

Crossing the kitchen, I move closer to her while still holding her gaze. "It was. What I did yesterday crossed a line, and I apologize for that."

"Crossed a line?" She scoffs, and then shoots me a disgusted look. "Ridiculous. But fine, if you think it was a mistake, then let's pretend it never happened."

With that anger pulsing in her eyes, she starts to turn away from me. Before I even know what I'm doing, I grab her arm and spin her back to face me. She starts in surprise, and then scowls up at me while yanking her arm out of my grip.

I lock hard eyes on her. "I didn't say that it was a mistake. I said that it was unprofessional."

An unreadable expression descends on her features.

For a few seconds, we just stare each other down in silence.

Then a calculating glint shines in her deep blue eyes. It makes my heart jerk.

"Not a mistake, huh?" she says.

Taking a step forward, she closes the short distance between us until she is standing so close that I can practically feel the warmth from her skin. Every nerve in my body goes on high alert.

Kayla keeps her scheming eyes on mine as she reaches up and wraps her hand around the back of my neck. With firm movements, she pulls my face down closer to hers. I let her.

My pulse beats erratically as she rises up on her toes and slides her lips along my jaw.

"So if I were to do this…" she begins, her breath caressing my skin with every word.

I flex my fingers and clench my jaw as she reaches my

mouth. Remaining only a breath away, she slants her lips over mine. If I move forward just a fraction, our lips will touch. And if that happens, I don't know how this morning is going to end.

"...would you stop me?" she finishes, her lips hovering dangerously close to mine.

My cock hardens, and it takes all of my willpower to stop myself from sliding my hands into her flaming red hair and claiming her lips until I've kissed her troublesome mouth into submission.

"Do you want me to?" I challenge instead.

She lets out a *hmm* that vibrates against my mouth. Neither a confirmation nor a denial.

Then she abruptly lets her hand drop from the back of my neck and retreats a step. Relief crashes through me, and I fight the urge to suck in a deep breath, because without those wicked lips so close to mine, I can finally think properly again.

That calculating look is back in her eyes as she cocks her head, her gaze now once again locked on mine. "What if I did it to someone else? Would you stop me then?"

"No." I stare her down. "Like I said, you can fuck whoever you want."

A sly smile spreads across her lips. "Even you?"

I snort. "You wouldn't be able to handle me."

"Oh really?"

Taking a step forward, I use my size to force her to back up against the kitchen table. Licking my lips, I drag a highly deliberate glance over her body. Her chest rises and falls with rapid breaths.

"Yes," I reply. Lifting a hand, I trace my fingers over her collarbones. "Because you're used to being in charge. You're used to people jumping to obey you." I quickly close my hand around her throat. "But in *my* bedroom, *I* give the orders. And you obey."

Her breathing hitches. I can feel her pulse fluttering underneath my fingers.

Keeping my hand around her throat, I stare her down for another few seconds. Then I release her and instead stab a commanding hand towards the chair beside her. And when I speak, I put unflinching power and searing authority into every single word.

"Now, sit your ass back down on that chair and finish your breakfast like a good girl."

Her eyes flash, and she jerks back as fury and indignation pulse across her features.

I chuckle and then wiggle my eyebrows at her while a smug smirk spreads across my lips. "Told you that you wouldn't be able to handle it."

17

KAYLA

From right next to me, I can feel Jace glowering at me. I just keep my eyes on the building ahead as we continue down the sidewalk.

Bright sunlight beats down from a clear blue sky, baking the city. The smell of warm asphalt hangs in the air, and sweat trickles down my spine even though I'm only wearing a short skirt and a light top in a thin white material.

If we had bothered to check the weather forecast, we would've known that there was a heatwave coming this week, and then we wouldn't have decided to pick this particular day. But we didn't check the weather forecast, so here we are, traipsing across the city and doing lots of odd jobs for businesses in exchange for them donating something to our silent auction.

Not that I'm doing much of the work. Or any of it, really. I took one look outside this morning and decided that I would not be performing any sort of demanding tasks in this kind of heat.

So I made a deal with Jace. In exchange for him doing all

of the work today, I have promised to not sneak away or ditch him for the entire rest of the week. And given that it's only Monday, I'd say that he is getting one hell of a great deal out of this bargain. But then again, given the size of the lawn he just mowed, I suppose that I am too.

"You'd better hold up your end of the bargain, little demon," Jace threatens as he casts me a look from the corner of his eye while we continue towards the next business on our list.

We decided that it would be more efficient if our entire event group split up so that we could cover four times as many businesses instead of going to one at a time as a group. Right now, I'm very glad that I pushed for that strategy since it means that the rest of my group will never know that I didn't actually do any of the work.

"I don't know what you're complaining about," I reply as I flick a nonchalant glance at him. "It's not that hot."

He turns to face me, that glower still on his features. "Not if you're standing in the shade, no. But if you're walking back and forth across a damn field with a lawnmower…"

"It was just a lawn."

"The size of a football field!"

"Now you're just being dramatic."

Locking eyes with me, he stabs his finger at me in warning as he repeats, "You'd better hold up your end of the bargain. No bullshit this entire week. Or I swear to God, I will fucking handcuff you to your bed and leave you there."

Lightning shoots through me at the memory of what he did the last time he handcuffed me, but I manage to keep the expression off my face as I instead flash him a smile full of challenge. "If you handcuff me again, I'm going to call the police and tell them that you kidnapped me."

A villainous smile curls his lips. "Good luck with that. My family owns the police department in this city."

"Oh really? I bet I could buy them out from right underneath you."

"You forget, my family is rich too."

"Not as rich as mine."

"True. But we can also threaten to kill their loved ones if they don't do as we say." His eyes gleam as he gives me a wicked grin. "And money plus the threat of a dead loved one trumps just money every day of the week."

I scoff.

He smirks. "Face it, little demon. You've been outmaneuvered. So keep your end of the bargain or find yourself handcuffed and with no police coming to save you."

Scoffing again, I make a show of rolling my eyes at him. But I can't stop the smile that pulls at my lips.

Usually when I flaunt my wealth or power, people get uncomfortable. Especially men. They grimace faintly and shift their weight and try to change the subject as quickly as possible. But not Jace. He never seems to find it off-putting when I throw my weight around. Instead, he just meets me with the same energy. And I have to admit, I quite like that.

With that smile now fully on my lips, I try to turn away so that Jace won't see it. But it's too late. He has already seen it. Thankfully, he doesn't point it out. Instead, a soft smile blows across his own lips.

We close the final distance to the next business in comfortable silence.

It's a car dealership. Not one of the fancy ones. Just a regular one that normal people buy their cars from. I spoke to the owner, Richard Dalton, on the phone last week, and he has agreed to donate one of his cheapest models in exchange for some help. And for the publicity that comes with being featured at a silent auction hosted by none other than the Ashford heir, of course.

"Ms. Ashford," Richard Dalton exclaims as he comes bustling out of the door the moment we set foot on the massive parking lot in front of the building.

We weave through the sea of cars while he hurries towards us. He reaches us halfway across the parking lot. His brown hair is damp at the temples, and sweat slides down his neck. Given that he is wearing not only a dress shirt but also an actual suit jacket on top of it, I'm not surprised.

"I'm so honored that you want to include my humble business in your venture," he says as he shakes my hand.

His palm is also a bit damp. I smile while discreetly wiping my hand on the side of my skirt after we finish shaking. Jace, who as usual misses nothing, doesn't even bother hiding the amusement on his face.

"Of course," I reply. "I'm so glad that you wanted to be a part of it." Clearing my throat, I motion towards Jace before he can start outright grinning. "This is Jace, he is the one who is going to be helping you with…" I frown. "I'm sorry, what was it that you needed help with again?"

Mr. Dalton draws a hand through his hair and lets out an embarrassed laugh. "I never said, because I hadn't figured anything out yet." He straightens and then gives both me and Jace a nod. "But I have now. Come with me and I'll show you."

Turning around, he motions for us to follow as he starts towards the other side of the parking lot.

Sunlight gleams in the spotless windows of the cars that we pass as we make our way towards the side that is framed by both the street we took to get here and the one that runs perpendicular to it.

Jace leans closer, a smirk on his face, and whispers, "Need a handkerchief?"

"Shut up," I hiss, and cast a quick look to make sure that Mr. Dalton didn't overhear.

A soft chuckle escapes Jace's throat. I shake my head at him as we walk the final distance to the spot that Richard Dalton was apparently heading for. Both Jace and I stop when he does. My gaze drifts over the space before us. Or rather, over the cars before us.

There are two entire rows of cars lined up in the otherwise empty part of the parking lot. And all of them are covered in what looks like mud. Or maybe wet sand.

Richard turns to us and gives us a smile that almost looks a little apologetic. "My newest shipment came in yesterday." He motions towards the cars behind him. "But as you can see, the car carrier trailer that brought them here got caught in some really terrible weather. So the rain and the sand turned the cars into... Well, as you can see, they're not particularly clean anymore."

"And you need our help to wash them," I say, my eyes still on the rows of dirty cars.

Mr. Dalton clears his throat a bit self-consciously. "Yes."

I turn towards Jace, a wicked grin on my face. "Well, you'd better get to it then."

For a while, Jace just continues staring at the cars. Then he drags his gaze to me. I smile and bat my lashes at him in my best imitation of innocence. He narrows his eyes at me.

"The bargain," he says, his voice coming out low and full of threats, as he gives me an expectant look.

I roll my eyes and wave a hand in the air. "Yes, yes. I promise that I will keep my end of the bargain."

"You'd better."

The dark promises in his tone send a ripple down my spine.

Blocking it out, I instead give Jace one more smirk and then start towards the little patio a short distance away. It looks like a place where the staff can go to smoke on their break, or something like that, because there are several chairs waiting there in the shade. I sit down in one of them while Mr. Dalton shows Jace where the water and buckets and sponges are.

Once the owner has finished, he hurries back to the main entrance across the parking lot. I lean back in my chair, cross my ankles, and watch as Jace stands there on the asphalt, staring at the mass of cars.

He glances up at the blistering sun above. Then he heaves a sigh.

And then he grabs the hem of his white t-shirt and yanks it over his head.

My heart skips several beats.

After dropping the shirt on the ground, he rolls his shoulders back and walks over to the hose. I stare at the way his muscles flex when he grabs the hose and turns on the water.

Water sprays through the air, hitting the nearest car. The drops glitter in the bright sunlight as they fill the air like mist. But I can't take my eyes off Jace.

God damn it. Did he have to be this fucking hot? It's such an unnecessary complication.

On the street, a few passersby slow their walk as they watch Jace as well. Some leave the sidewalk and drift onto the parking lot. But they're looking at Jace more than the cars, so I'm not sure if they're actually here for a vehicle or for the free show.

Once Jace has hosed down the nearest car, he grabs a sponge and dunks it in a bucket of water and car shampoo. White foam drips from his strong hands as he lifts it up. I stare, completely transfixed as he starts washing the car.

The muscles in his chest and arms shift as he runs that sponge back and forth, and his hard abs tighten as he twists slightly.

My thighs clench, and I have to adjust my position in the chair as a throbbing sensation starts in my clit.

Fucking hell, is this what his naked body would look like in bed too? Is this how his lethal muscles would flex if he were to grip my thigh and hoist it up before thrusting into me?

Images of Jace above me and below me and in front of me in all kinds of positions flash through my mind.

I grip the armrest hard and press my thighs together.

God damn it. I should not be thinking about things like this. What Jace and I did at that costume party three days ago was a one-time act of insanity. Nothing else.

It doesn't matter that he's the hottest fucking guy I've ever seen. It doesn't matter that he makes me laugh. It doesn't matter that he never makes me feel bad about the fact that I'm rich and powerful. It doesn't matter that he goes to the trouble of making breakfast for me every morning. And it certainly doesn't matter that he made me feel like I was bursting with sparkling pleasure when he made me come on that red couch.

All that matters is that I need to get rid of him.

My heart flutters as Jace reaches forward over the hood, his perfect body making the move seem effortless.

Next week, I amend in my head. I need to get rid of him, but not until next week. Because I did promise that I wouldn't pull anymore bullshit this week if he did all the work today. And a deal is a deal.

A low whistle of approval sounds from right next to me. "Damn."

I start in surprise and whip my head to the left to find a woman about my age dropping down into the chair beside me. She's wearing a blue polo shirt with the logo of the car dealership embroidered on it, which means that she no doubt works here. I narrow my eyes as I study her face.

With her eyes locked firmly on Jace's half-naked body, she cocks her head and smiles. "I'd tap that."

An absolutely irrational flash of jealousy and possessiveness burns through me like wildfire.

"He's my bodyguard," I snap, the words coming out with much more bite than I intended.

The woman next to me doesn't seem to notice, however. Because she continues ogling Jace as if she's imagining what he looks like in bed. A sly smile blows across her features as she gives me a knowing glance.

"Oh you lucky girl," she says.

I squeeze my hand into a fist and resist the urge to stab her.

18

JACE

To my surprise, Kayla actually kept her end of the bargain. She didn't try to sneak off even once during the entire rest of the week. So when her father's guards came to relieve me for my day off, I wasn't nearly as exhausted as I have been all other Sundays.

After sleeping in my own bed back at Blackwater, I went through several workout routines and some target practice, and I still feel like I'm bursting with energy. In a good way. It's not the restless energy that has plagued me for years. It's more of an excited one.

I scan the shelves as I walk down one of the aisles. Normally, I wouldn't bother going to a grocery store downtown like this, but this specific one has a lot of ingredients that are difficult to find in a mainstream store. And Eli and Raina are coming back today after being away for the past four days on an out-of-state assassination, so I figured I'd do the cooking.

Though in all honesty, it's mostly because Eli and Raina can't cook for shit. At least not unless you count Raina's insane ability to make different kinds of poison as cooking. Which I'm pretty sure she does. And since I have no intention of being poisoned this particular Sunday, I will be making the food instead.

I only have a vague idea of what I want to make, so I study the contents of the shelves as I continue down the aisle, looking for inspiration.

When nothing sparks my interest, I rake my fingers through my hair and round the corner into the next aisle.

And slam right into someone's shopping cart.

"Watch it," a familiar voice snaps.

I blink in genuine surprise. But before I can so much as open my mouth, two guards are already descending on me.

They stop short a couple of steps away when they suddenly realize who I am.

The girl on the other side of the shopping cart stares at me, her mouth slightly open.

"Jace," she says, sounding just as surprised as she looks.

I glance from her to her guards and then to the aisle of food around us before frowning at her in confusion. "What are you doing here, little demon?"

Kayla stares at me in silence for another few seconds. Then she gives her head a short shake as if to clear it, and then waves a hand at her guards. They immediately retreat to the end of the aisle, giving us space. Since I'm here, they know that no one will hurt her even if they are standing farther away than they normally would.

"What does it look like?" Kayla replies, apparently having recovered, as she raises her eyebrows and motions expectantly down at the shopping cart. "I'm buying groceries."

"I thought today was family day," I retort, shooting a

pointed look towards her guards. "Shouldn't you be at your parents' house?"

She sighs, sounding slightly annoyed. "He was called away for an urgent meeting, so family day was cancelled."

"So you're…?" I wave a hand towards her shopping cart.

"I'm cooking for my event planning group."

"Your event planning group? You mean Aurora, Jenn, and Lionel?"

"Yes." She gives me a look full of challenge. "So?"

Yes, *'so?'*, indeed. Why does the thought of Kayla cooking for Lionel make me want to shoot someone in the face? Preferably that slimy little fucker Lionel himself. It shouldn't bother me. Kayla is just a job. A means to an end. She can cook for her friends whenever she wants. It makes no difference to me.

Irrational jealousy twists inside my stomach like snakes.

No. Fuck this. Kayla is not going to cook for Lionel fucking Henderson.

"So this is what you're planning to serve?" I ask instead, making a show of looking down into her shopping cart.

That immediately makes her defensive. Probably because she, just like Eli and Raina, doesn't actually know how to cook. From what I've seen these past few weeks, she either eats out or has food delivered from some fancy catering company that her family has a partnership with.

"What of it?" she retorts, crossing her arms and giving me a sharp look.

I continue studying the groceries she has picked, trying to figure out what on earth she's planning to make. Then surprise jolts through me.

Meeting her gaze again, I arch a surprised eyebrow. "Italian?"

"Yes." She sounds almost a little self-conscious.

Amusement ripples through me, but I keep it firmly off my face and instead frown at her. "Do you even know how to cook?"

"Of course I do."

Giving her a dubious look, I pick up one of the ingredients that I know for certain is really difficult to get right, and hold it up in front of her face. "What are you planning to do with this?"

She snatches it out of my hand and slams it back down into the cart again. "I'm sure I can Google it."

"No, no, no." I shake my head at her and then lift my hand to beckon at her guards. "I'm not letting you desecrate my native cuisine like this."

"I... What are you...?" She frowns in confusion as her guards return. "What—"

"I'll take it from here," I tell her father's guards. "You can head home or to your other assignments or whatever. I'll guard her the rest of the day."

Surprise flits across their faces as they exchange a glance. Then they look to Kayla for confirmation. She continues scowling at me for a few more seconds before turning to meet their eyes. Heaving a resigned sigh, she gives them a nod in confirmation.

They nod back in acknowledgement. Then Ryan, the tall dark-haired one, gives her an apologetic grimace while pulling out his phone.

"I'll call it in, but Mr. Ashford will no doubt need to hear it from you as well, ma'am," he says.

"Yeah, you're right," Kayla replies with another sigh. "Call him up."

While they call Trent Ashford to clear the guard change, I pull up my own phone and send a text to Eli.

Me: *Change of plans. There was an emergency so I need to handle Kayla's security today too.*

He replies within seconds, which means that they must already be home.

Eli: *"Emergency." Right. Tell Kayla I said hi.*

Me: *No. And what's with the quotation marks?*

Eli: *Just that next time you tell Kaden that he's whipped, I'll remind you of this.*

Me: *Fuck you. I'm not whipped. I'm working.*

Eli: *And you owe me dinner.*

Me: *Who says I was going to make you dinner?*

Eli: *Why do you think I invited you over?*

Me: *Asshole.*

Eli: *Bastard.*

Me: *I'll see you next weekend.*

Eli: *Yes, you will. And you'd better bring food or I'll kick your ass.*

Me: *Come try it.*

Eli: *Or Raina will slip poison into your whiskey.*

I heave a deep sigh, because I know he's not kidding about that one. Raina would never outright kill me, of course. But she's an incredibly skilled chemist so I know that there are lots of other things she could put into my drink that would make me do whatever she wanted without it being fatal.

With a faint smile tugging at my lips, I shake my head at my unhinged brother and his even more unhinged girl as I type out a reply.

Me: *Fine, I'll make you dinner next weekend.*

Kayla finishes her call with her father right as I slip my own phone back into my pocket as well.

Her father's guards give the two of us a nod, button their suit jackets, and then stride away. Kayla relaxes the moment they're gone. I convince myself that it's only because they were making her stand out with their highly conspicuous black suits in a grocery store on a Sunday afternoon.

Grabbing the shopping cart, I start down the aisle before she has realized what's happening.

"Hey," she calls as she scrambles after me. "What are you doing?"

I grab some things from her cart and put them back on the shelf. "You can't use these."

"Why not?"

Picking up some others, I put them back as well. "And this brand is shit." I select another one from the shelf next to it. "These are better."

Crossing her arms, she mutters something under her breath and does her best to glower at me as she follows me around the grocery store. I return the nonsensical ingredients she had put in her shopping cart before I arrived to save the day, and instead fill it with food that will actually taste good together.

"I thought today was your day off," she remarks.

"It is."

"I could've done this on my own."

"Because you know so much about making Italian food."

"Yes."

"Uh-huh." Stopping in the middle of the aisle, I level a stare full of challenge on her. "Look, do you want to give everyone food poisoning or do you want my help?"

Drawing her eyebrows down, she glares at me. But I swear to God there is a smile threatening to spill across her lips too.

"Fine," she says, and throws her hands up in an overdramatic gesture. "I'll let you help me. Just a little."

Which means that I will be cooking the entire meal while she sits on a chair, drinks wine, and drools over how hot I look when I cook.

Just the way I want it.

19

KAYLA

God damn, the boy can cook. My soul flutters every time I take a bite of the food, and I have to actively stop myself from moaning. The taste is absolutely incredible. Not to mention how fucking hot he looked while he was making it.

"This is absolutely delicious," Jenn blurts out between enthusiastic bites. Her blue eyes are wide as she stares at me from across my kitchen table. "Did you really make this?"

A sheepish smile spreads across my mouth, and I scratch the back of my neck. "Uhm, no. Jace did, actually."

Jenn, Aurora, and Lionel all whip around to stare at Jace, who is sitting across from me at the table. Shock pulses across all of their faces as they gape at him.

"*You* made this?" Jenn asks, sounding as surprised as she looks.

"It was a team effort," Jace replies, a grin on his mouth, as he winks at me.

Unexpected warmth ripples through me, and I let out a soft laugh.

Team effort. Right. The only thing I contributed to this meal was picking out the wine. Since I have no idea what I'm doing around food, Jace ended up cooking the entire meal on his own while I sat at the kitchen table drinking wine. And staring at his forearms. And staring at the way his messy curls fell down over his forehead when he was looking down at the cutting board. And staring at the light that sparkled in his eyes when he tasted the sauce to make sure it was seasoned perfectly. God, who knew a man could look so hot while doing something as simple as making food?

"I just picked out the wine," I admit, a smile on my mouth, as I nod towards Jace. "Jace made all the food."

"It's incredible," Jenn says to Jace, her eyes glittering as she takes another bite.

Aurora gives him a knowing smile over the rim of her wine glass. "Gotta love a man who knows how to cook."

There is a genuine smile on Jace's lips as he raises his own wine glass in a salute. Red and golden light from the setting sun reflects against the windows of the building opposite ours and shines into my apartment. It casts warm light over Jace's handsome features as he smiles. My heart does a strange summersault in my chest.

"Why do you even know how to cook?" Lionel suddenly asks, almost sounding a bit suspicious as he frowns at Jace.

While setting down his wine glass, Jace turns and leans forward a little so that he can meet Lionel's gaze since they are seated the farthest from each other. No one is sitting at the head of the table. Instead, Jace and I are sitting opposite each other on the right side of the table while Jenn and Aurora are seated opposite each other on our left. Lionel is sitting on Aurora's other side, which puts him alone there at the left side of the table.

"What do you mean?" Jace asks, a slight frown on his face.

Lionel gestures at the food on our plates. "I mean, you don't exactly look like someone who knows how to make something like this."

"And what does someone who knows how to cook look like?"

"I don't know," Lionel snipes back. "Not like you."

He sounds defensive. And angry. Which I find very strange. But Jace doesn't seem bothered by it at all. He lifts his broad shoulders in a shrug and flashes us all a grin.

"Well, a man's gotta eat," he says. "And in order to eat, you need to know how to cook." A sharp glint full of challenge creeps into his eyes as he once again leans forward and locks eyes with Lionel. "Or are you one of those men who expect your girl to cook for you?"

Lionel's cheeks flush an indignant shade of red as he splutters, "No. Of course not."

Jace lets out a huff of amusement and leans back in his seat, nonchalantly swirling the wine in his glass before taking a sip.

Before Lionel can retort, Jenn expertly switches the topic. "We should probably start planning the next step for our silent auction. We have secured the items that will be auctioned off. Now, we need a venue."

"Exactly," Aurora picks up.

Lionel shoots one last glare at Jace, but then joins the discussion as well.

I keep my eyes on Jace.

This is one of the things that I find so interesting about him. The contrasting sides of him and how effortlessly he can shift between them. On the one hand, he's carefree and full of laughter and excitement. Like a golden retriever. Which is why I call him Sparky when I want to mess with him. But at the same time, he's also cunning and confident and incredibly dominant.

My heart starts racing at just the memory of that one command he snapped at me to prove a point earlier. *Now, sit your ass back down on that chair and finish your breakfast like a good girl.* God, I wanted to slap him when he said that. But mostly, I wanted to slap myself because of how my heart flipped and my pussy throbbed.

While only listening to Aurora with half an ear, I let my gaze drop back down to Jace's forearms. The way his muscles flexed when he was chopping ingredients and whisking the sauce and lifting the pans while making dinner earlier was so hot that my mind drifted down all kinds of really dangerous paths. And now, I can't get those thoughts out of my head.

Suddenly realizing that I'm staring, I snap my gaze back up.

And find Jace smirking at me with a knowing glint in his eyes.

I scoff, trying to play it off, but I can't stop my cheeks from heating. Hopefully, it's not visible in the dancing candlelight and the already red and golden hues from the setting sun.

Blocking out those inconvenient thoughts, I drink deeply from my wine glass and instead return my attention to the discussion about how we are going to find a venue for our silent auction.

But even after we have finished dinner, and Aurora, Jenn, and Lionel have left, and we have cleaned up in the kitchen, I still can't get those forbidden thoughts completely out of my mind.

Indecision twists inside me as I linger in the living room,

watching Jace retreat into his bedroom. As usual, he doesn't close the door fully behind him.

I should head back into my own bedroom too. Should call it a night. I have classes in the morning. And I've been drinking. Not that I'm drunk or anything. But still. It's Monday tomorrow. I should do the responsible thing and get ready for a week of studies.

The memory of how fucking hot Jace looked when he was cooking blows across my vision again.

Fuck it. I start towards his bedroom. I'm not going to do anything. I'm just going to ask him something. Just one question. And then I will leave. Then I will do the right thing and be responsible and not further muddle this already complicated relationship that we now have.

I make sure that he can hear me coming towards his room so that he has the chance to shut the door in my face if he wants to.

He doesn't.

Walking inside, I find him standing by the dresser on the other side of the room. Shirtless.

Electricity shoots up my spine as Jace sets down the shirt he has just taken off and turns to face me. Light from the ceiling lamp falls across his muscular chest when he stops. Heat pools inside me, and I suddenly forget why I'm here.

Jace arches an eyebrow. "Did you need something?"

I clear my throat, scrambling to compose myself again. "Yes."

"And that is…?"

"When you said that I wouldn't be able to handle it, what does that mean?"

He blinks, looking a little surprised by the direction this conversation just took. Then a sly smile spreads across his lips instead as he flicks a knowing glance up and down my body. "It means exactly what I said. You wouldn't be able to handle me."

Irritation flickers through me. "Based on what?"

His expression hardens and his voice pulses with authority as he snaps, "Get on your knees."

I start slightly at the utter command in his voice, and then scowl at him.

He smirks. "See? Whenever I tell you to do something, your first instinct is to refuse."

"That doesn't count." I glare at him. "You did that knowing full well that it would surprise me."

"Whatever you need to tell yourself." Suspicion suddenly blows across his features as he narrows his eyes at me. "Why are you even asking this, little demon?"

I hold his gaze. "Maybe I'm curious."

"About what?"

About what it would be like to fuck you. What it would be like to be utterly dominated by you in a way that I have never experienced with anyone. And most of all, I'm curious to know if I would like it as much as I suspect that I would.

But I can't say that, of course. So I reply, "Curious to know if I can actually handle taking orders from someone."

"Hmm."

He continues studying me in silence for another few seconds. My heart is suddenly pounding in my chest.

Outside the windows, a car alarm goes off. The piercing sound is the only thing breaking the stillness before someone eventually shuts it off. I flick a quick glance around the bedroom.

All of my other bodyguards always kept it neat. Jace doesn't. There are four bats leaning against the wall next to the windows, a few clothes scattered on the dresser, and a shirt that has even slipped down to the floor. And the bed is unmade. For some reason, the sight of those messy sheets makes my pulse race even more.

"Alright," Jace says at last.

I snap my gaze back to him. His face has become an unreadable mask, but his eyes are intense as he watches me.

"You want to test if you can follow orders?" he asks, though it's more of a statement.

Making sure to keep my features neutral, I lift my shoulders in a nonchalant shrug. "Yeah."

"Take off your shirt." The force of the command cuts through the air like a blade.

I start in surprise. A devilish smile curls his lips, as if he was expecting that reaction. Then he raises his eyebrows, his expression dripping with challenge.

Flashing him a sharp smile to match his own, I hold his gaze while reaching down to grab the hem of my shirt. My heart slams nervously against my ribs as I start pulling off my shirt. But there is also an insane thrill to this whole situation that makes my spine tingle.

Warm air kisses my naked skin as I slip the shirt over my head and then toss it to the floor. I can practically hear my heart pounding in my chest as I stand there, wearing only a bra and pants now, while Jace watches me with eyes intense enough to sear through my very soul.

"Pants too," he orders without breaking eye contact.

With my eyes locked on his, I start unbuttoning my pants and then slowly slide down the zipper. He never takes his eyes off mine. And he doesn't look at all affected by what I'm doing.

That sends a pang of self-consciousness through me.

Given how experienced Jace is, this is probably nothing special to him. *I'm* probably nothing special.

Those thoughts make my insides twist painfully, but I manage to keep my expression neutral as I slip my hands underneath my pants and start pushing them down.

After guiding them over my ass and down my thighs, I bend forward to push them all the way down my legs and then step out of them. Pushing the garment to the side with my foot, I straighten once more while trying to keep my heart from thundering too hard.

Right as I straighten, I catch Jace flexing his hand and clenching his jaw. As if he has to physically brace himself for what I look like in only my underwear.

It makes heat flood my cheeks again, and I can't help another flash of self-consciousness. Shifting my arms, I discreetly try to cover myself a little.

"Don't cover yourself up," Jace snaps.

I jerk back in surprise at the roughness of his voice, and let my hands drop back down by my sides again.

"You're the most gorgeous woman I've ever seen, so there is no reason for you to hide."

My mouth drops open. For a few seconds, all I can do is stare at him. Did those words actually come out of his mouth? Is that what he truly thinks?

Panic flashes across Jace's features. As if he hadn't meant to say that. Then he clears his throat, and the unreadable mask is back on his face again.

But I'm not about to let him get off that easily, so I open my mouth to comment on it. However, right before I can, Jace issues an order with such utter authority that it pulses through my very soul.

"Now, get down on your knees and crawl to me."

At first, I can only feel the power of that command vibrating through the air.

Then his words sink in.

Jerking back, I gape at him in disbelief. "What?"

He pushes off from the drawers and strides across the room, power rolling off his broad shoulders as he advances on me. I scramble a step back in surprise. Jace just keeps coming, forcing me to stumble backwards to keep from getting mowed down by him.

My back hits the smooth wall with a thud.

Jace keeps moving until he is standing barely a step away. His bare chest is so close to my naked skin that I can feel the heat radiating from him. My heart hammers against my ribs. It's so loud that I'm pretty sure he can hear it.

Lightning skitters across my skin as he places two fingers underneath my chin and tilts my head back so that I meet his gaze. I draw in a shuddering breath as he lets his hand drop back down again. But he doesn't step back. He remains standing there, so close that I can almost feel his body against mine.

"Outside these walls, everyone you meet might jump to obey your every order," he begins, his eyes searing into mine. "But in here, you obey *my* commands. So when I tell you to crawl, you fucking crawl. Understood?"

Fire rushes through my veins, and my clit throbs. My heart is beating so hard that it feels as if it's going to break free from my chest. No one has ever spoken to me like this before Never.

No one has ever dared to give me orders. And I would never have deigned to respond to such a thing. It would've made me furious. But as I stare up into Jace's stunning face, all I feel is a dark thrill coursing through my spine.

Jace towers over me. And his muscular body blocks out everything else in the room. Physically, I wouldn't stand a chance against him. He could make me do whatever he wanted with just physical force. And the fact that he doesn't even use his sheer size and strength to dominate me, the fact that he only uses his voice to assert his authority, somehow makes this whole situation even hotter.

He knows that he's powerful, and he doesn't need to prove that. And that kind of confidence is so fucking hot.

"I said, *understood?*"

"Yes," I breathe, feeling as if my whole world is tilting on its axis.

Challenge glints in Jace's eyes as he demands, "Yes, what?"

My thighs clench and my heart stutters. "Yes, sir."

He leans down, slanting his lips over mine until I can feel his breath dance over my mouth when he says, "Good girl."

A shudder rolls through my whole body.

He braces his hand against the wall next to my head as he moves closer. My breasts brush against his bare chest with every breath now. His lips hover over mine. Almost touching. Almost kissing. I drag in unsteady breaths. Jace places his other hand on my hip. A tiny moan escapes my throat.

In the span of a heartbeat, Jace yanks his hand off my hip and pulls back.

The move is so sudden, and so unexpected, that I start. And the loss of his nearness is so jarring that all I can do is to blink at him in stunned surprise as he takes several steps back.

"Test concluded," he announces. A cold smile slides home on his lips as he gives me a dismissive look. "And guess what? You failed. You talk a lot, but when push comes to shove, you won't actually *do* it. Which means that you can't handle it." He jerks his chin towards the door. "Now, go to bed."

Anger roars through me like flames. Shoving off from the wall, I stalk towards him. "Do you want to know what I think?"

"No. But I have a feeling you're about to tell me anyway."

With a vicious smile full of challenge on my lips, I stride forward. He holds my gaze, letting me back him towards the bed.

"I think *you* are the one who can't handle it," I counter.

He chuckles as he comes to a halt right in front of the bed, and then gives me a look pulsing with warning. "You are out of your league, little demon."

"Oh, I don't think so." Stopping before him, I wrap my hand around the front of his belt and give it a firm yank. "I saw you when I straightened after I took my pants off. You almost blew your load just seeing me in my underwear." I smirk at him. "So imagine what will happen when I do this."

Before he can retort, I release his belt and instead reach up behind me to unclasp my bra.

A ripple shoots through his body as I toss my bra aside, leaving my tits on full display only a step away from him.

"Kayla," he says, his voice now full of warning.

"Or this," I say as I slide my hands into my panties and push them down.

The muscles in his jaw tick as I step out of my panties, but he keeps his eyes firmly locked on mine. "Put your clothes back on."

I shoot a pointed look down at his cock, which is straining against his pants in a way that must surely be painful. "Why?" I taunt as I meet his gaze again. "Can't handle it?"

"You—"

"You talk a lot," I interrupt, echoing his own words to me

and putting even more mocking into my tone. "But when push comes to shove, you won't actually *do* it."

He moves before I can react.

In one fluid motion, he grabs me, spins me around, and shoves me down on the bed. My body is still bouncing on the soft mattress when he appears above me.

Heat spears through my core as he straddles me, the rough fabric of his jeans scraping against my naked skin. Leaning forward, he braces both hands against the sheets on either side of my head as he gets right into my face.

Fire burns in his eyes as he locks them on me. "Is this what you want? Huh? For me to pin you to the bed and tell you what a good girl you are?"

Lust pulses through me, but I manage to keep the mocking expression on my face as I reach up and slide both hands through his messy curls. My heart flutters. Fuck, his hair feels just as soft as it looks.

"No," I say, smirking up at him as I slide my hands through his hair and down to the back of his neck. "I want you to *do* something. But you won't." Challenge bleeds into both my tone and my smirk. "Because you can't handle it."

A shudder rolls through his body as I trace my fingers along the back of his neck. I do it again, and I'm rewarded by the same incredible shiver of pleasure. He licks his lips and flexes his fingers in the sheets.

"You talk a lot of shit for someone within kissing distance," he says, his voice hoarse.

I yank his mouth down to mine.

Lightning crackles through me as our lips clash. Jace moans into my mouth. The sound makes my heart skip a beat.

His mouth becomes furious, *desperate*, as he claims my lips with a possessiveness that leaves me breathless. I rake my fingers down his back as he pushes his tongue into my mouth, dominating it with demanding strokes. My head spins.

I roll my hips, grinding my bare pussy against the coarseness of his jeans.

Another moan rips from deep within his lungs.

I draw my hands down the side of his ribs and along the top of his pants.

And I swear a fucking *whimper* escapes his chest this time.

My heart swells and pleasure pulses through my soul at the sound of it.

Jace takes one hand off the mattress and instead places it on the side of my neck and jaw in a highly controlling and possessive move.

While he steals the breath from my lungs with desperate kisses, I unbuckle his belt and then unbutton his pants before shoving the zipper down. He kisses me furiously while I start pushing his pants down. But I don't get far because I can't reach much more than that when he's pinning me to the bed like this.

With a groan of frustration, Jace reluctantly tears his mouth from mine and sits up. I gasp in desperate breaths while he quickly shifts to the side and strips out of his remaining clothes.

My eyes widen as I take in the size of his cock.

No wonder he's so cocky and full of swaggering arrogance about his sexual prowess. He has the goods to back it up.

"So that's why everyone wants to fuck you, huh?" I tease, but my words end up coming out breathless.

A truly devilish smile spreads across his lips as he grabs my thighs and spreads my legs wide, exposing my pussy completely to him. It sends a dark thrill down my spine. But he doesn't return to his position on top of me. Instead, he settles himself on his knees between my spread legs. His eyes glitter as he leans forward.

"No." He smirks at me. "*This* is why everyone wants to fuck me."

And then he licks my pussy and swirls his tongue around my clit.

Electricity shoots through my every nerve, and I gasp as I arch up from the bed and try to close my legs. Jace's strong hands remain firmly on my thighs, keeping them spread wide open for him.

Taking my clit into his mouth, he rolls it between his lips.

Pleasure spears through me.

"Jace," I gasp, trying to close my legs again as a sudden burst of embarrassment pulses through me.

No one has ever done something like this before. What if he hates it? What if I taste bad? What if he thinks it's gross? What if he thinks *I'm* gross?

Feeling very self-conscious, I try to close my legs again.

"You don't have to—" I begin, but then my words are cut off by a moan as Jace takes my clit into his mouth again.

"Fuck, you taste so good," he murmurs against my pussy.

Heat sears my cheeks and pools at my core at both his words and the way his voice vibrates over my sensitive skin.

He draws his tongue down along my pussy. I suck in shuddering breaths and slide my hands into his hair as pleasure flickers through every nerve in my body.

Jace pushes his tongue inside me.

I gasp up into the ceiling. Gripping his hair hard, I moan and squirm on the soft sheets as he fucks me with his tongue.

"Jace," I pant.

He swirls his tongue around my clit again.

"God," I gasp.

His soft chuckle vibrates against my clit. "That's better."

Sliding my hands deeper into his hair, I flex my fingers in his soft curls as he licks and teases and fucks me with his tongue until the tension inside me is so intense that I can barely see anymore.

"Jace," I moan. "Jace, I'm going to—"

Pleasure shoots through my limbs like bursts of electricity.

My legs shake underneath his strong hands as the orgasm sweeps through my body. My clit throbs between his lips as he continues pleasuring me while I writhe and gasp on the sheets.

Once the last waves have faded, I just lie there on the mattress, staring up at the ceiling and wondering how the hell I have managed to go through my entire life without experiencing something as incredible as that.

Then reality trickles back in, and I realize that Jace is still kneeling between my spread legs with his cock painfully hard.

Raising my head, I meet his eyes. Embarrassment laces my voice as I say, "I'm sorry. I couldn't... I couldn't stop it."

He frowns at me in genuine confusion. "Why would you want to stop it?"

"I—"

My words are cut off by a sharp breath as he draws a light hand over my pussy. But his fingers are gentle as he strokes my sensitive clit until pleasure once more starts building inside me.

"Answer me," he demands.

It takes a few seconds before I remember the question. My chest heaves as I wiggle on the sheets while he slides his fingers down to my entrance.

"Because I came before you had a chance to come too," I reply, shooting a look towards his hard cock.

He frowns at me in silence for a second. Then understanding apparently floods his system, because his eyes widen. While tracing my entrance with his fingers, he sighs and shakes his head.

"Jesus Christ," he mutters, and then gives me a look. "You really haven't been fucking the right kind of guys."

"What—" I begin.

But right then, he pushes two fingers inside me. I arch up from the bed and then grip the sheets hard. My heart slams against my ribs as Jace carefully adds a third finger, stretching me gently.

"The lady comes first," he declares, as if that's the most obvious thing in the world. "At least once. Preferably twice. Then the guy can chase his own release. What kind of selfish idiots have you been fucking if they have made you think that they're supposed to come first?"

"I, uhm…" I begin, but my mind is scrambled by the feeling of Jace's fingers inside me.

"Now, are you on birth control?"

"Am I—" A moan tears from my chest and I grip the sheets hard as he scissors his fingers inside me. "What…?"

"Birth control."

Stars flicker before my eyes, but I manage to press out, "Yes. Yes, I'm on birth control."

"Good." He withdraws his fingers and shifts into position above me so that he is bracing himself on the mattress on either side of me instead. His brown eyes glitter as he flashes me a sly smile while brushing the tip of his cock over my entrance. "Because I want to feel you, all of you, when I show you how those other guys *should've* fucked you."

"I—"

He thrusts his hips.

My eyes widen as his thick cock slides into me. I release the sheets and instead wrap my hands around his biceps. Or I try to, at least. I can't reach all the way around. But I dig my fingers into his muscles as he slowly pushes his cock deeper.

He's huge, so faint pain flickers through me with each inch. But he moves slowly, being careful not to hurt me. I shift my hips slightly, creating a better angle.

Pleasure ripples through me when he pushes deeper this time.

Jace keeps his eyes locked on mine, studying the emotions on my face.

With one final push, he sheaths himself fully.

My heart hammers against my ribs at the feeling of him filling me completely like this.

"Fuck, you're perfect," he blurts out, sounding astonished.

I suck in a small breath, suddenly finding it difficult to breathe properly.

Jace doesn't move. He just keeps his cock buried inside me like that, allowing me time to adjust to his size.

Leaning down, he steals a kiss from my lips while murmuring, "So perfect."

My very soul flutters as warmth fills my body.

Pleasure flickers through my veins again as Jace starts kissing his way down my throat while he pulls his cock out halfway. I drag in unsteady breaths. His lips brush over my throat and down to my collarbones. Then he shoves his cock all the way inside again.

I gasp, and a jolt shoots through me. But it's a good jolt.

Squirming on the sheets, I shift my hips to match his thrusts as he pulls out and then slams into me again while he kisses a trail down my chest. Moans spill from my lips.

When Jace hears it, he starts up a faster pace.

I tighten my grip on his biceps as he begins thrusting into me with steady commanding moves. Pleasure pulses through me with each thrust. He flicks my nipple with his tongue. I whimper and dig my fingers harder into his muscles.

His movements become harder. Faster. More demanding.

My chest heaves as he pounds into me while he kisses his way back up my throat. Taking one hand off the mattress, he traces it around the curve of my breast before his fingers find my sensitive nipple.

Bright spots dance before my eyes as he rolls my nipple between his fingers while his lips brush over my throat and his massive cock creates insane friction inside me.

The sheer amount of stimulation makes my brain feel like it's melting.

I suck in desperate breaths as Jace pounds into me.

Tension whirls inside me like a storm as I careen towards another orgasm.

Lifting my hips, I meet him stroke for stroke as he fucks me hard and dominantly. Such a contrast to the softness of his lips on my throat and the gentle teasing of his fingers on my aching nipple. And the combination of it makes it feel as if I'm about to burst with pleasure.

Fucking hell, this man is a god. He works my body as if he knows it better than I do.

I writhe on the soft sheets and flex my hands around his biceps as the edge of the orgasm draws closer. My breaths come in short bursts.

Jace slams into me, hitting a spot deep inside, at the same time as he pinches my nipple.

My eyes fly open and pleasure explodes through my body.

I gasp as my pussy tightens around his thick cock.

A sly smile graces his lips as he lifts his head from my throat and watches as pleasure floods my features.

With powerful thrusts, he keeps fucking me through the orgasm until it feels as if my body is going to unravel from the prolonged stimulation. Then he picks up some more speed, finally chasing his own release. I slam my hips up into his and slide my hands up to his shoulders. Then I rake them down his muscled back while he pounds into me. A moan escapes his throat. I draw my fingers along his ribs. His eyes flutter.

My body rocks back and forth on the bed from his powerful thrusts.

Then a dark groan tears from deep inside him, and pleasure floods his features as well.

I watch, still high on my own release, as light bursts in Jace's eyes when he comes. His cock pulses inside me.

It's the most insane thing I have ever experienced. It feels as if my soul has floated away from my body, leaving it utterly spent and bursting with pleasure. I just want to do this again. And again.

I want him to tell me to get down on my knees and crawl to him. Because the next time he says it, I'm going to fucking do it. I want to feel everything that this absolute god of a man can make me feel.

A flash of panic cuts through the blissful haze in my mind, shattering those sinful thoughts like broken glass.

With that sense of panic clanging inside me like giant alarm bells, I stare up at Jace's stunning face.

Oh fuck. How am I supposed to go back to thinking of him as just my bodyguard now? How am I supposed to go back to thinking of him as just an annoying problem that I need to get rid of?

Fucking shit. What have I done? I shouldn't have done this. I should never have crossed this line.

My heart pounds like a battle drum in my chest.

Some lines should not be crossed, because there is no uncrossing them.

And this was definitely one of them.

20

JACE

For some reason, I thought everything was going to change after that stupidly impulsive and absolutely incredible night four days ago. Partly because of her. But mostly because of me.

These past six years, I have fucked a lot of people as a way to appease the restlessness in my soul. And I always get bored. Sometimes, I get bored before I even get to their bedroom. Sometimes, I get bored halfway through. But I always, *always*, get bored afterwards. Because none of them ever mattered. Nothing in my life ever mattered.

So I was terrified that I would start feeling like that about Kayla now as well. I'm supposed to spend the entire rest of the semester guarding her, so how would I survive that if that damn restlessness and boredom returned?

But it didn't.

Not even for one moment.

Kayla might be infuriating and frustrating and a downright little demon, but she is never boring.

Quite the opposite.

She's fascinating.

Her fierce spirit. Her stubbornness. Her energy.

It's as if it feeds my soul. As if *she* feeds my soul.

And these past four days, she has leveled up in her attempts to drive me crazy.

Which is the other thing that surprised me after our glorious night together.

Kayla is acting as if she hates me even more now. As if she's even more angry and petty and wants to get rid of me even more. Which makes absolutely no sense. Because I'm fucking excellent in bed. And I know that she enjoyed herself as much as I did. I could read it clear as day in her eyes. Feeling her naked body against mine as I drew pleasure from her soul blew my fucking mind. And I know that the experience blew her mind too. It was written all over her face. So the fact that she is trying even harder now to ditch me took me a little by surprise. But it doesn't bother me too much.

She's probably just angry that I was right. That she couldn't handle me. That she couldn't handle it when I told her to get down on her knees and crawl. While I, just as I said, could handle *her* perfectly.

Strolling along the sidewalk, I check my phone to make sure that the little dot on the map is still heading in my direction. It is. I pick up the pace slightly so that I will reach the corner of the alleyway before the little red dot reaches that spot.

The sky visible between the tall buildings is painted with streaks of deep red and purple. Soon, the sun will dip entirely beyond the horizon. But I will have acquired my target well before then.

I jog the final distance as I notice the little dot picking up speed as well. However, I'm far faster so I reach my destination first.

Drawing myself up by the wall right next to the mouth of the alley, I wait.

Two seconds later, the sound of rapid footsteps comes from inside the alley. I remain where I am, listening as they draw closer.

After locking my phone screen, I slip it back into my pocket.

The footsteps reach the mouth of the alley.

Darting forward, I grab my target, spin her around, and slam her up against the wall inside the alley.

Kayla lets out a huff as her back connects with the red bricks.

Then shock pulses across her gorgeous face as she stares up at me with wide eyes. I keep one hand around her throat, pinning her to the wall, while the other traps her right wrist against the wall next to her head as well.

"You," she splutters, staring at me with such a stunned expression that I almost laugh.

I smirk down at her. "Hello, little demon."

She yanks adorably against my grip on her wrist. Which naturally makes no difference whatsoever. When that doesn't work, she wraps her left hand around my wrist and tries to force my arm away. I tighten my fingers around her throat in response. She snaps her gaze back to my face and shoots me a glare, but stops trying to push my arm away.

Letting her free hand drop back down by her side, she stares up at me with eyes full of annoyance and frustration. "How do you always do this? How do you always know whenever I sneak out?"

"Seeing as you *always* try to sneak out, it's not really the secret you think it is."

She stomps her foot in anger and throws out her free hand in exasperation. "Then how do you always find me?"

Easy. I put a GPS tracker in her watch.

After the first hellish week she put me through, I realized that she always wears the same wristwatch. And she doesn't just wear it sometimes. She *always* wears it. So one night, I planted a GPS tracker in it while she slept.

So now, whenever she manages to sneak away, I just follow the little red dot on my phone. And *abracadabra*, there she is. Just like magic.

I'm not about to tell her that, though. So I just smirk down at her and lift my shoulders in a nonchalant shrug.

"I'm just that good."

She scoffs. "Always so arrogant."

"It's not really arrogance when you can back it up."

Grinding her teeth, she yanks against my grip on her wrist. "Just let me go."

"I will. Once you apologize for sneaking off and making my job harder."

"I don't give a shit if I make your job harder."

"Then I suppose I don't give a shit if you spend the night pinned to the wall in this alley."

A growl rips from her throat, and she once again tries to use her free hand to bend my fingers off her wrist. I tighten my hand around her throat until I'm almost cutting off her air completely.

My eyes are hard and full of authority as I stare her down. "You give me shit, and I'll give you shit."

She glares back at me with eyes like hellfire for another

few seconds. Then she angrily yanks her free hand back down. I let her breathe properly again.

"Now, apologize," I demand.

I know that she hates this. Which is why I love doing it. I love riling her up and watching her get all flustered.

"Fuck you," she snaps.

Shaking my head, I tut as if I'm disappointed. Though in reality, I love it when she fights me like this. There truly never is a dull moment with this little demon around.

"Really?" I say, making a show of looking surprised. "You had no problems following orders last Sunday. Some of them, at least." I let a teasing smirk slide home on my lips as I give her a knowing look. "Should I tell you to take off your clothes again? You responded very well to that command."

Red flushes her cheeks. A low snarl rips from her lungs as she struggles hard against the wall. But she's no match for my strength, so she's not going anywhere unless I allow it.

"You fucking arrogant bastard—" she growls, but I cut her off.

"If this is you trying to apologize, you're off to a terrible start." I shrug. "Just saying."

Another frustrated noise tears from her chest, and she stomps her foot on the ground again. "Just get off me!"

"I will. When you apologize."

"Fine!" The word rips from her throat as she glares up at me with furious eyes. "I'm sorry."

I grin down at her. "See? Was that so hard?"

"Just let me go."

Since she did indeed apologize, I do release my grip on her. Though I would've preferred a more sincere apology. Perhaps a bit of groveling. But we'll work our way up to that.

Her blue eyes flash as she gives my chest a shove that does absolutely nothing to push me back.

"I hate you," she growls as she slips out from between my body and the wall.

Angry footsteps echo between the brick walls as she starts stomping away. I chuckle and follow her.

"No, you don't," I reply with a grin.

And then I make sure to walk as close to her as physically possible all the way back to her apartment.

21

KAYLA

The walk back home didn't do anything to help me cool off. In fact, it just made me even more angry. Especially since Jace walked so close to me that I felt like I was being suffocated by his massive body hovering over me. It got to the point where I even tried to physically push him farther away, which of course didn't work. And that just made me even more furious.

Stalking into my apartment, I try to slam the door shut before Jace can get through. Or to slam it right into him. Or preferably both.

Neither plan works.

He just yanks up an arm and grabs the door before it can hit him. I grind my teeth as I release the handle and storm across the threshold. Jace follows with a casual smile on his face, as if none of this fazes him in the slightest. Nothing ever does.

"I've said it before, little demon," Jace begins from behind me as he closes and locks the front door. "If you're civil, I'm civil. So stop trying to ditch me."

Stopping in the middle of the living room, I whirl around so fast that I almost knock over the potted plant next to the couch. Anger still courses through me, and the casual expression on Jace's features is just making it worse.

"Then stop following me everywhere!" I snap back at him.

Jace shoots me a look while closing the distance between us. "You know I can't do that. It's literally my job to follow you everywhere."

Deep down, I know that he's right, of course. He has literally been hired to follow me everywhere. And none of that is his fault. But I'm too angry to be logical. Especially since Jace is... well, Jace.

I can never slip away from him like I always managed to do with my other bodyguards. And I can't make him frustrated and drive him to quit like I did with all the others. And worst of all, he has somehow managed to make me like him, which none of the others ever even came close to doing.

And I fucking hate him for that.

"Then quit!" I scream back at him in response. The words tear out of my lungs with both anger and desperation.

Emotions flicker across Jace's features for a second. But it's too fast for me to decipher. Then that casual expression is back on his face again, and he shrugs.

"Can't do that either," he says.

Frustration rips through my insides as I stare up at him and snap, "I don't want you here!"

"Unfortunately for you, that's not up to you."

"I don't *need* you! I don't need a fucking bodyguard."

"Your father seems to disagree."

"My father." I practically spit out the words. Rage still courses through me like molten fire, and I start pacing back and forth on the floor, because if I don't do something to expend all of the restlessness inside me, I'm going to explode. It feels as if lightning is flashing through my veins as I turn my head to meet Jace's eyes while I continue pacing. "My father is acting as if we're in the mafia. We're a fucking real estate family! No one is going to assassinate me."

Jace nods a couple of times, as if conceding the point. "No—"

I throw out a hand. "See? Even you agree with that."

"But," he continues, cutting me a look as he picks up from where I interrupted him. "Someone might kidnap you and hold you for ransom. It's not as dangerous as being assassinated, obviously, but it's still an experience that I assume you want to avoid."

"Kidnapped?" Stopping my pacing, I give him an incredulous look. "No one is going to kidnap me."

He crosses his arms over his broad chest as he stares me down. "Your family is one of the richest families in the entire state."

"So?"

"So, that gives desperate idiots a motive to kidnap you in order to extort money from your father."

"Are you even listening to yourself?" Staring up at him, I shake my head at him in complete disbelief. "Are you actually hearing the words coming out of your mouth right now? Kidnapping a rich heir and holding them for ransom?" An exasperated sigh rips from my lungs, and I stab a hand at his chest. "No one does that! This isn't some crime drama on TV."

"Yes, they do. These kinds of things do happen. More than you think."

Anger sears through me, and I give his chest a shove as I glare up at him. "I know that you don't live in the real world, but *I* do. Your world might be full of spies running across rooftops and highspeed car chases and sniper rifles and all that action hero stuff you see on TV. But my world is not like that. My world is just business classes and annoying homework and coffee with my friends and loud parties full of drunk rich kids."

"Once again, your father seems to disagree, since he hired me."

"He's wrong! And he wouldn't even be acting like this if it weren't for—" I cut myself off before I can say too much.

But Jace, the always fucking too perceptive Jace bloody Hunter, picks up on it immediately. His gaze sharpens as he narrows his eyes at me. "If it weren't for what?"

My fingers drift to the watch on my wrist and I unconsciously start fiddling with the strap. The rage bleeds out of me as old memories wash over me instead. I heave a sigh, suddenly feeling completely drained. I glance down at the watch.

"Nothing," I reply, my voice coming out soft and quiet.

Jace wraps his hand around my jaw, tilting my head back up. His brown eyes are full of authority as he locks them on me. "If it concerns your safety, I need to know."

"It doesn't." I slap his hand away. "So just drop it."

Concern pulses across his face, and it makes my throat close up with emotions I can't handle right now.

"Kayla—" he begins, but I cut him off.

"I said, drop it," I snap. Gathering rage around me like a shield, I shoot him a withering glare. "And leave me the fuck alone, because I don't need a bodyguard."

Before he can reply, I spin on my heel and stalk towards my bedroom. Grabbing the handle, I yank the door open. I only manage to get it halfway up before a hand appears on the pale wood.

I jerk back in surprise as Jace plants his palm against the door and slams it shut before I can escape into my room. Whirling around, I find him right in front of me. With one hand on the door, he traps me between it and his muscular body.

"If you don't want to talk to me, that's fine," he growls down at me, finally sounding as frustrated as I've felt since this fight started. "But stop being stupid about your own safety. If someone tries to kidnap you—"

"*If* someone tries to kidnap me," I cut him off, venom dripping from my words, "I will just do what I have done to every single bodyguard I have ever had. I will slip away and escape."

He scoffs and gives me an incredulous look. "You think you can handle a kidnapping attempt? On your own?"

Grinding my teeth, I give his chest a hard shove. "Yes, you arrogant son of a bitch. I'm not nearly as helpless as everyone seems to assume."

His free hand shoots up and wraps around my wrist, stopping my next shove. His eyes bore into mine as he stares me down. "I'm not saying that you're helpless. I'm saying that it's very difficult to stop, or escape from, a kidnapping attempt unless you're a professional with extensive training."

"Yeah, well, I have spent my entire life escaping from overbearing men who think they can keep track of me."

Yanking my wrist out of his grip, I twist around to grab the handle again. Then I pull, trying to open the door.

Jace keeps his palm firmly on the door, holding it closed, for another few seconds while he stares down at me as if he is making a point. I yank on the handle again.

At last, he takes his hand off the door and steps back.

Pulling the door open, I stalk across the threshold and into my room before turning around to face him again. He just stands there on the pale hardwood floor, watching me with an unreadable expression on his face.

Guilt twists inside me again, because I know he doesn't deserve my anger and rudeness. But I don't care. I want freedom. I want my life back. So I put as much venom into my voice as I possibly can and spit out some final parting words.

"I don't want you. And I don't need you. I can take care of myself. So leave me the fuck alone."

Then I slam the door shut in his face.

22

JACE

Lying on top of my bed, I stare up at the pale ceiling while Kayla's words echo inside my skull over and over again.

He wouldn't even be acting like this if it weren't for—

If it weren't for what?

Has there been an attempt on her life before? My heart clenches at the mere thought.

Rolling over, I grab my phone from the nightstand. The streetlamps outside cast pools of yellow light on the walls and ceiling, illuminating my otherwise darkened bedroom. I meant to just lie down on my bed for a couple of minutes to compose myself after our fight before I headed into the shower, but I've remained here for almost an hour now. Because I can't get our fight out of my head. Several parts of that fight, in fact.

After sitting up so that my back is resting against the headboard instead, I start searching the internet for news articles about Kayla. I try everything I can think of.

Kayla Ashford. Assassination attempt. Kidnapping.

Assault. House fire. Mugging. Basically any crime I can think of that would explain her words. But nothing comes up.

Based on the nonexistent news articles, nothing dangerous has ever happened to Kayla Ashford.

But that doesn't necessarily mean anything. Families who are as rich as the Ashfords would've made sure to keep things like that out of the news.

Which is the other part of our fight that I can't get out of my head.

She truly believes that assassination attempts and kidnappings don't happen in real life. And there are two reasons for that assumption. If it's an assassination, the hitman might be skilled enough to make it look like an accident. And if he's not, or if it's a kidnapping instead, the family is often rich and powerful enough to make sure that it doesn't end up on the news. After all, no one wants their private family matters to be blasted across national television for strangers to pick through.

So assassination attempts and kidnappings do happen. Especially to people like Kayla. And it's important that she understands that.

Dropping my phone on my chest, I slide a hand underneath my head and stare up at the pools of light in the ceiling while my mind churns.

If I only knew what *'He wouldn't even be acting like this if it weren't for—'* actually meant, things would be a lot easier.

I tap my finger against the back of my phone as I keep staring up at the ceiling while I sort things through in my mind.

"Ah, fuck it," I say with a sigh as I at last make a decision.

Picking up my phone again, I open the group chat that my brothers and I have, and send a message.

Me: *I need your help.*

For about a minute, nothing happens. But it's only early evening, and I know that neither Eli nor Kaden is away for an assassination right now. Not with Kaden's wedding happening in two weeks. Rico might be in a meeting, depending on if there has been some kind of urgent matter, but he usually tries to keep normal working hours so that he and Isabella can actually have a life too.

At last, a reply comes in.

Eli: *Beg us.*

Narrowing my eyes, I glare at the screen. Is he serious?

Another message quickly follows. From Kaden, this time.

Kaden: *Yes, Golden. Beg us.*

"Motherfuckers," I mutter at the screen as I roll my eyes at my annoying older brothers.

But I really do need their help, so I keep my curses to myself and instead give them what they want.

Me: *Please.*

Eli: *Ha. Told you she's making him desperate enough to beg. Now pay up, Kaden.*

Kaden: ...

Kaden: *Fine.*

An exasperated sigh escapes my chest, and I scowl down at my phone as I send an annoyed message back.

Me: *A bet? Seriously? You assholes.*

Eli: *You bailed on me and Raina last Sunday. We almost starved to death without any food.*

Kaden: *And you called me whipped. Three times this week alone. You had it coming, Golden.*

"Bastards," I huff.

But I can't quite stop a smile from tugging at my lips. Because they do have a point. Being the youngest means that

I've spent most of my life doing everything I can to mess with them. And if I may say so myself, I am incredibly good at it too.

A message from Rico pops up on the screen as he at last joins the conversation too.

Rico: *You seriously thought he wasn't going to beg? How could you not see that coming, Kaden? My grandma could've seen that coming and she's blind in one eye. Not to mention that she's dead.*

Kaden: *It's Jace. He's fucked and dumped more people than I've tortured. And that's saying something.*

Rico: *True.*

Eli: *Can't argue with that.*

I glower at the screen. I can practically see their smirks through the phone. Shaking my head, I let out something between a huff of grudging amusement and an exasperated sigh. Then I send a message back.

Me: *Fuck you all. Are you going to help me or what?*

Their responses are immediate, arriving one after the other within the span of a few mere seconds.

Eli: *Naturally.*

Kaden: *Anything.*

Rico: *Name it.*

Warmth spreads through my soul and I smile down at the screen. Yeah, they might give me as much shit as I give them. But they have my back when I need it.

23

KAYLA

"Are you a duck or what?" I mutter.

Jace blinks and then looks down at me in genuine surprise. "What?"

I just raise my eyebrows expectantly. "A duck."

A group of young women who look like tourists suddenly stop on the middle of the sidewalk to look down at what's presumably a map on one of their phones. Jace effortlessly steps out into the street and even manages to swerve around a stray arm that someone flings out to point at the building across the street. After stepping back up onto the sidewalk, Jace falls in beside me again.

Faint amusement tugs at his lips as he frowns down at me. "Do you usually just skip past the beginning of a conversation and simply start it in the middle? Or did I finally manage to block out the sound of your voice for the past few minutes?"

I roll my eyes at him. "Funny."

"I know." He grins and wiggles his eyebrows before shooting me another questioning look. "It still doesn't explain the duck comment, though."

Drawing a hand over my hair, I fix my ponytail while we turn the corner and start down another street. It's Friday evening, pleasantly warm, and most people got paid yesterday, so the streets are full of people out for a night of fun. I dodge a couple who cut past right in front of us to get to the Italian restaurant on our left.

"It's just..." I begin, not even sure how to phrase this. "Nothing ever bothers you. It just runs right off you like water on a duck."

He raises an eyebrow in silent question. "What would bother me?"

"I don't know. Our fight last night? Everything I do?"

A soft chuckle escapes his chest, and he gives me a knowing look. "I grew up with three older brothers who are all various degrees of unhinged. Last night wasn't exactly the first time someone called me a waste of space and slammed a door in my face."

I wince, and guilt seeps through my chest.

"You should've seen Kaden when he was thirteen," Jace continues, a smile full of mischief on his face. "Such a drama queen." He tilts his head to the side. "Though to be fair, I did steal his knife collection and hid it for like three days. He almost tore our house apart trying to find it." Another smug chuckle rolls from his chest. "Good times."

Pain slices through my heart, and I fiddle with the strap on my watch.

God, I wish I had that. A brother that I could drive absolutely crazy with my stupid pranks but who would still always have my back.

Swallowing past the lump in my throat, I glance up at Jace and say softly, "I don't think you're a waste of space." I clear my throat a bit awkwardly and then add, "I just don't want you in mine."

"Oh, trust me, I'm aware. But unfortunately for you, I am in your space. And I will continue to be for another few months. So let's just make this as easy and hassle-free as we can, okay?"

"Fine."

He dramatically presses a hand to his chest and stares down at me in a show of exaggerated shock. "Did you just agree with me? Oh, what a momentous day." He starts patting his pants as if looking for his phone. "Hold on, I need to call the scholars so that they can put this in the history books. Kayla Ashford, the most stubborn woman on the planet, finally agrees that Jace Hunter, the hottest, funniest, and all around most exceptional guy to ever walk this earth, is right. This really needs to be written down."

A laugh escapes my throat before I can stop it. Quickly drawing my eyebrows down, I give him a shove and my best attempt at a glare. "Don't push it."

He just grins back at me.

On our left, a small café at last appears. I turn towards it. Sidestepping a guy in a suit, I cut across the sidewalk and head for the door.

"Hold on," I say to Jace over my shoulder. "I just need to use the restroom."

Before he can reply, I pull open the door.

Warm air and a faint scent of incense meet me as I step across the threshold. Since I know that Jace will follow, I hold the door up to him before walking inside.

The small café is dimly lit, full of dark wood and green plants in wicker baskets. About half of the tables are occupied, and most people in here are either reading a book or typing on a laptop.

I approach the counter. "Hi."

"Oh, Ms. Ashford," the girl behind it says with a smile since I've been here several times before.

Smiling back, I motion towards where the restrooms are located. "Sorry, is it okay if I just use the restroom."

She nods. "Of course. Go right ahead."

"Thanks."

I cast a glance over my shoulder to check what Jace is doing. As expected, he has taken up position about halfway across the room. His perceptive eyes scan the entire space for threats.

Amusement ripples through me. This is a café that the quiet and well-behaved university students go to when they don't want to spend the night at home. The only threats in here are the ones they read about in their books.

Only dark wood panels watch me as I walk down the short hallway towards the restrooms.

But when I reach the door, I walk right past it and open the 'employees only' door instead. With three quick strides, I'm across the empty breakroom and to another door.

Fresh air washes over me as I open it and slip out into the alley behind the café.

A victorious grin spreads across my lips.

I've done this exact trick with like six other bodyguards, so the cashier already knows that I didn't go to the bathroom. It will take Jace a few minutes to figure that out, though.

Through the side window, I can just barely see the back of his head where he's still standing in the middle of the café.

Because of what we just talked about, I almost feel guilty for pulling this disappearing act on him. *Almost.*

Excitement pulses through me like sparkling waves.

Jenn said that a bunch of people were heading to the meadow tonight, so if I can just get to a taxi before Jace notices that I'm gone, he will never find me. He'll spend all night searching through the city while I'm finally enjoying a night of freedom with my friends out by the woods.

"Sorry," I whisper, still looking at the back of Jace's head from outside the window.

Then I take off.

Hurrying down the alley, I make my way towards the street on the other side of the building. Not the one we came from, since that is probably the first place Jace will check.

My dark blue dress flutters around my thighs as I jog the final distance to the mouth of the alley, and I can't stop a wide smile from spreading across my face. Finally. I will finally have a night all to myself.

With that excitement still bouncing around inside me, I round the corner and stride out onto the sidewalk on the next street.

A hand grabs my arm.

My stomach lurches as I'm yanked to the side.

Irritation burns through me. How could Jace have possibly managed to get here before me? I saw him in the café less than a minute ago, and the only way here is through the alley that I used.

I let out a huff as I'm slammed chest first up against the wall. Twisting my head, I get ready to snap at Jace.

Panic crashes over me like a bucket of ice water.

Three men wearing black masks surround me.

I open my mouth to scream.

The guy pushing me up against the wall quickly yanks up his hand and locks it underneath my jaw, snapping my mouth shut. A moment later, the man on my right gags me with duct tape. I fight and try to yank the tape off or at least push myself away from the wall, but the third guy grabs my wrists and shoves them together behind my back.

Fear and panic pulses through my chest like electric currents as what feels like zip ties are yanked shut around my wrists.

I try to scream through the gag, but only muffled sound makes it out.

Then the world goes black as someone blindfolds me too.

The purse with my phone and keys and wallet is quickly yanked away from my shoulder.

My heart spasms as I'm lifted off my feet. Bucking my hips, I thrash wildly to get free. But it's like trying to fight against immovable steel bands. I kick my legs and wiggle furiously while screaming behind the duct tape. My pulse thunders in my ears.

A jolt shoots through me as I'm heaved down again. But it's not the ground that I land on. It's hard but covered in some kind of soft fabric.

Dread spikes through me.

A trunk. This is the trunk of a car.

I land on my stomach, and before I can even start trying to twist around, hands appear on my ankles. Within seconds, my ankles have been zip tied together and secured to my bound wrists, leaving me in a hogtie.

The loud thud of a trunk being shut cuts through the air like an executioner's blade.

It's followed by more thuds as car doors are slammed shut.

Then the sound of an engine.

The floor of the trunk vibrates slightly underneath me as the car speeds away.

Twenty seconds.

That was all it took.

In the span of a mere twenty seconds, I've gone from excitedly skipping out of an alley to being blindfolded, gagged, tied up, and locked in the trunk of a car.

Terror washes through me. Yanking and pulling, I try to kick against the trunk, but I'm so tightly hogtied that I can barely even wiggle. Let alone move my legs.

A sob rips from my throat, muffled by the gag.

How the hell did things go so wrong so quickly?

In the movies, the victim always sees the van pulling up. They always have time to scream. To fight. To draw attention. It shouldn't go down like this. It shouldn't just happen quietly in the span of a few seconds.

If I had just had time to scream, Jace would've heard me.

Regret washes over me, and I thump my forehead against the floor.

Jace. How long before he figures out that I'm not in the restroom? How long before he finds the street where I was taken? Is there even something back there to find? Some kind of clue that will help him figure out that I've been kidnapped?

Another wave of regret crashes over me. It's mixed with anger and fear and desperation. Those feelings swirl inside my mind, pulling at me until I feel like I'm drowning in a cold black sea. The car keeps driving, taking me farther and farther away from any chance of a quick rescue.

Something between a snarl of rage and a sob of panic rips from my lungs, and I thump my forehead against the floor again.

This isn't even supposed to happen! People don't just get kidnapped. *I* don't get kidnapped. This—

The car stops.

Because of the anger and fear, I have no idea how much time has passed since I was thrown in the trunk.

I twist my head, listening intently as car doors are once more opened and closed.

Then fresh air whooshes over me as the trunk is popped open as well.

My heart hammers against my ribs. Craning my neck, I try to see something, anything, through the blindfold. But it's impossible.

I suck in a sharp breath through my nose as someone grabs me and lifts me up.

Since I know that we're still outside, I immediately start trying to scream through the gag and wiggle my way free again.

The guy just throws me over his shoulder, as if I'm no more challenging than a weak child, and starts walking.

Behind me, the trunk is slammed shut again. I strain my ears for any clues as to where I have been taken, but I can barely hear anything over the loud pounding of my own heart.

I should never have left the café. I should've stayed home tonight. I should've—

A door is opened.

The soft winds disappear, which means that we must have moved indoors. Footsteps sound on the floor as my captors continue walking across whatever room we're in. Then another door is opened.

Dread spikes through me as we suddenly start down a set of steps.

Oh God. Are they taking me to some kind of torture chamber?

Does that actually happen? I thought people didn't get

kidnapped except in movies, but apparently they do, so maybe the torture basements are real too.

I suck in shuddering breaths through my nose as the guy carrying me sets me down on a cold stone floor. I try to crawl away, but barely manage to wiggle.

Shock clangs through me as someone suddenly cuts the zip ties from my ankles. Yanking my legs back down, I roll over and get into a kneeling position. But before I can get to my feet, I feel the barrel of a gun against my forehead.

I stop moving immediately.

My heart slams against my ribs and blood rushes in my ears.

But one of the other men just cuts off the zip ties around my wrists too and then moves me until I'm sitting on the floor with my back against the wall instead. The gun stays at my forehead while my captors grab my wrists and raise them above my head.

Metallic clicks echo through the room as my wrists are handcuffed to the wall above my head.

Then the gun disappears.

Twisting my head from side to side, I try desperately to catch a glimpse of something. But I'm still blindfolded. And gagged. And now I'm handcuffed to the wall of someone's basement.

My heart thrums in my chest and panic crackles through my veins.

A sob threatens to rip from my lungs.

Oh God, what have I done?

I wish Jace was here.

24

JACE

Standing in Eli and Raina's basement, I watch Kayla where she sits blindfolded, gagged, and handcuffed to the wall. Eli, Kaden, and Rico stand beside me, studying her as well.

Then Rico turns to me and raises an eyebrow in silent question.

I shake my head. Let's give her another minute to truly think about the consequences of her actions.

After our fight last night, I figured it was time to show her exactly why she needs a bodyguard. Which was why I asked my brothers for help yesterday. Then it was only a matter of letting her sneak away from that café and sending a text to Eli, who was already waiting in the car with Kaden and Rico. They did the rest.

Eli has slid his gun back into its holster and is now smirking down at my shackled little demon while Kaden shoots me a look full of wicked approval. Rico just shrugs in response to my headshake and turns back to watch her as well.

The short blue dress she's wearing has been pushed up a little so that it only covers her upper thighs, and her ponytail is a lot messier now than it was earlier.

A faint smile blows across my lips.

She looks incredibly hot when she's handcuffed to a wall like this.

We wait in silence for another minute until I'm certain that Kayla has thoroughly revised her ridiculous notion about being able to stop a kidnapping attempt on her own.

Then I at last move forward so that I'm standing right beside her, lean down, and grab the edge of the duct tape across her mouth. She flinches slightly when my fingers brush her cheek, but then she sits completely still while I gently remove the tape.

She doesn't try to scream. Only works her jaw a couple of times and then closes her mouth again.

I give her an approving nod even though she can't see it.

Despite the panic that no doubt clangs inside her, she has managed to properly think through her situation. Eli put a gun to her forehead earlier, so she knows that at least one of her captors has a weapon. And doing something that would antagonize someone with a gun, like screaming, is a terrible move. Especially when you're also blindfolded and handcuffed to a wall.

Staying quiet was the right move here, and I'm going to praise her for that.

As soon as I have finished lecturing her.

Reaching behind her head, I remove the blindfold and drop it to the floor on top of the discarded piece of duct tape.

She blinks a couple of times and then quickly flicks her gaze across the room now visible around her.

I know what she sees.

It looks kind of like a torture chamber. There are chains and manacles on the walls, and some pieces of furniture that really don't belong in a normal basement.

But I know for a fact that Eli and Raina use this space more for their own insane sex games than anything else.

And to be fair, this particular basement isn't even that bad. Kaden and Alina's is much worse.

Kayla's blue eyes do one quick sweep across the room, which reveals my brothers standing there on the floor, and then she snaps her gaze to me.

For a few seconds, it's as if her brain can't process what she's seeing.

Then realization floods her features.

Her eyes widen with absolute bafflement and her mouth drops open.

"You," she blurts out, staring up at me. "You, you..."

I grin down at her from where I'm standing next to her. Then I arch an eyebrow at her and give her a look dripping with challenge. "What was that thing you said about not needing a bodyguard?"

Anger flashes across her face like a lightning strike, and she yanks wildly against the handcuffs while screaming, "I'm going to fucking *kill* you!"

From a few steps away, Eli lets out a low chuckle.

"Me?" I press a hand to my chest in a show of mock outrage as I hold Kayla's gaze. "*I* didn't do anything." Twisting around, I motion towards my brothers. "Meet your kidnappers. Eli."

My eldest brother says nothing, just continues watching her.

"Kaden," I continue.

Kaden gives her one of his psychopath smiles.

"And Rico," I finish, with a nod towards him.

Raising two fingers to his brow, he gives her a lazy salute.

Hellfire burns in Kayla's eyes as she drags her gaze back to me. I swear I can hear the actual noise from how hard she's grinding her teeth.

"You had your brothers kidnap me?" She practically spits out the words.

I hold her furious stare. "Yes."

"I'm—"

"And did you see how easy it was for them to take you?" I cut her off, my voice hard.

Rage flashes across her features again, and she yanks hard on the handcuffs. "I swear to God, when I get out of these handcuffs, I'm going to—"

"Give me a minute, will you?" I say to my brothers.

Rico nods. "We'll be upstairs. The girls should be back soon anyway."

While he starts towards the door, and the short hallway and the stairs beyond it, Kaden gives me a knowing look while a little smirk tugs at his lips. I narrow my eyes at him, but he thankfully doesn't say what I know that he's thinking.

Eli does, though.

"You make a mess, you clean it up," he warns, shooting me a long look as he starts towards the door as well.

Shock, and a little fear, pulses across Kayla's face. She probably thinks that he means blood. But I know that that wasn't the fluid that Eli was thinking about.

I shoot my annoying brothers a glare, which just makes them grin like the unhinged psychos that they are. However, they thankfully disappear out the door and close it behind them without making any more comments.

Staring at the now closed door, I shake my head at them

and their twisted dirty minds. That was not why I brought Kayla here. I did it to teach her a lesson.

"I'm going to fucking kill you," Kayla growls behind me.

Amusement ripples through me, and I have to take a second to smile before I wipe all traces of mirth from my features and turn around to face her.

Moving so that I'm standing right in front of her, I cross my arms over my chest and level a hard stare down at her. "And how, exactly, are you going to accomplish that when you're handcuffed to the wall in my brother's basement?"

"As soon as I get out—"

"And how are you going to get out?" I hold her furious stare with merciless eyes. "Huh? You're entirely at my mercy now."

Her eyes flash like lightning strikes, but she has no comeback for that because she knows that it's true. So instead, she just lets out a long string of curses.

"This is what I've been trying to tell you," I push, still holding her gaze with commanding eyes. "You might be excellent at sneaking away from your own bodyguards, but against a team of trained professionals out to kidnap you, you don't stand a fucking chance. That's why I need to be there to protect you."

"I wouldn't need protecting if you hadn't sent your psycho brothers to kidnap me!"

"You needed to see how easy it is for a trained professional to take you. And how fast it can happen."

Apparently, she has no quick comeback for that either, since that is also true, so she switches to threats. "The moment I tell my father about this, he's going to fire you, you arrogant son of a bitch."

"Why would he do that? He approved it." Cocking my head, I flash her a grin. "He said that it was, and I quote, *a good training exercise for her.*"

Another snarl rips from her throat, and she struggles against her shackles again.

Uncrossing my arms, I start towards her. Because of the handcuffs, she can't move from where she is sitting on the floor. But she *can* move her legs.

The moment I get within range, she yanks her leg up in an effort to kick me in the balls. But since it's the only possible attack she can accomplish in that position, I anticipated it and grab her ankle mid-air.

Moving her leg to the side, I step in between her legs instead before I release her. She can kick all she wants, but I'm out of reach in this position.

She bares her teeth at me.

I close the distance between us until my boots almost brush against her pussy. Then I crouch down to her level. She pulls against the manacles again.

Grabbing her chin, I hold her head immobile while I lock serious eyes on her. "Against people like me, like my brothers, people who know what they're doing, you are out of your league. You're smart. You're strong. You're stubborn. And that's a good thing. But it doesn't matter in situations like these."

She just glares up at me in angry silence, because once again, she knows that I'm right. She has experienced it firsthand now.

"Admit it," I say. "In situations like these, you need my help."

A muscle feathers in her jaw as she grinds her teeth again.

"Admit it," I demand.

She just continues staring up at me in stubborn silence.

I heave a deep sigh and release her chin. Placing my palms on my thighs, I get ready to push to my feet. "Alright, then. If you can do everything on your own, then have fun trying to get out of this basement. I'll see you in the morning."

Alarm pulses across her features, and she flicks a quick glance between the handcuffs trapping her to the wall and the door across the room. I straighten and start to turn around.

"Wait," she says. It sounds as if she had to drag that word from the depths of her soul.

Pausing on the floor between her legs, I arch an eyebrow in silent question.

She forces out a long angry sigh. Then she presses out, "You're right."

"About what?" I coax.

Her fingers curl as another wave of angry frustration flits across her face. "It *was* easy for your brothers to kidnap me. And if you had been there, things would have turned out very differently."

"Which means…?"

A downright murderous expression flashes across her face, and she grinds out her next words between gritted teeth. "That I need your help."

I grin. It's a grin full of smug victory that makes lightning flicker in her eyes again.

"Glad we're finally on the same page," I say, just to rub it in even more.

Sliding a hand into my pocket, I pull out the keys to the handcuffs.

Anger still in her eyes, she says nothing as I at last unlock the manacles.

They fall open with two distinct clicks.

Kayla immediately shoots up from the floor.

And attacks.

25

KAYLA

Shooting up from the floor, I throw my whole weight into it as I tackle Jace. It makes him take one step back. One. Single. Step. Another snarl rips from me as I shove at his muscular body again.

"Fucking bastard!" I scream at him.

I can't believe that I wished he was here just mere minutes ago when he was the one who had orchestrated this whole thing. I'm going to fucking kill him for this.

He chuckles and then tilts his head to the side as if conceding the point. "Yeah, I know." Seriousness blows across his features as he fixes me with a commanding stare. "But you needed a practical demonstration. You're good at slipping your own bodyguards, but you do need them for situations like these. You need *me*."

"The only thing I will be needing is a shovel for when I bury your body."

"You—"

Yanking up a hand, I gasp and point to the door behind him in shock.

He immediately whips around.

Smug victory pulses through me. I can't believe he fell for that.

But I don't waste a second. Hooking my foot behind his ankle, I yank his leg out at the same time as I tackle him again. This time, because his balance is off from how he's twisting towards the door, he actually goes down.

Both of us tumble to the ground as he topples backwards.

He hits the stone floor with me on top of him. The impact is forceful enough to knock the breath out of him.

While he is busy sucking air back into his lungs, I throw my arm out and reach for the manacles attached to a ring in the floor a short distance from us. If I can just get it around his wrist, I've won. And then I will make him fucking crawl.

My fingers brush against the cool metal of the shackles.

But before I can grab them, my arm is yanked back as Jace grabs me and twists his hips. I suck in a sharp breath between my teeth as I'm flipped around. My back hits the cold stone floor with a thud. I yank up my hands, but Jace locks his fingers around my wrists, slamming my hands back against the ground above my head. His massive weight is now settled firmly between my spread legs.

"Clever," he says. Mischief glints in his eyes as he grins down at me. "And so close to succeeding."

Pulling against his grip, I smirk up at him. "I can't believe you fell for that. I thought you said that you were smart."

"When have I ever said that?" He raises his eyebrows in a show of confusion before a smirk tugs at his own lips as well. "Charming? Yes. Funny? Without a doubt. Hot? As hell. But smart?" He tips his head from side to side as if considering. "Not particularly." His eyes turn serious. "At least not when it comes to you."

My heart skips a beat.

And I'm suddenly acutely aware of all the places where our bodies are touching.

His warm brown eyes are locked on mine as he continues. "So yes, if you ever want to distract me, pretend that there is a threat to your safety. Because I will *always* react to that."

It's suddenly difficult to breathe. His intense eyes, his protective words, and the way his body is pressing against mine make my heart pound. I drag in unsteady breaths.

He leans closer.

My pulse flutters as he slants his mouth over mine. And when he speaks, his breath caresses my lips.

"But be careful not to do it too often," he whispers against my mouth. "Or I might decide to handcuff you to me again. For your own safety."

His eyes glitter, and a sly smile curves his lips. He's so close that I can almost feel that smile against my mouth. My chest rises and falls with uneven breaths.

Jace skims his lips over mine. "And because you look so fucking hot in handcuffs."

I crush my mouth against his.

A moan tears from deep within his chest.

The sound of it makes my soul vibrate.

Wrapping my legs around his waist, I roll my hips against his. Another desperate sound escapes his throat.

While kissing me senseless, he releases his grip on my wrists and instead slides his hands down my body. A shudder of pleasure ripples through me at his possessive touch. Grabbing the hem of my dark blue dress, he starts pushing it upwards. I lift my ass off the floor to help his efforts while I reach towards his belt.

Lightning skitters across my skin as he strips me of my

clothes while I do the same to him. His hands are firm on my body, moving my arms and adjusting my hips and legs with complete authority. It makes my clit throb with need.

The stone floor is cold underneath my bare back, but I can barely feel it when Jace's naked body hovers over mine. The heat that radiates from him is like sunlight.

I throw my head back, exposing my throat to him as he kisses his way down my neck while he drags his cock through my wetness.

My thighs clench.

He slides his hands up my arms, moving them up above my head. I draw in shuddering breaths as his lips brush over that sensitive spot below my ear while he positions the tip of his cock against my entrance.

Then two clicks sound.

I gasp and snap my gaze up to my hands.

My eyes widen at the handcuffs that are now locked around my wrists and secured to a metal ring set into the floor. The same handcuffs that I had planned to shackle Jace with earlier.

Narrowing my eyes, I drag my gaze back to his.

He smirks down at me. "Told you that you look hot as fuck in handcuffs."

"You—"

My retort is cut off by a gasp as Jace pinches both of my nipples. It's then immediately followed by a moan as he rolls my sensitive nipples between his fingers. I writhe on the floor underneath him.

Still toying with my nipples, he leans down and steals a savage kiss from my lips. "And I fucking love it when you squirm."

I bite down on his bottom lip.

He just grins against my mouth and shifts his left hand so that he is bracing it on the floor instead. Then he shoves his cock inside me.

Gasping, I arch my back as his hard length fills me. He draws out a little and then thrusts in again.

A moan tears from my lungs.

"So perfect," he murmurs against my lips.

Pleasure shoots up my spine as he slams into me, creating the most insane friction, while his right hand pinches and then rolls my nipple again. I yank against the handcuffs, trying desperately to get my hands down to his body. But I'm completely trapped.

All I can do is to just take whatever he gives me.

And the feeling is exhilarating. Handing over power to Jace like this is so fucking intoxicating that I feel like every nerve inside my body is filled with crackling electricity. Pleasure pulses through my soul as he switches his pace, going faster and harder.

Moans spill from my lips as his thick cock sends a jolt of lightning through me when it hits a spot deep inside.

Jace shifts his weight and moves his left hand until his fingers brush over my nipple, joining the efforts of his right hand. I suck in rapid breaths as he expertly plays with both of my nipples while his cock slams into me.

The sheer amount of stimulation makes my brain flicker.

I pull against the handcuffs again as pleasure spikes through me.

"Oh God," I gasp.

Black spots dance before my eyes.

He pinches my nipples, making me whimper and squirm and yank desperately against the manacles again.

Then he slides his hands down my sides and grabs my

hips. With confident moves, he angles my hips into a slightly different position. Then he thrusts into me.

My eyes fly open, and I suck in a sharp breath.

Because of the angle, his cock grinds hard against my clit with every thrust while he also hits even deeper inside me.

Holding my hips in that position, he starts up a brutal pace.

Pleasure builds inside me until I feel like I'm going to shatter from the tension trapped in my soul. I desperately want to run my hands through Jace's soft curls and then rake my fingers down his back. Desperately want to make him moan and squirm. Make him feel like his brain is melting the same way that he is making me feel with every dominant thrust of his hips.

But I can't.

I'm completely at his mercy. My body is his to do with as he wishes. And by God, it's the hottest fucking thing I have ever experienced.

Pleasure streaks through me like tiny lightning strikes as his cock hits that perfect spot inside me over and over again. I moan and writhe as tension thrums inside me. The edge is so close. Oh God. It's—

"Come for me, little demon," Jace commands.

Release crashes over me.

My pussy tightens around his cock and my clit pulses as pleasure ricochets through my body. Incoherent moans spill from my lips, and I yank hard on my restraints. Jace tightens his grip on my hips, holding my trembling body steady while he fucks me through the orgasm.

But when the final waves die down, he doesn't stop. He keeps going until another wave of pleasure starts building inside me. My heart feels like it's going to give out.

"Oh God," I whimper. My body feels as if it's coming apart at the seams. "Jace. Please."

"You can take it," Jace says, his voice dripping with power and confidence.

Lust and pleasure pulse through me at the simultaneous command and praise.

His fingers dig into my hips as he holds me steady, mercilessly fucking me towards another orgasm.

I suck in shuddering breaths as tension once more crackles inside my soul. My heart hammers in my chest. Curling my fingers into fists, I try to remember how to breathe as the edge of that second orgasm draws closer.

He slams into me.

And release once more explodes through my veins.

I arch up from the ground as an even more intense orgasm shoots through my limbs. My legs shake from the sheer force of it. Stars dance before my eyes.

Then a dark moan tears from Jace's chest.

His cock pulses inside me as he comes as well.

With that incredible moan of his still echoing inside my skull, I drag in breaths that don't seem to contain enough air. I'm pretty sure my soul has floated away from my body. Or maybe it's my mind that has left. All I can feel is Jace's perfect body against mine and his thick cock buried deep inside me.

Soft lips brush over my jaw. Then Jace's warm breath caresses my skin as he murmurs two words that make my already throbbing clit start pulsing again.

"Good girl."

26

JACE

Kayla draws her eyebrows down in an adorable attempt at a scowl as she puts her dress back on and then brushes her hands over the dark blue fabric to smooth it down. Since that dress and her underwear were the only things she needed to put back on, she's already done getting dressed while I've only just pulled my jeans up. My belt clinks as I start buckling it while I glance around for my t-shirt.

"This changes nothing," Kayla announces, with that adorable little scowl still on her gorgeous face. "I'm still going to kill you."

I raise my eyebrows at her in a show of confusion while I let a sly grin spread across my lips. "For what? Giving you three consecutive orgasms?"

Her cheeks turn an incredible shade of red. "No, it—"

"Oh, that's right. It was *four* consecutive orgasms, wasn't it?"

"No," she snaps, still looking flustered. "For having me kidnapped. I will get back at you for this."

Before I can reply, she spins on her heel and stalks towards the door. Her long red hair flutters behind her like a stream of liquid fire as she yanks open the door and storms out into the short corridor before the stairs on the other side.

Then she lets out a yelp. From in here, I can't see what caused it, but this is Eli and Raina's house so it can't be anything dangerous. Well, not anything too dangerous. Alright, nothing overwhelmingly dangerous. Actually, scratch that, this house belongs to my most unhinged brother and the craziest fucking girl I've ever met. There are *plenty* of dangerous things in this house.

After a second of stunned silence, Kayla blurts out, "Who are you?"

"Who am I?" Raina says from what sounds like halfway down the stairs. She sounds suspicious, which is really bad. "Who the fuck are *you*?"

Ah, shit. I hurry over to where my shirt is and snatch it up.

On the other side of the door, Raina raises her voice and calls, "Eli! There's some girl in our basement. Did you put her here for a specific reason or should I get the poison?"

"What the fuck," Kayla exclaims, sounding horrified.

While pulling on my shirt, I quickly make my way to the door. Strolling out into the short corridor, I flash Raina a grin while motioning towards Kayla. "She's with me."

"Oh, that's right!" Eli calls back from upstairs since he obviously couldn't hear my answer. "I forgot to tell you. We kidnapped Jace's girl."

Kayla jerks back and then whips her head towards me.

I groan inwardly and clear my throat a little self-consciously at the way my infuriating brother just referred to her as *Jace's girl.*

On the stairs, Raina relaxes. "Oh."

I breathe a sigh of relief since it would have been very difficult to explain to Trent Ashford that I also managed to get his daughter poisoned after I fake kidnapped her.

Kayla shoots me a vicious glare before turning back to Raina.

"I'm not his girl," she snaps.

Amusement flickers in Raina's piercing green eyes, and she shoots a pointed look down at Kayla's legs. "The fact that you have his cum dripping down your thigh would suggest otherwise."

I choke on my breath.

Kayla snaps her gaze down to her legs where a thin stream of cum is indeed sliding down her skin.

Her entire neck and face turn flaming red.

Raina smirks like the little villain she is and then simply turns around and starts back up the steps, her long black hair swaying over her back as she moves.

"Come on," Raina says without turning to look. "There's a bathroom upstairs."

With embarrassment still staining her cheeks bright red, Kayla quickly wipes the trail of cum from her thigh and hurries after Raina. I shake my head at both of them as I follow.

The night outside is dark, but Eli and Raina's house is brightly lit and full of noise. Or at least, the living room is. While Raina shows Kayla where the nearest bathroom is, I saunter through the hallway and into the living room.

It's an elegantly decorated room, completely at odds with the sex and torture chamber basement. And I know that it's all Raina's efforts, because Eli doesn't give a shit about interior design. He just wants whatever Raina wants.

God, all of my brothers are so whipped.

When I walk into the room, I find all three of them sprawled on the couches made of dark wood and deep green fabric. Light glints in the golden candleholders along the low coffee table, and in the whiskey and wine glasses littered on the dark wooden surface too.

Alina sips from a cocktail, her gray eyes glittering in the warm candlelight, where she sits in an armchair. Her long blonde hair spills down over the rich green backrest. To my left, Isabella pulls out a bottle of red wine from the liquor cabinet. Her shoulder-length auburn hair sways slightly as she straightens, but her blue-gray eyes are as sharp and perceptive as ever as she turns to look at me when I walk through the doorway.

"Did you make a mess?" Eli asks, a wicked smirk on his face where he lounges on the couch with his feet up on the coffee table.

"Of course not." I flash him a grin full of challenge. "Jeez, didn't you know? You're supposed to come *inside* her. Not paint the walls with your cum." Tutting, I shake my head. "Classic rookie mistake"

On the couch opposite him, Rico chokes on his whiskey while Kaden snickers into his own glass.

Eli narrows his golden eyes at me, making the scar through his eyebrow tighten. "Careful now, little brother. Remember whose house you're in."

Strolling over to the couch, I reach behind it and pull out a bat. "Since when has that ever stopped me?"

Surprise pulses across Eli's face as he sees the bat, and he sits up straighter and turns so that he can see it properly. With that stunned look still on his features, he snaps his gaze back up to my face and demands, "Where the hell did you get that from?"

"I put it there last time I was here."

"You can't just hide random bats in our house."

"Why not?"

"Because—"

"I want to go home," Kayla suddenly says from the doorway. The embarrassment on her face is gone now, replaced instead by cold command as she locks eyes with me. "Now."

Raina breezes past her in the doorway and walks towards where Isabella is still standing on the floor. While Isabella's sharp eyes assess Kayla, Raina casually plucks the bottle of wine from her hand and strolls over to the couch. Isabella shifts her gaze away from Kayla and instead rolls her eyes at Raina, who flashes her a grin in reply.

After grabbing two wine glasses, she starts filling them up while casually saying, "Was this your first kidnapping?"

Silence falls over the room.

In the doorway, Kayla starts slightly when everyone turns to look at her.

"Uhm, yes," she replies when she realizes that the question was directed at her.

"Ahh," Raina says with a contented sigh as she leans back and takes a sip from her wine glass. "The first kidnapping is always the most exciting."

Disbelief pulses across Kayla's face. "Exciting? I thought I was going to die!"

Raina snorts as if that's a ridiculous reaction.

"If I remember correctly," I begin, flashing Raina a knowing smile. "The first time we kidnapped *you*, Eli put a gun to your brother's head and made you crawl up to our feet and kiss our boots while groveling for forgiveness."

Across the room, Kayla snaps her gaze to me, shock

evident on her face. Eli groans on the couch while Raina narrows her eyes at me.

And because I simply can't help it, I lie through my teeth and mess with her even more as I add, "I still have those boots. Saved them in that exact condition just to preserve that memory."

"Do you know what *I* still have?" Raina says, her voice turning lethally sweet as she holds my gaze. "That poison that I used to make *you* grovel. I could go and get it if you want?"

"Don't antagonize her, Golden," Eli says. Amusement and deep love flicker in his eyes as he glances to his girl. "You know how it ends."

Yeah, I do, unfortunately. And since I don't want to spend the next few months checking every piece of food and drink I consume for poison, I just roll my eyes and stop baiting her. Raina takes that as a victory and flicks her hair behind her shoulder, looking entirely too smug.

"Golden?" Kayla suddenly echoes. Her brows are furrowed as she sweeps her gaze over my family. "Why do you call him that?"

Pushing off from the couch, I spin the bat in my hand and rest it on my shoulder as I start towards her. "Don't listen to them. You wanted to go home? Let's go."

"Fine," she replies, annoyance settling back on her features. "Just one more thing."

Her eyes turn sharp as she drags them over my brothers, holding each of their gazes in turn for a few seconds before moving on to the next one. Eli and Rico exchange an amused look in return while Kaden just looks back at her, his eyes dark.

I glance between her and them. "What are you doing?"

"Memorizing their faces," Kayla replies, her eyes still on

my brothers. "So that I know exactly who to target after I'm done getting revenge on you."

Three things happen almost simultaneously.

Isabella pulls a gun and levels it straight at Kayla's temple.

Fury flashes in Raina's eyes as she shoots to her feet and declares, "I'll get the chemicals to dissolve her body."

And Alina pushes up from her armchair and says, "Great, I'll prep the bathtub."

I groan in exasperation and rub a hand over my forehead, massaging my brows.

Shock and panic pulse across Kayla's face, and she yanks up her hands while making calming motions. "Wait, wait, wait. Hold on. What the fuck is going on?"

"What's going on?" Isabella echoes, her voice full of threats. While still holding her gun steady against Kayla's temple, she motions towards my brothers. "If you touch them, *any* of them, I will shoot you in the head."

"And then I will dissolve your body with fast-acting chemicals so that there is nothing left of you for anyone to find," Raina adds, a smile full of poison on her lips.

"And I will make sure that we all have airtight alibis," Alina finishes.

For a few seconds, Kayla just stares at them in utter shock and confusion, as if she can't figure out if they're joking or not. They just stare right back, dead serious.

Then Kayla turns and gapes at me, disbelief pulsing in her eyes. "What the *fuck* is wrong with your family?"

On the couch, Eli, Rico, and Kaden just laugh and raise their glasses to their girls in a synchronized salute full of approval and loving pride.

I heave another exasperated sigh and put a hand on Isabella's arm, pushing it down and lowering the gun.

"Jesus fucking Christ," I mutter. Then I sweep a pointed stare over all six of them. "Way to introduce yourselves, guys."

Kaden lifts his shoulders in a nonchalant shrug. "You're the one who asked us to kidnap her."

I tip my head to the side. "Good point." Shifting my bat to my other hand, I wrap my arm around Kayla's waist and start pulling her with me. "Anyway, we should get going so that she can take out all of her rage on me instead of making empty threats directed at you."

"Wait," Raina says, her green eyes still locked on Kayla. "So you're not actually planning to hurt Eli?"

"And Rico," Isabella adds.

"And Kaden," Alina finishes.

Kayla flicks a glance between the three of them as if she's not sure how she's supposed to reply to that.

Lowering my mouth to her ear, I whisper, "They were serious about the killing and dissolving and alibis stuff, just so you know."

Her gaze darts to me for a second before she looks back at the three murderous women in the room.

"Uhm, no," she replies hesitantly. "I'm not actually planning to come after any of them."

"Good," Raina says, and plops down on the couch again.

Isabella slips her gun back into her pants and strolls over to steal one of the wine glasses that Raina filled earlier. Once more seated in the armchair, Alina reaches for her cocktail again.

Equal parts exasperation and amusement flicker through my soul.

Next to me, Kayla stares at them all as if she can't figure out what to make of this anymore. Her eyes are wide and her mouth is slightly open, as if she's still reeling. Blinking, she shakes her head a couple of times.

I huff out a soft laugh at how absolutely bewildered she looks, and then I start pulling her with me through the doorway.

Before we can disappear, Eli calls after us. And I can hear the wicked grin in his voice.

"See you at the wedding!"

That seems to be the final straw that makes Kayla's sanity snap. Whipping her head around, she stares at me with an expression full of confusion and exasperation and utter frustration.

"What fucking wedding?"

27

KAYLA

Since it's a Monday afternoon, the library is packed with people. Sunlight streams in through the tall windows, illuminating the pale marble floor and the wooden bookshelves that fill Ivy River's grand library. We got lucky because a group was leaving just when we arrived, so we managed to get one of the tables set along the wall of windows.

Next to me, Aurora is explaining something to Jenn and Lionel, who are sitting across the table from us. I know that I should be paying attention to what they're saying, but I'm having trouble concentrating on anything because I'm still so embarrassed about what happened at that wedding two days ago.

I thought I was going to be able to quietly sneak off while everyone was busy watching Kaden and Alina. But no. What did I manage to do instead? I caused an armed standoff between two assassin families.

My cheeks heat again just thinking about it, and I shoot a

quick glare at Jace where he is standing a couple of steps away from our table.

He could have at least warned me that every single person in that damn church was going to be armed.

As if he is thinking about that day too, Jace slides his gaze to me. A smirk tugs at his lips. I shoot him another scowl before returning my attention to my friends.

"We need a venue that's big enough to fit all of the items," Aurora argues from the seat next to me.

Jenn raises an eyebrow from the chair opposite her. "Do we? I mean, really. Do we actually need to physically put all of the items in there? What about the car? Are we really going to put a car inside a building?"

A pensive expression blows across Aurora's face, and she sits back in her chair. "Right. The car. I kind of forgot about that."

"Why don't we just put a picture of the car in there instead?" Lionel says, looking between me and the Carlisle sisters.

On my left, Jace snorts.

Lionel snaps his gaze to him, displeasure flickering in his gray eyes. "What was that?"

Jace arches an eyebrow at him. "A picture? Seriously?"

"I wasn't planning on just sticking it up on a wall," Lionel snipes back. "I was thinking in a nice frame. On a table."

"A frame?" Jace snorts again and shoots him a look full of mockery. "Well, then that changes everything. Great idea, Lionel."

Sarcasm practically drips from his voice, and it makes Lionel sputter in anger as he trips over his words in his haste to retort. I shoot Jace a warning look, which he just answers with a quick smirk in my direction. I narrow my eyes at him.

"Who even asked for your opinion, *bodyguard?*" Lionel spits out that last word as if it's an insult.

"You did." Jace raises his eyebrows as if that should've been obvious. "I didn't say anything. I just scoffed. And *you* asked me to elaborate."

"Jace," I cut in before Lionel can retort.

He turns to me. "What? You didn't think the picture idea was good either. None of you did."

Lionel turns to us, as if expecting us to defend him. Jenn and Aurora grimace apologetically when he looks to them.

"It doesn't matter," I say to Jace. Annoyance ripples through me. Because he's right. The picture idea was terrible. But I don't want to admit that. So instead, I finish with, "Just drop it."

"Exactly," Lionel says, turning back to Jace again and flicking a dismissive look up and down his body. "Why are you even here?"

"Why are *you* here?" Jace counters, fixing him with a hard stare full of contempt. "Have you actually contributed anything to this group project? Or are you just skating by on all of their hard work?"

Anger and indignation flash across Lionel's face, turning his cheeks and neck red. Curling his lips in disgust, he keeps his eyes on Jace as he says, "Can't you tell your dog to go home, Kayla?"

Jace moves before the final word has even left his mouth.

Lurching forward, he grabs Lionel's wrist and yanks it up in the air behind him while gripping Lionel's neck with his other hand.

A bang echoes through the library as Jace slams Lionel's cheek down against the table.

Jenn and Aurora jump in surprise, and every single person within range turns to stare and gasp at us.

"Call me dog one more time," Jace says, forcing Lionel's arm farther back. "I fucking dare you."

A cry of pain rips from Lionel's throat, and he whimpers on the table.

I shoot to my feet and lock furious eyes on Jace. "That's enough."

"It will be," Jace replies, his own merciless stare still locked on Lionel. "When he apologizes."

All around us, people are staring at us and filming us and whispering behind their hands.

Mortification crashes over me like a tidal wave.

People are going to be talking about this for weeks.

I just wanted a normal fucking university experience! And yet, I constantly end up drawing attention. Everywhere I go. All the time.

Because of him.

Because of all of them. The middle-aged men in suits who stood out like signal beacons on campus. And now Jace with his overprotective hitman bullshit. I just want him gone. I want them all gone. I want my fucking life back!

Spinning on my heel, I start stalking away from the table without a word.

"Kayla," Jace says.

The command in his voice makes me grind my teeth in annoyance. Ignoring him, I simply continue striding towards the doors.

If I stay, Jace is going to force Lionel to grovel for forgiveness. And I'm done being a spectacle for all the shocked students in this library. The only way to separate Jace and Lionel right now is for me to leave. Because then, Jace will follow.

"Uhm, Kayla," Jenn calls after me. "Wait. I have a venue for us to look at tomorrow."

"Great," I reply without slowing down or turning to look. "Just text me the address and I'll be there."

"Oh. Uhm. Okay."

The sound of a table scraping against the floor comes from behind me. Then Jace's footsteps echo against the marble. I simply keep walking.

"That's right," Lionel calls, his tone mocking. "Run after your mistress like the dog you are."

Jace's footsteps stop.

Lionel lets out a terrified squeak.

Then Jace's footsteps start back up again.

I still don't turn to look.

Everyone else does, though. All the students and faculty members that I pass turn to stare at me as I walk out of the library.

Embarrassment burns through my cheeks.

I'm going to fucking kill Jace when I get home.

28

JACE

The heat of her rage could've powered a mid-sized town for an entire month. I could feel it vibrating through the air like heat waves during the entire walk back to her apartment. Though I don't really understand what she's so angry about. Lionel is a dick. He had it coming.

Following her into the apartment, I close and lock the door behind us. I expect to hear Kayla's angry footsteps continue towards her bedroom. But instead, they stop in the living room. Halfway between my bedroom and hers.

I heave a deep sigh before turning to face her. *Here we go*.

"In the morning, you're going to call my father and tell him that you quit," she declares.

Scoffing, I stride away from the door and towards her. "No."

Fury flashes like lightning strikes in her eyes at my arrogant tone. As I close the distance between us, I study her. She is angry. Really, really angry. It radiates from her entire being with such intensity that I'm almost surprised that I can't see real flames flickering along her red hair.

Drawing my eyebrows down in genuine confusion, I demand, "What's your problem with me?"

"You!" She throws her arms out in rage as I come to a halt in front of her. "*You* are the problem. First you had me kidnapped by your psycho brothers and had me handcuffed in a basement."

"You didn't seem to mind the handcuffs during the second part of that night."

Her eyes flash, but she doesn't take the bait. Instead, she stabs her finger into my chest. "And then you dragged me to that wedding where I almost caused a mass shoot-out."

"How is that my fault? *You* are the one who caused the standoff."

"You could've warned me that you were all armed."

"It was a church full of hitmen. You seriously expected us not to be armed?"

A snarl rips from her throat, and she gives my chest a shove. "And now you embarrassed me in front of the entire university!"

"*I* embarrassed you? Lionel—"

"Lionel is my friend. And you don't get to treat my friends like that."

Wrapping my hand around her wrist, I stop her from shoving me again while I lock hard eyes on her. "Lionel is a leech."

"He—"

"He's not with you because he wants to be your friend. He's with you because he wants something from you."

She jerks back as if I had slapped her. And I immediately regret saying that. Even though I know that it's the truth. There is nothing genuine about Lionel Henderson. He's only trailing after Kayla because he wants something from her.

And I'm pretty sure it's financial security in the form of a very advantageous marriage.

"You don't know anything about me," she snaps, and yanks her hand back. "Or him. Or my other friends."

Guilt twists inside me, because I suddenly realize that this is a topic that she's self-conscious about. My expression softens, and I raise my hands in surrender.

"Look, I'm not saying that people don't like you for you," I explain. "I'm just saying that *Lionel* is a selfish asshole who doesn't deserve to be your friend."

Cold fury burns in her eyes as she flicks a mocking look up and down my body. "As opposed to you?"

The words hit harder than I want to admit. Because I did actually think that we had started to become friends in a way. But I make sure to keep my expression blank as I just stare back at her.

"I'm just doing my job," I say tightly.

"No, you're not!" She throws out her arms again. "You're being obnoxious and difficult—"

"As opposed to you?" I throw back in her face.

"You're ruining my life!" Her chest heaves with rage as she stares up at me. "It's not my fault that you're the screw-up of your family who got stuck with babysitting duty while all of your brothers are out doing cool hitman stuff. It's not my fault that you don't measure up to the rest of your family. So stop trying to ruin my life too."

Her words hit me like a knife to the gut.

For a second, all I can do is to stand there and stare down at her while something crumbles inside me.

She jerks back, as if realizing what she just said.

But I don't care.

I simply turn around and walk towards my bedroom.

"Jace," Kayla says from behind me, her voice strained. "Wait. I didn't—"

The door lets out a soft thud as I shut it completely behind me.

Standing there on the other side of the door, alone, I let the blank mask slip from my face. Raking my fingers through my hair, I tilt my head back and draw in uneven breaths.

Fuck. It feels as if my chest is caving in.

I drag in another breath and walk over to the drawers by the bed. Yanking one open, I grab the bottle of whiskey I've kept in there. I haven't felt the need to drown out my thoughts ever since I started this job, and I know that I shouldn't drink when I'm technically still on duty, but her words just... hit too close to home.

Slumping down on the floor, I sit with my back against the side of the bed and drink straight from the bottle while staring out the window. Purple and red streaks from the setting sun are reflected in the windows of the building across the street, and the sounds of cars honking echo outside.

I drink from the whiskey bottle again.

Because Eli, Kaden, and Rico are so effortlessly skilled at everything, I've grown up always feeling like I have something to prove. That I need to prove that I'm as good as them. It's the curse of being the youngest sibling.

But it's more than that.

All of them are completely fine with just continuing on the legacy of the Hunter family and the Morelli family, as if the thought that they could do something else is not even worth considering. And it makes me feel as if there is something wrong with me. Why else would I be the only one who is angry about not having a choice in the matter?

Kayla said that I was the screw-up of the family. That I didn't measure up to the rest of them.

Pain stabs through my chest.

Because she might be right.

Gripping my shirt right over my heart, I curl my fingers into the soft fabric so hard that my joints ache.

Fuck, what if she *is* right.

I have always been terrified that my brothers would think that I don't measure up to them if they ever found out my true feelings about being forced onto this path. And now they know. So is that how they see me now?

Bringing the bottle back up to my lips, I drink deeply again. The whiskey burns on its way down, but the feeling is gone too quickly. And the alcohol still hasn't helped me numb the ache in my chest.

Kayla called me a duck once. Said that everything just runs off me like water on a duck. Most people think the same thing when they meet me. And for the most part, they're right. I have an ego the size of North America and way more confidence than should probably be legal. But there are also some things that I am incredibly insecure about. And this is one of them.

I tilt my head back and heave a deep sigh.

Sitting there on the floor, I stare at nothing as I raise the bottle to my lips once more while trying to fight off the suffocating emotions in my chest.

A soft knock comes from the door.

I blink, realizing that the room is now dark around me. The sun must have set. Only yellow light from the streetlamps outside shine in through the windows and illuminate parts of the walls. I glance down at the bottle in my hand, noticing that it's almost half empty.

Another knock comes.

I ignore it.

"Jace," Kayla says from the other side of the door, her voice gentler than I have ever heard.

It sends another stab of pain through my chest.

"Jace," she repeats. "Please."

I take another drink.

"Please can I come in?" she says.

Remaining on the floor, I say nothing.

The door is opened anyway. It brings with it the smell of food. But I don't have enough fucks to give right now, so I just keep staring out at the window.

Soft footsteps sound on the floor.

Then Kayla appears next to me. I can feel her looking down at me, but I don't bother turning towards her. A soft and very miserable-sounding sigh escapes from her chest.

She sits down next to me. Resting her back against the side of the bed, she stretches out her legs along the floor. She's so close that her thigh almost brushes against mine.

"I'm sorry," she says softly.

And then she holds out something to me. Tearing my gaze from the window, I glance down at the item she's holding out to me with both hands. It's a bowl. One of her normal kitchen bowls. Filled with something… vaguely edible-looking.

I shift my gaze up to her face.

My heart clenches.

She looks genuinely sorry. And a little miserable.

"What's that?" I ask, nodding down at the bowl she's still holding out to me.

"It's food."

"You don't know how to cook."

She winces. "I know. But you like food. And I wanted to…

well, I wanted to apologize. And to do something… well, give you something… that you would like."

The way she's floundering makes my heart warm a little. I've never seen her like that before. Never seen her this… vulnerable. And the fact that she's even showing me this side of herself, for the sole purpose of apologizing to me, is undeniable proof that she actually means every word.

After setting the whiskey bottle down on the floor beside me, I reach out and take the bowl from her still outstretched hands. There is a fork stuck into the food. It looks kind of like pasta. Except the long noodles have been broken into small pieces. Which is an absolute sacrilege.

Spearing some of the floppy bits with the fork, I bring it to my mouth and eat.

I almost choke. Coughing, I force myself to swallow the bite. Did she drop an entire tub of salt in the pot or what?

Next to me, Kayla grimaces and squirms a little on the floor.

Holding her gaze, I drink some more whiskey to wash down the taste of salt before I announce, "This is terrible."

An apologetic look flashes across her face.

"Seriously." I arch an eyebrow at her. "Are you trying to apologize or poison me?"

Alarm pulses in her eyes, and she opens her mouth to no doubt apologize again and reassure me that she is not trying to poison me.

Then she notices the smile on my mouth.

A huff of amusement rips from her throat instead. With a smile pulling at her own lips, she gives my shoulder a soft shove and then turns so that she is facing forwards again, looking out the window. Her leg moves a little closer to mine.

"I really am, though," she says, gazing out at the dark night outside. "Sorry, I mean. I really am sorry."

I set the bowl of overcooked and oversalted pasta down on the floor.

"I didn't mean that," she continues. "It was just a shot in the dark. I've grown up feeling like I always have so many expectations to live up to, so I used that and hoped that it would hit you as hard as it would've hit me. But I didn't actually mean it."

She fidgets with the hem of her shirt for a few seconds.

"Actually," she continues, and then she at last glances towards me. "That's not the entire reason. I also chose that specific insult because I was jealous."

Confusion pulls at my brows. "Of what?"

"Of what you have." She heaves a deep sigh and rakes her fingers through her hair. "Back at your brother's house, when we were all in the living room, I was angry because of the kidnapping. But I was also angry because I was jealous. I saw how much they love you, how much you all love each other, and I just... I just want a family like that too."

"Don't you have—"

"Anyway," she interrupts, looking away and clearing her throat in a way that signals that she really doesn't want to talk about that. "So that was why I said that to you in the living room just now. I was angry and frustrated and jealous. And I'm sorry."

I keep my gaze on the side of her face until she finally turns back to meet my eyes again. "Apology accepted."

Relief flickers across her beautiful face.

But I keep speaking. "*If* you tell me what it is that I have done to make you hate me so much."

She winces. Drawing her legs up, she braces her elbows on

her knees and slides her hands through her hair once more. Then she lifts her head again and glances at me. There is something between a grimace and a smile on her face.

"I don't hate you," she says. "I actually like you. Which is what makes me hate you."

A surprised laugh escapes my throat, and I frown at her. "What does that mean?"

"It means that I like you as a person, but I still don't want you here."

"Ouch."

She laughs, somehow sounding both amused and miserable at the same time. Heaving another sigh, she shakes her head and lets her legs slide back down to the floor. "It's just... I don't want a bodyguard. I want freedom."

Uncomfortable emotions start crawling up my throat, because I realize that I know exactly what she's talking about.

But she must have misinterpreted the expression on my face, because she hurries to explain again. "So it's not you that I hate. It's the situation." Desperation floods her beautiful blue eyes as she holds my gaze. "Do you have any idea what it's like to never have the freedom to choose what your life looks like?"

My heart squeezes painfully, and my throat constricts.

Fuck, I never thought about it like that. I never realized what living like this must be like for her. Never having a moment of privacy. Always having someone looking over her shoulder and checking what she does and who she talks to. It must be suffocating her.

This job, guarding her like this, is my ticket to freedom. But in doing so, I'm taking away hers. I'm essentially trading her freedom for mine.

Guilt slices through me.

"Yeah," I reply, the word coming out a bit more strained than I would've preferred. "I do."

But I still can't quit. I need to make it to the end of the semester so that I will be able to choose my own future. And even if I were to quit, Mr. Ashford would just hire someone else, so it still wouldn't make a difference in Kayla's life.

So quitting is out of the question. But there is something I can do.

"I'm sorry," I say.

She blinks in surprise. "For what?"

"For being a jerk. For deliberately staying closer than I actually have to in order to ensure your safety. I'm very good at what I do. I don't need to be standing right on top of you to protect you." I nudge her leg with mine and give her a small smile. "Look, I can't quit. Your dad will just hire someone else. But I promise that I will give you more space from now on."

Her eyes light up like glittering starlight.

The sight is so beautiful that my heart almost stops.

"Really?" she says, sounding both hopeful and a little guarded. As if she's afraid that I will take it back.

I nod. "Really."

She smiles as brightly as the moon.

A mischievous smile spreads across my own lips as I hold up a finger in the air and add, "*If...*"

She nods, ready to agree to whatever demand I'm about to present. "Anything."

"If you promise to never break pasta like this again." With a glint in my eyes, I shake my head at her. "It's an absolute sacrilege."

She laughs. A real genuine laugh that ripples through the air like silver bells.

And the sound of it makes my heart stutter.

29

KAYLA

My entire soul feels light. Like it's sparkling with energy. After our talk last night, Jace really did keep his word. During all of my classes today, he stayed at a distance, watching over me but not crowding me.

I know that he's there, of course. But now I only see him if I look for him. It's honestly pretty astounding how someone as big as him can make himself practically invisible if he wants to. And he really does try to make himself invisible. The only time he broke cover and appeared at my side was when Lionel tried to persuade me to take a walk with him, just the two of us, during lunch. Within seconds of Lionel putting a hand on my arm, Jace was there, looming over him like a god of death.

It startled Lionel so much that he actually jumped. He left quickly after that, glaring daggers at Jace. I had rolled my eyes at Jace then, but in all honesty, I didn't really mind.

In truth, I also find Lionel a bit annoying at times. I know that he likes me and that he's trying to flirt with me, but I'm not really interested. Actually, I'm not *at all* interested.

Especially since my thoughts have started drifting more and more to the man who challenges me and sees me and understands me and helps me in ways that no one else has.

While still continuing down the street, I instinctively glance over my shoulder, looking for him. For Jace.

He appears immediately. He always does that, as if he can tell when I'm searching for him and he wants to check if I need help. Since I don't, I just give him a small smile. The answering one on his own mouth makes my pulse flutter.

Turning back to the busy street ahead, I continue towards the address that Jenn sent me yesterday. It's down by the river, which is not my favorite place to be, but since I left the library so abruptly yesterday, I figured I could at least come and see the building she has found for our venue.

I glance down at my phone occasionally to make sure that I'm heading in the right direction.

Thick clouds cover the heavens and gray light filters down, painting the city in unusually bleak hues. The weather has started to cool a little now. It's not particularly cold, but I still went home after afternoon classes to grab a light jacket. I'm not sure how long Jenn has planned for us to be here, but with the clouds, the wind, the closeness to the river, and the setting sun, it might be a chilly evening.

When I reach the correct address, I find Aurora, Jenn, and Lionel already there and waiting for me. Aurora gives me a cheery wave and the other two smile as I close the final distance. While I walk, I study the buildings that run alongside the river. They look like residential houses.

"I'm not late, am I?" I say by way of greeting, glancing between them.

"Oh, no, not at all," Jenn replies with a smile, and then bumps her shoulder against Aurora's. "We were just early."

"Yes." Aurora shoots her sister a look full of mischievous teasing. "Because *someone* is a time pessimist."

Jenn matches that look. "Better than being a time optimist."

My insides twist a little with jealousy at their easy banter, and I try my best not to look towards the river while I fiddle with the strap on my watch.

"No bodyguard today?" Lionel asks, his eyebrows raised in surprise as he makes a show of looking behind me.

That thankfully cuts off the sibling banter between Jenn and Aurora. Letting my hand fall away from my watch, I draw in a breath to steady myself and then give Lionel a smile.

"Oh he's here," I reply.

Twisting slightly, I look over my shoulder. As if on cue, Jace appears. He crosses his arms over his broad chest and levels a hard stare on Lionel that I can feel from all the way over here. Lionel scoffs.

I turn back to the three of them and then motion towards the building on my right. "Though I have to say, I'm a little surprised. Where on earth did you find a venue here? I thought these were all residential houses."

Jenn blinks, looking confused. Then realization pulses across her features, and she lets out a breathy laugh. "Oh, right. You left before we..." Her gaze darts to Lionel, who was as much at fault for my leaving as Jace was. "Anyway. I wasn't talking about a building." With a bright smile on her face, she sweeps out her arm in a theatrical way and gestures towards the river. "I was talking about *this*."

My heart stops as I turn to look at what she's pointing to.

A boat. Or rather, a yacht. But it doesn't matter how big it is. What matters is that it's on the river. My heart starts pounding in my chest. I don't want to be here.

"It's owned by a friend of the family, so we can borrow it for a night," Jenn says. "I figured we could park the car here on the street right by the boat, and then bring all the other items onto it so that..."

She keeps talking, but I can't hear anything over the roaring inside my head.

An arm is suddenly linked with mine.

"Come on, I'll show you what it looks like on deck," Jenn says.

Her voice sounds like it's really far away even though I know that she's right next to me. I want to scream at her to stop, but I can't make my voice work. So all I do is to try to control my breathing as she leads me and the others onto the yacht.

Blood pounds in my ears. I draw in shallow breaths.

"Okay, so here's what I'm thinking," Jenn begins.

Then she slips her arm out of mine. It leaves me standing right next to the railing on the boat's outer side. Right next to the open river.

My heart beats so hard that I think it's going to crack my ribs.

"What if we put a drinks table here?" Jenn says, motioning with her arm. "And then..."

Her voice fades as memories crash over me. Throwing out a hand, I grip the railing to keep from toppling over.

My gaze snaps to the watch on my wrist.

Then to the water right below.

Blue eyes stare up at me.

My lungs freeze and ice spreads through my veins.

Waves lap against the side of the boat. The water looks gray in the gloomy light from the overcast sky. And I swear I can see him there. Floating. Bobbing in the water. Lifeless blue eyes staring unseeing up at the sky.

I can't breathe. I can't—

"Kayla," Lionel suddenly says from right next to me, his voice cutting through the memories that threaten to drown me. "Are you okay?"

"No." The word tears out of me like a bullet.

It startles both him and the Carlisle sisters enough that the deck falls completely silent.

Fuck. I should've... I shouldn't have snapped the word like that. God damn it, I need to pull myself together.

Forcing a deep breath into my lungs, I tear my gaze from the river and pry my hand off the railing. While letting my arm drop back down by my side, I turn to face the rest of my group. But I can't stop my other hand from drifting over to my watch.

"I, uhm..." Fiddling with the strap of my watch, I look from face to face and then clear my throat. "I just... don't like boats."

Lionel's expression changes. Becomes more focused. More intense. "Why not?"

I know that he's worried. That he can see that I'm not okay. But I don't want to explain why. I don't want to tell him that story. But I don't know how to explain it away either.

Thankfully, I don't have to. Because Aurora follows up with another question almost right after Lionel has finished speaking.

"Do you get seasick?" she asks from halfway across the deck, her pale brows raised and genuine concern on her pretty face.

"Yes," I blurt out, a bit more forcefully than I had intended. Then I nod several times too for emphasis. "Yes, I get seasick.

And what if some of the guests get seasick too? Not to mention the risks of having an event this close to the water. What if someone drinks a little too much and falls in? We can't risk that. The boat was a great idea, Jenn, but we really should be looking at something else. Some kind of building."

The words tumble out of me faster than normal. Lionel watches me with slightly furrowed brows, as if he notices that I'm off my game right now. But Jenn only scrunches up her face in thought for a few seconds.

"Huh," she says, tapping her chin. "I didn't think about that. But you're right. We won't have any insurance to cover it if someone drops something expensive in the water or, like you said, falls in."

"Yeah, so we should probably..." I motion towards the street.

Jenn nods, looking thoughtful.

"Well, luckily for you," Aurora begins with a bright grin. "I have another location for us to check out too."

"Great," I reply, again a bit too quickly. But I cover it with a forced smile as I motion for us all to get off this damn boat. "Then let's go."

Aurora is practically skipping as she hurries to catch up with Jenn. She elbows her sister in the ribs while teasing her about how her idea is so much better.

With my heart still slamming in my chest, I walk as quickly as possible across the deck. Lionel falls in beside me.

His gray eyes are full of worry as he searches my face. "You sure you're okay?"

"Yeah," I reply. Then I realize that I'm fiddling with my watch again, so I force myself to let my hands drop back to my sides. Painting a smile on my face, I turn to meet Lionel's eyes. "Yes, I'm fine."

He holds my gaze for another few seconds. But then he thankfully just nods. “Alright.”

I nod too.

Jace, who was standing right by the entrance to the yacht while we were on it, discreetly moves farther away as we reach the street.

My heart aches and my body feels numb. And I suddenly want Jace right next to me instead. I want his warm body beside me. I want to see his easy smile. His brown eyes that always sparkle with so much life.

But I don’t know how to tell him that.

So in the end, I just follow Aurora towards the next venue location in silence. My fingers fiddle with my watch. And lifeless blue eyes continue floating before my vision.

30

JACE

A scream shatters through the night. I'm out of bed and halfway through the apartment with a gun in my hand before the sound of it has even finished echoing off the walls. I snap my gaze around the kitchen and living room while I run, but everything is dark and still and completely undisturbed. As is the front door.

Another scream erupts from inside Kayla's bedroom.

I yank open the door and barrel inside, gun raised and my eyes sweeping across the space.

Kayla is thrashing on the bed, her arms and legs tangled in the pale sheets.

Moving quickly, I scan her bedroom for signs of an attacker before I shoulder open the door to her bathroom and doing the same.

But everything is empty and quiet.

Confusion and terrible worry courses through me as I dart back into her bedroom.

"Kayla—" I begin.

Another cry rips from her lungs, and she throws her head from side to side.

My heart almost stops as I notice that her eyes are still closed.

They're closed. Which means that she's still asleep. There is no attacker. She's… having a nightmare.

Both relief and even more worry pulse through me at the same time.

Setting the gun down on her dresser, I hurry over to the bed.

Whimpers spill from Kayla's lips as she twists and tosses on the bed. Her long red hair has fallen across half of her face like a curtain, but I can still read the anguish on her features clear as day.

Pain spears through my heart.

Climbing onto the bed, I kneel next to her on the mattress and reach towards her shoulder. But then I pause, hesitation crashing over me. Fuck, how should I wake her? Am I even supposed to wake a person when this happens? Didn't someone say that was dangerous? Or was that only for sleepwalking? Fuck, I don't—

Another cry rips from her throat.

And it damn near tears my soul out.

I can't watch her suffer like this. I have to wake her.

Gripping her shoulders, I give her a firm shake. "Kayla."

She thrashes in the sheets again.

"Kayla!" I snap, fear infusing my voice with unflinching command.

She snaps her eyes open, and her hands fly up towards mine and wrap around my wrists so hard that I'm pretty sure it's going to leave bruises. But I don't care. She can hurt me as much as she wants, as long as I never have to watch her suffer like this again.

"Victor," she gasps, her eyes wild and darting all over the place. "Victor, don't!"

Panic flashes through me, and I release her shoulders in a heartbeat. Oh God, did someone hurt her? Is that what the nightmare was about? Maybe I shouldn't be touching her like this. Fuck, did I just make it worse by grabbing her like that?

Her own hands remain around my wrists, her fingers digging into my skin hard, as she sits upright. "Please, don't. Victor—"

"It's not Victor," I blurt out. "It's Jace."

Dread and panic whirl inside me like a storm as I kneel there on the mattress next to her. Because I have no idea what to do. Despite all of my training, I have no fucking clue how to help her. No clue what I should be doing to make this better. So all I can do is sit there and hold her gaze, trying to force a sense of calm that I don't really feel into her body. I've never felt so useless in my entire life.

She blinks then. "Jace." It's barely more than a whisper.

"Yes. It's Jace. I'm here." I hold her frantic gaze. It takes all of my self-control to keep my voice steady. "I'm here, little demon."

Her eyes dart around her darkened bedroom, as if finally taking in her surroundings. She blinks several times. And her hands remain wrapped hard around my wrists. Then her gaze returns to me.

"Jace," she breathes.

I nod. "Yes."

Her chest heaves.

She glances around her bedroom again. The terrible fear and panic in her eyes is starting to fade. But I still remain completely motionless, letting her mind catch up and finish shedding whatever horrible nightmare she was trapped in.

After a few seconds, her gaze lands on my bare legs. I'm only wearing a pair of boxers since I shot straight out of bed when I heard her scream. Then she shifts her gaze up to my arms.

Surprise pulses across her features when she realizes that she's gripping my wrists. She quickly releases me. My bones ache from how hard she was squeezing my wrists, but I can barely feel it. All I can feel is an overwhelming worry for Kayla.

"Are you okay?" I ask gently.

She drags her gaze up to my face. Emotions pulse across her features.

"No," she gasps out.

And that single word sounds like it was wrenched from the depths of her soul. I can't bear it. I can't stand the way her voice breaks or the pain in her eyes.

Wrapping my arms around her, I pull her trembling body towards me and hold her tight.

A sob rips from her throat.

Then she wraps her arms around my chest and hugs me closer to her.

And then she cries.

She cries so hard that her body shakes in my arms. Her cheek is pressed against my chest, so I can feel her tears against my skin as they pour out of her. Can feel every heart-wrenching sob that rips from her lungs. Every tremor that rolls through her body.

Pain slices through me, tearing at my soul and damn near ripping my heart from my chest.

Holding her tightly, I stroke a hand down her hair and kiss the top of her head. "I've got you, little demon. I've got you."

Another sob racks her frame, and she tightens her arms around me, clinging to me as if I'm the only thing holding her together right now.

My heart aches.

I don't know who this Victor is, but I'm going to fucking kill him if he is the reason for her pain.

31

KAYLA

My heart pounds in my chest. It's so loud that it rattles my bones. I can still feel the water clinging to my skin. So much colder than it was before that moment when my life changed. Can still feel the seaweed brush against my ankle. The current pulling at me. The sharp rocks digging into the soles of my feet as I run along the side of the river. Can see the darkness. That horrible fucking darkness that obscured everything. And then those glassy blue eyes.

Another shudder racks my frame, and I tighten my arms around Jace's firm body, trying to use his warmth to chase away the chill that has seeped into my bones. His strong arms envelop me like a barrier against the rest of the world.

Resting his chin on the top of my head, he continues stroking my hair while murmuring softly, "I've got you."

A sob escapes my lips.

Oh God, I have never let anyone see me like this. This weak. This pathetic.

But it was that damn yacht on the river. Standing so close to the streaming water. It was haunting me all evening. And now it followed me into my dreams as well.

I shiver.

The feeling of that cold water washes over me, stealing the warmth from my soul.

"Jace," I gasp. "I need to… I need to feel something. Please, make me feel something else."

He immediately shifts his head, bringing his lips down to my neck. A shudder, but one of warmth and pleasure this time, ripples through me as he kisses that sensitive spot below my ear.

"Whatever that nightmare was about, it wasn't real this time. It wasn't happening to you again." He kisses that spot again before continuing down the side of my neck. "*This* is real. This is where you are. You and me."

A small whimper slips past my lips.

Jace shifts us over, gently laying me down on the bed while he straddles my hips. He draws his strong hands along my arms, positioning them so that my hands are resting against the mattress beside my head. His warm and muscular body is a solid weight against my own, and the feeling of it keeps me from breaking apart completely.

I suck in an unsteady breath as he draws his hands down my arms again while his lips continue brushing over my throat. Another pleasant shudder rolls through my body as his steady hands slide down my sides. He stops once he reaches my ribs, and just holds me like that. And the feeling of those strong, confident hands against my body grounds me. I release a deep sigh.

Jace kisses his way over my collarbones, and every brush

of his lips sends tingles down my spine. It chases away the coldness that was clinging to my bones. Another whimper spills from my lips as he lightly grazes his teeth over my skin.

My heart is now beating hard in my chest, but for a different reason.

Warmth spreads through my body as Jace keeps his commanding hands on the sides of my ribs while he kisses his way back up my throat. Lightning skitters across my skin as he slides his lips along my jaw. Then he slants his mouth over mine.

Raising my hands, I slide them through his soft curls and pull his lips down to mine.

A pulse of heat surges through me.

Jace rolls his hips and kisses me back as if it was the sole reason he was put on this earth. Oh God, the way this man kisses. His tongue swoops in, dominating mine, as he lays complete claim on my lips. I moan into his mouth. My fingers curl in his hair, gripping it hard before I rake my fingers through it again just to feel those soft strands brush over my skin.

Jace answers by deepening the kiss.

He kisses me until my head is spinning. Until I can't breathe. Can't think. Can't remember why I felt so cold and panicked only minutes before.

My pulse slows and my body relaxes.

I've got you, he said.

Yes. Yes, he truly does.

Once my body is no longer tense and trembling, Jace breaks the kiss. But he doesn't pull back. Instead, he rests his forehead against mine, his eyes still closed.

"Tell me what you want," he whispers.

My throat closes up at the emotions in his voice. I slide my hands down to the back of his neck and then over his broad shoulders. His body is so warm underneath my palms. Jace Hunter truly is like the sun. Like my own private sun, capable of chasing away the coldest and darkest of memories.

"Just hold me," I whisper back.

He nods, his forehead moving against mine. Then he gives me one more kiss, a soft and gentle one, before he rolls over and lies down next to me. The mattress sways underneath me as he shifts before settling his weight.

Once he's lying on his back, he slides an arm underneath me and pulls me to him. I roll over on my side and drape my arm over his muscular chest. He holds me tightly and tilts his head down to kiss my forehead again.

Pleasure curls around my spine.

For quite a while, we just remain like that. I can feel his heart beating against my palm where I rest it on his chest. It's steady. Unshakable. Just like he is.

Suddenly, I get the overwhelming urge to tell him. To tell him what the nightmare was about. What happened when I was a kid. Why I hate rivers. Why my father insists on having a bodyguard monitor my every move even though I would never do something so terribly stupid again.

I open my mouth to speak.

A pulse of self-consciousness ripples through me, and I hesitate.

It's not his burden to bear. It's not his job to listen to my sob stories. Him just being here right now, holding me because I asked him to, is more than he needs to do already.

So I close my mouth again.

But Jace, always so incredibly perceptive Jace, must have

been able to somehow read all of that on my face. Tilting his head down, he meets my gaze with those warm brown eyes of his.

"Do you want to talk about it?" he asks.

I swallow against the lump in my throat at how unreasonably kind this man is to the girl who has done nothing but make his life hell since the moment I met him.

"Yes," I manage to choke out in reply.

He says nothing. Only watches me, waiting in silence while I swallow again and gather my thoughts.

"I, uhm…" I begin, blowing out an unsteady breath. "I had a brother. Victor. He… died."

Pain floods Jace's eyes. "I'm sorry."

I nod, acknowledging it, while sorrow rips through my soul. I draw in another shuddering breath, waiting for it to pass, before I can manage to continue. "He was just one year older than me, and we were inseparable. Best friends. We did everything together. We raised so much trouble. Fun trouble."

A wistful smile blows across my lips as those old memories swirl through my mind.

"We didn't have bodyguards as such back then," I continue. "But we had people who watched us. To make sure we didn't get into too much trouble." Pain and regret slices through me, but I force myself to keep speaking. "One day, when I was eight and he was nine, we snuck away. Like we had done hundreds of times before. Victor wanted to go to the river that ran through the grounds at our summer vacation house. So we did."

My heart starts to pound again. Jace instinctively tightens his arm around me.

"At first, we just swam in the river like we always did. But then he wanted to go to a better spot. A more fun spot, he said. So I followed him to a place where massive boulders lined the riverbank. Almost like cliffs." My voice starts to tremble and I choke out my next words. "He wanted to jump from them and into the river."

Understanding fills Jace's eyes, but he says nothing. Only keeps watching me in silence. As if he knows just how badly I need to tell this entire story. How badly I need to share it with someone else. Someone who might be able to understand.

"I told him not to." Tears prick behind my eyes as I hold his gaze. "I *begged* him not to. I told him that it was too dangerous. I told him that we should go back. I even took his hand and tried to physically pull him back." Pain spears through my heart. "He just grinned at me, gave me one of those troublemaker winks that he had given me thousands of times, and then ran towards the cliffs."

A sob rips from my chest. I drag in a breath and have to clear my throat before I can continue.

"He hit his head on the way down. I rushed down to where I could wade into the river and then I..." Lingering panic pulses through me, as if I'm still there in that river, desperately searching for my brother. "I tried to find him. I dove in, over and over again, but I couldn't see him. The water was so dark."

Jace's eyes are full of pain and sadness as he holds my gaze.

"When I couldn't find him, I realized that the current might have pulled him away, so I ran down along the water." I swallow, the spikes of pain inside me almost unbearable. "I found him by the riverbank farther down." Coldness spreads through my soul again, and I press myself harder against Jace's warm body. "Even after all these years, I can still see his glassy blue eyes staring unseeing up at the sky while his body bobbed there in the shallow water."

The agony and sorrow in Jace's eyes deepen, and he hugs me tighter.

I wait for him to say the same thing that everyone else has said. The therapists I went to as a kid after that, the few friends I've told over the years, my parents. They've all said the same useless thing when I've told them this.

It wasn't your fault.

I know that it wasn't my fault! But it still doesn't change the fact that Victor is dead. That he died that day in the river. That I found his corpse bobbing in the water and staring up at the sky with dead eyes when I was eight years old.

But that's what they all do. That's what they all say. And I hate it when people immediately start trying to fix it. To fix me. To give me a quick solution so that we can move on from this awful topic. *It wasn't your fault, so let it go.* That's what they're essentially saying. Every time.

That's the problem with a lot of people. They don't know how to listen. Truly listen. They're only listening while waiting for their turn to speak. And sometimes, I don't want to hear what they have to say. Sometimes, I just want to tell someone and have them hear it and acknowledge it. I don't need them to come up with a solution for me. I just want to share the burden for a moment.

Jace's eyes are brimming with sincerity as he holds my gaze and says, "I'm so sorry that that happened to you. And to your brother."

I stop breathing as I wait for the inevitable *but*.

It never comes.

No 'but it wasn't your fault' and no 'but if you do this or

that you'll get over it' or anything like it. Nothing. Just a true heartfelt acknowledgement of my pain.

He hugs me tighter to his chest.

My heart almost breaks.

Whatever woman Jace ends up marrying, no matter who she is, she will still never be good enough to deserve him. No one will ever be good enough to deserve this incredible man.

32

JACE

For a long while after that, I just lie there on her bed, holding her close. She rests her hand on my chest, and I'm almost surprised that she can't feel it through my ribcage how much my heart is breaking for her.

Jesus Christ, to have gone through *that,* and at such a young age…

I suppress the urge to shake my head.

If anything had happened to Eli or Kaden or Rico, I don't think I could've survived it. But Kayla watched her brother die, found his body, and she has somehow still managed to fight her way out of that pitch black hole of sorrow and become such a radiant person full of life and fire.

"So that's why Dad is insisting that I always need to have a bodyguard with me," she says eventually.

Her voice sounds more like her now. Strong. Determined. Confident. As if she has let the grief wash over her and has now reached the other side again. It strengthens something in my own heart.

"To make sure that nothing happens to me," she continues.

"To their one remaining child. But there's no need for that, because I will never do something as stupid as that again."

I search her face, noting the lingering pain there. "So you have always had a bodyguard looking over your shoulder? Ever since then?"

"Yes." She raises her chin, and even though her blue eyes are now full of steel again, I can still hear the frustration and desperation lacing her voice. "Every day. My entire life. I have been watched, monitored, every single minute of my life." Her expression softens, and she gives me an almost apologetic smile. "Which is why I've been giving you so much shit."

An answering smile blows across my own lips. "Well, to be fair, I've been giving you a lot of shit too."

"Yeah. You really have."

I let out a surprised laugh as she gives my chest a playful shove. Then her eyes turn serious again.

"Can I ask you something, though?" she says.

My stomach dips at the tone of her voice, but I nod. "Of course."

"Why did you take this job?"

Indecision flashes through me. I hadn't planned on telling her this. But after all that she has just shared with me, how can I not?

So I clear my throat and hedge, "After what you just told me, this is going to make me sound like a petulant child."

To my surprise, she just smiles at that and raises an eyebrow while her eyes glitter with mischief. "As opposed to your default state which is naturally the very picture of maturity?"

A laugh escapes my lungs, and I nudge her with my hip. "Funny."

"It's one of my many amazing qualities." She grins. Then

her expression turns serious again, and she cocks her head as she studies my face. "Just tell me. Why did you accept the job to be my bodyguard? From what I understand, you're still in the middle of your senior year. So why ditch that to babysit me?"

"I, uhm…"

Raising my free hand, I rake it through my hair. I don't even know how to start. Kayla just keeps watching me with those big blue eyes. I heave a sigh and decide to just go for it.

"Look, the people in my family have been hitmen for generations. So I'm expected to become one as well."

Her eyebrows climb higher. "You can't choose a different profession?"

"No." I grimace. "My father made that clear very early. And I… I didn't handle that so well. My brothers have no problem with it, but the fact that I don't have a choice in my own future almost broke me. Which led me to… engage in destructive activities." I clear my throat. "Anyway, long story short, my father made me a deal. If I successfully handle this bodyguard job, he will let me choose whether or not I become a hitman."

Shock pulses across her beautiful face. "That's what you have riding on this? Your entire future?"

"Yeah."

With that stunned disbelief still swirling in her eyes, she pushes herself up on her elbows so that she can meet my gaze fully. "So wait, let me get this straight." Lifting a hand, she motions between us. "We've been giving each other absolute hell… when in reality, we both just want the same thing. Freedom."

A laugh rips from my lungs, because she's absolutely right.

Still chuckling at that realization, I nod. "Yeah, it would appear so."

"Huh." She sounds astonished.

The mattress bounces underneath me as she drops back down and then twists so that she's lying on her back next to me instead. For a little while, we just stare up into her pale ceiling. The sun is starting to rise now, casting its first rays over the sleeping city around us.

"How about this?" She turns her head so that she's looking at me again. "We stop making each other's lives hell."

"I can get behind that." I raise an eyebrow at her. "So… we're civil?"

She flashes me a devilish grin that makes her eyes glitter like jewels. "Civil-ish." Then she winks. "Wouldn't want things to start getting boring around here."

A laugh, full of both surprise and happiness, escapes my throat. "No, we wouldn't want that."

33

KAYLA

The building is almost empty, but somehow still full of noise. I glance towards where Jenn and Aurora are carrying, carting, and sometimes outright dragging in the variety of items that we have managed to obtain for our silent auction. It's happening on Friday evening. Two days from now. My pulse speeds up at just the thought.

I'm not usually nervous about presentations or assignments like this. I know that I'm good at what I do and that I always get high grades on anything I turn in. But this assignment is different. Not only because it's an actual event and not a paper that can just be handed in, but also because it's a group project. That means that there are too many variables. Too many things that can go wrong.

Though to be fair, I couldn't have pulled this off without the others. Aurora really came through for us with this building. It's the perfect venue for our silent auction. And Jenn has been incredible at getting all of the items organized and delivered here.

My gaze drifts towards where Lionel is unpacking some white linen tablecloths. He hasn't contributed much to this project, to be honest. Sometimes, he seems more focused on trying to flirt with me than actually participating in this project. Well, *that* and staring daggers at Jace when he inevitably shows up to ruin his attempts to get some alone time with me.

Maybe I need to talk to Lionel about that.

Not that I owe him an explanation or anything. But it might make things easier if I just outright tell him that I'm not interested in dating. Not him anyway.

While pushing another table across the floor, I sweep my gaze around the massive high-ceilinged room. Apart from the furniture and items we're currently unloading, there is almost nothing in here. But Jace has somehow still managed to make himself invisible.

It makes warmth and gratitude flood my chest. He truly has been doing his outmost to make me feel as if I'm not being constantly monitored. And it works. I'm not feeling as stifled anymore. It also helps that I now know why *he* is here. Why he is doing this job.

As if he can feel me searching for him, Jace appears and raises an eyebrow at me from across the room. I shake my head in response to his silent question. He just shoots a pointed look towards the heavy table that I'm pushing across the floor, and then arches his eyebrow again. A soft chuckle rolls from my chest, but I shake my head again. I've got this.

He rolls his eyes as if he thinks I'm being stubborn for no reason, but then flashes me a bright smile and moves back to where he was hiding in plain sight earlier.

My heart flutters erratically behind my ribs.

I don't know what Jace and I are now. He's still my

bodyguard. He still works for my father. But we're somehow also… more. Friends, maybe.

The table grinds against the floor as I push it the final distance to the other table that's already waiting by the wall. I frown at myself, at my own confused emotions, as I move around the table and adjust it so that they line up better.

Are Jace and I friends? We talk to each other and mess with each other as if we're friends. But friends don't kiss the way we do. Friends don't *fuck* the way we do.

A flicker of insecurity ripples through me. Because friends also don't get paid to spend time together. And Jace is here to do a job. I'm a job assignment.

Fuck, why does it all have to be so complicated?

"It's really starting to take shape now," Lionel suddenly says from right behind me.

Surprise pulses through me, because I was so wrapped up in my own tangled thoughts that I didn't hear him approach. While adjusting the table one last time, I look up and then turn towards him.

"The event, I mean," he continues, and gestures with one hand at the building around us. His other arm is carrying a couple of white tablecloths. "It's so close to being finished."

I flick a quick glance around the mass of items and tables that are still waiting in a cluster on the floor. We're not even halfway done yet. But I return my gaze to Lionel and give him a smile anyway.

"Yeah, it really is," I say.

He smiles back while dropping one of the tablecloths on the table next to us before he shifts the other one in his arms and holds out one side of the long white fabric to me. I take it silently. It flutters in the air as we spread it wide before draping it over the first table. Then we grab the second one and do the same.

"About the car," Lionel begins as we smoothen out the creases. "I think I've found a good spot for it outside, but I want to know what you think."

"Great," I reply.

At least he's contributing something.

After brushing my hands over the soft linen one more time, I straighten and pull out my phone. From across the table, Lionel blinks at me in surprise as I type a quick text and send it.

Me: *Going outside to decide a location for the car.*

The reply comes back almost immediately.

Jace Hunter: *And giving me a heads-up instead of just sneaking off? Wow. Now I really am impressed, little demon. I was just going to make you dinner tonight, but now I think I'll throw in dessert too.*

An absolutely ridiculous grin spreads across my mouth. But I don't care, because there's a sparkling warmth filling my chest. Still smiling like an idiot, I slip my phone back into my pocket.

"What was that all about?" Lionel asks.

A jolt shoots through me because I had almost forgotten that he was here. Clearing my throat, I quickly wipe the grin from my face and instead lift my shoulders in a casual shrug.

"I was just giving Jace a heads-up that we're going outside so that he can follow," I reply while we start towards the door.

Lionel's expression immediately darkens with annoyance. "Does he always have to follow you around like a shadow? It makes it very difficult to have any actual conversations with you when he is always standing a step away, glaring at me as if he's planning to murder me."

Amusement ripples through me at the mental image. Because that is exactly what Jace looks like whenever Lionel tries to get me alone.

But the emotion is quickly followed by a flicker of frustration. I didn't want to have this conversation right now, and certainly not here, but it looks like it needs to be said.

Softening my features, I glance over to meet Lionel's eyes as we continue towards the door. "Look, I'm sorry if I've been sending mixed signals."

I know that I haven't, and I know that I have nothing to apologize for, but I phrase it like that anyway because most men truly have such incredibly fragile egos.

"But I'm not really looking for a relationship right now," I finish gently, and give him an apologetic smile.

His cheeks flush a deep shade of red. "Oh. No, it's not… I'm not…"

He fumbles when he tries to open the door, and it takes two more tries for him to grab the handle and push it down. While stepping outside, he frantically waves his hand several times in the air, as if telling me to disregard his words and actions.

I just watch him with my eyebrows raised as I step out into the darkened parking lot beside him.

"That's not what…" he begins before trailing off again, his cheeks still flushed with embarrassment. "I wasn't trying to imply…" Straightening his spine, he clears his throat and seems to compose himself. Then he gives me a smile. "It's alright."

I'm not sure what I'm supposed to say to that. Of course it's alright. I have no obligation to date him or to indulge his attempts at flirting. I don't owe him anything.

So what I end up saying is simply, "Good."

He winces, as if he realizes that he probably should've said something else. Then he quickly changes the subject instead.

"Anyway, so after the event on Friday, I was thinking that we all should go out to celebrate," he says. "As a group, I mean. There's a drinks-and-a-show type of place that's supposed to be really good, and I just think it could be fun."

"That sounds great."

"Good. Great. I'll… I'll set it up."

He flashes me a smile and then quickly moves on to talk about the car again.

I suppress the impulse to laugh.

Well, that went better than expected.

34

JACE

The silent auction ran like a well-oiled machine. Though that was not a coincidence. The event ran smoothly because Kayla made sure it did.

Standing by the wall a short distance away, I watch as she issues orders to the catering company she hired, telling them to start clearing everything away. The final attendants have already left, and the only people still in the room now are the caterers, Kayla's event group, and the professors who came to assess the event.

Warm light from the chandelier above shines down on the pale wooden room. It makes Kayla's deep blue dress shimmer when she turns around to speak to Jenn. Her long red hair ripples down her back. The sight knocks the breath from my lungs. God, she really is gorgeous.

"Jenn," Kayla says. "Do you have the list of—"

"Yes," she replies, waving a piece of paper in the air.

"Good. Lionel, the guy who won the car is coming to pick it up tomorrow, which means that we need to move it into an actual parking space for tonight. I cleared it with the building manager and we can use the one at the back. Get to it."

Fire flickers inside me.

Fuck, she's so hot when she takes charge and bosses people around like this. If she was mine, I would—

I stop myself before I can finish the thought. Because she's not mine. She's a job assignment.

Confusion whirls through me.

Isn't she?

I nod to myself. Yes, she is a job assignment. Then that confusion is immediately back again. Because she's also not just a job assignment anymore. I don't know what we are, but I know that the line has been crossed. And things have become muddled.

I'm here to keep her safe. And I do. No one will ever hurt her as long as I'm here. So I am doing my job. But is it wrong that I also… care about her? That I like the way she challenges me? That I love the way she makes me laugh? That I would worship every inch of her body if she asked me to?

Before I can find the answer to those questions, the two professors who were here to assess the event suddenly start approaching Kayla and the others. Even though they're just her teachers, I still edge a little closer as the two men move towards her.

Lionel and the Carlisle sisters hurry over to where Kayla is standing. All of them look slightly nervous as the professors reach them.

"Well," says the man in the gray suit as he claps his hands together. "What a splendid event this was."

Kayla and her friends release a whooshing breath of relief. Smiling broadly, they exchange quick looks while the second professor nods in agreement.

Pride swells in my chest. Which is ridiculous, because I have no logical reason to be proud since I didn't actually contribute anything to this event. Well, except maybe the car washing and all that. But still. I am proud. Of Kayla. She truly is a born leader.

"To be honest," the first professor continues, a slightly sheepish smile on his face. "We expected that you would rely mostly on your, uhm… assets."

At their confused look, he clears his throat before elaborating.

"We all know that Kayla has access to quite the fortune, as well as a vast network of connections, so we thought you would take the easy way out and just use that. But you didn't." He flashes them a bright smile. "You worked hard on your own to make this a success."

Standing a short distance from them, I can't help but scowl at the professor. What the hell kind of comment was that? In my opinion, that's a very strange way of looking at the world. If someone has money and connections, why would it be considered wrong to use them?

It would be like saying that people who are born beautiful are cheating because they can get modeling jobs or acting jobs easier than people who are not. Yes, it's mostly luck that determines if you're born into a wealthy family or born with great looks. And yes, it sucks if you end up getting dealt a bad hand. But if you do manage to get lucky, why is it wrong to use the power and wealth you have?

God knows that I wouldn't have been able to get away with even half of the shit I do if I wasn't a Hunter. But why should I feel guilty about that? I am who I am.

My insides twist as a thought that I have been avoiding flashes through my mind.

Yes, I am a Hunter. And while that comes with lots of advantages, it also comes with expectations. Now, I'll soon be in a position to choose my future. All I need to do is to finish out this semester as Kayla's bodyguard, and then I can choose whether to go back to Blackwater and become a hitman or to do something else with my life.

And that is the question, isn't it?

What do I actually want for my future?

I study Kayla while the professors continue giving them feedback on the various stages of the event.

Is this what I want? To be a bodyguard?

Uneasiness slithers through my gut. Because I know, in my heart, that being a bodyguard is not what I want. Standing around for hours, just watching the same person for a threat that might never come is not what I want for my life.

If it had been anyone but Kayla, I would already have been bored out of my mind. But she keeps me on my toes. And she makes me want to be close to her all the time.

But being a bodyguard for someone else? Fuck, I think I would shoot myself in the head before the first week was over.

A hint of regret flickers through me.

Because if I'm being completely honest, I miss Blackwater a little. I miss the fights, the adrenaline, the plotting, the power plays. I actually like that world. The world of a hitman.

So is that the future I want then?

I don't know.

The only thing I do know is that I don't want to spend my life being someone's bodyguard. Because the only person who I would want to be a bodyguard for is Kayla, and I don't actually want to be her bodyguard because what I really want to be is her—

I quickly shut down that line of thought before I can finish it. Before I can admit, even to myself, what is getting more and more impossible to deny. What I truly feel.

Dragging a hand through my hair, I heave a sigh and banish all thoughts of the future for now.

This is getting too fucking complicated.

35

KAYLA

Pleasant murmuring and clinking glasses fill the air around us. I glance around the room while a waitress sets down four wine glasses on the table before us. I have to give it to Lionel, he did pick a beautiful bar for our celebration.

Round tables made of dark wood dot the floor across the entire room leading up to the small stage at the front. Glittering chandeliers hang in the ceiling, filling the space with warm light. And there are candles on every table.

"Well then, boys and girls," Aurora says as she picks up her wine glass. There is a bright smile on her lips as she looks between me, Jenn, and Lionel. "Here's to our ridiculously successful silent auction!"

We all raise our wine glasses as well. Jace is standing a short distance away, and I'm suddenly struck by the feeling that he should be here too. At the table. After all, he is the one who secured all of the items for me. And also because—

"To our ridiculously successful silent auction," Jenn and Lionel echo, cutting off my train of thought.

I quickly repeat those words as well while we all clink our glasses together.

Aurora drinks deeply before letting out a contented sigh and leaning back in her seat. "We're definitely going to get a fantastic grade on this assignment. Did you hear what they said about our organizational skills and time management?"

"Yeah." Mischief glitters in Jenn's eyes as she jabs her elbow into her sister's ribs. "Not that *you* contributed much to the time management part."

She gasps dramatically and mimics clutching her pearls. "You wound me, sister."

Both of them start laughing. I smile too, but my fingers still drift to my watch and I fiddle with the strap. As the main Ashford heir, my brother was supposed to get this watch when he turned thirteen. Now, I got it instead.

Pain slices through my chest.

Normally, I can function every day without thinking too much about it. But after that unexpected trip to the yacht on the river, those old memories have been surging up more and more. Those old hurts. Not just for the fact that I lost my brother that day, but also because I lost any chance at a normal childhood. A normal life. A normal family.

I don't think I've truly realized until now, until I saw Jace interact with his brothers and their girlfriends, how much I desperately yearn for that too. Yearn for the feeling of belonging. Of being a part of something.

My hand falls away from my watch as I glance towards where Jace is standing a short distance away. He gives me a small smile that makes butterflies erupt in my stomach.

It eases the pain in my soul.

"So, what kind of show is it?" Jenn suddenly asks.

I flash Jace a quick smile before returning my attention to the conversation around the table.

"You said it was a drinks-and-a-show kind of place," Jenn continues, and gestures towards the small stage ahead. "What kind of show is it?"

"Oh, uhm," Lionel replies after swallowing his gulp of wine. Setting down his glass again, he scratches the back of his neck. "I'm not actually sure. I've just heard that it's good."

"I think we're about to find out," Aurora says, and nods towards where a man in a dark blue suit has just walked onto the stage.

A round of applause sweeps through the room, and everyone stops talking and instead turns towards the man.

"Welcome," he says as he comes to a halt at the front of the stage. With a conspiratorial smile on his face, he spreads his arms wide. "To a night of mysteries. A night of miracles. A night where we breach the veil between the living and the dead."

I suck in a sharp breath. Oh God. No. Don't tell me this is a—

"My name is Caesar Ordell and I am a bridge between our realm and the place where our loved ones are waiting," he continues. "I can help them speak to you from beyond the grave."

Ice spreads through my veins.

On my left, Jenn shoots Aurora a pointed look, which she replies to with an eye roll. I could probably have understood what that look meant if my brain had been working properly, but right now, all I can focus on is how cold my chest suddenly feels.

"Let's see who we have here with us today," Caesar says as

he drops down from the small stage and starts walking between the tables. "Who the spirits want to talk to today."

People look towards him with bright eyes, as if they're hoping he will come to them. Wrapping my hand around my wristwatch, I squeeze it hard while desperately hoping that he won't come to our table.

Caesar stops at a table halfway across the room and starts talking to a woman about her grandmother. Jenn and Aurora whisper to each other and Aurora rolls her eyes again as Jenn nudges her in the ribs. On my other side, Lionel just watches with mild curiosity. None of them seem to have noticed my panic.

I can feel Jace's eyes burning holes in the side of my head, but I don't dare to turn and look at him. Because if I do, this calm façade that I somehow still manage to present to the rest of the world is going to shatter like broken glass.

"I'm feeling another connection," Caesar says.

My heart leaps into my throat as he starts moving in our direction. Blood pounds in my ears as he stops right in front of our table and locks eyes with me.

"From a brother," Caesar says, his blue eyes firmly on mine. "Victor."

I suck in a short breath.

Both Jenn and Aurora turn to stare at me, shock pulsing across their faces. They didn't know about Victor. Nobody does. Because I never talk about him.

"I see... water," Caesar says, his eyes compassionate as they search my face. "A lake."

I stare back at him.

"No, a river," he amends.

I swallow.

"You were both very young."

My throat starts to close up.

Caesar gives me a look of sorrow. "He says that the current was too strong."

Shock pulses through me. How could he possibly know that?

"He knows that you tried to save him."

I have to press my mouth shut to stop my bottom lip from trembling. Panic tears through my soul, and my gaze darts around the room behind Caesar. Oh God. How can he know all of this? Is Victor actually here? Please don't tell me he's really here. I don't want to—

"He wants me to tell you that it was not your fault. He says that he would have gone in anyway."

My eyebrows draw into a small frown.

"He would've jumped in anyway," Caesar says, holding my gaze.

A sob rips from my throat.

Shoving my chair back from the table, I shoot to my feet and rush towards the door.

I can't be here. I can't. I don't want to hear this. I don't want *them* to hear this.

Tears blur my vision as I race through the room and towards the door.

Lionel must have shot to his feet and left at the same time because he is at my side immediately, placing a gentle hand on my elbow and leading me towards the back door.

"I'm so sorry," he says, his voice breathless. "I didn't know. I didn't know that this was a… that your brother had…"

Another sob escapes my lips without permission. I want to yank my arm out of his grip because I don't want anyone to touch me right now. I just want to be left alone. But I can't find the strength to do it, so I just stumble along as he quickly walks us towards the back door.

"Let's go outside," he says gently. "The alley out here is usually empty, so no one out here will be staring at you if you want to… take a second to compose yourself."

I shake my head.

I don't want to compose myself. I want to cry my eyes out. I want to go home. I want a hug. And comfort food. And someone who will let me break down without making me feel like I'm embarrassing myself.

Lionel grabs the handle and starts pulling the door open.

Before he can even get it halfway open, Jace slams his palm against the door and shoves it shut again with a bang that reverberates through the air. Lionel lets out a yelp as Jace grabs him by the collar and yanks him away from me. The force of it sends Lionel stumbling backwards and crashing into the wall hard enough to rattle the paintings along the corridor.

"What the hell are you—" Lionel snaps, his voice furious. But then he cuts himself off when he straightens and finds Jace standing between me and him like a murderous demon. Shooting Jace an angry glare, he instead says, "I was trying to help her!"

"You've done enough," Jace growls. Violence pulses from every inch of his carved body as he stares Lionel down. "Now, get the hell out of my sight before I snap your fucking neck."

"I didn't know!" Desperation bleeds into Lionel's voice. And it pulses on his entire face as he looks to me, his eyes pleading. "I didn't know that this was a psychic reading. I didn't know that your brother drowned and—"

"Get. Out."

Lionel flicks his gaze back to Jace, who looks to be one

second away from pulling the gun that I know he always carries concealed in his clothes.

I still haven't said a word. I just can't muster enough energy to open my mouth. So all I do is to look at Lionel, silently begging him to just leave. Fine, he didn't know about the psychic and about my brother, but I still don't want to talk to him right now.

Anger flickers in Lionel's eyes, and he shoots another venomous stare at Jace. Then he spins on his heel and stalks away. He throws open the front door on the other side of the corridor and then disappears out into the night without a second look back.

I slump back against the wall.

My heart is still pounding in my chest.

Resting the back of my head against the wall, I stare up at the light in the pale ceiling above. The air conditioner hums faintly into the suddenly pressing silence.

"How could he have known all that?" I whisper. To Jace or to the ceiling or to no one at all. Pain clenches my heart. "He must be a real psychic. There is no way he could've known that. Which means that Victor was really here and..."

A sob rips from my throat before I can finish the sentence.

"No, he's not."

I snap my gaze down from the ceiling and turn my head to look towards the sound of the new voice. Jace has spun around as well.

Jenn gives me a sympathetic smile as she and Aurora walk down the hallway and approach us.

"No, he's not psychic," Jenn repeats.

"But he knew about Victor," I protest as they come to a halt in front of me.

Jace has moved so that he is standing beside me, but he

looks much less inclined to throw Jenn and Aurora out than he did Lionel.

"He probably saw on the guest list that you were coming and researched you," Jenn explains. Her eyes are serious but also lined with sympathy as she gestures between me and the main room down the hall. "He probably thought that making a grand impression on you would be great publicity for his show, so he checked you out."

Next to her, Aurora nods. "We didn't know about your brother, but now that we knew what to search for, it only took us a couple of tries to find it."

Holding up her phone, she shows me an old news article from the local paper where our summer house was located. I glance away from the picture of Victor it shows.

"But that only says that he drowned," I argue. "How could he possibly have known that it was a river? That he jumped in? That I was there too? That I tried to save him?" Dread and pain sear through me, and I slash my hand through the air. "He couldn't! Not unless Victor was..." I choke on the words.

Jenn and Aurora share a look. Embarrassment, but also immense empathy, blows across Aurora's face as she turns back to meet my gaze.

"Look, I..." she begins, pushing her blonde hair back behind her ear. "I was really close with our grandpa. And when he died, I... Well, long story short, I became really into this." She shoots Jenn a serious look. "And I still believe that true psychics do exist."

Jenn just nods, as if she won't argue with that.

Aurora turns back to me. "But most people, and especially the ones who do these kinds of shows, are con men."

"But how could he *know*?" Emotions claw at my chest like sharp talons. "There is no way for him to—"

"He did what's called a cold reading," Jenn interrupts. Her voice is firm but not unkind. Holding my gaze, she raises her eyebrows. "Remember what he said? First, he said that it was a lake. But then you scowled at him. Just a little. And he said *river* next. That's when you swallowed."

I blink at her in confusion and surprise.

"I was watching you closely," she explains, and her eyes dart towards Aurora. "I learned all I could about these kinds of cold readings so that I could explain it to Aurora and break her out of her..." Clearing her throat, she shifts her gaze back to me. "Anyway. He didn't know about the river and the current and all that. He guessed, and then used the micro expressions on your face to determine if he was right. If you swallowed or if your mouth dropped open a little or your eyes widened a fraction. Or if you frowned or scowled or pulled back."

Disbelief tumbles through me. And for a few seconds, all I can do is to stare at her. "He... He *guessed?*"

Both Jenn and Aurora nod. Jenn looks determined while Aurora is looking at me like she understands exactly how I felt back in that room, and exactly how I'm feeling right now.

Rage burns through me. Hot enough to torch this whole building.

"He guessed," I repeat, fury seeping into my voice. "He pretended that my brother was here, talking to me from the other side? He *pretended.*"

"Yeah."

Another wave of rage roars through me. He put me through all of that pain and hurt and emotional upheaval for a *show*? He exploited my grief for money? For publicity?

"I want to kill him." The words rip from my soul with enough force to make me taste blood. Fury flickers like lightning strikes through my body as I look from Jenn to Aurora to Jace, who is watching me in silence. "I want him dead. Can we make that happen?"

God, I can't believe I went through all of that shit, all of those emotions, and it wasn't even real. It was just a scam. People like that don't deserve to—

"Well, yeah," Jace replies. There's a casual expression on his face as he motions vaguely at himself while glancing between me and the Carlisle sisters. "I could… I'm a… You know."

And a broken and yet full laugh rips from me at the sight.

God, where has this absolutely extraordinary man been all my life?

36

JACE

The scent of melted cheese and herbs and freshly baked baguettes with garlic butter fills the kitchen and living room as I plate the creamy pasta dish I made and then break the baguette in half, putting one half on Kayla's plate and the other on mine.

I stopped on the way back from the psychic reading to pick up some ingredients, and a ready-made baguette that I could just pop in the oven, since I had a feeling that Kayla needed some comfort food. She didn't say it, but I could see it in her eyes. And food is the perfect cure for heartache.

Lifting the plates, I turn towards the table. Kayla is sitting there with a glass of wine, looking lost in thought. But she looks up when she sees me approaching the table.

Happiness pulses across her face when she glances down at the food.

The sight of it almost stops my heart, and I can't suppress the smile that spreads across my lips. After setting down her plate, I walk around the table and drop down into the chair opposite her. A soft thud sounds as I set down my own plate.

She picks up her knife and fork, but then stops. Her gaze darts up to my face, as if waiting for me to tell her that it's okay to start eating. An amused breath escapes my lips, and I motion with my hand for her to go ahead while I try the wine.

She grins and then digs into the food.

A small moan spills from her lips, and she closes her eyes for a second as she chews.

My heart does a backflip in my chest.

God, I love watching her eat. I love cooking for her. I love how happy it makes her.

Setting down my wine glass, I pick up my own utensils and dig in as well. And damn it's good, if I may say so myself. I really am an excellent cook. My brothers really should be paying me when I grace their tables with my extraordinary food. Suspicion flickers through me while I chew because I suddenly realize that that's probably why they all invite me over so often. Especially around dinner time. And with a surprising amount of ingredients waiting in the fridge. Huh. Clever.

"I don't actually want him dead, by the way."

I blink, pulled out of my thoughts about my sneaky brothers, and look up to meet Kayla's beautiful blue eyes from across the table.

"The psychic," she clarifies. "I don't actually want to kill him."

Alarm pulses through me. "You don't?"

"No. He's a scumbag but…" She shrugs. "Anyway, I just thought I'd clarify that."

"Oh. Shit." Dropping my fork back onto my plate, I shove my hand into the pocket of my jeans and yank out my phone. "Hold on."

She jerks back and blinks at me in shock. "Wait, are you serious?"

I shoot her a glance over my phone while I send a quick message to the group chat I have with my brothers, telling them to stop our preparations.

"Well, yeah," I reply as I slide my phone back into my pocket. Lifting my shoulders in a shrug, I hold her gaze with a mix of bewilderment and seriousness. "You said you wanted him dead, so..."

Candlelight dances in her astonished eyes as she looks back at me. "You would actually do that? You would kill someone for me?"

"Of course I would."

"No, I don't mean in a bodyguard-protecting-me-from-dying kind of way. You would actually kill someone for me, someone who isn't a direct threat, just because I asked you to?"

"Yes."

I would do a lot more than that. In fact, I don't think there is anything I wouldn't do for her.

Kayla Ashford is unlike anyone I have ever met. She is fire and life and explosions of color. And she has somehow managed to blast her way into my heart with air horns and snarky comebacks and creative escape attempts and with her intelligence and endurance and power and how she never apologizes for who she is. How she owns herself and the very world around her.

And she does own everything. My heart included.

"You know, I've been thinking..." she begins, suddenly sounding uncharacteristically uncertain. "I wouldn't actually mind it if you stayed a little closer to me from now on."

My heart leaps into my throat and hope flares up inside

me, bright as a star. But I try to temper it as I carefully reply, "I thought you didn't like feeling your bodyguard looming over you all the time."

"Maybe I don't feel like you're just a bodyguard anymore."

I can barely breathe. "Maybe I don't feel like you're just a job assignment either."

Her eyes light up, and I swear I can see relief pulse across her face. I almost laugh. How could she not have known that I felt the same? That I've been feeling this way for weeks? Granted, I haven't even dared to admit it to myself. But still.

"So maybe, instead of lurking in the shadows, I want you to sit next to me in class and at lunch and all that from now on." She pauses for a second before adding, "Like a boyfriend."

My heart bursts, and a wide grin spreads across my mouth. "Like a boyfriend, huh?"

A grin full of challenge slides home on her own lips as she raises her eyebrows. "Unless you don't think you can handle me?"

Pushing up from my chair, I lean over the table and wrap my hand around her jaw. Her eyes dance with mischief as I lean closer, a sly smile on my lips. "Oh, I think I can handle you just fine, little demon."

She steals a vicious kiss from me and then laughs against my lips. It's a laugh full of villainous promises and epic challenges. And it makes my whole soul come alive.

37

KAYLA

I slam the front door shut behind me. Whirling around, I advance on Jace while raising a finger in the air.

"That," I say, stalking towards him, "was so fucking hot."

Jace leans back, half sitting on the edge of the kitchen table, and crosses his ankles. His brown eyes glitter and a smirk plays over his lips as he watches me. "You thought so, huh?"

"Yes." I stop barely half a stride away. So close that I can feel the heat from his body. Tilting my head back, I lock eyes with him and raise my eyebrows pointedly. "Though next time, maybe be a little more discreet when we're sitting right opposite Aurora, Jenn, and Lionel."

Amusement pulls at his lips, and he arches an eyebrow as well. "You're the one who literally told them that we were heading home so that you could fuck my brains out."

Heat washes through me. Not embarrassment. Just pure fire that licks through my veins and makes me feel invincible. This past week since Jace and I decided to admit how we really feel about each other has been the most exhilarating week of my life. Yes, Jace still watches over me as a bodyguard, but it's a choice now. He's close because I want him close. And fucking hell, I want him more than close. All the time.

"Yes, well," I reply, holding his gaze while that fire pools inside me. "How else was I supposed to react? When you called me a good girl."

Drawing his hand up my throat, he takes a firm grip on my jaw and tilts my head farther back. His eyes gleam as he leans closer. "You like that, huh?"

He brushes his lips over mine.

My spine tingles.

"Maybe I will call you that again," he breathes against my mouth.

A shudder of pleasure rolls through me, and I try to lean forward and claim his lips, but his grip on my jaw keeps me firmly in place. He smiles against my mouth, teasing his lips over mine again without actually kissing me.

"Take off my shirt," he says.

My clit throbs at the command in his voice. Lifting my hands, I draw my fingers along the top of his pants, gently brushing his bare skin.

I'm immediately rewarded by a shudder rolling through his body.

I grin against his mouth.

"The things I will do to you," he whispers against my lips, his hand still wrapped around my jaw.

With that wicked smirk still on my mouth, I slip my hands underneath the fabric of his white t-shirt and start slowly pushing it up his stomach. The feeling of his sharp abs underneath my palms makes my thighs clench.

I take my time drawing my hands over his lethal body, caressing every sharp ridge and tracing every curve, until another shudder of pleasure rolls through him.

"Oh, you truly are a little demon," he murmurs against my lips.

Pulling me closer, he claims my mouth with a hard kiss. Then he releases my jaw and instead grabs the hem of his shirt, which is now bunched around his chest. With a firm yank, he pulls it over his head and tosses it down on the floor next to us.

My gaze immediately rakes over his bare chest. Need sears through me as I run my eyes over his muscular frame. Fuck, he really is gorgeous.

"Your turn," he says, his voice full of wicked promises.

I drag my gaze up to his perfect face and find him watching me with a sly smile on his lips.

"Take off your shirt," he orders. "And back up a few steps. I want a good view."

A jolt shoots through me. I'm still not used to people giving me orders like this, but fuck I do love it when it comes from Jace. With heat flickering in my belly, I follow his commands and take a few steps back so that he can see me properly. Then I reach for the buttons on my shirt.

Jace's cock is already straining against his pants before I have even unbuttoned the first one.

I flash him a grin as I move on to the next one. Taking my sweet time, I carefully unbutton each one. Jace narrows his eyes at me, the promise of vengeance dancing in them.

Once I've finished with all the buttons, I draw my hands up my body and towards my shoulders. Jace clenches the edge of the table that he is still leaning against when I trace the curve of my breasts. Hunger burns in his eyes as he watches me.

Pushing the shirt off my shoulders, I let it flutter to the floor behind me.

Jace draws in a long breath as if to steady himself. It just makes me grin wider.

"Your jeans too," he says.

There is still unflinching command in his voice, but it's also rough and laced with need now. God, I love seeing how much I affect him.

Keeping my eyes locked on his, I undo the button on my jeans and then slide the zipper down. His fingers tighten around the edge of the table. I slip my hands underneath the fabric of my jeans and start pushing them down. Slowly. Ever so slowly.

Jace draws in another long breath through his nose, his hands gripping the table so hard I swear I can hear the wood crack.

I flash him a devilish smile. Then I guide my pants over my ass and down my legs. Once both my pants and socks are off, I straighten again in only my underwear.

Fire burns in Jace's eyes as he drinks in the sight of me in nothing but lingerie. He runs his tongue over his bottom lip. His massive cock is straining so hard against his pants that it must surely be painful.

With his fingers still gripping the edge of the table, he drags his gaze up to my face again. "Fuck, you're gorgeous."

I gasp at the breathless tone of his voice and the sheer desperation and amazement in his eyes as he stares at me.

"Take off your underwear," Jace suddenly orders, his voice rough. "You have five seconds."

I arch an eyebrow. "Or what?"

His eyes glint with delicious threats and wicked promises. "Are you sure you want to find out, little demon?"

A dark thrill rolls down my spine.

"One," he says.

I quickly strip out of my remaining clothes.

He lets out a low chuckle of approval as my panties and bra hit the floor.

Every nerve in my body feels like it's crackling with electricity as he takes his time studying every inch of my now completely naked body. His gaze is so intense that I don't know whether I want to cover myself up to prevent him from burning holes through my very soul or if I want to stride over to him and yank his own pants off before I shove him down on the table and fuck his brains out.

"Get down on your knees."

The command pulses through the air. I draw in a sharp breath at the sheer power dripping from his voice. Shifting my weight, I press my thighs together as my clit throbs.

Jace smirks at me. "I said, on your knees."

My heart pounds in my chest as I slowly lower myself to my knees on the floor. Jace remains where he is, leaning against the table with his ankles crossed and his fingers curled around the edge. But his eyes track my every move, study my every curve, as I kneel there on the floor a few strides away.

"Now, crawl to me."

I blink, my eyes widening in surprise.

His voice drops lower, darker, as he stares me down. "Do not make me tell you again."

My pulse thrums and anticipation curls around my spine. Fuck, I never thought I would be doing something like this. Ever. But I'm so turned on right now that I can barely breathe.

Bending over, I place my palms on the smooth hardwood floor.

And then I crawl.

Desire burns in Jace's eyes as he watches me crawl towards him on my hands and knees. Releasing the edge of the table, he straightens and widens his stance. I crawl until I reach him. Then I stop, kneeling right before his feet.

Tilting my head back, I meet his commanding stare. Power rolls off his broad shoulders and pulses from his muscular body as he towers over me.

My heart is slamming against my ribs and my pussy is throbbing with need. If he doesn't start touching me soon, I'm going to shatter.

"Take off my belt," he orders.

I reach up and wrap my fingers around his leather belt. Satisfaction blows across his handsome features as I fumble while trying to quickly unbuckle it. Faint metallic clinking fills the air as I finally get it open. Then I pull on one side, sliding it out of the belt loops.

Once it's out, I get ready to place it on the floor. But Jace stops me with a single sentence.

"Offer it to me."

Surprise flits through me. I glance between the leather belt and his face. "What are you going to do with it?"

He only answers with a villainous smile that makes my heart skip a beat.

I shift my weight as the throbbing in my clit gets even more intense. The orders, the dominance pulsing from his entire being, the power difference between us right now, the sheer thrill of not knowing what he is going to do next, it has made me so high-strung and turned on that I can barely stop myself from squirming on the floor.

While pressing my thighs together, I hold up the belt with both hands, offering it to him.

A sly smile full of satisfaction curls his lips. "Good girl."

Pleasure streaks through me like lightning and a shudder racks my frame.

Jace closes his hand around the belt and lifts it from my palms. "Now, take out my cock."

My heart is thundering so hard in my chest that I can barely hear anything over the loud pounding. I shift my weight again, trying to relieve the ache between my legs.

Moving my hands to the front of his pants, I quickly undo the button and slide the zipper down. Then I push the fabric aside and slip my hand into his underwear.

A low moan escapes from both my throat and his as I close my hand around his cock. I free it from his underwear and draw my hand along the hard length.

Another moan and a shudder rip from him.

He slides the belt around my neck and then slips it through the buckle before pulling it tight. The leather is pressing against my skin where it encircles my throat. Jace winds the other end around his hand two times. My core throbs at the utter dominance in that move.

His eyes dance with wicked delight as he levels a commanding stare on me. "Do you want me to fuck you?"

"Yes," I gasp out, my whole body already thrumming with anticipation. I slide my hand up and down his cock again while a devilish smile spreads across my lips. "I want you to fuck me so hard that I forget my own name."

Sparks flicker in his eyes. But all he says is, "Yes, *what?*"

I narrow my eyes at him.

He holds my stare. Waiting. Daring me to disobey his final order.

"Yes, sir."

Satisfaction pulses across his face, and he smiles. Using the belt around my neck, he pulls me to my feet and presses his lips against mine.

"So. Fucking. Perfect," he murmurs against my lips between hard, possessive kisses.

While kissing him back with equal furious passion, I draw my hand up and down his cock again. He moans into my mouth. I laugh against his lips.

He answers by spinning me around so that I'm facing the table instead. In one terrifyingly smooth and efficient move, he bends me over the table, widens my stance, and tightens his grip on the belt still around my neck.

My heart is slamming so hard against my ribs that I swear I can hear it through the table. Lightning crackles through me as Jace's cock brushes over my ass when he steps up behind me. His free hand lands on my hip.

I press my forehead against the smooth tabletop as Jace traces the curve of my hip before slipping it down between my body and the edge of the table. A gasp rips from my lungs as he draws his fingers over my pussy.

"So wet already," he muses.

But I can hardly concentrate on his words because he rolls my already throbbing clit between his fingers with such precision that black spots dance before my eyes. I clench my hands into fists and moan into the table.

"Do you like it when I boss you around?" he demands.

Lights flicker in my brain, and I squirm against the table as he toys with my clit. Fuck, I can't even remember how my lungs are supposed to work. Am I even breathing?

He pulls on the belt, making me raise my head from the table and tilt it backwards. "Answer me."

"Yes," I manage to gasp.

"Yes, what?"

"Yes, sir."

"That's right."

He keeps me like that, bent over the table and my neck craned, while he continues playing with my clit until I'm whimpering. Pleasure thrums inside me like a storm.

But just before I can reach the edge of release, he abruptly pulls his hand back and instead gives my ass a firm slap.

I gasp. Both pleasure and pain flicker through me, driving my already high-strung body insane.

"Get up on your toes for me, little demon," Jace orders.

I comply, immediately rising up on my toes to give him better access. A moan spills from my lips as he draws his hard cock through my wetness. He does it again.

"Please," I beg.

The teasing is unbearable. Tension is still pulsing through my soul with no release. It feels as if I'm coming apart at the seams. I need him. I need him to fuck me already.

Another whimper slips out of me as he tortures me again. "Please, sir."

His free hand wraps around my hip.

Then he slams his cock into me.

I gasp at the feeling of him finally inside me. He winds the belt around his hand again, tightening my leash and forcing me to keep my back arched and my head tilted back like that. Then he slowly draws out. And then thrusts in again.

A moan tears from deep inside me at the incredible friction it creates.

I brace my palms on the smooth tabletop as Jace starts up a savage pace.

Pleasure shoots up my spine with every thrust of his hips.

My pussy throbs with need. When I'm bent over the table with his belt around my neck like this, all I can do is to once more just take whatever he gives me. And I've come to realize that I fucking love it. I love it when he dominates me. I love feeling his massive body pressing against mine and knowing that he can do whatever he wants to me. Because I know that Jace will never abuse the power that I'm giving him. He will only ever use it to make my body tremble with pleasure.

Tension builds inside me like a cresting wave as Jace slams into me hard enough to make the table grate against the floor. I suck in short, shallow breaths as electricity flickers through my veins with every thrust. The thrumming tension keeps mounting. I clench and unclench my hands as the insane friction brings me closer and closer to the edge. Light dances before my eyes. My body practically vibrates with tension.

His cock hits the perfect spot deep inside me.

Again.

And again.

Lightning flashes before my eyes, frying my brain and turning me into a moaning, whimpering mess. The pulsing tension inside me is so intense that I can barely see straight. I gasp air into my lungs as Jace slams into me.

"Come for me, little demon," he commands.

Release explodes through me.

A breathless cry rips from my lungs as pleasure shoots through my every vein. I throw out an arm and grip the edge of the table hard as the orgasm crashes through my body with enough force to make my legs shake. White light flashes before my eyes as Jace continues fucking me through the pulses of pleasure.

My inner walls flutter around his cock as he pounds into

me with such possessiveness and dominance that I feel as if my mind is floating in the clouds.

His cock pulses inside me and a desperate groan tears from his lungs as release crashes into him as well.

Bent over the table, my chest heaving and my heart slamming against my ribs, I try to remember how I, just a few months ago, could possibly have thought that my life was complete without this. Without him.

God, there is no one who makes me feel as complete as Jace Hunter. No one who makes me feel as strong and smart and beautiful. No one who challenges me as much as he does. No one who sees all of me, even the broken and weak sides, and still looks at me as if I'm the most perfect thing this universe has ever created.

When the last waves of the orgasm have faded, I don't feel exhausted. I don't feel spent. I feel like I'm bursting with fire.

Pushing up from the table, I turn to face the man who barreled his way into my life with his ridiculous jokes and unshakable confidence, and who has somehow managed to make me feel both safe and free at the same time, and for the first time in over a decade.

That cocky little smirk that I fucking love is playing over his lips as he looks down at me. His strong hands are gentle as he removes the belt from around my neck and drops it on the floor. I flash him a wicked grin.

"My turn," I say, and lock my hands around the back of his neck.

Jumping up, I wrap my legs around his waist. He knows exactly what to do, and immediately slides one arm underneath my ass and the other behind my back. I kiss him hard. Furiously. Possessively.

Mine. This incredible fucking man is mine.

I slide my hands up from his neck and draw my fingers through his soft curls. He moans into my mouth as he carries me away from the table. I bite his bottom lip before tangling my tongue with his again. He squeezes my ass and rolls his hips against me.

My back hits the living room wall with a thud.

Keeping my legs wrapped around his waist, I roll my hips right back against him until he's moaning into my mouth again. I grip his hair hard and kiss him deeply as I—

The front door bursts open.

I whip my head towards it.

Stunned blue eyes stare at us with a mix of shock and disbelief.

Horror crashes over me like a cold black wave.

"Kayla," my father blurts out.

His shocked gaze snaps from my naked body to Jace. To his bare chest. To his pants hanging halfway down his hips. To my legs around said hips. To his arm underneath my ass and the other one around my back. And to the very damning way that Jace is bracing my body against the wall in a position right above his cock.

Jace's mouth has dropped open in shock as he stares back at my father with equal disbelief.

Fury replaces the shock on my father's face.

Panic replaces the shock on Jace's features.

And dread replaces the shock clanging through my own soul.

"Jace Hunter," my father growls. "I hired you to protect my daughter. And instead, you… you…" His face is red and his voice is shaking with anger as he stares at Jace as if he wants to murder him. "I'm going to fucking kill you."

Then he lunges for a kitchen knife.

38

JACE

He didn't kill me. But I wish he had. Because now, I have not only lost my only chance to choose my own future, I have also lost Kayla.

By the time I had managed to put Kayla down, pull my pants back up, and secure the knife that Trent Ashford tried to bury in my heart, his bodyguards had shown up and leveled two guns at me. I wasn't shot. But I was fired and escorted out of the building.

I tried to call and text Kayla afterwards, but she never replied. Probably because she is dealing with the fallout from this whole mess. Or maybe she hates me now. Because what I do know is that Kayla now has a new bodyguard who has been given orders to shoot me on sight if I ever come within six feet of her.

The small scrap of freedom she managed to carve out is now gone.

And so is mine. In fact, Dad almost killed me for messing up his business relationship with Trent Ashford.

So now I'm back at Blackwater University. With no freedom. No Kayla. And no one to blame but myself.

I slam my fist into my opponent's stomach.

He crumples to the ground.

I know that the basement around me is full of people, full of guys who usually show up for our underground fight club, but I can't see them. Can't hear them. All I can hear is the sound of my mind cracking and all I can see is Kayla's panicked face as I was marched out the door at gunpoint.

Dropping down, I straddle my opponent and raise my fist. Then I slam it into the side of his jaw.

Fuck. Fuck. Fuck. Why did Trent Ashford have to pick that fucking day to visit? And why were we so fucking careless? We could've waited until the semester was over. Then I could've quit my job as her bodyguard and then we could've started dating. I could've had both Kayla and my future.

But now I have neither.

I have nothing.

Without her, everything is meaningless anyway.

I slam my fist down. Again. And again.

"I yield. Please, Hunter. I yield. Hunter. Please. I'm begging you."

It takes another few seconds for the words to register. For me to realize where they're coming from. *Who* they're coming from.

My head is whirling like a tornado.

I blink repeatedly before my eyes fix on the guy lying underneath me.

Blood trickles down from his nose and lip. Panic and fear flash in his eyes. One hand is raised, palm up, in a show of surrender. The other is frantically tapping the floor beside his body. Tapping.

I stare at that hand.

Tapping.

Tapping *out*.

Oh fuck. How long has he been trying to surrender? I didn't even hear him.

I can't hear fucking anything over the roaring in my own head.

Scrambling off him, I stagger to my feet.

My opponent crawls backwards until he can rest his back against the concrete wall behind him. Tilting his head back, he tries to stop the blood from dripping down his chin.

Chaos and restlessness rip through my soul.

I need another fight. Turning with jerky movements, I search for the guy who was going to fight me next. My eyes lock with his.

Fear flashes across his face.

In a heartbeat, he drops to his knees and taps his hand against the floor. Submitting before the fight has even begun.

Rage sears through me. I need a fight. I need to do something to expel this storm I'm currently drowning in.

My gaze sweeps across the rest of the crowd.

Every single person in the room drops to his knees and taps his hand against the floor in submission.

A snarl rips from my lungs.

They all surrendered before a fight could even begin.

I hate them for it because I need a fight so fucking badly that I can barely breathe anymore. Can barely think. Can barely see.

But I also understand them. This isn't the first time I've spiraled like this, and the other times didn't end very well for the people who were brave and stupid enough to agree to fight me.

When Kaden was here, he always deliberately provoked fights with me so that I could get the anger and restlessness out of my system before things got too bad. But Kaden and Eli and Rico have all graduated now. So this year, there has been no one to stop me from spinning out of control.

I've spiraled into these mad episodes a couple of times before, and everyone in this fight club has learned to recognize the signs. They know when they can fight me safely and when they should bow out before it even begins because all of the safeguards in my brain have already been fried.

And I fucking hate them all for it. But I can't blame them.

So I spin on my heel and stalk towards the stairs.

There is a half empty bottle of whiskey on a low table by the wall. I think I brought it, but I can't remember. I snatch it up anyway as I storm up the steps.

Shoving the door open, I emerge on a dark lawn.

Winds whirl around me, pulling at my hair as I start back towards my house.

I lift the bottle to my lips and drink deeply.

Then I glance down and notice that I'm not wearing a shirt. Was I wearing one when I left the house? I can't remember. And it doesn't matter.

Nothing fucking matters anymore.

Kayla is gone. My future is gone. Everything is gone.

Pain stabs through my heart. It's so intense that I stumble a step to the side and have to brace myself on someone's fence. Squeezing my hand into a fist, I press it hard over my heart in an attempt to stop the ache.

It doesn't work.

I suck in a shuddering breath and then drink deeply from the bottle again.

Pushing off from the fence, I start towards my house once more.

My entire body feels empty. Hollow. Like there is nothing inside of me except the pain echoing in the void.

What's the fucking point of anything?

I fucked everything up.

I ruined Kayla's shot at freedom and got her stuck with another damn man who is going to be looming over her shoulder and watching her every move in a way that makes her hate her own life. I ruined my own shot at freedom by proving to my dad that apparently I can't be trusted to be professional and responsible. I strained Kayla's relationship with her parents. I strained my relationship with my own parents. And I doomed mine and Kayla's relationship before we could even get it off the ground.

There was a right way to go about this. And what we did wasn't it.

Raking my fingers through my hair, I take another swig from the bottle as I stagger up the driveway to my house.

It has been three days and I haven't even worked up the fucking courage to tell my brothers about this. If they don't already think that I'm nothing but a fucking screw-up, they're going to think so now.

The front door thuds as I slam it shut behind me. I don't bother locking it. If someone wants to break in and attack me, let them. I don't fucking care. I even wish they would.

In fact, I desperately want to go over to the Petrov house and provoke Anton and his twin cousins into a fight. They still dislike me enough that they would do it.

But Alina would be angry if I hurt her brother and cousins. And if I made Alina upset, Kaden would skin me alive.

I wouldn't actually mind if he did that, though. But what I

wouldn't be able to handle is the disappointment that I would see in his eyes. I could survive his fury. But I couldn't survive his disappointment.

The couch creaks in alarm as I slump down on it. I raise the bottle again and drink deeply.

Part of me wants to stalk right into Trent Ashford's office, put a gun to his head, and tell him that Kayla is mine regardless of what he thinks of our relationship.

But I can't do that to Kayla. I can't make her choose between me and her father. I don't want her to have to choose. She has already lost too much.

So I would rather self-destruct than be the reason that she loses even more of her family.

Resting the back of my head against the couch's backrest, I stare up into the ceiling. The house is dark and silent around me. So at odds with the roaring chaos in my own mind.

I want to beat someone unconscious. I want to throw this bottle across the room just to hear the glass shatter. I want to set the house on fire. I want to do something that will relieve the oppressive restlessness that is threatening to shred me to pieces from the inside.

But I can't.

So I do the only thing that I can to numb the pain inside me.

I sit there on the couch. And I drink.

39

KAYLA

When I heard that Jace lives at a campus for hitmen, this was not at all what I was expecting.

I stare at the rows of beautiful houses complete with small yards that line the road. There were a bunch of larger buildings closer to the entrance and the middle of the area that looked like apartments, but in here, it's all freestanding houses.

Checking the text I received on my brand-new phone, I make sure that I have the right house before I walk up to the door. It really would be such a shame if I ended up getting shot in the face just because I rang the wrong doorbell.

The house before me is stunning. It's elegant and made of dark wood, and there is a yard that wraps around the house. A black Range Rover is parked on the street outside, which should hopefully mean that Jace is here. It's also nine o'clock on a Saturday morning, so he won't be in class at least.

Stopping just outside the door, I raise my hand and ring the doorbell.

Nothing happens.

I frown at the door.

Maybe the doorbell isn't working?

Raising my hand again, I decide to knock instead.

No answer.

A scowl pulls at my brows.

I knock several more times.

Still no answer.

Heaving an annoyed sigh, I try to simply shove the handle down and pull the door open instead.

To my utter surprise, it works.

For a few seconds, I just stare at the now open door in confusion. The guy lives at a university for assassins, and he leaves the front door unlocked? What the fuck is he thinking?

Shaking my head at his carelessness, I walk across the threshold and into the hallway beyond.

The inside of the house is as beautiful as the outside. Floor and walls made of smooth dark wood, an elegantly curving staircase at the end of the hall, and ornate lamps in the ceiling. It looks like something straight out of my world. The world of the obscenely wealthy.

Or it would have, if it wasn't so fucking messy.

I step over a bat that is lying on the floor in the middle of the hallway. Making my way farther in, I glance into a room on my right. It turns out to be a study, which is surprisingly neat and clean. But there is no sign of Jace, so I move on to the doorway on the left instead.

Shock pulses through me as I step into a combined kitchen and living room.

The walls and floor in here are also made of dark wood, there is a grand dining room table in the middle of the room, a kitchen island and stainless-steel appliances in the kitchen side on my right, and a cream-colored couch in front of a large TV on the other side of the room. It would be a beautiful space if, *again*, it wasn't so fucking messy.

Empty glasses and whiskey bottles litter the kitchen island. There is also a bat there. And another one on the floor next to the table.

I sweep my gaze over the room in disbelief.

Then my gaze snags on the couch.

A mop of messy brown hair is spilling out over the backrest.

I move towards it. While passing the bat on the floor, I bend down and pick it up. Just in case.

But when I reach the couch and walk around it, my suspicions are confirmed and I do indeed find Jace there. The sight of him still shocks me, though. Not because it's him, but because of how he looks.

There are dark circles under his eyes, and he is scowling even though he is clearly asleep. His knuckles are bloody, he is shirtless, and there is blood splattered across his bare chest as well. An empty bottle of whiskey sits on the low coffee table in front of him, but no glass.

He looks… broken.

Pain spears through my heart at the thought. It's so intense that I almost lose the grip on the bat.

But then it's immediately followed by a flash of anger.

No. He does not get to self-destruct like this just because we had a setback. Yes, things went to hell. And yes, with hindsight, we should've done things differently. But it's nothing we can't fix.

Stepping up next to him, I poke him with the bat.

His eyes snap open and he shoots up from the couch.

My stomach lurches as he spins me around, yanks the bat

out of my hand, and slams me up against the wall. A huff rips from my lungs at the impact, and I blink repeatedly.

Jace is standing right in front of me, one hand buried in my collar and the other gripping the bat.

For a few seconds, his eyes are wild and unfocused, as if he still hasn't figured out what happened or where he is or who I am.

Then he blinks.

Blinks again.

Realization slams into his face like a shovel.

Jerking back in shock, he releases my shirt and stumbles a step back. The bat slips from his hand and clatters to the floor.

"Kayla," he blurts out, his wide eyes still staring at me as if he can't believe that I'm actually here.

I cough air back into my lungs and then smoothen down my shirt. "Yeah, I really should've seen that coming after the air horn episode. Surprising you when you're sleeping really is a terrible idea."

Jace is still gaping at me. "You're here."

I arch an eyebrow. "Very observant of you."

"You're here," he just repeats, sounding absolutely dumbfounded. "How…? Why…?"

Ignoring his questions, I nod towards the empty whiskey bottle on the table. "Did you drink all of that last night?"

He glances at the bottle before meeting my gaze again, still looking bewildered. "Uhm, yeah. I think so."

"Where is your shirt?"

"I'm not sure."

"Is that blood?"

His gaze drops down to his bare chest and the blood

splattered there. Then he meets my gaze and shrugs. "It's not mine."

I roll my eyes. "It's cute how you think that's supposed to be comforting."

At long last, a hint of light returns to his eyes. The sight of it makes my heart jerk. A grin ghosts across his lips for a second, and he rakes his hand through his messy hair.

Keeping the stern look on my face, I stride over to the sink and grab a glass from the cabinet next to it. After filling it with water, I walk back to Jace and shove it into his hand. He blinks at me, confused.

"Drink that," I order. "Then go and take a shower."

His eyebrows shoot up.

I raise mine too as I demand, "Did I stutter?"

Now, he's properly grinning. The sight lifts the weight that had been pressing down on my chest.

Raising the glass to his lips, he drinks it all in a few long gulps.

"Good," I say as I take the empty glass from him. Then I stab a hand towards the doorway. "Now, go shower."

His eyes glitter as he chuckles. Then a sly smile pulls at his lips and he rakes a deliberate glance over my body. "Have I told you how fucking hot you are when you're bossy?"

My spine tingles and I can barely manage to suppress a grin of my own. But I keep my hand pointed towards the door and simply say, "Shower."

With that smile still on his lips, he raises two fingers to his brow in a mock salute. "Yes, ma'am."

I laugh softly as he strolls out the door.

While he showers somewhere upstairs, I walk around the living room and kitchen, idly studying it. When I'm done with that, I move on to the room across the hall. It's the study that is neater and cleaner than the rest of the rooms downstairs. I drift along the shelves, looking at the titles on the spines.

"Find anything interesting?" Jace suddenly asks from behind me.

"Not really," I answer as I begin to turn around. "But I haven't…" I trail off as my gaze lands on Jace.

His brown curls are still damp from the shower, and they have been swept back from his face in the hottest fucking way I have ever seen. And to top it all off, he's only wearing a pair of sweatpants.

I stare at his sculpted body. At the lone drop of water that runs down from his hair, over his neck, and then down his bare chest. At the absolutely sinful V that disappears down into his pants.

Heat pulses through me.

"Ah," Jace says, sounding entirely too pleased with himself. "I see that you've finally found something interesting."

With great effort, I tear my gaze from his body and snap it back up to his face. Then I arch a pointed brow in silent question.

He just shrugs casually as he saunters towards me. "You only told me to shower. You didn't specify that I had to put on a shirt afterwards."

His eyes glint as he closes the distance between us until he is standing so close that my back is pressed against the bookshelves behind me. He trails two fingers up my throat before placing them underneath my chin, tilting my head back so that I meet his gaze. Lightning skitters across my skin at his touch.

"And now that you're properly distracted," he begins, a wicked smile on his face. "I can finally trick you into answering my questions. Namely, how are you here? Where is your new bodyguard?"

A matching grin spreads across my own mouth as I give him a knowing look. "Oh, he's probably still waiting for me to come out of a café restroom."

Jace raises his eyebrows in surprise.

I chuckle. "Oh, I've pulled that same trick on at least half a dozen bodyguards before you." I narrow my eyes at him. "Though no one else has been as annoyingly perceptive as you."

I can practically see Jace's ego inflate. But before I can poke a hole it in again, a serious expression blows across his features, and he studies me with intense eyes.

"But I thought..." he begins and then trails off before finishing with, "when you didn't answer my calls or texts."

Slipping a hand into my pocket, I pull out the brand-new phone that I had to get after Dad confiscated my old one. Jace glances at the phone, and understanding floods his face without me even having to say it.

"Oh," he says.

"Yeah." I slide my phone back into my pocket. "And I couldn't exactly find your phone number again by just searching for it on Google. Since you're... well, *you*."

He grimaces. "I was worried that you blamed me for screwing things up for you and getting you stuck with another overbearing bodyguard."

"Why would I blame *you* for that? I'm the one who suggested that we should start dating even though you were still working for my father." I roll my eyes at his silliness, and slap his chest with the back of my hand. "Moron."

A relieved laugh escapes his lips. Then that seriousness returns, and he searches my face again. "So, where do we go from here? You're still stuck with a new bodyguard who will shoot me on sight."

"Yeah, Dad is... kind of pissed."

"Kind of?"

"Okay, very pissed. But that's probably because he actually saw us naked like that. If he'd just heard about it, he wouldn't be nearly this furious."

"Thank hell he didn't walk in when I had you bent over that table then." His eyes gleam with mischief. "Or when you were crawling up to me naked."

Mortification crashes over me at just the thought of my dad seeing that. "Oh God. I think I would've shot myself if he had seen that." Shaking my head, I shove that horrifying thought aside. "Anyway, yes, he's angry right now. But it will pass. And then we can start dating publicly again."

"And until then?"

"Until then, we'll have to keep our distance. We can talk on the phone, but I can't sneak off to see you. It will only work against us."

He heaves a deep sigh and rests his forehead against mine. "Fuck."

"Are you..." I begin. My heart is suddenly slamming in my chest, and I flex my hand nervously. "Are you okay with that? I mean, I remember that you told me that you're usually pretty... uhm, active."

Jace frowns down at me, confusion evident on his face.

"So, we don't have to be exclusive during that time if you don't want to—"

"What?" he blurts out as realization suddenly crashes over his features. "Of course we're exclusive. I would rather cut off my own cock than touch someone else."

My heart swells, and I'm momentarily lost for words. "Oh."

"And you, little demon," he continues. His fingers brush lightly over my throat. "You're of course allowed to touch someone else if you want to. But just know that if you do, I will hunt him down and kill him. Very slowly. And very, very, painfully."

A dark thrill ripples through my soul, and a devilish smile spreads across my lips as I hold his gaze. "Good. Then we're on the same page."

"Indeed we are. So—"

His words are cut off by a low moan as I trace my fingers along his bare skin right above his pants. A shudder rolls through his powerful frame. I slip my hand inside his pants and wrap my fingers around his cock.

A strangled noise comes from Jace's throat, and he throws out an arm to brace himself against the bookshelves behind me, as I tighten my grip and draw my hand up and down his shaft. It hardens immediately.

"So I suppose we're just going to have to make the most of our time today then," I say, moving my hand again.

Jace curls his fingers into a fist against the bookshelf and draws in a steadying breath through his nose. "We should—"

The front door is yanked open.

"Wake up, Golden," a now familiar voice yells from the hallway outside the study. "And get your ass downstairs before I beat you up for wasting my time."

Jace starts in surprise and tries to turn towards the door. But I keep my hand around his cock, stopping him from moving more than his head.

The front door is slammed shut again. Then three pairs of footsteps sound from the corridor, coming closer to us. I remain exactly where I am as I slide my hand up and down

Jace's cock again. His gaze darts to me. But before he can say anything, three men appear in the doorway.

Eli, Kaden, and Rico.

"Oh, you're up," Rico says, his words a lot less threatening than Eli's were. "Great."

I draw my hand along Jace's cock again.

A shudder ripples through his body, and he bites his cheek to stop a moan. After a warning glance at me, he twists his head to look at his brothers.

"Yeah, uhm," he manages to press out. "A little busy at the moment."

I shift my hand up and down again, and a whimper almost slips past his lips.

They all frown. From that angle, they can't see me behind his huge body, so they have no idea that I'm jerking him off.

"Can you just..." Jace croaks, his hand clenching and unclenching on the bookshelf. "Wait in the living room for a minute?"

He sucks in a deep breath as if to steady himself. Right when it looks like he has almost composed himself, I tease his tip with my thumb.

His knees nearly give out.

"Please," he gasps out. And I'm not sure if he's talking to his brothers or me.

Kaden snickers, but Rico says, "Sure."

They all start to turn.

"Oh and, Kayla?" Eli suddenly says.

My heart leaps into my throat. Could they actually see me?

Leaning my head out from behind Jace's body, I meet the amused stares of his brothers.

"Driving Jace insane like that while he's trying to act

normal?" Eli says. Wicked delight glitters in his golden eyes as he flashes me a grin. "We approve."

All three of them chuckle. Rico even winks at me.

Warmth spreads through my soul.

And just like that, I feel like I'm a part of the family.

40

JACE

"The sheer amount of wicked, depraved revenge I'm going to inflict on you for that is going to be fucking biblical," I threaten Kayla as the two of us at last walk into the combined kitchen and living room to join my three infuriating brothers.

Kayla just laughs and then wiggles her eyebrows at me, challenge dancing in her bright blue eyes.

Huffing out a breath of grudging amusement, I shake my head at her. Little demon, indeed.

"That was fast," Eli comments as we enter the room.

They're all standing around the kitchen island. Eli is leaning over it, eating the leftover pasta I put in the fridge yesterday, while Rico is scowling at the mess of empty bottles and glasses that litter the surface. Kaden just watches me while he casually spins a knife in his hand.

"Yeah," Kaden picks up, his dark eyes glinting as he holds my gaze while speaking to Eli. "But isn't he kind of famous for always blowing his load too quickly, though?"

Kayla chokes on a laugh. I shoot her a sharp look before

shifting my glare to my brothers. As we reach the kitchen island, I also snatch up the bat waiting there and level it at them.

"I will crack your skulls," I warn.

Kaden snickers. Next to him, Rico rolls his eyes while Eli snorts. The bastard also continues eating my food.

"I was saving that," I tell him.

Eli just keeps eating. "That right?" Then he looks up and meets my gaze, golden eyes glinting with sly amusement. "Guess you should've been faster."

"I am not a quick draw, you motherfucker," I growl. "I will have you know that I am excellent at foreplay and—"

"No one wants to hear about your sex life, Golden," Rico interrupts.

"Unless it's to tell us that Kayla is making you wear a French maid costume," Kaden adds, a smirk on his face. His eyes are full of dark delight as he slides his gaze to Kayla. "Then I want to hear all about it."

I point the bat in his direction. "*You* are the one who is wearing the French maid costume, you whipped little—"

"Why do you call him that?" Kayla suddenly asks, interrupting our bickering.

We all turn to face her. There is genuine curiosity on her face as she looks at the four of us.

"Golden," she clarifies. "Why do you call him *Golden*?"

"Don't—" I begin, but my bastard of a brother cuts me off.

"Because he has the attention span of a golden retriever puppy," Eli says.

Narrowing my eyes, I glare at him.

Kayla bursts out laughing. Doubling over, she wraps her arms around her stomach and laughs so hard that tears line her eyes.

"Oh my God," she gasps out between fits of laughter. Bracing herself on the edge of the island, she straightens and wipes away tears of laughter before looking between me and my brothers. Her entire face is full of sparkling joy. "You're right! He really is just like a golden retriever puppy."

All three of my brothers chuckle. I shoot them death glares before leveling a threatening stare on Kayla.

"You, little demon, are already utterly fucked after what you pulled in the study," I remind her. "Are you sure you want to keep digging your own grave deeper?"

Her answering smile is full of brilliant challenge. Then she slides her gaze to my brothers. "When we first met, I called him *Sparky* for that same reason to piss him off."

Rico chokes back a laugh, and Kaden grins in a way that means he's going to remind me of this for all eternity.

Raking a hand through my hair, I heave an exasperated sigh and shake my head at them all. But just when I think I'm about to beat my dear brothers unconscious with my bat, Kaden speaks up again.

"He's practically never had an attention span longer than five seconds," he says, his dark eyes serious as he holds Kayla's gaze. "So the fact that he has kept such unwavering attention on you, and for so long, really is saying something."

Kayla's mouth drops open, and emotions pulse across her beautiful face. She turns to me.

But before she can say anything, Rico straightens in a flash and snaps, "Incoming."

We all whip around to stare out the window.

A car screeches to a halt on the road outside. Then an angry-looking man in his fifties jumps out and storms towards our front door.

Kayla groans. "Ah, fuck. That's my new bodyguard."

"Want me to bash his head in?" I ask.

She starts to laugh, but then realizes that I'm serious. While suppressing an amused smile, she shakes her head. "Uhm, no. It's probably best if I just leave."

Angry pounding comes from the door. Then the handle rattles as well, which means that one of my brothers must have locked the door behind them when they got here. Probably Rico.

"I'll, uhm..." Kayla begins as she turns to my brothers and gives them a smile that is somehow both apologetic and grateful. "I'll see you around."

They all nod.

Spinning the bat around, I rest it on my shoulder as I start towards the door with Kayla beside me. It's far too soon to let her go. In fact, if I had a choice in the matter, I would never let her go at all. But I don't want to mess up her relationship with her parents, so I suppress the urge to murder the man currently pounding on my door.

"We'll figure this out," Kayla says, brushing the back of her hand against mine.

That small touch sends a bolt of electricity up my spine. I flex my other hand on the bat in order to stop myself from grabbing her and keeping her here with me forever.

Forcing out a long breath, I manage to reply, "Yeah."

And then we're at the door. After unlocking it, I deliberately shove it open much harder than necessary. It forces the man outside to leap back to avoid getting hit by it. With the bat still on my bare shoulder, I glare out at the now flustered-looking bodyguard.

"Ms. Ashford," he says, his eyes locked on her. "You cannot simply..." Then he trails off as his gaze darts up to me.

I'm shirtless and very obviously closer to Kayla than six feet.

Alarm flashes in his eyes. Then hesitation. Then he seems to make a decision, because he clenches his jaw and pulls out a gun from inside his suit jacket.

He has only just managed to raise the gun and point it at me when fear crashes over his features instead.

Shoving the gun back into his jacket, he holds up his hands in a panicked show of surrender.

Twisting slightly, I glance over my shoulder to find my brothers standing in the hallway behind us. Both Eli and Rico are holding a gun, their weapons aimed straight at the bodyguard's forehead. Kaden stands between them, spinning a knife in his hand while a true psychopath smile curves his lips.

My heart squeezes tight.

But I turn back to the bodyguard.

"Yeah, you should probably pretend that this never happened," Kayla says to him while lifting her shoulders in a nonchalant shrug.

"Ms. Ashford," he replies, his voice stern. But then his gaze drifts to the bat in my hand, and he seems to change his mind about what he had been about to say. "We should leave. Now."

Kayla scoffs and then simply turns towards me. Wrapping a hand around my jaw, she yanks my face down to hers and kisses me so possessively that I think my heart stops beating for a second.

Then she releases me and takes a step back, across the threshold and out the door.

Behind her shoulder, the bodyguard is staring daggers at me.

Kayla just flashes me a grin, winks, and then saunters away.

My heart slams against my ribs as I stare after her.

Fuck, I think I love this girl.

No, I don't *think* I love her. I love her. I love Kayla Ashford so fucking much that I would burn the world down for her.

Standing there, I watch the love of my fucking life disappear as the ill-tempered bodyguard drives her away.

It takes me another few seconds to compose myself after that. Dragging in a deep breath, I rake a hand through my hair and remind myself that she's not gone. That this is just temporary.

Then I at last close the door.

When I turn around, my brothers are no longer standing there. Instead, I can hear faint clinking sounds from inside the kitchen. I walk towards it.

Someone has cleared all the empty bottles and glasses from the countertops. I approach the kitchen island that Eli, Kaden, and Rico are once more standing around. Kaden slides a glass of water towards me. It stops right before the edge. I pick it up and drink half of it in one go before setting it down again.

Then panic slams into me. I jerk upright and whip my head towards where Kayla is already gone. "Fuck! I forgot to get her new phone number."

"Calm down," Kaden says. "I already have it."

Spinning back around, I stare at him with raised eyebrows. "Why do *you* have her phone number?"

He holds my gaze, a knowing look in his dark eyes, and raises an eyebrow at me. "Who do you think told her where you live?"

It takes a few seconds for his words to register. Then understanding trickles through me. I blink, stunned. "Oh."

For a while, no one says anything.

"Why didn't you tell us?" Rico eventually asks into the suddenly pressing silence.

There is no accusation in his tone. Instead, he sounds almost a little… hurt.

It makes pain and guilt worm their way through my chest.

Setting the bat down, I drag a hand through my hair and lift one shoulder in a self-conscious shrug. "I don't know."

"Bullshit," Eli says.

I snap my gaze up to his face.

Anger flickers in his eyes, and the scar down his brow tightens as he scowls at me. "You got fired, Dad threatened to kill you and sent you back to Blackwater, and you didn't even tell us. We had to find out from *him*."

"I just—"

"And you've spent the past five years spiraling out of control because you don't want to be a hitman, and you didn't tell us that either."

"That had nothing to do with you," I try to protest.

"Shut up," he snaps. Lightning now flashes in his eyes that are always lined with a hint of insanity. "Do you even realize how much of *our* shit you've had to deal with over the years? And during all that time, you've apparently been carrying around your own shit by yourself. For years. Without telling us." His eyes are full of command as he stares me down. "Why?"

"It doesn't matter."

He slams his hand down on the counter hard enough to make my glass jump. "Just fucking talk to us!"

"Because you're all always so perfect!" The words rip out of my soul with the force of a gunshot.

All three of my brothers jerk back in surprise and blink at me.

My chest is suddenly heaving. Raking my fingers through my hair yet again, I force oxygen into my lungs. Then I have to force myself to let my hands drop back down. I clench my fingers into fists.

"You're exactly the sons that Dad wanted," I say, holding their stunned stares. "The legacy that Dad wanted. And I… I didn't even know if I wanted to be a hitman. So I started self-destructing. With the fights and the alcohol and the sex. Anything to take my mind off it. Which just made him even more disappointed in me. Made him see me even more as a failure. And you…" I slash my hand through the air, motioning at all of them. Desperation leaks into my voice. "I didn't want you to see me as a weak pathetic failure too."

The silence that descends on the kitchen is so loud that I can hear it ringing in my ears.

Outside the windows, the sun has crested the rows of buildings along the street. Pale morning light filters into the room, creating patterns on the dark wooden walls.

My brothers just stare at me for another three heartbeats.

Then Eli shatters the silence like a smashed mirror. "You fucking moron."

Embarrassment crashes through me, and I start to turn away. His hand shoots out. Grabbing me by the arm, he turns me back towards them.

"I'm serious," he says, anger and disbelief pulsing from every word. "How the fuck do you not know?"

All I can do is to just hold his stare. Waiting for whatever cutting remark is about to pass his lips.

His eyes are dead serious as he stares me down. "We've never considered you a failure."

"And we sure as hell have never thought you were weak," Rico adds.

I draw back, stunned, and glance between the three of them. Eli finally releases my arm and instead rakes both hands through his hair and shakes his head as if he can't believe my stupidity. And Kaden has even stopped spinning his knife. It's now back in its sheath as he holds my gaze from the other side of the island.

"Why do you think we give you so much shit all the time?" Kaden asks, his eyes boring into mine.

"Because I'm your annoying little brother who is always too loud and too careless and too restless and too much of a fucking screw-up?" I reply.

"Because you're the best of us," Kaden says, his voice dead serious.

"You always have been," Eli adds.

Rico lets out a soft chuckle. "We're all fifty shades of fucked up. But you've somehow still managed to remain exactly who you are. A fucking ball of sunshine who carries the rest of us. After what happened with my parents, you, with your easy smiles and your insane ability to make the world feel lighter, were sometimes the only thing that kept me breathing. That kept me from being crushed underneath the weight of it all."

My throat starts to close up, and I swallow, not sure what to say.

Rico gives me a small smile. "It's the real reason we started calling you *Golden*."

My heart suddenly feels like it's both bursting and squeezing hard at the same time. I drag in an unsteady breath.

trying yet again to swallow against the thickness in my throat.

"You've always had our backs," Eli says, his gaze steady on mine. "And we have yours. Against *everyone*."

Kaden gives me a faint smile that almost seems a little sad. "All you had to do was say the word."

Before I can make my brain work properly, Eli pulls up his phone and abruptly hits dial. The sound of the line ringing fills the silent room as he puts the call on speaker before placing the phone on the kitchen island between the four of us.

After three signals, someone answers.

"Eli, is something wrong?"

My heart jerks in my chest as I recognize the voice. Jonathan Hunter. Our father.

"Yeah, something's wrong," Eli replies.

"Tell me."

"Jace's future."

I snap my gaze up from the phone and stare at Eli. He just holds my gaze while waiting for our dad to respond.

A deep sigh comes from the other end of the line. "Jace will finish his studies at Blackwater."

"No, Jace will get to choose if he wants to finish or not," Rico says, his voice full of calm authority.

"Rico?" Dad says, sounding confused. "Look, this isn't—"

"Or we will disown you," Kaden finishes.

I jerk back, my eyes wide as I stare at the three of them. No one threatens Jonathan Hunter. No one.

Kaden just flashes me one of his psychopath smiles, as if silently saying, *I can do whatever the fuck I want.*

"You cannot disown me," Dad sputters. "I am your father."

"Yeah, we can, actually," Eli says casually.

"Jace gets to choose his own future, or you lose four sons today," Kaden warns.

Furious silence echoes on the other end of the line.

"What's it gonna be?" Rico demands.

"You do not threaten me," Dad growls, anger dripping from every word. "Jace stays at Blackwater."

Defiance and steel resolve pulse through my soul. Straightening my spine, I raise my chin and level a hard stare down at the phone.

My brothers are right. I'm done letting him dictate what I can and can't do. He is just a man like the rest of us. And any man can be threatened. You just need to figure out what the right leverage is. Luckily for me, I know exactly what will make our unbendable father fold like a pretzel.

With a vicious smile on my lips, I say, "How do you think Mom is going to react when you tell her that she will never see any of her kids again?"

Kaden, Eli, and Rico all look up at me in surprise. Then a smirk spreads across Kaden's lips while Rico gives me a slow nod.

Eli flashes me a grin of approval and silently mouths, "*Nice.*"

The silence on the other end of the line is deafening.

Then Dad curses.

All four of us grin like devils at each other.

"Fuck," Dad says, and lets out a low whistle under his breath. "You really are my sons, aren't you?" He heaves a defeated sigh. "Fine. Jace gets to choose."

Then he hangs up before we can gloat.

I stare down at the phone for a few seconds while those words echo through my mind.

I get to choose. My freedom is back. My future is back. Now, all I need is Kayla, and everything will be perfect.

Swallowing thickly, I look up and meet my brothers' eyes. "Thank you."

The words come out sounding more choked than I had hoped for, but they don't comment on it.

Instead, Kaden simply smirks at me and starts twirling his knife in his hand again.

"Anything for you, Golden," Rico says with a wink.

"But now, you *really* owe us dinner," Eli adds, his eyes gleaming as he grins at me.

I laugh.

And finally feel that decade-long restlessness fade from my soul.

41

KAYLA

The coffeeshop is bustling with activity when I walk in. Chatter and laughter mix with the whirring and hissing from the fancy coffee machines behind the counter. I scan the pale wooden tables until I find the people that I'm looking for.

Jenn is sitting next to Felicia, one of the girls that we met at that party all those weeks ago, and they look to be engrossed in a deep discussion about something. Across the table, Aurora is laughing at something that Mitch said. Ever since they met during that drinking game we played, they've been casually flirting whenever they see each other. Aurora hasn't said anything, but I think they might be on the verge of dating. Lionel is sitting in the chair next to Mitch, looking thoughtful as he stares unseeing at the table while he absentmindedly uses his straw to stir his iced coffee.

I stride up to them and pull out the chair opposite Lionel. They all turn towards me.

Aurora's beautiful face lights up with a bright smile. "Kayla! You came."

"Of course I did," I reply, smiling back at her.

She winces apologetically. "It's just… after what happened with Jace and your dad and all that, I wasn't sure if… Well, if your freedom of movement had been impacted."

"I'm an adult. He can't exactly ground me anymore." I chuckle and give her a knowing look. "Not that he didn't try."

"Well, I never doubted you for a second," Jenn says as she slides an iced coffee towards me.

Taking the drink she must have ordered for me when they arrived, I give her a grateful smile and a nod. Since I showed up to school with a different bodyguard this week, I had to tell them what happened with Jace. At least the short version of it. They understood. Normal twenty-year-olds don't have to worry about their parents' approval or opinions, but for people like us, who are so intricately connected to our family businesses, it's a little different. It's one of the few downsides of being a rich heiress.

"Yeah, uhm, speaking of…" Lionel suddenly says. He leans to the left and then the right, scanning the space behind me, before his surprised gray eyes meet mine again. "Where *is* your new bodyguard?"

A villainous grin spreads across my mouth. Leaning back in my chair, I cross my ankles and flick my hair behind my shoulder. "Probably still sitting on the couch in my apartment, guarding me while I'm taking a nap."

He jerks back and blinks in surprise. Aurora laughs loudly enough to startle Mitch, who then glances between me and her since he's not really all that familiar with my situation.

I smirk and take a sip from my iced coffee. "It's really not that difficult when you've been doing it your whole life."

At least not unless it's Jace keeping watch.

Pain stabs through my heart.

God, I miss Jace.

Aurora laughs again. Jenn shoots her a look that seems to say, *I told you so*. Felicia just shakes her head in confusion.

Then Aurora goes back to flirting with Mitch and Jenn resumes her discussion with Felicia. It sounds like they're talking about a fantasy series. Or maybe an anime. But I can't really focus on what they're saying because my mind keeps drifting back to Jace.

While taking another sip of coffee, I discreetly glance at Lionel. Since we're sitting opposite each other, I thought he was going to start up a conversation the way he usually does. But thankfully, he seems to read my mood and instead simply pulls up his phone and focuses on that as he types something.

Relief flickers through me, because I'm suddenly not in the mood to talk to anyone.

I miss Jace.

It's ridiculous, I know that. I'm not a kid. I don't need anyone. I'm stubborn and independent and I can take care of myself. But I still miss him.

And I didn't realize just how much I've come to love having him in my life until he's suddenly gone from it.

I love his stupid jokes and his swaggering confidence. I love his silly lectures about how breakfast is the most important meal of the day. I love the food that he makes for me. I love his brilliant smile and his glittering brown eyes, so full of life and energy and mischief. I love how he always makes my life feel easier. Lighter. Even during the dark moments. I love how he never backs down. I love that he is never intimidated by me. By my wealth or my power or status. I love that he sees me. That he gets me. I love—

Stunned realization pulses through me, and I sit back in my chair. Blinking, I stare at the brick wall on the other side of the coffeeshop while that sudden realization finishes echoing through me.

I don't just like Jace. He's not just someone that I plan to date and see how it goes. I already know how it will go. Because I can't imagine my life without him in it.

Holy fuck.

I think I love this guy.

"Kayla," Jenn suddenly says. Her pale brows are pulled together in a slightly worried frown. "You okay?"

Clearing my throat, I give my head a quick shake to clear it before I snap my gaze back to Jenn. "Yes. Yes, I'm okay. Sorry, I just spaced out a little."

She smiles, and then asks me what I think about a character that I have never heard of. While she explains who it is, and then launches into a whole discussion about him with the rest of the table, I do my best to engage and talk and nod like an active participant. But my mind is still echoing with that realization from earlier.

I think I love Jace.

Even after we've finished our coffee and said goodbye, I can't get the thought out of my head.

Sliding my hands into my pockets, I stare unseeing at the sidewalk ahead of me as I walk back to my apartment. My mind continues churning and my heart is pattering in my chest.

I've had boyfriends before, of course. When I was younger. But I don't think I've ever loved anyone before. Not like this. And it terrifies me. Because now, I suddenly have something to lose. What if Jace doesn't feel the same? What if he's—

The back of my neck prickles.

Yanked out of my thoughts, I blink at the street ahead. But everything is empty and quiet. This is one of the more deserted parts on the outskirts of campus, so no one else is walking along the sidewalk. And there are no cars coming towards me either.

But that strange feeling in my stomach doesn't go away.

I glance over my shoulder.

A nondescript blue van rounds the corner and starts coming down the street.

It shouldn't be an odd occurrence. And yet...

Where have I seen that van before? *Have I* seen that van before?

And it's driving much slower than is needed on this road.

A sudden pulse of panic shoots through me, and I yank up my phone and hit call.

Jace picks up after only two signals. "Kayla, are—"

"I think there's a van following me," I blurt out. "I think I saw it outside the coffeeshop when I left and it's here now and it's driving really slowly and—"

"Kayla," Jace interrupts. His voice is sharp. Clear. Alert. "Is your bodyguard there? Are there any other people around you right now?"

"No."

"Get to a crowded area. Now."

Fear and panic whirl through my chest like a storm as I whip my gaze around the street, trying to figure out where I will find people. This road has nothing but small university shops, which are all closed now since it's evening. I cast another glance over my shoulder.

My heart leaps into my throat.

"Oh God, it's speeding up," I blurt out as the van suddenly accelerates and starts barreling towards me.

"Run!" Jace snaps

I break into a run.

My sneakers pound against the ground as I sprint towards the next cross street. The car roars behind me, coming closer. I'm not going to make it. The next street is too far. I'm not going to—

A narrow alleyway appears on my left. It's blocked by a tall wooden gate.

Skidding to a halt, I slam shoulder first into the gate, throwing my entire weight against it.

It flies open.

I dart forward, into the alley.

And nearly smack right into a stone wall.

Dread crashes over me like a cold wave as I skid to a halt in front of the wall. It's a dead end.

Car doors are being slammed and footsteps are pounding against the ground just a short distance from me. Racing back to the tall wooden gate, I throw it shut and press myself against it to stop them from following me in here.

"Kayla!"

It takes another second for me to even recognize that it's my name being called. Recognize who is calling it. And where it's coming from.

While still bracing my back against the wooden gate, I stare down at the phone still in my hand.

Jace. Jace is trying to talk to me. How long has he been trying to talk to me? What is he saying? I can barely hear anything over the blaring panic in my head.

Yanking my hand up, I press the phone to my ear again.

"I'm trapped," I gasp into the phone. "I'm trapped in a dead end and—"

A weight crashes into the wooden gate from the other side hard enough to make it rattle in its hinges. My shoes slide across the ground. Fear grips my heart like an iron fist, but I throw my body back against the gate, slamming it closed again.

"They're here!" My voice doesn't even sound like my own. "They've found me. I can't get out. I can't—"

"Listen to me!" Jace screams on the other end of the line, and I realize that he has been trying to say something but I've kept talking over him. "Are you wearing your watch?"

My panicked mind can't process his strange question. "What?"

The weight slams into the gate again, and I skid forward another inch.

"Answer the question," Jace snaps. "Are you wearing your watch?"

While digging my heels into the ground, I press my back against the wood behind me, desperately trying to push the gate fully shut again. My gaze darts down to the watch I'm always wearing. The watch that was supposed to have been my brother's.

"Yes," I blurt out.

Another weight slams into the gate.

"Good," Jace says. He sounds calm. Collected. In control. "No matter what happens, you must never take off your watch. Do you understand?"

"Yes—"

The gate is forced open almost an entire foot. Straining my legs, I try to stop it from moving but it's impossible.

"Jace," I gasp. "Jace, they're coming in!"

"Kayla."

His voice is so steady. So full of power and confidence and promises. I try to use his calm, his control, to force my own mind to stop panicking. To force my heart to stop beating like a battle drum in my chest.

"Listen to me very carefully," Jace says in that steady tone. "Don't fight them."

Two weights slam into the gate at the same time.

It sends me flying forward.

Wood cracks as the gate crashes into the stone wall of the building on my right. I whip around, stumbling to regain my balance.

And come face to face with two men in ski masks.

"They're here," I breathe into the phone as I back away.

But my back hits the wall behind me after only a few steps. The masked men advance on me. My heart is slamming so hard against my ribs that I think I've broken something.

Fear and panic course through my body like bolts of electricity as the two men pull out zip ties, a gag, and a black hood.

"Don't fight them," Jace says into my ear, but this time I swear I can hear his voice crack a little. "Do whatever they say. And never take off the watch. I'm coming for you."

42

JACE

I'm dressed for bloodshed and rushing down the stairs within a minute. I can barely hear anything over the roaring in my head as I lace up my boots while checking the tracking app on my phone.

I put a tracker in Kayla's watch months ago, so that I could find her if she ever managed to sneak away. I had almost forgotten about it. Until today. Until someone took her. Until someone took my Kayla.

I'm going to fucking kill them all.

Shooting to my feet, I snatch up a bat from the umbrella stand before I sprint out the door and towards my car. There are already six bats in the trunk of my car, but I toss this one into the passenger seat as I throw myself into the driver's seat and floor it.

Bats are good. But I need guns too.

I know that my brothers could hook me up with whatever I wanted. They would drop everything to come and help me with this. But it would take too long. And every second that Kayla spends at someone else's mercy is another second that my heart is fucking shattering in my chest. I'm getting her back. And I'm getting her back right now.

The car skids across the asphalt as I swerve into the parking lot right outside Blackwater University's nearest gun range. Leaving the car running, I shove the door open and dart towards the entrance.

Several people jump out of my way as I barrel through the door and into the gun range. The guy in charge of distributing the weapons jerks back and blinks at me in surprise as I stalk around the counter and shove him out of my way. Scanning the racks of weapons, I quickly locate what I need.

Snatching up a holster, I shove my arms through the straps and secure it around my chest. Then I start loading up on guns and ammo and silencers.

The guy, who is supposed to stop people from doing exactly this, stares at me from two steps away, his mouth working up and down but no sound coming out.

If I was anyone else, I would've been shot by now. But because of my family's connection to the Morelli mafia family, and the direct order from Federico Morelli himself that we are all untouchable, no one at Blackwater ever dares to deny me anything.

"Y-you're not supposed to," the guy finally manages to press out. "You can't—"

I yank up a gun and aim it at his forehead. "I wasn't asking."

He jerks back and his hands fly up in surrender. Fear flickers in his eyes as he stares at me and swallows. In fact, fear pulses in everyone's eyes when I spin around and stalk back through the indoor range.

Everyone in here is an assassin-in-training. So the fact that they all look like they're about to shit themselves says something about what I must look like right now.

But I don't care.

I don't care if I look like an unhinged maniac who is about to go on the worst killing spree of the century.

They took my girl.

I'm going to paint this whole fucking town with blood.

43

KAYLA

My heart is pounding so hard against my ribs that my chest aches. Drawing in deep breaths through my nose, I try to force my heart to stop beating so hard. So loudly. I can barely even hear anything over that panicked thumping.

I'm zip tied to a chair, my wrists and ankles secured to the metal legs and armrests, I'm gagged, and there is a dark hood over my head. The hard plastic edges of the zip ties dig into my skin. I can't move. I can't speak. And I can't see.

But I'm unharmed.

Back in that alley, I did what Jace told me to do. I didn't fight my abductors. I gave them no reason to hurt me. I handed over my phone when they told me to. I held out my wrists when they told me to. I stood there quietly and let them gag me and blindfold me and lead me into their van. I walked willingly when they pulled me out of the van again after we stopped. I sat down in this chair when they told me to. I let them zip tie me to it.

And because of that, I am unharmed.

They threw my phone on the ground in that alley and crushed it with a boot.

But I'm still wearing my watch. My completely analog wristwatch that is somehow still going to lead Jace here.

My heart squeezes hard.

Jace.

His final words to me echo inside my skull.

I'm coming for you.

Drawing in unsteady breaths through my nose, I try to block out my hammering heart and my racing pulse and instead focus on that one simple fact. Jace is coming for me.

The metallic creaking of a door being opened comes from somewhere on my left. My heart leaps into my throat at the sudden sound. I once more try to force it to calm down so that I can hear over the blood pounding in my ears.

Several sets of footsteps echo between the walls.

The door falls shut with a thud.

The footsteps continue in my direction.

I draw in shuddering breaths.

"I gave you three months to get your shit together and pay off your debt to me," a gravelly voice says. "And you're almost out of time now. I'm here because you promised that you could pay it all off tonight. With interest. And yet, *that* does not look like a mountain of cash."

It's a man, that much I can hear. But I don't recognize the voice at all.

I force myself to remain completely still as the man stops right in front of me. The other footsteps fall silent as well. My treacherous heart slams against my ribs.

"It's something better," another man replies. "It's a blank check."

This voice, I recognize. But before my panicked mind can

sort through the memories and place the voice, the bag is yanked off my head.

I blink against the sudden light from the fluorescents above.

When I open my eyes again, I find myself in a warehouse. A man in his fifties is standing right in front of me, staring down at me. His brown hair has started to turn gray but his brown eyes are hard. He is wearing an impeccable dark gray suit and a single gold ring on his finger.

My heart stalls. Because I know who this is. I had never heard him speak before, so I didn't recognize his gravelly voice. But I know what he looks like.

This is Gregor Doyle. He's a loan shark who runs one of the biggest gambling empires in this state. His business practices are as slimy as they are cut-throat.

"This is Kayla Ashford," the second man says. The man whose voice I recognize.

I tear my gaze from Doyle and flick it to the man standing next to him.

My eyes widen, and I jerk back in my chair, as utter shock slams into me.

"*Lionel?*" I blurt out. Or I try to. The gag muffles it into garbled mumbling.

Regret flickers in Lionel's gray eyes for a second.

He looks exactly like he did when I said goodbye to him outside the coffeeshop less than an hour ago. Stylish maroon pants, a white dress shirt, and his brown hair perfectly styled. Just like any other rich student at Ivy River. And not at all like a cold-hearted, double-dealing kidnapper.

I gape at him, disbelief ringing like bells in my head.

He shoots me an apologetic look before turning back to Doyle. "She is the sole heir to the Ashford empire. Her father will pay you whatever you want to get her back. You can demand enough money to clear my debt to you, with interest, ten times over if you want."

A scheming glint creeps into Doyle's eyes, and a sharp smile curls his lips as he studies me. "A blank check, indeed."

"So my debt is paid?"

"*When* I have received Trent Ashford's money," Doyle says as he locks hard eyes on Lionel. "Then yes, your debt will be paid and the price on your head will not go into effect."

Intense relief washes over Lionel's entire body. But I can barely process it because I can't get past the realization that Lionel kidnapped me. He fucking *kidnapped me* in order to clear his own debt to a gambling king.

And suddenly, all the fear inside me evaporates. Gone like smoke in a strong wind. In its place, burning rage flares up.

I'm going to fucking kill this son of a bitch.

"I assume you have his number?" Doyle asks Lionel.

The little weasel nods and pulls up a phone.

Doyle takes the offered phone. "Good. Then let's get some video proof."

He snaps his fingers at the two men who were standing silently a few steps behind him.

I study their faces and the way they move as they approach me. They're not the same men who kidnapped me, which means that these two must work directly for Doyle while the two who grabbed me must have been hired by Lionel.

The one with black hair walks up behind me while the one with the shaved head takes up position on my left.

My muscles tense.

But all the guy behind me does is to untie the knot and remove my gag.

I work my jaw and run my tongue around my mouth. Then I level a furious stare on Lionel.

"I'm going to fucking destroy you," I growl at him.

Regret flickers in his eyes again. "I didn't have a choice."

"Didn't have a choice? You—"

I stop speaking abruptly as the guy with the shaved head pulls out a gun and presses it against my temple.

"I'm not interested in your squabbles," Doyle says, and slashes a hand through the air while shooting an annoyed look at Lionel. Then his hard eyes lock on me. "When I start filming, you are going to say these words and these words only. *Please, Dad, give them whatever they want. They're going to kill me.*"

Anger courses through my veins like lightning, and I glare back at the loan shark.

He stares back at me. When I say nothing, he demands, "Understood?"

My first instinct is to tell him to shove that fucking phone up his ass. But then Jace's words pulse through my mind again. *Don't fight them. Do whatever they say. I'm coming for you.*

I glance down at my watch. I still have no idea how Jace is going to be able to find me. But I trust him. I trust him more than I have ever trusted anyone in my entire life.

So I keep my eyes downcast and tell Doyle what he wants to hear. "Yes, I understand."

"Good." He snaps his fingers. "Now, look at the camera."

The man behind me moves away so that he isn't visible, and the guy holding the gun to my temple shifts so that only his arm and the gun against my head will be visible. I draw in a deep breath and look up at the phone Doyle is holding. He nods.

"Please, Dad," I repeat as instructed. "Give them whatever they want. They're going to kill me."

Doyle nods again and lowers the phone. Then he turns to Lionel. "Keep her quiet."

Not waiting for a reply, he simply spins on his heel and strides away to no doubt call my dad and blackmail him into paying my ransom.

"How do you expect to get away with this?" I snap, whipping my head to stare at Lionel. "I know that it's you. I know that it's him." Motioning with my chin, I gesture at the man still holding a gun to my temple and his friend now standing next to him. "I know that it's them. I know what all of you look like."

Only silence answers me. Deafening, crackling silence.

Coldness spreads through my body as I stare at the three silent men.

"I know what you look like," I repeat.

But it's not a threat this time. It's a realization. A terrible, terrible realization.

I know what they look like. Which means that they can't let me walk out of here. Which means that as soon as they get the money from my father, they're going to kill me.

Oh God.

My heart rate speeds up until it's beating so fast that I'm sure it's going to rip out of my chest. I swallow as panic threatens to drown out everything inside me. They're going to kill me. The metal barrel pressed against my temple suddenly feels so cold that I swear ice is spreading through my veins. My body feels numb.

I glance down at my watch again.

Jace.

Jace is coming. I just need to stall for time.

Time.

I need time.

"Why?" I blurt out, desperate for anything that will keep the guy with the gun from pulling the trigger right now. My eyes are full of both panic and rage as I meet Lionel's gaze. "Why?"

He shifts his weight uncomfortably. "You heard why. I owe him money."

"Money? You have money! You attend Ivy River, for fuck's sake!"

"Not that kind of money." He shifts awkwardly again, and his gaze darts to Doyle's guards for a second before returning to my face. "With the interest, the amount just… kept growing. And if I didn't pay it off soon, he was going to put a price on my head."

"You—"

"Not everyone has unlimited wealth like you do," he suddenly snaps, cutting me off. Anger flickers in his eyes now.

I open my mouth to snarl back at him, but the guard pushes his gun a little harder against my temple. Forcing my rage back down, I draw in a deep breath and remind myself of what I'm doing. I'm stalling for time. So I have to keep him talking.

"How long?" I ask instead.

Lionel just glances away.

"Lionel," I say, letting some of that fear back into my voice. "You owe me this much. How long have you been planning this?"

He clears his throat and drags his gaze back to me. "Since the day I met you at that party where you climbed in through the window and fell on top of me. When you told me who you were, I… I knew that you were the answer to all my problems."

"So when we met at the coffeeshop…?"

"It wasn't a coincidence."

"But that was over two months ago!"

"Yeah." A hint of irritation flits across his face now. "I hadn't expected it to take this long. I thought I would be able to get you alone much sooner, but then there was… Jace." He grinds his teeth. "Do you know how many times I almost managed to get you alone? On campus, at all those parties, at the coffeeshop, in the parking lot when we were preparing for our auction. Hell, I even took us to that stupid fake psychic and paid him to target you so that you would run off all upset and alone."

Genuine shock pulses through me. He set that up? *He* set that up.

"But Jace…" A snarl rips from his lungs, and he shakes his head. "Jace was always fucking there. So…" There is a hint of smugness in his voice now. "I had to get him fired."

Realization clangs through me. "You tipped off my father. That's why he came to my apartment that day."

"Yes. And then you finally got a bodyguard who wasn't as obsessive as Jace, and I could finally text the people I had hired and tell them to grab you on your way home today."

"You—"

The door is shoved open. I snap my gaze towards it to find Gregor Doyle striding back into the room.

"Your father was very amenable and complied with all of my demands," he announces, a satisfied smile ghosting across his lips as he looks at me. Then he shifts his gaze to Lionel. "Your debt is paid."

Lionel releases a shaky breath of relief.

Doyle comes to a halt in front of me. His face is a blank mask as he waves a nonchalant hand in the air. "Now, let's wrap this up."

Dread explodes through my chest like cold poison.

I'm out of time.

44

JACE

The tracker in Kayla's watch led me to an abandoned warehouse on the outskirts of the city. Since the area is so conspicuously empty, I had to leave my car a short distance away and travel the final distance on foot.

Drawing myself up against a huge metal container, I glance around the edge and towards the building where Kayla's signal is coming from.

There are three cars parked out front. One is the blue van that I'm assuming they used to abduct Kayla. The other two are an expensive Audi with tinted windows and a discreet black sedan.

Two men who look like common thugs stand close to the van. Two men who look like professional security guards flank the building's front door.

I narrow my eyes. If you can afford that kind of Audi and that kind of hired security, there is no need to use common thugs for a kidnapping. Which means that there are two separate parties involved in this. That might complicate things.

I study the four people outside closely. The thugs don't appear to be carrying guns. But based on the bulges beneath the other two men's suit jackets, *they* most definitely are.

Pulling back from the container, I slip around it and approach the building from the back.

Since I have no idea what's going on inside, I can't just go in guns blazing. There is too much risk of Kayla being caught in the crossfire if this devolves into a straight up shoot-out. I have to be stealthy.

Red and purple streaks line the sky in the west as the sun slowly starts dipping below the horizon. I stick to the shadows as I run along the side of the building. My pulse thrums in my ears. Every second I spend out here is another second that Kayla is in there at the mercy of her kidnappers. I need to finish this quickly.

Reaching the edge of the building, I glance around the edge to check if the four men outside have moved. They haven't. The two guys by the van are still standing there, talking quietly to each other, while the two professionals stand on either side of the front door.

I pull back.

A quick look behind me reveals a set of crates stacked against the metal wall of the building. I back towards them while adjusting my grip on the bat in my hand. After stepping in behind the crates, I reach towards the metal wall and start tapping my fingers against it.

At first, nothing happens.

Then a voice comes from the other side of the building.

"Do you hear that?"

I keep drumming on the wall.

"Yeah," another man replies. "Go check it out."

With my fingers still tapping, I remain behind the cover of the crates.

Footsteps sound from around the corner. They stop. Then they continue forwards. Towards me.

I flex my fingers on the bat, shifting it into a two-handed grip, while I wait for him to get closer.

Then I take one quick step out.

And slam the bat into the side of his head.

Shock pulses across his face.

But it's already too late.

His hand drops away from the gun he was reaching for. Blood trickles down the side of his head where his skull caved in. He topples backwards, hitting the ground with a thud. His body spasms once. Then he goes limp, staring unseeing up at the sky. There is a stunned expression on his face, even in death.

"You find anything?" the other guy calls from around the corner.

The dead man remains dead on the ground, not answering his question. I step around the body while approaching the corner again. Blood slides down along the bat and drips on the ground.

Now, I just need to wait for the second professional to come and investigate why his partner isn't replying. Then I can—

A gunshot cracks through the air.

My heart stops.

The gunshot... It came from *inside* the building.

Ice spreads through my veins.

Kayla.

Throwing all caution to the wind, I yank out a gun and sprint around the corner.

The guard at the door spots me the moment I skid around the corner. He yanks up a gun, but I'm already holding mine. I squeeze the trigger.

A massive weight slams into me from the side.

My entire body jerks to the side, throwing off my aim. The bullet hits the guard in the shoulder. He screams in pain.

I slam shoulder first into the ground with one of the thugs on top of me. His arms are wrapped around my chest, but his grip is jostled when we hit the ground. I twist and fire again towards the guard, but he yanks open the door right on time. The bullet cracks into the metal door instead. And the guard is gone.

Ramming my elbow into my attacker's stomach, I manage to get him to loosen his grip enough for me to twist towards him fully. I yank up the gun to shoot him in the face, but the second thug is barreling towards us. Shifting my aim at the last moment, I fire towards the second thug.

He throws himself sideways right before the bullet tears through the air.

But that move bought the first guy two seconds to lunge for my gun. His meaty hands close around my wrist, trying to pull the weapon away from me. I kick my knee up into his side. It makes him shift his weight enough for me to yank out the bat that was trapped between our bodies.

With a snap of my wrist, I slam the bat into his side.

A howl of pain rips from his throat, and he jerks sideways from the force of the blow.

But the second thug has already reached us now.

Pain shoots through my wrist as he kicks the gun out of my hand.

Twisting my whole body, I throw my weight up and to the side, shoving the first thug off me.

With his weight finally gone from my chest, I drag in a deep breath while spinning around and getting to my knees. The second thug swings his fist at my head.

I slam the bat into the side of his knee.

It breaks his kneecap with a sickening *crack*.

A scream of pure agony shatters the air.

I shoot to my feet right before the first thug can struggle up from the ground as well, and smack my bat down on his back.

Only a choked gasp rips from him when I break his spine.

Spinning quickly, I use my momentum to put even more force into the strike to the second thug's head. He's struggling to stay upright after I broke his kneecap, and he barely manages to look up before I crack my bat into the side of his head.

Blood splatters across my face as his skull shatters.

The guy on the ground is still screaming in agony, now unable to move with his spine broken. I slam my bat into the back of his skull, crushing bone. He falls silent at the same time as his companion hits the ground, dead.

These were the two people who hunted Kayla into a dead end. They were the reason why there was fear and panic in her voice when she called me. Why she almost sobbed when she realized that she was trapped. They made her feel scared and helpless.

They deserved to die brutally and painfully.

The front door is shoved open.

In one fluid motion, I drop my bat, straighten, and pull out two more guns while diving to the side.

A bullet tears through the air where I was just standing.

While rolling to my feet, I raise my right hand and fire right as the guard from before steps out of the door.

His head snaps back as the bullet hits him straight in the forehead.

"Shit," someone swears from inside.

I sprint towards the outer wall and barely manage to skid to a halt next to it when another guard, this one with black hair, strides across the threshold, already squeezing off shots while he walks.

But I'm no longer standing where he's aiming. I'm standing to his right, where the door is not shielding him.

The moment his head is fully out the door, I fire one bullet straight through his temple.

He slams into the door he was holding up on the other side, and then crumples to the ground. His body remains there, keeping the door open. I stay where I am, one gun trained on the doorway and the other one down by my side.

"Hold your fire or I'll shoot the girl," a gravelly voice suddenly bellows from inside.

My heart lurches.

Kayla.

This is going to turn into a negotiation. Fuck. If only I knew how many people were still in that building. There is no way to make sure we both walk out of here if I don't know what I'm up against.

"Put your gun down and slowly walk over to stand right in front of the doorway," the gravelly voice demands. "Or I will shoot her."

Fuck. I need to know how—

As if she could read my mind, Kayla suddenly shouts, "Two! One armed."

My heart swells with pride.

But the incredible feeling is abruptly cut off as a thud sounds, follow by a cry of pain from Kayla.

Rage roars through me. It's so fierce that it nearly blinds me.

"You lay a hand on her one more fucking time, and I will break every bone in your body twice before I finally bash your head in," I growl.

"And why is that?" the gravelly voice calls back, now sounding wary and suspicious.

"Because Kayla Ashford is mine."

"And who the fuck are you?"

"Jace Hunter."

Silence descends on the deserted grounds.

Then I swear I can hear the man inside curse under his breath. No one wants the Hunter family as an enemy.

"Lionel fucking Henderson," he growls. "I should've done more than just shoot him in the leg."

Shock pulses through me. Lionel? Is *he* a part of this? Fuck, I knew it. I always had a bad feeling about him.

"Listen," the man calls, his voice now a lot less threatening and a lot more pleading. "I got pulled into this not knowing the true scope of it. So how about this? I walk out this door with Kayla. Then when I reach my car, I release her and drive away."

"Or I can just shoot you the moment you step outside."

"If you do that, I will take Kayla down with me."

"Choose your next words very carefully."

He is silent for a few seconds. "I walk out with Kayla, we go to my car, I release her, and then I leave. No one will hurt her."

Watching the doorway, I consider my options. I could try to take him out. But Kayla has already confirmed that he has a gun. And despite the fact that I am an excellent fucking shot, there is still a risk that he has time to squeeze the trigger before he dies.

And I can't take that risk.

"Alright," I reply. "Agreed."

Two seconds pass. Then a man with a shaved head walks out the door. He is unarmed and is holding his hands raised where I can see them. I frown.

His gaze darts across the area, then he notices me. Wariness is written in every line of his face, but all he does is to turn so that he is facing me while he slowly starts moving away from the door. He is wearing a black suit like the others, which means that he is likely a bodyguard to this man as well.

Then fiery red hair comes into view in the doorway.

My heart clenches as I stare at the side of Kayla's face.

Her gaze darts towards me where I'm standing directly on her right, but she doesn't turn her head because there is a gun pressed against the back of her skull. And a man's hand on her shoulder.

Fury burns through me.

I flex my fingers on the gun by my side and raise that as well. I keep one weapon trained on the unarmed bodyguard and the other on the man who is now stepping out of the building.

Red light from the setting sun falls across his face as he becomes visible.

Surprise flickers through me.

It's Gregor Doyle.

Rico has been talking about him several times in the past few months. Apparently, he has started to get a little too greedy. A little too sure of his power. A little too inclined to forget that no one operates an underworld business in this state without the Morelli family's blessing. And that blessing can be taken away just as easily as it was given. Which is what Rico has been talking about doing.

Doyle's brown eyes flick back and forth. Then he spots me to his right, and immediately shifts so that Kayla is facing me. His hand remains on her shoulder and his gun at the back of her head as he uses her like a human shield.

I'm going to fucking bury this guy.

He moves slowly as he starts backing towards his Audi with his bodyguard next to him. I follow, keeping my guns trained on them.

Kayla watches me with an expression I can't read.

My gaze slips down to her face for a second.

There is a bruise forming on her cheekbone.

Rage cracks into me like a lightning bolt, and my voice drops low and lethal as I ask, "Which one of them hit you?"

Since she can't move her head, she uses her eyes to look pointedly to her left. Doyle's bodyguard, who can't see that she has already answered my question, just continues backing towards the car with his hands raised.

I shoot him in the head.

"Fuck!" Doyle blurts out, jerking to a stop and ducking farther behind Kayla.

The bodyguard collapses to the ground in a thudding of limbs. Blood runs down his forehead from the small hole there.

I shift both guns to Doyle. But he is still hidden behind Kayla, and I can't risk him shooting her, so I let him start towards the car again. He is moving faster now, backing as quickly as he can without tripping on his own feet.

Kayla remains standing with her spine straight as he yanks open the driver's side door.

Then he leaps inside, slams the door shut, and floors it.

The tires screech against the road as he speeds away.

I'm just about to shoot at his car when Kayla's knees buckle.

Darting forward, I ram my guns back into the holsters across my chest and grab her.

Her body crashes into mine as she sways.

Then she wraps her arms around me. Tightly. A small sob escapes her lips as she buries her face in my shirt.

My heart almost breaks.

Holding her tightly, I feel her body shake slightly in my arms as she sucks in rapid breaths.

"I love you," she gasps out. "I didn't know if I would ever get the chance to tell you. But I love you."

The air is knocked right out of my lungs. My heart forgets how to beat normally and just flutters around inside my ribcage instead.

Drawing in a shuddering breath, I tighten my arms around Kayla and hug her back fiercely. "I love you too, little demon. I love you so much that I can barely breathe."

She lets out something between a sob and a small noise of happiness. Then a tremor racks her frame again. Aftershocks from the adrenaline that must have been coursing through her body like electricity ever since she first spotted that van.

All I want to do is to kiss her and tell her that I love her again and ask her if she's okay, but I know that that's not what *she* needs. Right now, she just needs a moment to process. To feel. To sort through her emotions. To let her brain come to the conclusion that she is here and she is safe and alive.

So I just stand there. And hold her.

It takes almost five minutes for her breathing to even out. And then once she is breathing normally again, she curls her fingers into the back of my shirt and grips the fabric tightly.

As if she needs to feel that I'm here. I stroke a hand over her hair and down her back.

At last, she draws in a deep, shuddering breath and relaxes her grip on my shirt.

"You came," she says, her cheek resting against my chest.

I smile. "Of course I came, little demon. I thought you knew by now. I will always find you."

I can feel her smile. "How?"

"I put a tracker in your watch the first week we met."

At this, she snaps her head up and stares up at me with such absolute bafflement that I actually chuckle. Light returns to her eyes, and she swats at my chest while taking a step out of my arms. I don't want to let her go. I never want to let her go ever again. But I force myself to let my arms drop back down to my sides and take a step back.

"You put a tracker in my watch," Kayla echoes. Her beautiful blue eyes are pulsing with something halfway between amusement and disbelief. "So that's why you were always able to find me when I snuck away. Not because you were actually some super talented bodyguard."

"Hey!" I put a hand to my chest in a dramatic show of mock affront. "I *am* super talented. And super hot. And super funny. And—"

"Yeah, yeah." She laughs. And the sound of it heals the cracks that had formed in my heart this past hour. "I'm starting to think that I was right. It really is going to get difficult for your ego to fit through the door soon."

"Oh, but I've already showed you, remember? All I need to do is turn sideways and—"

I stop as something moves in the corner of my eye.

Yanking out a gun, I spin towards the door to the building just in time to see Lionel drag himself across the threshold, past the dead bodyguard who is still holding the door open, and out onto the asphalt. His left leg isn't moving, and it leaves a red smear on the ground.

He stops when he sees us.

Fear slams into his features, draining his face of color.

"Please," he calls, his voice breaking with desperation.

I turn back to Kayla and arch an eyebrow. "Do you want to shoot him or should I?"

"He has already been shot," she points out.

"Yeah, how did that happen?"

"Doyle wanted to leave him with a reminder of what would happen if he ever were to owe him money again."

"That's why he did this? Because he owed Doyle money?"

"Yeah."

"Now I'm definitely going to shoot him." I hold out my gun to her. "Unless you want to?"

A vicious scheming glint creeps into her eyes, and she gently pushes my gun down. "No. I'm not going to kil him. I'm going to send him to jail."

My eyebrows shoot up. Jail? I want to torture that fucking bastard to death. Why would she just want to send him to jail? But ultimately, it's her decision. So I block out my thoughts of painful and murderous revenge, and instead give her a nod.

"And then I'm going to put a bounty on his head," she continues. The smile on her face is downright villainous now as she stares at where Lionel is still crawling across the ground. "The inmate who torments him the most each week, without killing him, will get paid. Every week. For the rest of Lionel's sentence."

Surprise crackles through me. It's followed by a massive wave of approval. A wicked grin spreads across my mouth as I look Kayla up and down. “Damn, you really are a ruthless little demon, aren’t you?”

She flicks her long red hair behind her shoulder. “He should’ve known better than to mess with the rich and powerful.”

A dark laugh rumbles from my throat. Wrapping one arm around her waist, I pull her towards me and claim those wicked lips of hers. “He should’ve known better than to mess with *you*.”

Burying her fists in my collar, she holds me tightly as she kisses me back with such fiery passion that I swear my heart stops beating. Then she chuckles against my lips, the sound pure devil, before she corrects the final two words of my statement.

“With *us*.”

45

KAYLA

Mom is hugging me so tightly that I can barely breathe.

After we handed Lionel over to the police, and after Jace did whatever it is that he does to make sure that he is not arrested for bashing people's heads in with a bat, he drove me home to my apartment. I needed a very long and scorching hot shower to wash off the memories of being grabbed and tied up like that. My wrists are still a little raw from where the zip ties were digging into my skin. But after I had gotten dressed, I rubbed some soothing gel on them.

Then I walked back into the living room and was practically ambushed by my mom and dad.

Apparently, Jace had called them while I was in the shower. And he has also made dinner.

"I'm so glad you're okay," Mom sobs into my neck as she continues hugging me. "I was so worried."

I hug her back. "Yeah, me too. But I'm okay now, Mom. I promise."

Dad, who was the first to swoop me into a crushing hug

the second I stepped out into the living room, is now standing awkwardly next to the kitchen table while Jace sets down plates full of food on it.

The entire room is filled with the mouthwatering scent of garlic and parmesan and fried mushrooms and herbs.

Dad clears his throat, looking very self-conscious, as he looks up to meet Jace's eyes while Mom releases me from her squeezing hug.

"I, uhm..." Dad begins, and then clears his throat again. "I wanted to apologize."

Jace looks up from where he's setting down the final plate, and frowns in confusion. "What for?"

"For firing you. For treating you like... like I did." He shifts his weight uncomfortably and scratches the back of his neck. "When Lionel called me, he made it sound as if you were... taking advantage of my daughter."

Fury streaks through me like lightning strikes at the mention of Lionel's name. At the memory of what he put me through today. And at the fact that he dared to interfere with my life in any way. That he almost ruined my relationship with Jace.

Waves of anger roll through me. Maybe I should double the bounty on Lionel's head?

"But I can see now that I was wrong," Dad continues. His blue eyes are full of misery and regret as he glances between me and Jace. "I was so, so wrong. And I'm sorry."

"It's alright." Jace shrugs and flashes him a smile. "I get it. You were just trying to protect her."

Dad winces. "As were you."

"Yeah." Before Dad can apologize again, Jace motions towards the table. "Now, please eat before the food gets cold."

Wood scrapes against wood as we all pull out chairs and sit

down around the table. Mom and Dad next to each other opposite me and Jace. Jace slides a hand over my thigh and gives my knee a little squeeze. It's such a casual gesture of affection that my heart stutters and I almost drop my fork.

After another nod from Jace to dig in, Mom and Dad start eating. But they stop halfway through the first bite and snap their gaze up to Jace. Astonishment pulses across their faces.

Dad swallows the bite. "This is… delicious. Did you make this?"

A small smile tugs at the corner of Jace's lips. "Yes."

"Wow," Mom says.

Dad nods.

Next to me, Jace is looking entirely too pleased with himself so I jab my elbow into his side. He just grins at me.

"Kayla," Dad suddenly says.

Dread rolls down my spine at the serious and almost painful note to his voice. I swallow and turn back to meet his gaze. "Yes?"

"We need to talk about your security." He gives me an apologetic look. "Today, more than anything, has demonstrated the need for a bodyguard."

"I don't want a bodyguard," I reply. And even I am surprised by the sharp steel in my voice. "I don't want to spend my entire life monitored and watched and shadowed by someone."

Dad winces. "I know. And I understand. But I don't know how else to keep you safe. That Gregor Doyle creature is still out there and he might want revenge. Not to mention that someone else might get inspired by his actions and try to kidnap you as well."

"Oh, I don't think you need to worry about that," Jace says before I can reply.

We all turn to him. He has already finished all the food on his plate, while I haven't even started eating yet. Jace notices this, and points towards my plate.

"You need to eat," he announces.

"I'm not sure if I can eat after everything that happened today," I reply, temporarily thrown off by the change in topic.

"That's exactly why you need to eat. Food is good for the soul. Our bodies are genetically wired to connect food with a feeling of safety. Because no one sat down on the savannah to eat while being chased by a lion. We only ate when we knew that we were safe. And that genetic wiring still remains. So when we eat, our body interprets that to mean that we are safe, and responds accordingly." Jace points to my plate again. "So, eating will make you feel better."

A stunned laugh rips from my chest. With both mirth and astonishment swirling inside me, I smile and shake my head at Jace. "Oh look, Mr. Public Service Announcement is back again."

He laughs and shakes his head at me as well. Then he leans in and steals a quick kiss from my lips. "Just eat."

"Alright, I will," I reply as he pulls back again. "If you explain what you meant by your 'I don't think you need to worry about that' comment."

A scheming glint shines in his eyes as he meets my gaze. "You won't be needing a bodyguard anymore. Not ever." Leaning back nonchalantly in his seat, he glances to my parents as well. "In fact, come tomorrow, none of you will be needing a bodyguard."

Confusion pulses across my parents' features. The same confusion swirls inside my chest as well, and I frown at Jace.

"What does that mean?" I ask.

"It means—"

His phone rings, cutting off his words.

With that sly smile still on his lips, he pulls out his phone and answers the call.

"Eli," he says.

Surprise pulses through me.

"You're all here?" he says into the phone. "Great, I'll be right down."

After ending the call, he abruptly stands up and pushes his chair back in. I scramble to my feet as well. My parents do the same.

"Wait," I blurt out. "Where are you going?"

He pauses. Sliding a hand through my hair, he leans down and slants his lips over mine. I can feel the wicked smile that spreads across his mouth as he whispers a sentence that makes my soul flutter.

"I'm going to show people what happens when they dare to touch something that belongs to me."

46

JACE

Blood runs down the side of my bat and drips on the ground as I walk. My hands and forearms are stained red, and blood is splattered across my face as well.

My brothers flank me as we stride out of the building that used to be Gregor Doyle's headquarters. Kaden is casually twirling a knife in his hand while Rico is still holding a gun. Eli's hands look like they have been dipped in red. I spin my bat, resting it against my shoulder as we walk.

Behind us, the building is on fire.

"Well, that should do it," I comment.

Eli and Rico chuckle while Kaden flashes me a wicked smirk.

I slide my free hand into my pocket and pull out my phone. Then I call our father. He answers after only two signals.

"You're done?" he asks by way of greeting.

"Yeah," I reply.

A loud *crack* sounds from behind us. Then part of the

building collapses. Embers swirl up and sail through the dark night as the burning wood crashes down.

"I think you can let the fire department through now," I continue.

"Will do."

"Oh, and by the way…"

He remains silent, waiting for me to continue.

"I have decided to stay at Blackwater."

For a few seconds, Dad says nothing. And when he finally speaks, there is a hint of guarded hope in his voice. "You have?"

"Yes."

As soon as I was officially given the choice, the answer was as easy as breathing. I love this life.

After this mission I just pulled with my brothers, my entire body is thrumming with energy. I fucking love this feeling. The adrenaline. The violence. The power. It makes my whole soul sing. I don't want a normal job. I want this.

"But then… why?" Dad asks, sounding confused. "Why go through all this trouble of changing my mind if it didn't matter?"

"It did matter."

"But it changed nothing."

"It changed everything! *The choice* was everything."

He is silent for a while. We have reached our cars now. My brothers turn to face me, waiting for me to finish the call. In the distance, the sound of sirens echoes across the dark city.

"Yes," Dad says eventually. "Yes, I'm beginning to see that now. Sorry I didn't realize sooner."

My eyebrows shoot up. "Hold on. Did you just apologize? *You*. The guy who never—"

"Alright, alright. Don't let it get to your head or I'll beat you up the next time I see you." He huffs out an amused breath. "Brat."

I chuckle.

"I'm proud of you," he adds, and then quickly hangs up before I can tease him about that too.

Shaking my head, I slip my phone back into my pocket while trying and failing to suppress the smile on my lips. My brothers watch me, their eyes gleaming in the light from the fire.

A drop of blood slides down Rico's temple as he raises an eyebrow at me. "So, what now?"

"Now, we go back home to our girls," I reply.

Grins spread across all of their faces.

Eli thumps the roof of his car with a hand. "Sounds like a plan."

With a nod, we all pull open the doors to our cars.

"Dinner at our house next weekend," Rico declares before slipping into the driver's seat. It's more of an order than a suggestion.

"You're cooking," Eli says, locking eyes with me as he climbs into his own car.

Kaden shoots me one of his psycho smiles as he pauses with his car door open. "And wear a French maid costume."

The others burst out laughing.

"Assholes," I call as they slam their doors shut.

Shaking my head, I watch as their black Range Rovers speed away. Only the crackling fire and the collapsing building hear me as I add two more words.

"Thank you," I say to my absolutely unhinged brothers. My brothers, who I now know, without a doubt, will always have my back. Against anything and everything.

After one final glance towards the burning building and

the absolute carnage that we left inside, I climb into my own car and drive back to Kayla's apartment.

She is still awake, sitting at the kitchen table alone and waiting for me, when I walk across the threshold. Jumping up from her chair, she takes two steps towards me before she screeches to a halt. Her eyes go wide as she flicks a glance up and down my body.

"Please tell me it's not yours," she says.

I blink in surprise for a second before realization filters through me. Oh. Right. The blood that is splattered across both my clothes and my skin.

"No, it's not mine," I assure her.

Relief washes over her features, and she closes the distance between us. Her body slams into mine so hard that she almost manages to knock me back a step. Wrapping her arms around me, she holds me tightly. I slide my arms around her and rest my chin on her head.

And at the feeling of having her in my arms, safe and completely free at last, the final tension and restlessness that had been coiled in my chest at last eases.

I draw in a deep breath, breathing in the scent of her.

"You will never have to worry again," I promise her. "You're free now. You never need to have a bodyguard looming over your shoulder and watching your every move ever again."

Something between a sob and a choked noise of joy and relief escapes her lips. Relaxing her grip on me, she takes a step back and then tilts her head so that she can meet my gaze. The emotions in her eyes knock the breath from my lungs.

"How?" she asks, sounding breathless. As if she can barely believe it.

I draw my fingers over her cheek, pushing a strand of hair back behind her ear. It smears blood over her perfect skin, but she doesn't seem to mind.

"We made a very bloody example of Doyle and everyone who was involved in your kidnapping," I explain. "So now, everyone knows that you and your parents are under the protection of the Hunter family. Anyone who touches you dies. Brutally and painfully."

Her stunning blue eyes light up, and then a truly devilish smile spreads across her lips. "And anyone who so much as whispers about pressing any sort of charges against the Hunter family will be buried underneath a mountain of lawsuits and ridiculously expensive lawyers."

My eyebrows shoot up.

"What?" she asks, fake innocence in her tone. With that wicked smile still on her lips, she takes a firm grip on my shirt and pulls my face down to hers. "I protect what's mine too."

Sliding an arm under her ass, I lift her up. She wraps her legs around my waist and locks her fingers together behind my neck.

"So..." she begins, teasing her lips over mine. "You're not my bodyguard anymore."

"No, I'm not."

Pulling back slightly, she cocks her head and meets my gaze, her eyes suddenly serious. "Does that mean that you're leaving?"

"Leaving?" I flash her a villainous smile as I hold her gaze. "Oh, you're not getting rid of me that easily, little demon."

An answering grin lights up her face.

I claim those perfect, sinful lips of hers with a kiss so possessive that it leaves her gasping.

"I thought you knew by now," I whisper against her mouth.

"There is nowhere you can go that I won't follow. You are mine. And I will always find you."

She kisses me back with such burning passion that my heart flips and my lungs cease.

This fierce, stubborn, powerful, scheming, and absolutely breathtaking little demon is mine. She barreled into my life like a crackling piece of dynamite and changed everything. She fills my soul and she holds my heart in the palm of her hand. She drives me crazy. She makes me sane. She is fire and energy. She makes me whole.

And I will never let anyone take her from me. Ever again.

EPILOGUE

TWO YEARS LATER

Golden light from the setting sun streams in through the glass walls of our penthouse. Far below, the city spreads out around us like a glimmering sea of lights and stone and steel. I smile out at the view before turning back to where Jace and Rico are standing by our marble-topped kitchen island, chopping vegetables and mixing herbs.

Isabella, Eli, Raina, and Kaden are sitting on the barstools on the other side of the island while Alina popped out to get the surprises that she and I have bought for our husbands.

Husband.

The word ripples through my whole soul like warm sparkles, and I glance down at the beautiful ring on my finger. Nothing has ever felt more right than this. Than him. Than us.

From across the room, Jace catches me looking at the ring and flashes me a sly smile. He looks just like he did when he walked into my father's office that first time. A white t-shirt that complements his muscular body, his brown hair effortlessly messy like he has just rolled out of bed, a grin on his face, and a bright sparkle in his eyes. The only difference is that he looks steadier now. Like he has finally found his place in the world. Which is here. With me.

I grin back at him as I close the distance to the kitchen island with the bottle of wine that I went to get.

Confusion trickles through me as I glance down at the bottle and find it already open. "I swear this wasn't open when I put it there."

All eyes slide to Raina. She continues drinking for another second before she realizes that everyone is staring at her.

"What?" she asks, raising her eyebrows as she looks from face to face. "I haven't touched it since I gave it to Kayla."

Isabella heaves a sigh and raises a hand. "It was me."

We all blink at her in surprise.

"*Raina* brought it," Isabella says while stabbing a hand towards Raina for emphasis. "I had to check it for poison."

Jace chokes out a laugh while Kaden snickers into his glass of wine. Eli just shrugs and nods as if that makes sense.

Raina, however, rolls her eyes and then shoots Isabella a look of exaggerated affront. "Oh, come on. It was *one* time."

"Yeah, well, I learned my lesson after that," Isabella replies.

"And it wasn't poison."

"No, it was like smoking psychedelic mushrooms. On steroids."

Rico chuckles while he continues grinding some herbs in a mortar. "I found her dancing naked in the living room when I got home."

While struggling hard to suppress a smile, Isabella shoots Rico a look that promises revenge before she shakes her head at all of us. "You guys are still the craziest people I have ever met. And I grew up in a literal cult."

Laughter ripples through the kitchen. Eli and Kaden even clink their glasses together as if that was the highest of compliments. Warmth spreads through my chest.

"Aww, come on," Jace says, grinning at Isabella. "You know you love us."

Her blue-gray eyes dance with light as she once more tries to hide the smile on her face while she sweeps her gaze over all of us. "Yes, I do. Unfortunately."

We laugh again. I top up her glass of wine before I refill my own as well.

"And speaking of love," I begin, and cast a glance between Eli and Raina. "You two are the only ones left now. Which makes no sense, because you were the first ones to get together. When are you getting married?"

"Ugh," Raina scoffs, and rolls her eyes. "Marriage is for normal people."

I arch an eyebrow at her. "You're not getting married?" With confusion flickering through me, I hold up my left hand to motion at the ring on my finger. "Then how do you stop people from flirting with your significant other if you don't have a visible mark of ownership?"

"I just poison them," Raina replies at the same time as Eli says, "I just shoot them in the head."

Silence falls over the kitchen for a few seconds.

Then Jace and I burst out laughing. Isabella once more shakes her head at us while Rico and Kaden exchange a knowing look and take a sip from their wine.

Eli and Raina, who were dead serious, just glance between us as if they don't understand why we're laughing.

Then a scheming glint creeps into Raina's green eyes, and she turns back to Eli. "I do like the sound of *visible mark of ownership*, though."

A considering expression has descended on Eli's features as well, and he nods slowly as he holds her gaze. "So do I."

"Perhaps we need to reconsider this whole marriage thing."

"Perhaps we do."

Before anyone else can say anything, the front door is opened. We all turn to look as Alina sweeps into the room, her long blonde hair fluttering behind her. Wicked glee pulses through me at the sight of the two large white boxes in her arms.

"Sorry it took so long," she says as she practically skips across the floor towards us. There is a matching smile full of wicked anticipation on her lips as well, and she winks at me as she reaches the island. "But I promise it will be worth it."

Kaden, who is casually spinning a knife in his hand, arches a dark brow. "What's going on?"

"We bought you gifts," Alina replies, that brilliant scheming smile still on her mouth.

She hands one of the boxes to me. The others shift their glasses aside so that we can put the boxes down on the island. Alina places hers in front of Kaden while I saunter over to set mine down in front of Jace. He pushes the cutting board aside and sets down the knife he was using to chop scallions.

"You have been talking about it for so long," I say. "So we figured that it was finally time for you to have your very own set."

Jace and Kaden exchange a look of confusion. Around the island, the others watch us with similar expressions of befuddlement. Eli cocks his head, studying Kaden's box next to him as if he is trying to see through the white cardboard. To Jace's left, Rico stops grinding the herbs and instead picks up his wine glass. A considering look blows across his features as he glances down at Jace's box while drinking from his wine.

"Well, open them," I say.

After Kaden slides his knife back into its holster, he and Jace exchange one more look. Then they shrug and grab the lid on their respective boxes. They lift them off at the same time.

Rico spits his wine across the counter.

Isabella gasps.

Raina grins like a little villain.

And Eli doubles over, his laughter booming across the apartment.

Absolute astonishment pulses across Jace and Kaden's faces as they hold up matching French maid costumes.

"I expect you to already be wearing it when I walk into our bedroom tonight," I tell Jace.

Alina gives Kaden a nod. "Same."

Eli is laughing so hard that it sounds like he's choking. Rico actually is choking on his wine as he tries to breathe and laugh and swallow at the same time. Across the counter, Isabella is pressing a hand over her mouth to stop her own laughter. But her shoulders shake with it.

Raina's green eyes glitter like emeralds as she raises her glass at me and Alina in a salute. "I think you just became my new favorite people."

Thuds echo across the room as Eli slaps his palm against the marble countertop while he continues laughing like he can't breathe.

Kaden narrows his eyes as he yanks out a knife and points it at his older brother. "I will fucking stab you."

Eli just laughs harder.

Alina and I exchange a smug grin full of victory.

"I know you've always been part of the family," Eli presses out as he tries to rein in his laughter. His golden eyes glint in the light from the setting sun as he looks between me and Alina. "But now, you're *really* part of the family."

Warmth spreads through my whole soul.

Jace drops the French maid costume back into the box and rounds the edge of the counter, advancing on me. His warm brown eyes dance with the promise of delicious revenge as he slides a hand up my throat.

Keeping a firm grip on my throat, he leans down and slants his lips over mine. His breath caresses my mouth as he lets out a low humming sound that makes my spine tingle.

"I'm going to make you crawl for this, you little demon," he breathes against my lips. And I can hear the smile in his voice. "You know that, right?"

A thrill of dark desire races down my spine. Burying my fist in the collar of his shirt, I hold him firmly to me as I whisper back, "Oh, I'm counting on it."

He chuckles, the sound vibrating against my lips. "I love you so fucking much."

I yank his mouth down to mine and claim his wicked lips for myself. He kisses me back like he's starving. Even after all this time, he always kisses me and touches me and fucks me like he simply can't get enough of me. It makes my heart flutter every time.

A sharp thud sounds right next to us.

"Keep it in your pants, Golden," Kaden says from the other side of the kitchen island. "No one wants to see your cock before dinner."

I laugh against Jace's mouth and then steal one last kiss before releasing him. Stepping back, I find one of Kaden's throwing knives buried in the cutting board right next to us.

Jace just brushes a lock of my hair out of my face and hooks it behind my ear before he turns towards his brothers.

There is a broad grin on his face as he says, "I know." His eyes glitter as he gestures down at his cock. "Because *this* just makes yours look so tiny in comparison."

Rico scoffs.

"Keep telling yourself that if it helps you sleep at night, *little* brother," Eli says, smirking as he adds emphasis to the word.

Jace shoots him a look full of challenge, but then simply yanks out the knife now stuck in his cutting board and points it in Kaden's direction. "And stop throwing knives in my kitchen."

"I'll stop throwing knives in your kitchen when you stop leaving bats in my house," Kaden retorts.

"You never know when you might need a good bat."

"Or a knife."

"Bats are far superior. You have the range. The strength. The..."

A soft laugh escapes me, and I shake my head as I watch them bicker about which weapon is best. Rico takes a long drink from his wine and then goes back to grinding the herbs while Alina carefully folds up Kaden's French maid costume, a glittering smile of anticipation on her face. Isabella inspects the wine bottle and casts a suspicious look at Raina before refilling her glass. But Raina is too preoccupied to slip poison into it because she and Eli have resumed their discussion about marriage.

Watching them all with a smile on my lips, I gently stroke the watch I'm still wearing. My brother's watch.

I think you would've liked them, I think to Victor, hoping that he can hear me. *I think you would've liked them a lot.*

Jace tosses Kaden his knife back and then bends down to pull out a bat that he had apparently hidden in one of our kitchen cabinets. He flashes me a brilliant smile and winks at me as he straightens. Then he turns back to Kaden and starts demonstrating something about how the bat produces force when he swings it.

My heart is so full that it feels as if it's bursting with light.

Not only did I manage to find the perfect man, I also gained three unhinged brothers and three insane sisters in the process. A family of my own. People who always have my back. People who I will protect with everything I have.

My gaze drifts back to Jace, and a smile blows across my lips.

This is everything I ever wanted.

He is everything I ever wanted.

The future is bright.

For all of us.

BONUS SCENE

Do you want know if Jace actually puts on that French maid costume? Then scan the QR code to download the exclusive bonus scene:

Made in United States
Orlando, FL
02 August 2025